T0198650

A Stained White Veil

ALSO BY THE AUTHOR:

Treasure

A STAINED WHITE VEIL

A Peachtree Street Chronicles Novel

Sam Biondo

iUniverse, Inc.
New York   Bloomington

A Stained White Veil
A Peachtree Street Chronicles Novel

iUniverse books may be ordered through booksellers or by contacting:

iUniverse
1663 Liberty Drive
Bloomington, IN 47403
www.iuniverse.com
1-800-Authors (1-800-288-4677)

ISBN: 978-1-4401-8105-4 (pbk)
ISBN: 978-1-4401-8106-1 (cloth)
ISBN: 978-1-4401-8108-5 (ebook)

Editor: Laurel A. Frazier

Printed in the United States of America

iUniverse rev. date: 10/22/09

For Susan, Laurel and Kris, and for my grandchildren.
The best fan club any writer could have.

BEGINNINGS

December 22, 1862
Washington D.C. U.S.A.

..........And, by virtue of the power and for the purpose aforesaid, I do order and declare that all persons held as slaves within said designated states and parts of states are, and henceforward shall be, free; and that the executive government of the United States, including the military and naval authorities thereof, will recognize and maintain the freedom of said persons...........

.......And upon this act, sincerely believed to be an act of justice, warranted by the Constitution upon military necessity, I envoke the considerate judgment on mankind and the gracious favor of Almighty God.

Abraham Lincoln, President.
Emancipation Proclamation

*   *   *   *

April 1, 1865
Richmond, Virginia, C.S.A.

"Shall we gather at the river, the beautiful, the beautiful river...."

Jefferson Davis, President of the Confederate States of America, squirmed in his seat in the first pew of the chapel as the congregation sang the old hymn.

The tall, gaunt leader of the Southern Cause had other matters on his mind at that moment, and the words of the spiritual were lost on him as he wished for the service to come to an end.

Davis reached up and touched the frayed fabric of his grey morning coat. In the inside breast pocket was the letter he had been handed by one of his aides minutes before the service had started.

It had taken Jefferson Davis only a few moments to memorize the most important words contained in the message from the Commanding General of the Army of Northern Virginia. Davis closed his eyes and silently mouthed the words: *Richmond has to be given up.*

Over and over, the terrible words repeated in his head. Finally, the embattled president of the Confederacy could take it no longer. He touched his wife's arm gently, and gave her a reassuring smile when she looked up from her hymnal.

The President stood and walked to the rear of the church. The congregation watched him, but kept up the song. Two aides in full dress uniform were standing at the doors which they opened to let Davis out into the early, spring-like weather. He looked up at the sky, otherwise bright and cloudless, which was stained by billows of dark smoke hovering above fires that continued to burn throughout Richmond. Thankfully, the Union gunners had again been ordered to allow the citizens of the Rebel capital to observe the Sabbath without the constant bombardment they otherwise endured every day.

As the doors closed behind Davis, he heard the singing come to an end, and the Reverend Jeremiah Chattsworth resumed his sermon.

Lt. Colonel Avril Newcastle, the president's chief aide-de-camp, stood talking among a group of officers at the bottom of the steps below the chapel entrance. The men went silent at the appearance of their leader, and Newcastle started to move toward Davis. But the president raised his hand slightly to hold him in his place, and came down the steps. He put his hand on the officer's shoulder.

"Let's walk this way, Colonel," he said, bidding the others to stay behind.

Jefferson Davis looked at the young man as they walked away from the church. Newcastle was shorter than Davis and looked up to his leader expectantly.

They are so young, Davis mused. *They are ever so much younger all the time.* But Newcastle had showed himself to be smart, resourceful, and trustworthy. They stopped walking once well away from the church.

"Colonel," Davis said. "Disturbing word has come from General Lee. I'm afraid things are not going well for him." He stopped to make sure Newcastle understood the importance of the words. "He has advised me that we must get away from Richmond. I'm afraid the city is no longer safe as our Capital." Both men knew what this meant. The dream was nearly dead.

"We must put 'Grey Phoenix' into effect, Colonel," Davis said, gravely. "And we have little time to prepare. It will be necessary for the government to evacuate the city this very night."

Grey Phoenix was a plan so secret that only fifteen senior government officials knew of its existence, as did a few military personnel who would be charged with carrying out the plan.

Lt. Colonel Newcastle knew what was expected of him: he was being ordered to personally see to the assemblage and packing of the archives of the Confederacy, and, most importantly, to the removal of the remaining treasury, which consisted of gold bars hidden in vaults deep beneath the three major banks of Richmond. The paper currency he would leave behind. It was worthless, now.

Once the gold and official documents of the Confederacy were delivered to the railhead outside the city- the only railhead not yet destroyed by the Yankee gunners- where the president and his family would be waiting, Newcastle and his detachment would round up the most important officials of the government and their families, and deliver them to the train. By early morning, the government would be located aboard a line of railroad cars far from Richmond, and the city would cease to be the capital of the Confederate States of America.

"Colonel," Davis said. "I pray you; do your job quickly and quietly. We cannot afford a panic among the citizenry. Even though many of our people are finding their way out of the city, others stay here because *we* have remained throughout the siege. We cannot risk our ability to leave Richmond if there were to be a wholesale panic and desertion."

They both knew that they were leaving the city and its people to the mercy of the Union soldiers. They had no choice. Without the gold and the government safely away from Richmond, there was no Confederacy.

"Do not despair, Colonel. We shall live to fight another day, and that is what matters now. Davis gave his aide a reassuring smile. "I will see you tonight."

The president of a collapsing nation turned and walked back to the church alone, his head down, his heart heavy.

*   *   *   *

April 3, 1865
Office of the President, C.S.A.
Richmond, Virginia, C.S.A.

Abraham Lincoln, 16th President of the United States of America, was alone in the office formerly occupied by his opponent of nearly four years.

Jefferson Davis was gone, along with his government, and many parts of the capital city they had abandoned less than two days ago were ablaze.

The Union army had become a "bucket brigade" around the core of the city, and the fires were slowly being extinguished, one by one.

Many of the fires had been started by the Yankee gunners who had attempted to take Richmond by siege, but some had been deliberately set by the retreating Rebels, who were intent on leaving Billy Yank with a scorched earth.

The room was quiet now, the big guns silent. Lincoln wondered what the last weeks had been like for Davis, presiding over a city under great duress. The President of the United States had not had to endure a bombardment of his own capital city, yet he knew the horrible toll that this war had taken on him. It could only have been worse for Davis.

There was a knock on the door, and Major General Irwin Gordon Holt entered the room. "Sir," he said gently, trying to minimize the invasion into what must be a momentous occasion for the Commander-in-Chief. *My God, he looks tired,* Holt thought, watching the tall, gaunt Lincoln closely.

"Yes, General?" Lincoln answered.

Holt was not happy about the President being here only a day after the Rebel army had pulled out. There was still a chance of snipers and disgruntled Confederate loyalists much too close for his safety.

"Sir," Holt said again, "your escort will be ready for the trip back to Washington in about an hour."

"I was thinking," the President said, already anticipating Holt's reaction, "that it might be prudent to extend our visit to Virginia for a few more days."

"Sir," Holt said, shaking his head emphatically, "I cannot recommend that, Mr. President. There are very serious numbers of Rebel troops only a few miles from here. I cannot guarantee your safety!"

Lincoln smiled. This was a fight he would not win, and he knew Holt was right. There would be much to do in the coming years to heal the country. He had to think of the future and not take needless risks.

He changed the subject. "Has Major Martin reported yet?"

"He has, Mr. President, just a few minutes ago." General Holt hesitated. "I'm afraid you were correct to assume that the Rebels would loot the banks. Whatever gold the Confederacy still has is gone."

Abraham Lincoln sighed, tiredly. "It would seem that Jeff Davis plans to continue the fight."

Holt said: "If I may, sir?"

Lincoln nodded, and Holt opened the door to the outer office and motioned to someone to come in.

A portly man, middle aged and balding, with a ruddy complexion, shuffled slowly into the room carrying his hat in nervous hands. He bowed to Lincoln.

"Mr. President, this is Hiram Edwards. He runs the general store down the road from here," Holt nodded at the man, and said, "Mr. Edwards has been an informant for us since the war began. He is a loyal American, and his information has been very helpful to us."

Lincoln looked at Edwards and smiled. "Your country owes you its deepest gratitude, sir."

Edwards glanced at Holt, a smile flitting across his face. "Honored, sir," he said to Lincoln with another bow.

The General said, "Mr. Edwards saw wagons on the road late the night of the First, sir. Not unusual of course," Holt continued, "under the present circumstances. But there were many more than usual, and some of the carriages were loaded with women and children, and other wagons were carrying trunks that didn't look military, but were being driven by soldiers. Mr. Edwards?"

"Yes, sir," the man said, taking Holt's cue. "I got curious about them soldiers drivin' civilians around, so I follows them. They went to the railhead southwest of the city limits." He looked at Holt, who nodded encouragement. "There was families there, you know, wimmin' and they kids, and wagons that had already been unloaded of whatever they was carryin'. They was boardin' a train in a big hurry. Most of the folks what left Richmond since the siege started just left by horse or carriage or wagons. These people was all together, and they had them a train waitin' on 'em."

"And, where do you think this train was going," the President asked, glancing at Holt.

"Well, now I can't know for sure you understand, but them train tracks go straight through Danville and end up at Montgomery, over in Alabama."

"Thank you, Mr. Edwards," the General said.

Hiram Edwards bowed once more and backed out of the room as Holt closed the door after him.

"Danville," the President said, quietly.

"There's a good chance, sir," Holt said. "And, if it's true, President Davis may be trying to meet up with General Lee, who still has a sizeable force in the field."

"What can we do?"

"If Lee is going to Danville, Phil Sheridan is going to be close by."

General Phillip Sheridan's Union cavalry had decimated the heartland of the South, from the valleys of western Virginia to Atlanta, while with General Sherman on his march to the sea. Now, he was hard on Lee's heels.

After a moment, Abraham Lincoln said, "We must get word to Sheridan. If he can beat Lee to Danville, we will have the Confederate government in our grasp."

Lincoln sat heavily into the chair across the desk from where Jefferson Davis would have been sitting had it been just a few days earlier. "I still believe Davis will try for Mexico," he said, softly. "But if he does, and if he gets across the border with his treasury, this war could go on for a very long time. Maybe long enough to destroy any chance of reconciliation."

✳   ✳   ✳   ✳

April 7. 1865, Near Dawn
North of Fikes Ferry, on the Catawba River
Alabama, C.S.A.

The rains that had swollen the creeks and rivers of the southeastern Confederacy throughout March of 1865 continued unabated during the first week of April, 1865.

It was like that now, as a steady drizzle combed through the large, old pines, splattering noisily into the puddles that continued to expand and turn the road north of Fikes Ferry into a sea of mud.

In the haze and rain, the scout was almost indistinguishable from the great brown mare. An oilcloth slicker was draped over his shoulders, surrounding him like a cocoon, and his old slouch hat covered his face.

The horse snorted as if attempting to clear water from its nostrils. The rider wiped away rain from his own face, but it didn't help much.

Fool's errand, he thought. *Them Yankees, they ain't comin' today.*

But, General Forrest had put the scout on the road north of the town to watch for movement by the Union commander, General James H. Wilson, and his nearly 13,000 troopers. He kept to the middle of the road, something he would never have done earlier in the war, but, *them Yankees ain't comin', not today.*

General Nathan Bedford Forrest and his cavalry had become a guerrilla force, cut off from John Bell Hood and his Department of Alabama, Mississippi, and East Louisiana forces, which were still fighting the Yankees in Tennessee.

Forrest had been sent by Hood to Selma, Alabama to help bolster the garrison defending the town, but Wilson's overwhelming forces had pushed Forrest's rag- tag troops aside as if they weren't even there. The town had fallen in just two days.

The next day, April 3rd, the two forces had met again outside Northport, and once more, Wilson's troopers had smashed into the Confederate cavalry, which quickly collapsed and scattered to the winds.

That Forrest, the scout thought. He had fought beside the general for four years now.

The man was whip- smart for sure, even though he'd had little schooling. He was ruthless, too, wealthy, with vast land holdings, and had been a major slave trader in the years before the war. He cussed like a field hand, but fought like a tiger, and the men of Bedford County, Tennessee had flocked to his ranks when he assumed command of the Brigade.

The defeats at Selma and Northport had been the first of his military career, following a long line of victories. The scout had been there for every one of them, at first as a trooper, but as his skills as a tracker and hunter, honed in the hills of East Tennessee had come out, he had served through most of the war as chief scout.

Lightning lit up the western sky and the rumble of distant thunder followed. The scout looked out from under the water soaked hat and studied the sky. The clouds, barely lighter than the sky itself, were moving slowly, west to east. The rain was going to come harder, he thought.

I just want to go home, the scout mused, for the hundredth time. *This here war is over and we done lost it.* Hard times lay ahead for the common soldier of the Confederacy.

He knew the common soldier wasn't fighting because of the darkies, and the few who had a little schooling might have heard of State's Rights, but they weren't in this here war because of that, either. They were fighting because the men of the mountains of North Carolina, and the low country of South Carolina and Georgia, of the hot plains of Texas, and the swamps and bayous of Louisiana and the gulf coast, and the stately plantations of Virginia didn't like being told how to live their lives. Far was the distance between the mind of the common soldier and the officers who led them.

The scout let out a bark of laughter, something else he wouldn't have done while on his stealthy business at an earlier time. *Now, that General Forrest, he had a passel a' Niggra's working his fields, or at least he used to.* In the mind of Nathan Bedford Forrest, the gap between white and black was as wide as an ocean.

Maybe the scout had felt that way once. Now, he just wanted to go home to Tennessee and lick his wounds. He wondered about his woman and the boy. He hadn't seen or heard from them in over a year. No way to know if they were still alive.

The horse slopped through the soft, rutted road. In the distance, the rumble of thunder came again. The sound rolled over the scout. This time it didn't stop.

The scout pulled up on the reins, and lifted the hat from his head, pointing his grizzled face into the wind like a hound smelling for a rabbit. The thunder kept coming, and grew louder.

He cursed, and looked around for an escape route. A flash of lightning lit up a hole in a fence line to his left, exposing a copse of trees above it, maybe fifty or sixty yards away.

He drove his spurs into the mare's shanks and pulled hard on the reins. The animal responded, and he guided her through the gap in the fence, and up into the stand of trees.

It was a thick stand of firs and the sodden branches whipped at his legs, but he was able to bury himself deep enough to hide, yet close enough to the edge of the tree line so that he could see the road through the increasingly heavy rain.

The sound of the thunder, now distinguishable as horses hooves, grew louder and louder. The scout felt a rising sense of fear traveling up his spine, and realized it was a sensation he had not felt in a long time.

God damn it, he thought. *I damn near rode right into them Yanks.* He lowered his head against the animal's neck and pulled down on the reins so that she wouldn't whinny.

The sound grew to an ear splitting level as the first horsemen came into view, heading south down the sodden road.

The scout tried to count the ranks of Yankee cavalry as they passed before him, but he quickly lost count. The Union and unit flags were furled so he couldn't make out who they were, but it had to be Wilson's people.

They had come after all.

Rank after rank passed the scout's position. So many that they blurred together in the mist and splashing, muddy water.

It took almost a quarter hour for the cavalry to pass. They were headed straight for General Forrest's position at Fikes Ferry, and they were now between the scout and the Confederate forces. Forrest would be outnumbered maybe twenty to one.

The scout watched the last of the massive force pass. It struck him that they were so confident, they hadn't put scouts of their own out in front of their column.

Six, maybe seven miles separated Forrest and disaster.

The sound of the Yankee cavalry became muted as they moved away, and soon the scout was left with only the pounding of the unrelenting rain in his ears.

He gave a quick thought to warning his people down the road, but knew in an instant that it was hopeless.

Fool's errand, he thought again, and pulled the oilskin tighter around his shoulders.

Glancing up at the dark sky, the scout pulled out of the trees and turned the mare north again, towards Tennessee.

✱   ✱   ✱   ✱

April 7, 1865
General Lee's Headquarters
Amelia Courthouse, Virginia, C.S.A

Robert E. Lee, Commanding General, Army of Northern Virginia, slumped back into the chair, removed his eyeglasses, and laid them gently on the table.

He closed his eyes and rested his grey head against the chair's back.

Four officers, his principle aides, stood motionless, trying not to intrude on the General's mood.

It is nearly done, he thought. *Four long years, so many fine young men dead, and now it is nearly done.* He opened his eyes and picked up the letter lying before him on the table. Lee did not put on the glasses, but stared at the fuzzy words without needing to read them again.

The letter, written personally by U.S. Grant, Commanding General, Army of the Potomac, U.S.A., had arrived under flag of truce some two hours earlier.

I am so tired, Lee thought, as the words he had memorized ran over and over in his head.

After four long years, "Sam" Grant, holder of one of the worst academic records in his class at West Point, was offering to accept the surrender of an army led by a man who had not only achieved a perfect record at the Point, but had once been its commandant.

So long ago.

And, today had brought word of another disaster at Sailor's Creek, not far from Lee's present headquarters, where his men had been defeated yet again. Worse yet, six general officers had been captured, including Lee's son, George Washington Custis Lee.

Lee rested his head and closed his eyes again. *Where is President Davis? Where is our government? Does it exist anymore?*

Lee's attempt to meet up in Danville with Davis had been thwarted by the fast moving columns of Phillip Sheridan's cavalry, who had cut off the Army of Northern Virginia from the 'new' capital of the Confederacy. Lee had no way to know if the President had been captured.

Lee felt an overwhelming melancholy enveloping him. *Where have all the victories gone?* The South, always outnumbered by the North's manpower, factories, navy, and of course, money, had never-the-less stood Lincoln's grand armies on their ears for over two years, and no true Southerner had even considered final defeat as a possibility.

And then, the tide had turned for good at Gettysburg, Pennsylvania, during the ill-fated invasion of the North. It was Lee's biggest gamble of the war. He had begun to believe that his forces were invincible. Instead, they had been decimated. But to his men, Lee remained god-like.

What would he do now? He was cut off from his political leaders, the President at best a fugitive, and possibly in irons, and the gold the army needed to continue the fight, out of his reach.

When it had become evident that he would not reach Danville, the General had turned his army toward Lynchburg, which would also take him near the passes through the Blue Ridge Mountains, the final escape route.

The Yankees were closing in. True, he had some thirty-five thousand soldiers in his ranks; a sizeable force under other circumstances, but they were exhausted, short on ammunition and food, low of spirit, and facing a rested, well armed, and well fed Union force of vastly superior numbers.

We can fight and end this war with a valiant struggle to the death, Lee thought, *but, who will rebuild our beloved South? Can we afford to lose even one more good man?*

Lee knew that this was an impossible situation. Even if he surrendered, the word would not reach other commands in theatres of war far from here for days. More men would die.

Who would rebuild the South? The landed gentry had been decimated, slavery was abolished, *and that is a good thing,* Lee knew, *but who will rebuild the South if I let more of our young men perish needlessly for a cause already lost?*

Finally, his decision made evident by circumstances, General Robert E. Lee sat forward in his chair and put on his glasses. "Colonel Pemberton," he said, motioning to his aide. "My writing case, if you will."

Pemberton retrieved the leather bound case and laid it before Lee.

"I will have a dispatch for you to carry, personally, if you would, Colonel. You will need to prepare a flag of truce."

Lee began to write, as Pemberton looked at the other officers in the room.

"I will need to meet with General Grant to discuss the surrender of the army," Lee said, "but it will be necessary to know the terms he is offering before such a meeting can take place."

The statement could not have been a total surprise, but Pemberton and the others were stunned to hear the words finally spoken out loud.

"You had best prepare to depart, Colonel. I will have the letter ready for you in a few moments," Lee said.

"Sir….," Pemberton started, ready to argue the case for continuing the campaign.

"Colonel," Lee raised his hand to stop him. "There is nothing left for me to do but to go and see General Grant," he said, sadly, "and I would rather die a thousand deaths."

*   *   *   *

April 9, 1865
The Wilmer McLean House
Appomattox Courthouse, Virginia, C.S.A.

General Ulysses Simpson Grant extended his hand to the elegantly uniformed Robert E. Lee. Looking up slightly into the eyes of the taller Lee, the disheveled Grant motioned to two chairs and a small table in the parlor of the abandoned house.

The two enemies, who had once been comrades in arms, sat down, and an aide to Grant put a black leather folder containing the surrender terms on the table between them.

Grant ignored the folder for a few minutes and passed pleasantries with the uncomfortable Lee.

Finally, Grant said, "General Lee, it is in the best interest of the country that we initiate the complete cessation of hostilities throughout the South as soon as possible."

Lee, momentarily unable to look directly at Grant nodded, slightly.

"The country cannot begin to heal while warfare continues," Grant added, leaning forward across the table. "Sir," he said, "President Davis cannot be allowed to continue the war from afar. Can you tell me where he is?"

Lee knew exactly what Grant was asking. He knew the General gave not one whit about Davis or his government. There was no government without the gold Lee knew Davis was carrying with him. Lee shook his head sadly. "General Grant," he said. "I have no idea where my government is. I promise you, sir, I do not know."

Grant was disappointed, but he believed the man. "I thank you for your candor, General Lee," he said.

A few minutes later after receiving a guarantee from the Union commander that his men could return home freely to await parole, Robert E. Lee formally surrendered the Army of Northern Virginia.

Out on the steps of the house as he prepared to leave, Lee stood face to face with Ely Parker; a full- blooded Seneca Indian who had been Grant's scout throughout the war. Lee touched the brim of his hat, and walked down the steps towards Parker.

"I am glad to see a *real* American here," Lee said.

Parker put his hand out to Lee, who took it, and shook it solemnly. "We are *all* Americans, General," Parker said.

✳   ✳   ✳   ✳

April 26, 1865
The Birmingham Road

Luddy Quinn had brought the news. The Yankee cavalry, about fifty strong, was heading east, just like Forrest and his thirty horsemen. The Yanks were on the Birmingham Road, and the Rebels were riding parallel and to the south, with only about a mile separating the two forces.

Three days earlier, a lone rider wearing tattered farmer's clothes and riding a mangy looking mare stumbled into Nathan Bedford Forrest's picket line in the middle of the night. After convincing the sergeant in charge that he was actually looking for the General, he was brought back to the little clearing deep in the woods about twenty miles west of the Georgia line, where the rag-tag troopers, wrapped in oilskins and huddled against each other for warmth, were trying to fight off the damp chill that permeated the night air.

The rider, actually an out- of- uniform soldier, was amazed at his good fortune in finding Forrest at all. He delivered to the General a letter he had kept hidden in the hollow of his boot heel, which was an order directly from the President of the Confederacy, Jefferson Davis.

Since he had received the letter directing him to meet Davis in Georgia, at a location not mentioned in the letter, but delivered by the President's emissary, so that the meeting place would not easily fall into the hands of Union soldiers should the rider be captured, Forrest had been moving his people eastward towards Georgia, ducking columns of Yankee cavalry along the way.

Now, the Confederate forces found themselves trapped into plodding along in muck and mire south of the Birmingham Road. The constant rain, seemingly with them for days at a time, was ending, and the mist that had helped them hide like shadows was lifting, taking away the protection of the poor visibility.

A shadowy figure came out of the mist just ahead of Forrest, who was leading the small column. He put up a hand to signal that they were stopping, and waited for the shadow to merge into the shape of Sergeant Quinn.

Quinn pulled up and looked at Forrest. "They's still right with us, sir. Headin' east, and in no partic'lar hurry."

"Damn," said the General, softly. "We don't break outta' this, we'll never make the rendezvous in time, Luddy."

"General," the scout said. "Nears I can tell, there's a lot of open territory ahead of us. But lest we get away from those fellers, ain't no way we can make up time."

"What are you suggesting, Sergeant?"

Quinn looked away, picking his words carefully. "Ain't my job to do the suggestin', sir. But if you was askin' me what I would do, I think we need to stop them Yanks from goin' where they's goin' before they get ahead of us."

General Forrest smiled, knowing the answer before the words were spoken. He looked up into the darkening sky. "'Bout two hours to full dark," he said. "Come another hour or so, the Yanks will be looking to make camp."

Forrest was quiet for a minute, and then he said, "You know, Luddy, they might be gettin' ready to break off in some other direction. We could wait them out."

Quinn shook his head. "They's goin' east, and that's a fact."

Forrest nodded. "I agree. We'll need to hit them after they settle down for the night."

Forrest signaled to his men to remount.

"Luddy, you go on back and watch 'em close. We'll come on slow, and wait for you to report their position after they make camp."

Sergeant Quinn nodded, and without further comment, touched the brim of his hat, pulled his horse around and headed back in the direction of the Yankee patrol.

It was fully dark when Quinn found the Confederate horsemen again.

"Yanks are over to our left flank, General," he told Forrest. "'Bout quarter mile up. Found a clearing just off the road and made camp." Quinn huffed, disgustedly. "Don't have no pickets out, lit a fire, and eatin' hot food just like they's on a damn picnic."

"Good. Let's hope they stay that way for an hour or so. Any sign of other Yankees patrols?"

Quinn scratched his beard. "Didn't see nothin', our people nor theirs. I think we're all out here alone, sir."

Forrest knew without asking, that the sergeant would have run a circle at least a couple of miles out from the Union camp to make sure.

"Okay," the General said, "let's get ready. We'll leave the horses here and move up on foot, let them get settled down and full of that hot food. Then we'll hit 'em."

They formed two lines, one along side the other, with Forrest and Sergeant Quinn up ahead, and started forward toward the Union troopers. As they neared the encampment, Quinn motioned back to the others, and they hit the ground, crawling some fifty yards through the mud and brush, until Quinn signaled again, and they held their positions.

Forrest and Quinn moved up another hundred feet or so, toward the edge of the tree line above the Birmingham Road on their bellies, until they were overlooking the enemy's camp fires.

Fools, Forrest thought to himself. The Union commander had left his men totally exposed and unprotected. Johnny Reb had the high ground, and every one of the Yankees was exposed to the possibility of gunfire. But, they were also a force twice the size of Forrest's. He needed to make sure the enemy was as unprepared to fight as possible when he attacked.

They watched the encampment for another half hour as the Yankees ate their dinner. The smell of the food, plain as it was, flooded over Forrest and his men. It had been a long time since hot food.

The two Rebels slid backwards through the brush as slowly and quietly as possible, until they reached the rest of the men, who were now both wet, and cold. Forrest signaled them into a tight group.

"Sergeant Quinn will take half of you around behind the Yanks," he said. "The rest of you will follow me back to the top of the bank overlooking the road. We'll fire two rounds into the camp, making sure to hit as many of them as we can. Then, Quinn and his men will run up on the camp from the rear and hit 'em with another round."

General Forrest let that sink in for a moment. "After Quinn's men fire, we will attack with sabers and revolvers from both sides. Understand?"

There was assent all around.

"We'll give you plenty of time to get around, Sergeant, but don't dawdle. I want to be up the road and out of here before we get more company. Make sure your men stay back and hug the ground until we fire our two rounds, hear?"

Luddy nodded, got up, and started tapping the shoulders of the men who were to follow him. Each man checked and reloaded his British-made rifle, the only real value the South had received from the negotiations with

Great Britain on the possibility of the British joining with the Confederacy against the North. Those negotiations ended after the bloody catastrophe at Gettysburg, when it became evident that General Lee would now be fighting a defensive war against a vastly superior enemy.

The sergeant and his men snuck away into the mist- covered woods, and headed east to a point where they could safely cross the road and flank the Yankee camp, while Forrest waited a while before advancing to his point of attack. No sense taking a risk of being discovered before Quinn was in place.

After a while Forrest signaled to his men, and the small group slithered their way to the ridge overlooking the road and the camp on the other side. The men hugged the ground, peering over at the Union troopers, who were in various stages of bedding down.

A few hung around the fires, smoking and talking. General Forrest squinted into the dark, trying to pick out officers in the light of the fires. *Take out the officers first, if possible.* This would be a risky deal if they didn't drop a lot of the Yanks with the three volleys.

Forrest wiped the sweat from his eyes. Off to the west, a short distance from the encampment he heard a low whinny. The Yankee horses. He wished he had back the three men he had left behind with his own mounts, but someone had to keep the horses quiet, and then bring them along fast after the attack so they wouldn't waste time getting out of here.

It had been about an hour or so since Luddy Quinn and his men had headed out to surround the Union troopers. Forrest touched the man closest to him, and signaled to pass the word to get ready. In the dark, he could see his men sliding their rifles up to shooting position, and he did the same.

The general drew a bead on what appeared to be an officer standing with three other troopers by the closest fire. The man was laughing at some remark. Forrest took one more look across the camp. *Can't wait no longer,* he thought.

His finger tightened on the trigger until it couldn't bear the tension any longer, and the explosion came quick and loud. Almost at the same moment the weapons alongside him followed suit. The smoke and smell flooding from the cartridges engulfed the Confederate line. Forrest and the others reloaded, took aim again and fired their second round into the enemy camp. Their first round had taken out all the standing Yankees, and the second hit many more as they rose up from the ground at the sound of gunfire.

The Union troops had been caught by their folly of feeling invincible in their position, but they were professional soldiers, and the camp showed signs of organizing a defense. That was when Luddy Quinn's men sent their round of death from the ridge to the south into the backs of the troopers who had risen to face the attack.

More men pitched over, struck by the withering fire. The Yankees were now in disarray.

"Now!" Forrest yelled at the top of his lungs, and his men dropped their rifles and grabbed the revolvers and sabers at their sides. In a moment, they were up and charging down the incline to the roadbed, and a second later they were crossing over and slamming into the staggered enemy.

The sound of clashing bodies and sabers, punctuated by a revolver's discharge here and there, was like a thunderclap and lightening strike all at once.

Forrest found himself face to face with a giant of a man, a scream of anger gushing out from between his beard and moustache. The man lunged at the Confederate commander with his saber. Forrest parried the blow with his own weapon, and fired two shots into the man's belly. A look of surprise erupted on his face, and he dropped to the ground.

Forrest caught sight of Quinn going blade on blade with another trooper about twenty feet away, just as he was attacked himself by another Yankee. Forrest slashed his blade across the neck of the overmatched man, and was alone again as the enemy slumped to the ground, his head nearly severed. All around him there were sounds of battle and screams of pain. They became one.

Within a few minutes, the din of battle lessened as fewer and fewer mini-battles went on. Forrest had no one left to fight, and he took a quick look around the encampment. He looked around the dimly lit battleground, seeing one, no, two of his men down, but there could be others.

As quickly as it had begun, the fight was over. The sound of gunshots and clashing blades was abruptly overtaken by a silence broken by the moans of the wounded.

Forrest stood by the biggest of the still-burning fires, trying desperately to warm himself. A pot of spilled coffee- *real* coffee by the smell of it, lay on the ground at his feet. *Damn waste,* he thought.

Luddy Quinn came up next to him. The two looked at each other.

"We got three dead, two wounded, but not too bad, sir," the sergeant reported. "They can ride."

General Forrest nodded slowly, his own adrenalin coming down. "The Yankees?"

The sergeant expelled a slow breath. "Few still alive, but they ain't gonna' make it."

"Let's get the horses down here and get movin'," Forrest said as he rubbed his hands in the fires warmth. "Morgan!" He called out, and the man came trotting over. "Get some of their grain for our horses," he said. "We're gonna' need it by tomorrow."

The man saluted. Suddenly, there was a loud "pop," and Morgan's jaw disintegrated in a gush of bone and blood, spraying the front of Forrest's face. The look of surprise on Morgan's face turned grotesque as his eyes rolled back into his head, and he dropped to the ground.

Quinn grabbed Forrest and tried to drag him down, but the general fought him off and stood his ground. Off in the distance, he saw two shadows that he knew were Yankee horsemen pulling out into the roadway, and heading west at a furious gallop, as some of his own men fired useless pistol shots after them.

God damn it. The Yanks had men with their horses, just like I did. Just like they ought to!

Forrest hadn't given any thought to the horses. Now two riders were barreling their way towards wherever more Yanks were down the road, and another of his men was lost for no reason.

"Luddy," Forrest wiped the dead man's blood from his face and said. "We best get out of here, and I mean right now!"

✶   ✶   ✶   ✶

April 28, 1865
Bones Tavern
Washington County, Georgia, CSA

President Jefferson Davis extended his hand to the mud- splattered apparition who had just come through the door into the small, sparsely furnished room. "Please sit down, General Forrest," he said, motioning to a chair. "Thank God you were able to join us here safely."

"Thank you, sir," Forrest answered, dropping heavily into the seat. The exhaustion in his face told the story of his hard journey from Alabama.

"Your men and horses are being tended to as we speak, and Horatio will have some food and drink for you momentarily."

Nathan Bedford Forrest nodded his thanks.

"You made good time reaching us with the weather conditions such as they are," Davis said.

"It was dumb luck that your messenger found us," Forrest said. "What forces we still have in Alabama are pretty spread out."

What forces we still have..... Davis thought. "Yes," he said, simply.

Horatio, Davis' Negro servant, knocked lightly on the door, and entered. He had been with the president all his life; as a playmate when they were children, and as manservant now. Although Abraham Lincoln's Emancipation Proclamation had technically freed him, Horatio had never considered leaving his post. The Davis' were his people.

"Thank you," the President said as Horatio finished laying out a meager plate for Forrest, and poured him a small beer. The general ignored the servant.

Forrest attacked the food and Davis left him to it for awhile. When the general sat back in the chair, the edge off his appetite, Davis said, "I am sure you are wondering why I sent for you?"

Forrest shrugged. "I guessed you were ready to move away from here and head for Mexico," he said, in a matter of fact tone. "We will need to move out as soon as possible, sir. The Yankees are bearing down on…."

Jefferson Davis was shaking his head, his hand up to stop the general. "No," he said. "You will not be escorting us to Mexico, General Forrest. I cannot leave my family, and I will not abandon the people who gave up so much to help govern our country." Davis shook his head sadly. "You know we would never make it through the Union army for such a great distance."

Forrest sat forward in the chair. "Sir, we cannot continue this fight without you bein' in Mexico with us!"

The President sat quietly for a long minute. Finally, he stood, and walked to the little window that looked out over the dirt lane that crossed in front of the tavern. "General, it is important, I agree, for the Union cavalry to *believe* that we are attempting to escape to Mexico. But frankly, it is my opinion that, even if we were successful in such an attempt," he came back to face Forrest as he went on speaking, "unless we were to arrive across the border with a large number of troops, we could not protect our treasury from Maximilian."

"But," Forrest protested, "the Emperor has offered us safe haven and a place to attack the North from!"

"Yes, I know," Davis interrupted. "Think on it, General. The Mexicans are still enraged over the Texas incident in '36. Would they want to risk another war with the United States? Over us? In our dire condition? They will certainly remember that we could not get the British to join us when we were winning. We cannot help them regain their territory lost in the Mexican War. No, I do not trust Maximilian's motives."

Forrest's despair showed on his face. "Then, what are we to do? Are we to give up trying to regain control of our world? Our sacred way of life?" He was on his feet now. "Sir, you have eluded the damn Yankees for hundreds of miles. Are you simply going to give up now?"

Davis motioned Forrest back to the chair, his hand on the General's arm, calming him. "There was a purpose to your journey here," he said. "Please let me explain."

They sat down again.

"No, General Forrest, I have not given up the dream of restoring our way of life. But, I am afraid we cannot win this war army against army. The North seems only to get stronger, and we get weaker every day." Davis hesitated before delivering more bad news. "Have you heard that General Johnston has surrendered his forces in Tennessee?"

The look on Forrest's face told that he had not. He hated Joe Johnston and had called the man a coward to his face. But, surrender?

Davis smiled a sad smile. "It is a strange thing," he said. "I never agreed much with a word that came from Abe Lincoln's mouth, but the man led his country to a crushing victory over us, and, because of the act of a madman actor; an act I believe will haunt the South for a hundred years, he will not be here to govern over his defeated foe."

"And, damn his retched soul to Hell!" Forrest cried out. "He took everything from us! I have no sympathy for that cursed bastard. The South must have its slaves to survive," he said, trying to calm himself. But the bitterness rushed from him. "There are few of us left, but we must prevail! And we need you, sir. What are you going to do?"

"As I said, General, I have no wish to give up, but we cannot carry on as we have. I am taking my people across to the coast. It has been arranged for a ship to meet us at Cumberland Island. They will take us to Haiti, where we will continue the fight in ways political as well as military."

"But, sir," Forrest said, "you can't provide safety for yourself or the gold you carry for hundreds of miles. You were damned lucky to find enough wagons and horses in Danville to get you this far. You *will* be captured!"

President Davis did not answer.

"All right, sir," the General said with a sigh of resignation. "We will endeavor to get you and your party to the coast."

"No," Davis said, shaking his grey mane. "You will not be traveling with us, General. I have a different task for you." Davis sat back in the chair. "The best service you can render to your government and your country now will be to draw away as many Union cavalry as you can from our route of escape. That is why you will leave here in the morning with wagons loaded with several crates."

Now Forrest understood. "But," he said softly, "*not* with the gold."

"No, General, not with the gold. We will carry the gold with us as long as we can. If the coast becomes unreachable, we will hide it. If we are successful in reaching Haiti, you and your men…and any others you can round up, will join us later from Mexico."

Forrest said, "But sir, where could you hide that much gold? Its weight alone will make it impossible to carry with you for any great distance."

Davis ignored the remarks. "If that becomes the case" he went on, "when it is safely hidden, I will get word to you of its location, so both of us will know where to collect it later for resumption of our…war. But in order to hide it, we must convince the Yankees that the gold is with you, on its way to Mexico."

The two men were quiet for a moment. "Damn Lincoln to Hell," Nathan Bedford Forrest said again.

President Jefferson Davis stood and offered his hand to one of his last remaining commanding officers. "General, we may all meet in Hell before this is finally over."

$$\ast \quad \ast \quad \ast \quad \ast$$

May 3. 1865
Along the Birmingham Road
Near the Alabama-Georgia Border

Two days of unusually hot weather followed by another day of chilling rain had caused a continuous, steamy fog to rise from the soggy ground. Sergeant Quinn heard rather than saw the Bluecoat cavalry that had been slowly making its way along the road west toward Birmingham for almost an hour.

Quinn, his head barely visible above the top of the hillock, spat tobacco juice into a puddle a few feet from where he lay. There was no fear of being spotted some fifty yards from where the enemy marched, but *anyways, it takes a hellofalot to scare this 'ol Tennessee boy these days.* But just to be on the safe side, he hunkered down a little deeper into the soft ground. No, he wasn't much scared of the long line of troopers up ahead; their chances of seeing him were no better than his chances of clearly making out even one enemy face through the mist. But he *was* worried about whether the Yankee commander had put out flankers who might come up behind his position.

It didn't really matter. Luddy Quinn, sergeant in General Nathan Bedford Forrest's cavalry, had seen enough. Crawling backwards for about ten yards to get deeper into the mist, he rose up to his haunches and drifted back into the woods. It was already getting dark, and it took him several minutes to find the tethered horse he had left far from the road.

Quinn mounted and guided the mare through the stand of pines, and down into a little valley. The sound of water rushing through the wide, but normally shallow creek, led him to the middle of the valley. He turned his mount westward, and went hunting for Forrest, and the rest of the Rebel horsemen.

About two miles west he pulled up and listened intently, trying to separate the sound of the rain drops falling through the trees, from the sounds of men and horses. It was pitch black now, with only the shadows of the swaying, high-topped pines visible against the blue-grey of the stormy sky.

When the hooting sound of an owl broke through the rain, Quinn relaxed and spurred the mare on. A short distance ahead, a horseman broke from cover and pulled up alongside the sergeant.

Quinn touched the brim of his hat and relaxed his grip on the reins. "General," he said, offering a soggy salute.

"Welcome back, Sergeant," Forrest answered. "What's the situation?"

"Bad's we figgered. Thousands of Yanks headin' west, sir." Quinn said. "Worst is, they done took the Birmin'ham Road away from us for sure."

General Forrest sighed. "Damn Yanks seem to have an endless supply of men, don't they, Luddy?"

"General, we can't use that road, and they keep pourin' more and more troopers into this area. Sooner or later, this rain is gonna' end, and they gonna' see us." Quinn stopped to think about what he wanted to say. He nodded towards the wagons hidden in the woods. "When they do, them wagons ain't gonna' make it easy for us to get away."

Forrest was lost in thought. They sat there atop their mounts, the rain the only sound.

Finally, Quinn said, "What you wanna' do, General?"

Forrest pointed west along the creek. "There's a town just across the border in Alabama. Just this side, there's a plantation owned by Rupert LaGrange…"

"That the feller who was a state senator up in Montgomery when it was the capital?"

"That's him," the general answered. "Maybe five, six miles from this very spot. He'll put us up or find us a place to hide 'til things settle down." He was thoughtful again. "This here creek bed's mostly hardpan. We'll use it for a road, follow it far as we can, and we'll dump them wagons before we reach Alabama."

Sergeant Quinn thought about that. "General, I know we can't carry that much gold on horseback, so I'll be guessin' there ain't nothin' but rocks in them crates."

"That would be a good guess, Luddy," Forrest said, in a near whisper, although the rain made it impossible for any of the others to hear him.

"Sir, I don't cotten' to dying for a bunch a' rocks what don't mean nothin'," Quinn said with a useless swipe at the water streaming down the brim of his campaign hat.

"Me neither," the Forrest said, "but for a little longer, that's gonna' be a real possibility."

$\star$ $\star$ $\star$ $\star$

May 12, 1865
Homer Smith House
Irwinville, occupied Georgia

"I would greatly appreciate it, Major, if you would address me as *President* Davis, if you do not mind!" He was on his feet now staring down the impeccably dressed Union officer. Davis' hands were shaking as he tried in vain to maintain his composure.

"Yes, I am sure you would," Major HenryAppleby said dryly. The short, mutton-chopped officer sat heavily on the chair, and smiled thinly. "But then I would be addressing you incorrectly." His smile turned into a sneer, and his voice rose. "You are president of nothing! You are but another Rebel prisoner, and have been for three days now, *Mr.* Davis, caught sneaking away from a war that *you* started. And, I expect, on your way to a date with the gallows! Now, sit down!"

The door flew open and Appleby scrambled to his feet, nearly falling off the chair. The two other soldiers in the room also snapped to attention as Ulysses Simpson Grant, Commanding General, Army of the Potomac, entered the room. Everyone fell silent, and Grant, standing in the doorway, casually lit the cigar that he carried in his hand. When the match went out, he finally spoke. "Good morning, President Davis," he said, and then turned to Appleby. "Major, there happens to be a bottle of very good Kentucky bourbon in the next room. The bottle and two glasses, if you please,"

Appleby nearly fell over himself with pleasure, and was back in a moment with the bourbon. Grant took the tray from him, set it on the table in front of Davis and filled the two shot glasses.

The general took one glass and carefully set it before the captive leader of the Confederacy, and took the other for himself. Appleby's crestfallen face belied his disappointment.

"That will be all for now, Major. You can return to your duties," Grant said, motioning to the other soldiers to leave the room with Appleby.

The door closed leaving Grant alone with his prisoner. "Armies are full of future politicians," he said with a rueful grin, and motioned Davis back to his chair.

Davis forced himself to relax. "I believe I have the honor of addressing General Grant?"

"I am not sure that it is an honor, sir, but, yes, I'm Grant."

The two men sat across the table for a long moment.

"General Grant," Davis said, "I am worried about Mrs. Davis and my sons..."

Grant held up his hand. "Do not concern yourself, sir. Your people have been billeted and given all necessary supplies. You will rejoin your family shortly. I am afraid your transport to Washington may be a few days off." Grant raised his glass, and Davis did likewise. "I promise you, President Davis, you and your people will not be ill-treated while you are our guests."

Jefferson Davis felt relief well up in his chest. "I thank you, sir. My wife has not been well. Our journey has been a harsh one."

"I will see to it that she and anyone else needing medical attention are seen by one of our doctors." Grant poured another round.

"I have missed good Kentucky bourbon," Davis smiled. "I was born there, you know."

Grant took the second shot, and then placed his glass carefully on the table. His face grew serious. "Mr. President, the war is over now, but our hardest job may still be before us."

"You speak, of course, of the reconciliation of our two nations," Davis said.

"I speak, sir, of reconciliation between the states of our Union." Grant sat forward in the uncomfortable chair. "We must stop thinking of ourselves as citizens of different nations. We are but one nation that has been at war with itself."

Davis did not reply. This was no time for a war of words. That, would be a war he could not win.

Grant took the bottle in hand, but did not pour. "Sir," he said, "this nation cannot recover and endure if the nations of Europe see us as a carcass to be stripped clean. We must start to heal our wounds immediately! Surely you can see that further bloodshed will be to the detriment of us all."

Davis knew where this was leading. He decided to bring the conversation to a head. "General Grant, you are asking me to end a war that you have already ended. We are defeated, sir! What more can I do?"

Grant studied the man for several moments. Then, he said, "Sir, I think you know exactly what I am saying. Somewhere out there is the remaining treasury of the Confederacy, which we know you brought out of Richmond." He finally poured more bourbon into the empty glasses, and stared hard into the eyes of his prisoner. "As long as that gold is out there, it can be used to continue a struggle that is officially over.....a struggle that has taken the lives of hundreds of thousands of *American;* not Northern or Southern lives, sir! *American* lives."

"Many of my countrymen do not see it that way, General Grant. Nothing will make them stop fighting for the life that has been taken from them," he said, quietly.

Grant shook his head. "You cannot possibly believe slavery will ever see the light of day again in this country. That way of life is gone forever."

"I doubt, sir, that you and I will live to see the true end of that question," Davis answered.

Grant ignored the remark. "President Davis, will you tell me where the Southern gold is?"

Davis stood and put his hands behind his back. He turned to look hard into the eyes of his conqueror. "General Grant, I expect the remaining forces of the Confederate States of America, *and* the gold you seek are well inside the borders of the sovereign country of Mexico."

✳   ✳   ✳   ✳

June 19, 1866, Midnight
George Geary Plantation
Near Pulaski, Tennessee

"I'm not a general anymore, Mr. Ellis." Nathan Bedford Forrest, late of the Confederate Army, tossed the remnants of the whiskey on the ground, and stared past his companion to the fire licking away at the raggedly constructed cross. They were in the fields far from the Geary plantation house. "Not a military man, but just a simple old soldier now embattled with the future, not the past."

"As are we all, sir," The speaker was Alton Henry Ellis, the scion of a Tennessee family that was of this place a hundred years before it became a part of the Union. "The question, I assume is how we preserve *our* future. Is it not?"

Forrest was becoming bored by the rhetoric. He was a man of action, not words, and the year since the armistice had taken effect had been an interminable nightmare. He nodded toward the mass of men encircling the now fully engulfed cross.

"We have given you the tool for your quest, Mr. Ellis. The Empire is in place. Now, what will you do with it?"

The man smiled, "It's already bein' done, General," he said, continuing to use the title. "The niggers around here are bein' kept in their place, all right. But we are not going to win the battle throughout the South right here alone."

He reached over and poured more of the sour mash into Forrest's mug.

Forrest knew where this was going, and he was silent for a long time. They watched the men around the fire, but their thoughts were elsewhere.

Finally, Nathan Bedford Forrest, one of the founders and leaders of the Ku Klux Klan, said, "Mr. Ellis, you are right. We will need a lot of money to win our fight." He tossed the liquor away without drinking. Everything tasted vile to him right now. "I suggest we find a way to raise the funds we need." He turned and walked away, leaving Ellis standing there.

They all think I know where the gold is. They think I'm keeping it for myself. I'm more dedicated to our Cause than any of those fools!

Forrest reached the makeshift corral where his horse was tethered, grabbed the reins, mounted, and sped away. *God damn you, Jeff Davis! You and your secrecy. Where in the name of God is that gold?!*

✳   ✳   ✳   ✳

December 6, 1886
The Garden District
New Orleans, Louisiana, U.S.A.

He could not open his eyes. Try as he might, he could not force his eyes to open, or his arms to rise from the bed, where they lay like lead weights at his sides.

The former president of the Confederate States of America felt the presence of the family members; his dear wife, and friends attending him, and heard their muted sobs. He could feel the air stirring as they moved around the bed. Certainly his dedicated manservant, Horatio was here, and old Dr. Pittman would be at the bedside, but Jefferson Davis could not open his eyes to acknowledge them.

He was dying. That much he knew, and the strokes had finally taken away his ability to die with the dignity his former position deserved. That was a lie, he told himself. Defeat and prison, though of a relatively short duration for one accused of treason as he had been, had taken away his dignity.

The last stroke had hit him a week ago while he was visiting the city from his home, "Beauvoir," located between New Orleans and Mobile. The doctor had pronounced him too ill to return home, and he had been brought to this house in the Garden District of the city. Even then, he had been able to speak yesterday to his wife. Now he could not.

It was of no consequence now, he knew. His heart, ravaged by the strokes, and an older, more hurtful pain that had begun in 1865 and had never lessened in its intensity, had taken a mighty toll. The last few years had not brought him solace. Some of his children were dead. This was life, and he was not afraid to die. But he could not shake the feeling, as he lay at the end of life's journey, that there was something left to do; something of great importance, something that he had *meant* to do before the strokes started coming. *Had he done so?* He couldn't remember. Again, he thought, *it is of no consequence now.*

His physical life was over. But his mind was still capable of rational thought. Yet, he could not bring forth the task that escaped him.

He remembered the conflict; the bloody conflict that preceded the death of his beloved South. At least he remembered some of it, and even then there were gaps.

But he did remember the Southern way before the battles raged and the way of life he had grown to love had disappeared. Nothing would bring it back.

No, the Confederacy had not come back. All the careful planning meant to provide a way for the South to rise again had come to naught. The close confidants who had helped him hide the remaining treasury of his collapsing government were mostly gone, or old and sick like their former leader.

No consequence. But, there was something that was important, and it would not come to him.

Jefferson Davis stopped caring, and let the last vestiges of a life unfulfilled slip away.

✳   ✳   ✳   ✳

November 29, 1922
Posted on the door, The State Capitol Building
Atlanta, Georgia, U.S.A.

We solemnly declare to all mankind: that the knights of the Ku Klux Klan, incorporated, is the original Ku Klux Klan organized in the year 1866, and active during the Reconstruction period of American history, and by and under its corporate name is revived, remodeled and expanded into a ritualistic, fraternal, patriotic society of national scope, duly incorporated (under the laws of the state of Georgia) in the years 1915 and 1916, and dedicated to the same principles and spiritual purposes as more particularly set forth in Article II, of the Constitution and Laws of the society........

The Imperial Proclamation

To the lovers of law, order peace and justice of all nations, people, tribes and tongues of the whole earth, Greetings:

I, and the citizens of the Invisible Empire, through me, make declaration to you:

We, the members of this order, desiring to promote patriotism toward our civil government; honorable peace among men and nations; protection for and happiness in the homes of our people; manhood, brotherhood, and love among ourselves, and liberty, justice and fraternity among all mankind; believing we can best accomplish these noble purposes through a mystic, social, patriotic benevolent association, having perfected lodge system, with an exalted ritualistic form of work and an effective form of government, not for selfish profit......do physically, socially, morally and vocationally:

Proclaim to the World:

That we are dedicated to the sublime duty of providing generous aid, tender sympathy and fraternal assistance amid fortune and misfortune.....amid the sable shadows of death.....

We invite all men who can qualify to become citizens of the Invisible Empire to approach the portal of our beneficent domain, join us in our noble work of extending its boundaries, and in disseminating the gospel of "Klancraft," thereby encouraging, conserving, protecting and making vital the fraternal relationship in the practice of an honorable clannishness; to share with us the glory of performing the sacred duty of protecting womanhood; to maintain forever the God-given supremacy of the White race; to commemorate the holy and chivalric achievements of out fathers; to safeguard the sacred rights, privileges and institutions of our civil government; to bless mankind and to keep eternally ablaze the sacred fire of a fervent devotion to a pure Americanism.

The Invisible Empire is founded on sterling character......., It is promoted by a sincere, unselfish devotion of the souls of men, and is governed by their consecrated intelligence. It is the soul of chivalry, virtue's impenetrable shield and the devout impulse of an unconquered race.

Done in the aulic of His Majesty, the Emperor of the Invisible Empire, Knights of the Ku Klux Klan, in the Imperial Palace, in the Imperial City of Atlanta, Commonwealth of Georgia, United States of America.

This, the 29th day of November, Anno Domini, Nineteen Hundred and Twenty-two, Anno Klan LVI.

William Joseph Simmons,
Imperial Wizard

CHAPTER I

———————— ▼ ————————

August 3, 2003
Amelia Island, Florida

I rolled onto my back and squinted through the blood that coated my face and flooded my eyes. I could see the weapon in Richard Barrett's hand as he aimed it at my chest. I was going to die, and Abby was going to die, too....

I awoke with a start as I always did when the dream came, and it still came often. I sat up in the lounge chair and rubbed my eyes to clear them of the sweat that was dripping from under my Ohio State cap. *Sweat*, not blood, but it still sent a shiver up my spine. The feeling didn't last long, and of course I knew that I was alive, and so was Abby Barrett, the love of my life.

She was standing some thirty yards from me, at the edge of the surf. Her slim form was there, her back to me and, had there been fifty women standing there in just the same way, I could have picked her out without hesitation. Abby was standing at the water's edge, wearing her big, floppy sun hat, absentmindedly swishing the foamy water with one foot as she read her paperback.

I leaned back in the chair and calmed myself as best I could. The umbrella over my head was useless against the sun and the thick, hot wind, and the temperature was near the one hundred degree mark, but it felt even hotter because of the humidity. It took a minute to bring myself down.

The dream was always the same: Cuba, the storm, several dead bodies surrounding me; some I recognized as friend, some foe, but all dead, just the same.

I looked out to the water's edge again. Abby was still there as I knew she would be, so I closed my eyes and thought back to how we had gotten here.

I had fallen in love with Abby back in Atlanta, where I was bartending at my brother, Pat's, Irish bar and grill. She was a student at Georgia Tech, and

I was trying to get a private investigations business going. Abby often visited *Ireland's Own* with her friends, and I fell hard, and strange as it still seems to me, she did too.

I had been born and raised in Cleveland, Ohio, attended Ohio State as a freshman football phenom wide receiver, and lost my ability to play on the very first pass thrown to me. While my leg and I were healing back in Cleveland, it gave my headstrong, opinionated, and wonderful Italian mother a chance to plan my "new" future. For some unknown reason, she Decided that meant a career as a PI, and, before I knew it, I was living above the restaurant in the Buckhead area of Atlanta, handling simple cases for Pat's friend and attorney, Max Howard.

Though I was a mess mentally and physically Abby brought reality and sense back into my life. Just as I could believe it was possible to be truly happy, she disappeared into thin air.

I could look at the beautiful face of Maria Barrett and know exactly what Abby would look like twenty-five years from now. Maria is elegant and cultured, the daughter of a wealthy Cuban tobacco plantation owner who, along with his and five other families, had escaped from their homeland one step ahead of Fidel Castro's henchmen when she was just a child. But before they left Cuba, the *patrons,* as the rich planters were known, hid the valuable possessions of generations of their families. They were betting that the people would rise up and throw the communists out quickly, so that they could come back to the land they loved. It never happened.

The first time I met Maria was the night I went looking for Abby, whom I had not heard from in the days following our first and only intimate encounter up in my room above Pat's bar. Maria told me that Abby was in Miami on family business concerning, as it turned out, the disposition of her natural father's parent's holdings to her and her brother, Carlos. But a few days later, while I was recovering from a run-in with a couple of unknown fists, I got a call from Abby's mom. Abby had been kidnapped in Miami.

What followed was like a Hollywood movie. I was told that Abby was being held for ransom, which turned out to be the hidden treasures of the patrons. Then came the crazy part: Maria Barrett wanted *me* to go to the ex-patriot community of Little Havana in Miami and ask the surviving Cubans who had conspired with her long-dead father to disclose the location of the treasure the kidnappers were looking for. Three days later, in defiance of all things reasonable, I was in Cuba trying to find a treasure that might not even exist, so that I could trade it for the life of Abby Barrett.

Somehow, it all worked out, but not before several people died; not before my sister-in-law's brother, Bobby Hemphill, who had gone to Cuba with me, saved my life, and nearly lost his own, and not before I took two bullets in my shoulder and thigh while trying to escape from the coast of Cuba with Abby, and an injured Bobby. And not before I killed the mastermind behind Abby's kidnapping: her step-father, Richard Barrett.

Its been seven months since all this happened, and now, in the dead of summer's heat, we found ourselves on this beautiful island, where my friend, Max Howard, had arranged a couple of condos so we could celebrate my recovery from my wounds.

I was jarred back to reality by the sound of a body dropping noisily into the lounge chair next to me. I squinted from under the bill of my ball cap and stared at the smiling, and somewhat silly, countenance of Bobby Hemphill.

"Don't you do anything quietly?" I said, giving him the evil eye, like I had learned at my grandmother's knee.

"Hell no, sport! Not on vacation, I don't."

"Well, that's just great," I answered with fake disgust.

Bobby is the younger brother of my sister-in-law, Charlotte June, or C.J., as she is know to everyone. A year ago he was the "lost child," at odds with his successful family and unsure of his place in the world. Then he went to Cuba with me, and eventually was forced to fire a .38 caliber slug into the head of a very large and dangerous man who was trying his best to squeeze the life out of me. I paid him back by almost getting him killed. But he helped me find and save Abby, and now he is my partner in our little business.

"Where's Sabine?" I asked.

"Gettin' her nails done," he answered. "Hey, what is it with girls gettin' their nails and hair done on vacation when they could do it back home anytime?"

Sabine Metaine is a gorgeous, mocha- skinned *Jamaica Air* flight attendant stationed in Atlanta, whom Bobby had met a few months ago. She's a native of Barbados whose mother is a *Bajan,* a native woman, and her father had been a French businessman who had lived on the island for years. Bobby was immediately taken by the tall beauty, and the two had been inseparable ever since.

"I'm sure I don't know," I said. "Actually, I find the mysterious side of women to be very interesting."

Bobby laughed. "Can't say you're wrong about that."

"You really like that girl, don't you?"

Bobby sat in silence for a moment, something he usually has trouble with. "I do," he said seriously. "I do really like that girl."

I smiled. "Good for you, Bobby."

He took a bottle of water out of the cooler and splashed some of the ice-cold liquid on his face. "Jesus, I thought it was hot back home, but this is murder." The use of the word, innocent as it was, brought the chill back.

I shook it off. "What say we try that seaside place for dinner tonight?"

"Fine by me," Bobby said, looking at his watch. "Leaves plenty of time for another little 'nap,' if you get my meanin'."

I pulled myself up from the chair and jammed his hat down over his eyes. "Whatever is wrong with you is no little thing," I said. "I'm taking Abby for a walk on the beach."

✳   ✳   ✳   ✳

The sound of the surf allowed me to sneak up behind Abby without her hearing me approach. I put my arms around her, resting my hands on her hard, bronzed belly and kissed the side of her neck.

"Hey, sweet cakes," I said, "hows about you and me find us a tall sand dune to hide behind so we can fool around?"

She pretended to ignore me and went on reading her book, but she put her right arm around my neck. "Watch it, stranger," she said. "I got me a boyfriend, and he's awfully strong, so don't bug me. Got it?" She laughed as I nuzzled against her and turned to give me a long, deep kiss. Her nearness and the sweet taste of her lips is always like a tonic to me.

"Let's take a walk," I said.

We started up the beach, walking along the edge of the incoming tide so we could avoid the hot sand. Our toes left deep ridges in the hard packed sand, as we walked arm in arm, just enjoying the noisy sea and each other.

Finally, Abby looked up at me from under the floppy brim of her hat. "Let's stay here forever," she said.

"Fine by me," I said, "but I might have to change careers since there is probably not a lot for an inexperienced guy in my line of work to do here. I was thinking that I might become a beach bum. What do you think?"

"All right, smart guy, I get the picture."

"Just for the record," I said. "There's nothing I'd like better, babe."

"Maybe some day," Abby sighed, leaning closer to me. "It was nice of Max to arrange this trip for us though, wasn't it?"

"Max is the best. I don't know where I'd be without him." I said, honestly.

"He's been so kind to my mother since the betrayal, too."

That's the way Abby speaks of her stepfather's willingness to put her life at risk in order to force her mother to give him the location of *el Tesoro,* the hidden treasure of her father and his friends; information he had not been able to find out during their marriage. He had raised Abby and her brother and a younger sister, his only child with Maria. Richard Barrett had been the only father she had ever known. And, when it all went bad, he tried to kill her.

"Max thinks the world of you both," I said.

"I know. We feel the same about him."

I hugged her tightly. "You still like me?"

"Hmm," she said, a quizzical expression crossing her face. "What did you say your name was, again?"

CHAPTER 2

▼

August 4. 2003
Amelia Island, Florida

Bobby took a mighty swing, and stared down the long fairway, his hand over his eyes like a visor, as his ball skittered along the ground and stopped thirty yards away from the divot hole where his tee, now blasted into splinters, had been a few seconds before. I shook my head as he dropped his driver and hung his head in shame.

"You know," I said. "It's a mystery to me how any well-bred son of a famous attorney, who happens to belong to Atlanta's most exclusive country club, *and* Augusta National to boot, could play so ugly."

Bobby picked up the club and trotted down the little hill from the tee box. "That's easy" he said. "My high school years were part of my 'rebel period,' so I never played golf with my dad. You know about my sterling performance during my very short college career, so you can guess how anxious he was to invite me to the club, right?"

"Bound to be fun." I said.

"Oh, yeah," Bobby laughed. "Anyway, this is about the best time of my life that I can remember, and we got three whole days left!"

Bobby let out a rebel yell which was under-appreciated by the golfers on a green close by.

"Very nice," I said, reproachfully, and drove our cart along the sixth fairway the short distance to his ball, dropped him off, and pulled back over to the cart path and waited for him to dribble a three wood a little closer to the green. He was in the middle of his backswing when my cell phone rang.

"Hey, Max," I said, recognizing the flashing incoming number as Max Howard's direct line in Atlanta.

"Shit!" I heard Bobby yell as Max spoke.

"Hey, Tommy. You guys doin' okay down there?"

"Great, Max. Everyone's having a great time. By the way, Bobby can't play golf for shit."

I waited for Max' big belly laugh but there was silence on the other end. After a few seconds I said, "How's everything back there?"

Still no response and I glanced at the phone's screen to make sure I hadn't lost the signal. I was beginning to feel something unpleasant deep in my gut, when Max finally spoke.

"You remember Willie Patton in my office, right?"

I felt a guilty relief that whatever he was about to tell me wasn't bad news about my brother, Pat, or his family. "Yeah, sure I do. We had a great time with Willie and Marti at your Fourth of July picnic. Why?"

Willie is a very bright, young black attorney; one of Max' "kids" as he calls his group of firebrands. I remembered his wife, a pretty blond with laughing blue eyes. They had been ecstatic about the pending birth of their first child, due around Thanksgiving, I think.

Bobby was back at the cart now, a quizzical look on his face.

"What is it, Max? What's going on?"

"He's dead, Tommy. Willie and his wife, they're both dead."

I was dumbfounded. It hardly seemed possible. "Jesus, Max. I can't believe it." I couldn't find the right words. "I'm so sorry to hear that. Was it a car accident?"

Max didn't respond immediately, but then said, "They were murdered. No, make that butchered, right in their bed, in the middle of the night." I thought his voice sounded strangled in his throat.

I looked at Bobby, and he gave me a silent "What?" I pressed the loudspeaker button on my phone so that he could hear our conversation.

"Max," I said, "murdered? Why? When did this happen?"

"It was night before last," he answered. "I been waitin' to get more details, and I just heard from Jake Berger a few minutes ago."

Berger is a homicide detective at the 14th Precinct in downtown Atlanta. He had worked on my case after I had been beaten to a pulp in the parking lot behind Pat's restaurant the night I had gone looking for Abby at her family's home.

"Jake's handling the case?"

Bobby broke in before Max could answer. "Hey, Max. What did you mean about them being 'butchered'? What the hell happened?"

"Hold on, Max," I said, as a twosome came up to the tee box behind us, and I waived them on. A couple of minutes later, they were rolling past us in their cart and we were able to continue. "Go ahead, Max, we're alone now."

"Well, from what Jake said, it was about the worst thing he'd ever seen." Max gave himself a few seconds before going on, and we waited in silence. "They were cut up pretty bad; stabbed several times each. No sign of resistance, so Jake figured they were held down by several assailants. It was torture, plain and simple. We don't know if they were dead when the worst of it happened, but, God, I hope so."

"What do you mean by the worst of it?" I couldn't really imagine what could be worse.

"The bastards cut the baby out, Tommy. They just opened Marti up like she wasn't a living, breathing human being. And, Willie, he had a wooden stake- Jake said it looked like a cross- they drove it right through his chest." Max sounded like he was lost in his own despair. "Right through his chest," he said again, as though to himself.

Max came back to us. "Jake wouldn't elaborate, but I think there were other things done to them that he didn't want to discuss over the phone, but he did say there was what appeared to be some kind of ritualistic drawings all over the walls. The bastards used blood to make those marks."

"Jesus," Bobby said softly. "How do you just pick out somebody and do that to them?"

"You don't," I said, shaking my head.

"Huh? I don't understand….."

"Tommy's right, Bobby," Max said, answering the question for me. "This wasn't a random killing. Willie and Marti lived on the third floor of one of several buildings at that large apartment complex over on Lenox, near the mall. They were due to move to their first new home in about a month." He gave it a moment for that to sink in. "Gangs of crazed killers don't wander around a complex that big carryin' stakes to drive through peoples bodies. No, they were targeted," he said.

"I agree," I said. "But, the question is, why? What possible reason would anyone have for going after the Willie and his wife?"

"I think I might know why," Max said. "But I prefer not to talk about it over the phone."

I was surprised by that, but I didn't push for an explanation. "What do you want us to do Max?"

"I need your help. Both of you, if you're willin'. I think I may have information that will lead to some answers, but much as I like and trust Jake Berger, I think his hands will be tied on this one."

"Why would that be?" I said, not understanding the implications of Max' comment.

"Let's talk about that in person." Max said with finality.

I looked at Bobby, and he nodded. "Okay. What do you want us to do, Max?"

"Come see me.…."

"We can be back in Atlanta in about seven hours," I broke in. Max Howard knew I would do anything for him, and I knew I could speak for Bobby.

"No, no. That won't be necessary. You're due back late Sunday, right?"

I said, "Yes, but…"

"Monday morning will be plenty soon enough," Max said. "Lord knows you all need a vacation, and by then I may have additional information from the police.….. and the coroner."

"Are you sure about this?"

"I am," he said. "And, Tommy, don't tell the girls. It'll only ruin their remaining time down there."

Max was right. It would serve no purpose to upset Abby and Sabine.

I sighed. "Okay, Max. We'll see you about 9 a.m. Monday."

"Good," he said, "and thanks."

The line went dead.

CHAPTER 3

▼

August 4, 2003, Evening
Amelia Island, Florida

I've gotten to know Max Howard pretty well. There was an anger building behind the soft voice and calm composure. But for now, the anger was being held in check by a smothering sense of sorrow and despair. He had lost one of his kids. The pain would lessen, and the anger would show itself later when he had the time to give in to it. Right now, I could imagine his fertile mind figuring a way to make sure this insane crime didn't go unpunished. I knew that he was putting his energy into that, and that alone.

Max had helped me get Abby out of Cuba, and kept her mother from falling apart during the excruciating events of those October days last year.

Thomas Patrick and Bobby Hemphill were going to be a part of this. I just didn't know how, and I couldn't even begin to guess what Max might know about why Willie and Marti had been murdered.

Neither of us felt much like playing golf after we finished our conversation with Max, but it would be hard to explain to the girls why we were back so early from the course, so we headed for the clubhouse bar. We didn't feel much like talking either, and we sat there just drinking beer and thinking our own private thoughts for a long time.

I knew Max was looking for us to be his eyes and ears.... and maybe much more, during what I was sure would become a personal quest for justice. And that was okay with me. But this was going to be very hard for Max Howard. I hoped that was going to be okay with him. I knew something about cases that became personal.

"How well did you know Willie and his wife?" Bobby broke in as our third round of Beck's Light arrived at the table.

"Didn't really," I said. "Outside of seeing him occasionally at Max' office, the July Fourth picnic was the first time we talked socially, and the first time I had ever met his wife."

"Max sounded pretty messed up."

"You know how close he is to his gang. To him this is like losing kin."

Bobby nodded. "Yeah, I guess. Especially the *way* they died." He shook his head. "*That* I don't get at all. Who *does* that kind of shit to people?"

"Come on, man," I said. "It happens every day, just not to people we know."

He was quiet for a while. "We're going to be in the middle of this, you know."

"That bother you?"

"Hell yes," he said, with a slight grin. "But not enough to keep me from being there for Max."

I smiled for the first time in two hours.

"Knew you'd say that."

The girls looked great, and they were relaxed and happy after their day in the Florida sun. We kept the conversation light as we sat down to a great seafood dinner overlooking the Atlantic. I had grown into a habit of telling Abby whatever was on my mind, but Bobby had agreed with me that it was best to follow Max' advice, and we kept the day's events to ourselves.

A couple of *The Bait Shop Restaurant's* specialty drinks, and I started to relax and enjoy the evening. The restaurant's name didn't do it justice, and each course was better than the last. I had to force myself not to over order from the terrific menu, but Abby and I finally settled on Lobster Newburg, while Sabine chose pan-fried sole with a Creole sauce and russet potatoes, and Bobby went for the Shrimp Alfredo. We started the meal with a shared house special salad prepared table-side. If I had worried that my appetite might have suffered from the news we had gotten from Atlanta, I needn't have. Or maybe it was because I was happy that Abby was having such a good time. Whatever the reason, we ate with gusto, moved on to dessert and an easy, lighthearted conversation, and a third bottle of wine.

It was dark outside, but from our table along the windows overlooking the beach, we could see the whites of the wave tops as they broke along the surf line. I found myself thinking, as I heard the girls giggling at one of Bobby Hemphill's bad jokes, that Abby was right. It would be great to stay right where we were. Maybe I would be able to escape some of the bad things that

I knew were coming my way when we got back to Atlanta. But, that's home for now. Whatever may come, it's where we belong.

Bobby started another lousy joke and the girls' boos ended my reverie, and I joined in.

"Jeez," I said. "Not only can't you play golf, but you've got a really bad comedy routine. Sabine, how do you stand this guy?"

She laughed, and her eyes sparkled in the candle's light. "I have no idea! In fact, Abby and I were discussing that very thing this afternoon." She turned and gave Bobby a pout, and said, "I'm so sorry, but you have absolutely no redeeming values."

He threw his hands in the air as we all laughed. "And these are my friends," he said. "What chance do I have?"

"Okay," Sabine purred, consolingly. "You are a *little* cute."

"No," I said, "he's a little short."

*   *   *   *

We said good night to Bobby and Sabine, and Abby and I walked down to the wooden stairs that went up over the protected dunes to the beach.

"Feel like a walk?" I asked, kissing her forehead.

"Hmm, let's just sit here for a little while and listen to the waves, okay?"

"Sure."

And we did, enjoying the salty ocean smell, not saying anything, but snuggling against each other and holding hands. Finally after a while, Abby yawned, and I knew she was ready to sleep.

As we got into bed, she turned to face me, and brushed my hair back from my face. "I love you, Thomas," she said quietly.

"I love you, too, babe. I always will, and I hope you will always be here for me to tell you so."

Abby gave me a crooked smile. "Why, Thomas Patrick. Wherever in the world do you think I would go?" She gave me a long, sweet kiss, and said, "Good night, silly boy."

I found myself wondering if Willie and Marti had been lucky enough to have had the chance to say, "I love you," one last time before they died.

*   *   *   *

The next morning Sabine joined us outside for breakfast on the restaurant's veranda, which overlooked the calm sea.

"Where's Superman?" I asked, with a smile.

"Still asleep," she giggled. "I don't think he's feeling too good this morning."

"Might have been those last few beers following those tequila shooters following the wine," I laughed. "Our boy had quite a night."

The waiter came over and took our order. The girls had the fruit plate, and I had the lobster omelet for the third day in a row. I know what I like, and I stick with it.

The day was going to be warm and humid, but at 8 a.m., it was still cool enough for us to enjoy sitting outdoors. The food arrived and we dug in, talking about nothing in particular, and basking in the light breezes.

"Maybe we should wake Bobby up," Abby said. "You know how he gets when he misses a meal."

"You guys!" Sabine laughed. "You make him sound terrible." Her mood changed a little, and she said, "Can I ask you something?"

"Sure," I said, and Abby nodded.

"You know, I really like Bobby. Actually," she said with a little smile. "I think it's more than that, and I think he feels the same, you know?"

"You might be right about that," I said, slyly, "but I doubt it."

Abby gave me a playful push. "You are such a bad man," she said. "Pay no attention to him, Sabine. What did you want to ask?"

"Well, I have some vacation time coming up in a month, and I'll be going home to Barbados to see my mother and little sister. I was thinking of inviting Bobby to come along. Do you think he would come with me, or would that be a little to...... pushy?"

"I think he will be more than happy to go with you," I said, honestly. "Very happy."

She smiled, again. "Really?"

"Really," I said.

"Oh, boy," Abby said, rubbing her hands together, gleefully. "Another beautiful island. Maybe we should go along to chaperone these two! What do you think, Thomas?"

I gave her a pained look. "Oh, great! Another vacation with Bobby Hemphill. Just what I need."

Just then an apparition came through the door onto the veranda, sporting mismatched clothes, a day's growth of stubbly beard, and a shock of uncombed hair. Bobby stumbled over to the table, and stared blankly at us as if we were strangers.

"Yeah," I said to Sabine, and pointed at my partner. "Mama's going to love *this.*"

The three of us burst out laughing.

Bobby looked at us in confusion. "What?!" he said.

✳   ✳   ✳   ✳

Abby and Sabine were standing in the surf talking girl talk. Bobby was stretched out in a lounge chair snoring deeply. I rummaged around in the towel bag we had brought down from our room, and found my cell phone down at the bottom. As quietly as I could, I got out of my chair, went up the stairs to the pool deck and called Max Howard back in Atlanta.

"How you doing, Max?" I asked, when he came on the line.

"Gettin' by, Tommy. I'm havin' lunch with Jake Berger a little later. He's got a copy of the autopsy reports for me, not that I'm sure I want to see them."

"Yeah, I know what you mean. I can't get this thing out of my mind either. You sure you want to wait 'til Monday to meet?"

"Monday will be fine, son," he said. "I still don't know much more than I told you yesterday, and I know Jake doesn't have any leads on who done this yet."

"It's still hard to believe." I thought again of Max' comment about having some information that might be pertinent to the murders of Willie and Marti. Whatever it was, he wasn't ready to talk about it yet.

"Yeah, it is, but it happened, and I can't just leave it like this."

I knew that was true, and it was just what I expected. The anger was coming. We talked a little while longer even though there wasn't much to say, and I finally let Max go.

The rest of the day was spent on the beach, and I tried to keep my spirits up, but the whole depressing situation was nagging at me. In my head, I was already back in Atlanta, preparing for whatever I could do to help Max.

That night after dinner, we went back to our rooms, everyone a little worn out by our long day in the hot sun. Abby came out of the bathroom ready for bed, and found me packing my clothes in the suitcase that I had thrown on the bed. She watched me for awhile, and then came over and took my hand. I looked up, and deep, dark brown eyes brought me back from my thoughts.

"Come over here, Thomas," she said, sweetly, leading me over to the couch. We sat down next to each other, and she took both my hands in hers.

"Now, Thomas, there is something bothering you, and you need to tell me what it is because I think it is troubling you very much." She patted my hand like a mother speaking to a child. "I can't help you deal with it if you won't tell me what's wrong."

I looked at her with admiration and consternation on my face. "How do you *do* that?!" I said.

"Do what?" she said, perplexed by my question.

"Know when something is on my mind!"

"What a silly question, Thomas! I love you! Of course I know. Besides, I have to watch out for you, don't I?"

I couldn't help myself, and I laughed. "And how about you? When do you worry about *you*?"

She looked at me with surprise. "Why ever would I do that?! After all, *you* watch out for me, right? Now," she said, brightly, "tell me what is going on."

And, I did. I kept the gruesome details out of my story, and I think she knew there was more to it than I was telling her, but she left it alone and didn't pry for details.

"How horrible," she said, quietly, when I finished. "They were so happy about the baby. Poor Max must be beside himself. And, think of their families!"

"I've never heard him sound like that before," I agreed.

We didn't say anything for awhile, but just sat there, holding hands.

"Max will get involved in trying to find the killers, you know. He won't let this terrible crime go unpunished." she said, matter-of-factly. "And, he is going to ask you to help."

"He already has, Abby, and I *have* to do this….."

"Of course you must, Thomas," she said. "You have to do everything you can to help Max."

I was relieved that she understood, and wouldn't try to argue me out of putting myself in possible danger. In my heart, I think I knew she wouldn't have asked me to back away.

"And Bobby will be helping you?"

I nodded. "He's fully committed. He'll do anything to help."

"Good. And thank you for telling me about this," she said, seriously, "but, I don't think we should tell Bobby that I know. I certainly don't think we should talk about this in front of Sabine. I think she is nervous enough about what he does for a living."

"Well, duh!" I said with a smile. "I wasn't even supposed to tell *you*, remember?" I got it settled in my mind right then and there, that Abby was so strong, it would never be possible, nor necessary, to keep anything from her. "You coerced it out of me with your feminine wiles!"

"Yes," she said proudly, "I did, didn't I? Okay, then let's pack in the morning, and we'll have a good breakfast, and then we can go back home so that you two can help Max."

I was beginning to understand just how lucky I really was to have this remarkable woman in my life.

I took her face in both hands and leaned close. She came to me with total willingness. I kissed her with all the love that was welling up in me, and then I kissed her again.

Abby moaned softly, and lay back on the couch, her arms above her head, her eyes closed. I pulled the satin slip that she likes to wear to bed slowly up over her head, and she lay naked before me. I began to kiss her body, starting at her neck and moving down to her beautiful breasts. I licked her dark areoles and caressed her hard nipples, taking them one by one into my mouth again, and again, lightly sucking on them as her breath caught.

Abby, her eyes still closed, ran her hands through my hair as I moved down her body, kissing her stomach, licking around her belly button, and trying with all my might to drink her in.

I stood and took off my shirt, then undid my belt and let my slacks fall away. Abby opened her eyes and looked at me, standing above her. She reached up and took my hand, gently drawing me down to her.

From then on, I could only think of Abby Barrett. The rest of the world, with all its horrors and pain, would have to wait.

CHAPTER 4

───────── ▼ ─────────

August 7, 2003, Evening
Atlanta, Georgia

Bobby and Sabine dropped us off in the parking lot behind Ireland's Own about 7:30, Sunday night. I ran our bags up to our rooms above the restaurant, and Abby and I went downstairs to let my brother, Pat, know we were back. I was happy to see Pat and C.J. sitting at a table, having dinner with their twin boys, "Big Foot" and "Monster Boy," the world's biggest four year olds.

"Any athletic scholarship offers for those two yet?"

"Oh, look," C.J. said, "Uncle Yankee Tom and Abby are back!" And the boys jumped off their chairs and rushed me like the future linebackers they were destined to become. I gave my sister-in-law a kiss, and Pat got up to give Abby a bear hug. She nearly disappeared against his 6'4", 250 pound frame that was actually forty pounds lighter than when he was playing for the Falcons.

Abby caught her breath and sat down next to C.J. Little Timothy jumped up on her lap and gave her a big, wet kiss. Watching my family take Abby into their hearts like this gives me a feeling of wholeness. Not that long ago, I wouldn't have thought that possible.

"Did you have a good time?" C.J. asked.

"We're moving to the beach permanently," I said.

"Oh, great," Pat said, with a grimace. "I guess you won't be taking any shifts behind the bar from now on then, huh?"

"Sorry, bro. I think I may be tied up for a little while."

Pat glanced at the girls, who were talking animatedly, and leaned closer to me. "Yeah, I know. Max was here last night. He's pretty messed up about what happened."

"He isn't the only one. Bobby and I are going to see him tomorrow."

"I told him he ought to let Jake Berger handle this, but I don't think he was listening."

"No," I said. "He's not going to let this alone, Pat."

We sat for a while, both thinking our own thoughts.

Finally, leaning closer to my brother so he could hear me, I said, "Heard from the folks?" Our parents still live in Cleveland, where Dad is a cop and Mom a housewife.

"Actually," Pat brightened, "I got a call from Rosie, and get this, our parents are in the Big Apple to see some shows. They went with a group from the Police Benevolence League for the weekend."

"Whoa!" I feigned horror at the news. "Connie and Seamus loose in the big city, huh?"

Pat laughed at the idea of dad on Broadway. "That's what I hear."

"And our little sis called on her own without you tracking her down?" Rosie is actually a year older than me, but loves playing the "little sister," gig, and is a very free spirit, with a terrific personality. "And, she would be getting away with what craziness while the folks are away?"

Pat let out a howl. "Nothing *I* want to hear about!"

"Hey, you guys!" C.J.'s voice came from the far end of the table. "Y'all stop raggin' on your sister, hear?"

Pat looked at me with amazement on his face. "How does she do that?" he said.

"Do what?" I asked, a quizzical look on my face.

"Hear what I'm sayin' when I'm practically whispering!"

I sat back, taking on a professorial air. "Well, I had the opportunity to ask Abby that very question in similar circumstances just the other day, dear brother."

"And?"

"I'm afraid, Patrick, that you aren't ready for that type of knowledge just yet."

"Yeah," Pat said, sitting back in his chair, and taking a drag on his beer. "Probably not."

✳   ✳   ✳   ✳

The sun broke through a cloudy sky, and the temperature was rising rapidly as the Monday morning traffic started to build. Bobby and I were heading down Peachtree Street toward Midtown. We made it to Max Howard's office by nine.

We were sitting in the main conference room, cut off from the lobby by a glass wall which had become opaque with the touch of a button, so now we couldn't see out, and no one could see into the room. We waited silently for Max. There wasn't much to say as we both ran over in our minds what we expected to hear from him.

It isn't a big law firm; fifteen lawyers and maybe another twenty people backing them up, and the entire office had a kind of pall over it. I had never experienced silence around Max' office. The kinds of cases usually handled by the firm carried an excitement and purpose to them that energized everyone. They helped people here. But the deaths of Willie Patton and his wife and child had taken the oxygen out of the air.

I was thumbing through a magazine someone had left in the conference room, and not really seeing what was on the pages, when the door opened and Max Howard came into the room followed by the ever-present Coral Mae Stone, his "right hand" assistant. Coral Mae, a tiny, elegantly dressed, grey-haired dynamo of some sixty years of age, was barely visible behind Max Howard's bulk. She had been with him since his early days as a new lawyer working for one of those giant Atlanta firms, and had resigned when he left, to help him start his own office two decades ago.

She finally broke free of his shadow and gave me a bright smile of greeting, as she put a large pile of multi-colored files in front of his place at the head of the big table.

Max gave us each a hearty handshake and thanked Bobby and me for coming in to see him.

We usually have our early morning meetings at Jimmy's, a Cajun place on Peachtree in the Midtown area, where Max likes to start his day with chicory-laced coffee and a big plate of beignets, the Louisiana-style donuts that he loves so much. He said they reminded him of his home town of New Orleans, and I like to kid him about the large amounts of powdered sugar that regularly dusted his ties. But this morning, his tie was spotless.

Coral Mae busied herself with opening the wall cabinet at the far end of the room, exposing a projection screen and, as if by magic, two more staff members bustled through the door, one carrying a small slide projector, which he set up in front of Max, and the other, a tray with a thermos of fresh coffee and fixings.

"Y'all help yourselves to the coffee," Max said to us. "Thank you, everyone."

In a second, we were alone, and the room was eerily silent again.

"How are you doing, Max?" I said, more to break the silence than anything.

"Well, I know I've been better, but we're getting' along, Tommy. The beach was good?"

"It was a great time," I answered. Bobby nodded in agreement. "Amelia's a beautiful place."

"Don't get there near enough anymore," Max said, as we struggled for normal conversation, but it was evident from the look on his face that there was a lot to say, and Max needed to get at it. I thought it might be easier if I introduced the subject.

"You said something on the phone the other day. Something about knowing why this happened to the Patton's?"

He nodded, slowly. "I think so. Let me start at the beginning, and see if we can agree on a course of action. I asked Jake Berger to come in a little later. He can fill you in on the crime scene, if that's okay?"

"Sure. Whatever you think is best, Max."

"Good."

He sat back in his chair, and began. "Willie Patton worked for me since the day he graduated from the law school at Georgia State, but he and his folks were from Nashville, originally. They moved here when he was ten years old, and his daddy got a job with an office cleaning company. Used to work in this very office building as a janitor. Now, he's one of the owners of the company. Willie's mama worked, too, when they were in Nashville, so little Willie and his sister spent their days bein' watched at the house of a woman they weren't related to, but called, Auntie Belle."

He took a drag on his coffee, and went on with his story.

"There was another little boy by the name of Carl Lee Wiggins. The two kids became such close friends over the years Belle took care of them, that they began referring to each other as 'cousins,' and they kept in close touch all these years Willie and his family have been in Atlanta. That's how this whole thing got started."

"This Wiggins was involved in the murders?" Bobby asked.

"Not the way you're thinking. Carl Lee Wiggins grew up to be a police officer in Nashville. That's where the files came from."

"Those files?" I asked, pointing to the stack on the table.

"These are copies of the originals," he said, pointing to the blue folders. "Carl Lee had evidently been doing a little extra-curricular investigating into some similar cases that had occurred over an eighteen month period. He isn't a homicide detective, just a street cop. The cases are compiled from six different states."

"So it wasn't his job or jurisdiction. Why was he looking into this stuff?" I asked.

Max poured more coffee for the three of us. "It was the similarity of the cases, and the fact that they appeared to be racially motivated that caught his attention."

"So," Bobby asked, "these were murders of black people?"

"That was what originally got Wiggins interested." Max opened the first file, and laid it before us. There was a picture of two young people- maybe mid-teens, on top of a small stack of letter sized papers. The girl was white, blond, and very pretty. There was a hopeful look on her face. It appeared to be a class picture or a professional portrait. The male was a young black man, about the same age. He was wearing a high school basketball uniform.

I looked at Max, waiting for an explanation.

"Those kids, Sandy Allen, and Maurice Tenley, are both dead," he said. There was no emotion visible on his face, as if it had all been spent.

"Jeez," Bobby said, quietly. "They were both killed?"

"They were. They lived in Richmond, Virginia, and were high school sweethearts."

"So," I said. "The 'similarity' to the other cases has to do with multiple murders

of white *and* black people, right?"

"Yes," confirmed Max.

"All young kids?"

"No, but they were all couples- some even married. And some of the females; some black, some white, were carryin' their partner's child." He pointed at the girl in the open file. e pointed zt thde girl in the open file.

I shook my head. "This girl can't be over sixteen."

"Fifteen, actually. The young man was seventeen and a star forward on the varsity team."

"So you're saying that there are a bunch of similar killings, not all in Nashville, that Carl Lee Wiggins put information together on?" said Bobby. "Why didn't he take it to his boss?"

"Why indeed," Max said. "Might be as simple as the fact that he had obviously overstepped the bounds of his duties, and got involved with stuff he shouldn't have cared about. Or maybe it was something else. Anyway, you can ask him yourself when you get to Nashville."

I looked at Bobby, then at Max. "We know where to find him?"

"We do, and you will be able to meet with him late tomorrow night. Anyway," Max said, getting back to his story and pointing at the stack of files, "whatever his reasons, he sent this stuff to the one person he knew he could entrust it to: Willie Patton."

I picked up the photo of the two dead kids and studied it for a few seconds. "What were the similarities, Max?"

"The victims were bound and gagged, stabbed several times," he hesitated. "And then, hopefully after they were dead, the bodies were mutilated- crude crosses used like stakes on the men and even worse atrocities visited on the women. There were ritualistic symbols made with blood on the bodies and on the walls- and, that's another thing. The murders all took place very late at night, and inside, as if the killers needed a lot of time for their.... work, and didn't want to take the chance of being interrupted by passersby."

"Those things all happened to your friends?" Bobby asked, shaking his head.

"Yes," Max said, softly.

"What was Willie supposed to do about all this?" I asked.

"Well, Carl Lee wanted Willie to look into the facts as he had found them to be. I think he was hopeful that we could go to the Feds and keep him out of it, you know, get *somebody* with some power looking into these cases at a higher level."

"Which," I said, "brings us to why the Patton family was killed. Do you think someone found out what Carl Lee and Willie were doing?"

"I do," Max said.

"Yeah," Bobby said. "But why butcher his whole family? Why not just go after Willie?" Bobby realized how crass that sounded. "Sorry, but you know what I mean, right?"

"Yes, I do," Max said. "And, I don't know the reason why. I hope Carl Lee Wiggins might help clear that up."

CHAPTER 5

▼

August 8, 2003, Afternoon
Atlanta, Georgia

I was packing up the files to take with us in a box Coral Mae had brought in after our meeting had broken up. Bobby was getting the car and I was alone, and feeling drained.

Jake Berger had come and gone, and nothing he had said had brightened the mood in the conference room.

We had spent the first hour with Jake looking at the slides Max had made of the pictures in the files. Blowing the pictures up had added to the gruesome nature of the photos. But Max had been right. The similarities between the crime scenes were unmistakable.

By now I had started to memorize some of the details of the different crimes, and I knew they were going to stick with me for a long time.

"And these same things happened to the Patton's?" I said to Jake.

"Almost as if the perpetrators used these other crimes as a stencil," he answered, as he took a file out of his brief case and laid it on the table. "These are the photos from the Patton home." He waived his hand over the other files. "They could be from any of the other places."

I shook my head. "How could this be? Doesn't this mean the killers have to be the same people? I mean, look at the symbols on the walls. They're almost identical."

The crude, bloody markings: a cross with a circle connecting the four directions of the posts, another circle, larger, with markings radiating outward along the circumference, like a sun throwing off rays, and the number 11, with an "x" crossing through it. There were other markings too bloody and smeared to make out, but still close enough to those in other case files to have possibly been done by the same hand.

Jake sighed. "It might mean that, but we really don't know for sure. The murders took place over a large geographical area."

Bobby was staring at the screen. Max had pulled up a slide of the eastern United States. Certain cities were marked with red stars. I caught the look on my partner's face.

"The crimes all took place in the South?" he asked.

"What?" Max looked at him.

"Look at the cities where these copycat murders took place," Bobby said. "Birmingham, Montgomery, Columbia, Nashville, Greenville, Richmond, Dallas, Little Rock, Norfolk, Memphis, and Atlanta….all Southern cities."

The stars marking the locations of the crimes Carl Lee and Willie had been investigating were all in the South.

"He's right," I said. "Can that be? Is it possible that this is happening only in our region, or is it more likely that Wiggins just didn't check anywhere else?"

"Good question," Jake Berger answered. "I'll check into that, but quietly."

Again, I thought about the comment Max had made about Jake during our first call when I was on Amelia Island.

"Why not call in the FBI right now?" I asked.

Jake looked at Max before speaking. "We think it might be best to follow this thing out for a while before we do that."

"We feel we owe it to the Patton's to get as strong a base of information as possible before we do that." Max added. We want to insure that if there is an investigation there won't be any way it can falter."

"That's right," Jake said. "Max and I agree that it would be beneficial to have you see where Mr. Wiggins might be going with this, and also it could help to have you interview the families and friends of the victims."

"So you think Wiggins is still actively involved?"

"We do."

"And you think it is better if this is done outside police channels." It was a statement and not a question. "And, I guess you think it's best to let this Carl Lee do the front work?"

"Yes," Jake said simply, and looked at Max, then back at me. "With your help."

I was bothered by his answer, but decided not to press for his reasoning. I trusted Max to have made this decision with Jake, and that had to suffice for now.

*   *   *   *

Max came into the conference room as I was finishing packing up the files, and sat down across from me.

"A sordid business," Max said, simply.

If he was going to elaborate on anything that had been said throughout our long meeting, it would be now, while we were alone.

"Anything else I need to know?" I asked, expectantly.

"I think we need to see what you get up in Nashville, Tommy."

Max reached into the inside breast pocket of his jacket and took out a thick, letter- sized envelope. He opened it and took a stack of bills and a piece of white paper out of it, along with two American Express cards.

"These are made out in your name and Bobby's, and the bills will come directly to the office," he said, handing me the cards. "And there's ten thousand cash there." He put the money back in the envelope and handed it to me. "In case you think it's better to use cash than the cards."

"Max," I said. "You don't need to do that."

"Tommy," he said earnestly. "I need you to go meet with the families of these victims. I need you to go wherever you have to go, whenever you need to. I told Carl Lee that I thought it might help to talk to those folks and that you were the best one to do that. If you have to pay for information, do it. Whatever it takes, son." He was silent for a moment. "These people, whoever they are, killed one of my kids. They killed his family, for whatever horrible purpose they had. That can't be allowed to go unpunished. I can't take the chance that this thing could go unpunished."

He sat back in his chair. "That's why I need your help, son. If you need more money, call Coral Mae if you can't reach me. Whatever it takes, no questions asked."

I know Max considers me one of his kids. And, I don't know if I could have ever gotten Abby safely out of Cuba without his help. I know he would do the same for me again if it were ever necessary. There was no way to argue the point with Max Howard. I put the envelope into my pocket.

He handed me the piece of paper that had been in the envelope. "This is where you meet Carl Lee at midnight tomorrow night. It's a bar in downtown Nashville, where the music clubs are located. It was his choice of location, and I think we better go along with him."

"Okay."

"And, thanks, Tommy," Max said, quietly.

I just nodded. I didn't really need to say anything else about it.

I finished packing up the files. "By the way, when is the funeral?"

"Willie's is 11 a.m. tomorrow, over in Decatur," he said. "Marti's is at 8 a.m. at Henson's Funeral Home in Midtown."

It took a few seconds for this information to register, and I thought I must have misunderstood him. "You mean they're having separate funerals? Max, how can that be? They were married, for God's sake!"

"Yes, but Marti's family would not agree to a joint service, or a joint burial for that matter, and Willie's dad wouldn't put his wife through a fight about it." He shook his head. "Like I said, it's a sordid business."

We were silent for a little while until the phone buzzed, and the receptionist let us know Bobby was waiting downstairs with the car.

I stood and shook hands with Max.

"When do you think you'll leave for Nashville?"

"I'm not sure why, Max," I said. "But I think I should attend the service for Marti Patton tomorrow morning, first."

CHAPTER 6

▼

August 8, 2003, Evening
Atlanta, Georgia

My mother has always called me "Thomas." She never uses a nickname for me, unlike my father, who often calls me "Tommy," or "Boyo," his favorite Irish expression.

Abby is the only other person in my world who always calls me by my formal name.

Except that one time.

I was sitting on the couch in our little living room above Ireland's Own, not ten feet from the spot where we had stood that night. In my mind's eye, I could see us holding on to each other, reveling in the contact of our naked bodies. We were about to share our first moments of love-making, and even now, nearly a year later, I can feel Abby's beautiful body pressed tightly against me. I can smell the sweetness of her hair and skin. I can feel the depth of my emotions as I held her against me.

It was then that she had looked up at me, the deep chocolate pools of her eyes damp with the moisture of her own feelings, looking through me to my very soul, and said, "Tommy?" with a simplicity and understanding that needed no answer from me.

We were standing there before me, like a hologram, and I squeezed my eyes tightly, wishing again for that last day of innocence; that last day before Abby had disappeared. That last day before the horrors of Cuba had begun.

I shook off the melancholy that was engulfing me. *Just a bad day,* I think to myself. *Abby will be home soon. It will be all right.*

I got up and grabbed another beer from the fridge, unscrewed the cap and took a long, deep pull.

Sometimes in the stillness of my room I still think of myself as that college freshman, just a jock, with no understanding of the real world, except for what I see on TV.

Desensitized to violence like any other American kid. It's all just a video game.

How did I get here? How did I get to the point of seeing the kind of terrible photos I had seen in Max' office today as a part of my daily routine? How did I get to the point where people have tried to kill me? How did I get to the point where I have killed?

If I keep this up, how long will it be before I am no longer the man Abby loves? That is my real fear. How will all this change me?

I glanced at the clock on the stove. It was almost 6 p.m. Abby would be back from the Georgia Tech campus where she has been scheduling her classes for the new semester, soon. She'll be hungry, but I don't feel like putting up with the hustle and bustle of Ireland's Own, so I dig through the freezer and find some chicken breasts and a package of frozen scalloped potatoes. There's a bag of fresh, cut-up lettuce in the fridge and a bottle of a California Chardonnay that she likes. Should do, I thought to myself, and I'll get to have her all to myself tonight.

This would be our last meal together for a while, and I want to make it nice, so I got out the "fancy" dishes and set the little table by the windows overlooking Peachtree Street.

Hard to believe I've actually learned to do some cooking since arriving in Atlanta, especially with my brother, Pat's, restaurant downstairs where the food has been free. I feel kind of bad now that I'm making a little money and rarely working any shifts behind the bar, but I know Pat and C.J. don't think a thing of it, and wouldn't take money from me anyway.

I started poaching the chicken so that it would defrost right in the covered pan. Once that happened, I'd add a little of the wine, some spices, a little virgin olive oil, and maybe a few sliced mushrooms. I start the oven to do the potatoes, and fix the salad except for the dressing.

Then I got another beer, sat on my old couch, and waited for Abby.

The room was getting darker, so I turned on the lamp on the end table next to the couch and got up to check on dinner.

I was adding the wine to the chicken when I heard the door open, and Abby called out.

"Thomas? Oh, something smells good! How did you know I'd be starving?"

I smiled, and the cloud I had been under lifted, just like that. "You're always hungry." I called out, and went to meet her.

"Hi," she said, warmly, as she put down some packages and wrapped her arms around my neck. "I always hoped I would fall in love with a man who could cook!"

She kissed me deeply, and I had to tell myself not to hold her too tightly, or seem too relieved to have her here in our little home. Abby Barrett is an amazing woman. She has an incredible ability to know when I am troubled. Tonight, I just want us to relax and be happy together.

I kissed her again and said, "The chicken calls. How about some wine?"

"Perfect!"

"You sure seem happy. Got all the classes you wanted?"

"I did," she said. "Every one, but it was close on a couple. The courses were closing out pretty quickly. I'm glad I didn't wait until tomorrow."

Abby kicked off her shoes and curled up on the couch with her glass of wine.

"Dinner in about five," I said, sitting down next to her. "Tell me about your day."

She gave me all the details about chasing down the courses she wanted, and told me about reuniting with old friends. It was obvious that Abby was excited about returning to Tech. It probably signified a return to a state of normalcy after the crazy year we had just gone through.

I kept my own dark day to myself as we ate, allowing us both to revel in her happiness. My turn would come, I knew, as she is always interested in what I'm working on. Besides, she is well aware of where I had been all day, and what I had been doing.

We finished dinner and I put on a pot of coffee. Abby helped me clear the table and took out some cookies that Maria Barrett's housekeeper, Patrice, had made for us on our last visit to Abby's mom's house. The place was like a second home to me, as I had spent my first few months after Cuba recuperating there under the watchful eyes of the Barrett women.

I brought two mugs of the coffee to the coffee table and plopped down next to Abby. She snuggled up against me and handed me a cookie.

"Now, that's what I call dessert," she said, and sipped the hot liquid carefully.

We were quiet for a few minutes, just enjoying being together. Then Abby asked me the question I had been dreading having to answer.

"Can you talk about what happened today?"

I smiled, wanly. "You asked that like you knew it had to be unpleasant."

"How could it have been anything else? That's why I wondered whether you were up to discussing it."

And we did. I tried to keep the worst of the details out of it, but I could tell she knew how bad it had been. I could tell from the way she listened, thankfully not asking for more details than I wanted to give.

"So this senseless killing of the Patton family is part of a larger pattern all over the South? How horrible," she mused.

"Hell, we don't even know if that is the extent of it," I said. "And even Jake Berger has no idea what this is all about."

"And Max thinks this policeman in Nashville can help figure this out?"

"I don't know what we'll find out from him," I answered. "All we know for sure is that he started this thing by investigating several murders with common threads. And sending that information to Willie Patton was probably why he and his family died."

"This Carl Lee must feel awful," Abby said, quietly. "When will you leave?"

"Max arranged for me and Bobby to meet Wiggins late tomorrow night, but I may be away for a few days. Max thinks it might be helpful to talk with some of the families and friends of some of the victims to try and find some common thread. I could be gone four or five days, maybe even a week."

Abby nodded. "Okay. I was going to spend some time with mom shopping for some things for Nina's school year. Maybe I'll spend a few days at home while you're gone."

"Maria would like that, and I know your sister would too."

"Then that's settled."

I told Abby where I had put some of Max' money so she would have it for anything she needed. She smiled for the first time since we started talking about my day at Max'.

"You know my mother," she said. "She won't let me put my hand in my pocket."

"It makes her happy to do things for you."

"I know."

"She almost lost you," I said, quietly.

"I know," she said, again.

Abby poured more coffee, and we sat quietly for a while.

"Can I ask you something?" I said, tentatively.

She put down her coffee cup and looked at me, quizzically. "Of course you can."

"What is it you love about me, Abby?"

She relaxed and smiled, pretending to be deep in thought. "Why, I guess that would be your fancy house and expensive cars, and monogrammed country club shirts…"

"Okay, I get it," I smiled. "But, that's not quite what I meant."

Abby looked at me, seriously. "Then, what is it, Thomas? What are you asking me?"

I took her hand and tried to explain what I had been ruminating about all afternoon.

"I guess it's just that, you know, when I got into this business there was a lot of minor stuff going on. Simple cases, that Max put me on, right? Then came the nursing home case and the horrible conditions those poor old folks were kept in, just so the owner could pour his money into gambling."

Crystal Harbor Nursing Home was a hell-hole being sued at the time by Max Howard's firm, and I had been hired to investigate what was going on. It was the first time I had been forced to physically confront someone, and, although we had been able to end the terrible situation, the whole process had a debilitating effect on me, personally.

"Then," I went on, "came Cuba. I don't have to tell you what that was like."

Abby stroked my face gently and nodded. We had both lost our innocence in Cuba.

"Now, there's this terrible thing going on and I know I have to keep my distance from it emotionally. But I guess that worries me, too."

She looked at me, and I could see she understood.

"You're afraid you will become hardened to this kind of inhumanity," she said simply. "And that will make me fall out of love with you."

I nodded. "I don't want to become some automaton, some unfeeling machine too used to horror to feel anything. You know, if you ever decided to leave me…"

She started to protest.

"No, wait. That is certainly not what I want. But if you did, for reasons of your own, I would have to live with that. I just don't want to ever drive you away."

Abby shook her head. "That's not you, Thomas. You can't be that way. But I understand and I can only offer this suggestion: please talk to me when you have doubts. Only silence, only keeping it inside, can cause us problems."

She smiled and I could feel her warmth wash over me.

"I'm here for you, sweetheart," she said. "I'm here for both of us, just like you are. There are two of us to handle whatever comes, okay? You need to remember that."

I took both her hands in mine, and kissed her lightly on the lips.

"What did I do to deserve you?" I said, softly.

"I ask myself the same about you. Every day."

We sat in silence again, just happy to be together.

After a while, Abby said, "So when will you leave for Nashville?"

"Probably around mid-day. Then, "I don't know why for sure, but I'm going to attend the service for Marti Patton in the morning. I don't know what I can possibly learn from going there, but I have the feeling that I need to see her family and the others who show up for the funeral."

"You're bothered by these separate burials, aren't you?" Abby asked.

"Yeah, I am."

CHAPTER 7

▼

August 9, 2003, Morning
Atlanta, Georgia

The night seemed to go on forever, and sleep came fitfully and in short bursts. For what must have been the tenth time, I glanced at the clock on the stand next to my bed. 5:40 a.m.

There wasn't much use in trying to go back to sleep until the alarm went off at 6:30. I turned it off and got out of bed as quietly as I could. Thankfully, Abby didn't wake up.

After a good twenty minutes in the shower, I dressed in the bathroom and gathered my

shaving gear and toothpaste and threw them into the small kit-bag I used when I traveled.

Abby was still sleeping when I tiptoed through the bedroom to the kitchen and made some coffee.

At 6:30, I kissed Abby softly on the forehead, picked up my bag sitting by the front door, went out into the hallway locking the door behind me.

I could hear the jumbled noises from Ireland's Own as I went down the stairs. I poked my head into the kitchen through the delivery door, and saw four of Pat's cooks preparing for the day's lunch business. I went through the kitchen and out into the restaurant. My brother was there sitting on a stool behind the bar, the *Atlanta Journal- Constitution* laid out on the bar top before him.

"Since when does the owner show up early in the morning when all the hard work is being done?" I said.

Pat yawned. "Since the Monster Boys decided they didn't really need to sleep and kept their parents up all night. Besides, why should they sleep at night, when they can sleep all day, right?"

He reached behind the bar and poured me a steaming cup of coffee.

"And what possible reason would a man of leisure like you have for being up at such a silly hour? Tennis match? Golf?"

"I wish. Going to a funeral, actually."

"Ahh," he said. "That's today, huh?"

"Yup. Not looking forward to it, either."

Pat nodded. "Max going with you?"

"I expect he'll be showing up."

We were quiet for a while. I drank some of the coffee and Pat refilled my cup and turned the page of his paper. But he had obviously been thinking about the day's events.

"Funerals are a lousy reason to have to get up early," he said.

"Yeah, especially this one. Evidently the families have agreed to disagree on having one funeral for Willie and Marti. They're having separate services and burials."

Pat looked up from the newspaper. "No shit?"

He flipped through the "Metro" section of the paper and found the obituaries.

"I'll be damned. I don't even see a notice in here about Willie's wife."

"You sure?" I said, puzzled. "That doesn't make any sense."

"Looks that way," Pat said. "What does Max say about all this funeral stuff?"

"What can he say?"

"Yeah, I guess," Pat said, shaking his head.

"Listen," I said. "Max is sending me and Bobby up to Nashville to meet with someone. After that, we may be going to meet some other people about this case. I'll probably be gone three, maybe four days. Abby's going to spend some time with her mom and sister, then come back here. Keep an eye on her for me, huh?"

"Sure, don't worry about her."

"Thanks."

Robbie Sedgwick, one of the bartenders, came through the kitchen door.

"My God, is this the end of the world?" he said, in mock surprise when he saw us together. "Anyway, donut time!" he said, and ceremoniously laid a box of *Krispy Kreme* donuts on the bar top, and sped away, back to the kitchen.

Pat and I studiously ignored the famous, enormously popular Southern favorite. He continued to peruse the paper. But I noticed his hand was starting to twitch a little.

"By the way," he said. "When are you going to marry that girl, sport?"

"Whoa! Where did *that* come from?"

"Well, you love her, don't you?" His hand was moving closer and closer to the box.

"Of course I do, but I need to be able to support her, too," I said, never surer of an answer to a question. "Pat, she's in college, and I'm trying to get a business on solid ground." I wasn't going to discuss the concerns I had finally been able to talk to Abby about last night.

Pat finally could stand it no more, and his hand dove into the square box of perfectly round, glazed donuts, one of which disappeared into his mouth in one bite. He pushed the box over to me, as if to relieve himself of guilt.

"Well, I wouldn't wait too long to ask her," he said in a muffled voice.

"Oh?" I said, as we both grabbed seconds. "And why not?"

"Because," Pat said. "Number one, she's great, number two, she seems to love you, and number three, you aren't that loveable. Your chances of finding another Abby are probably going to be limited. Besides, you lose her and mom will kick your ass…again."

"Hey, there was just that one time," I said, with a fake gloominess in my voice.

"Yeah, right. And, you're falling behind," he said, as another donut disappeared.

"I'm done," I said. But I studied the box. "*Krispy Kremes,* huh?"

"Hmm, tasty," he said, in obvious ecstasy.

I stared at the open and quickly emptying box.

"Little globs of fried fat, smothered in sugar," I said, studiously.

"Yowza!" Pat managed to say through his stuffed mouth.

"Concetta Rose Patrick would not be happy to see us eating this stuff," I said, envisioning our mother's horror at our gluttony.

"No, no she would not. Good thing she still lives in Cleveland, huh?" he said, as he inched the box a little closer to me, and grabbed another donut for himself.

"You are going straight to Hell," I said, with a sigh. "Well, maybe just one more."

Nothing positive comes out of a funeral, I thought to myself as the taxi driver wound his way through Peachtree Street's morning rush hour traffic. Bobby Hemphill would be picking up the suitcase I had left behind the bar at Ireland's Own before meeting me at the funeral home after the services for Marti Patton. That left me time to ruminate about unhappy things during the half-hour ride to Midtown.

Having been born of two ethnic groups considered to be "funeral professionals," I had been given insight into the intricacies of "The Wake" by my grandfathers. My mom's dad told me stories of the Italian funerals he had attended during his youth, which often included wakes held in the deceased's home. Besides the obvious drawback of scaring the crap out of any children who had to sleep with a dead body and the sickly smell of decaying flowers in their living room, these events were usually attended by waves of black-dressed, hired "wailers," who spent every moment of the visitation sessions screaming and crying and generally flipping out over the loss of the loved one. Sometimes, these wailers didn't even know the deceased.

On the other hand, as my leprechaun of a granddad on my father's side liked to say, there is no better party on earth than an Irish wake. Evidently, the usual Catholic wine, serving as the Blood of Christ, couldn't hold a candle to a good Irish whisky.

Seemingly, the moral of the two stories is that a funeral is for the living, not really for the deceased. A time to see, and be seen, to catch up on old friends and distant relatives and maybe, a chance to celebrate the fact that you aren't the one lying in a box.

If there is any truth to this concept, it appeared to be lost on the people who had gathered to say goodbye to Marti Patton.

After I had paid the taxi driver, I pulled self-consciously at the first tie I had worn in probably four years, and followed a group of people through the front doors of Henson's Funeral Home. The first thing that hit me was the heavy floral scent, an overpowering slap in the face that brought back less than happy memories of the wakes held for both my grandfathers, and my mom's mother, during my junior and senior years of high school. The second thing I noticed, as I checked the announcement board located just inside the door in the vestibule, was that there were two names listed. There was a Robert Meeker funeral commencing at Noon in Parlor "A," and one for a Martha Lee Harrison, at 8 a.m., in Parlor "B".

I knew I was in the right place and at the right time, so the only conclusion that I could draw was that the Harrison family was indeed Marti Patton's family, and that there was a concerted effort on their behalf to make any connection to her black husband, Willie Patton, disappear.

The hallway was densely packed with mourners flooding in and out of Parlor "B." There was no wall between the two areas, so it was pretty easy to find a spot near the rear of the hallway from which I could pretty much see the entire parlor area. At the front of the room I could see two tall lamp poles, some seven or eight feet apart, over the sea of people milling around. The tops of the poles had frosted lamps shaped something like flowers-maybe lilies- throwing off a low light. I couldn't see it, but I figured they flanked the coffin.

I couldn't see the family, but I wouldn't have known them if I had been able to. I decide that it would be best to just stay where I was and observe the scene, since I wasn't sure what I was looking for. I didn't see Max Howard.

People continued to mill around, and the air was filled with the buzz of muted conversations.

Suddenly, I felt the presence of another body within close proximity and I turned and nearly bumped into a wizened face glaring at me.

"Why, you're that comedian fellow from the television!" The face said. It belonged to an incredibly thin, female apparition of at least seventy- plus years. Her face was heavily lined and covered with a mask of cream colored make up. Her lips were a deep cherry red and sat smugly below a long, thin nose and eyes heavily lined with black eye liner. She wore a black dress with a heavy dose of pearls at her neck, and black gloves. The whole effect was covered by a big, floppy white hat.

"You're that Foxworthy fellow! Harold," she said to the elderly man to whose arm she seemed permanently attached. "It is, Harold, it's him!"

Jeff Foxworthy? I thought to myself. *The redneck comic?*

"Ahh… no, sorry," I said, in a low voice, as I tried to bring the conversation level down to 'funeral speak.' "I think you have me confused with a middle-aged, ahh…brown haired Southern guy."

"Oh, my," she said, a confused look on her face. "I'm so rarely wrong about things like that. Isn't that true, Harold?" The little man stared at the wall and appeared not to have heard any of this.

"We are Mr. and Mrs. Harold Montague," she said, with a haughty air. "You may call me Rita. And?" she said pointedly, and pushed her nose a few inches closer to my face.

"Sorry? Oh, yes, I'm Thomas Patrick. A friend of Marti and her husband."

"I see," she said, backing up a little. "You knew Martha's husband as well."

She gave her husband a knowing look, and he continued to ignore us.

"Yes, I did. And you are friends of Marti's family?"

"Heavens," the red lips said. "Why, we've known the Harrisons forever. We sponsored them for membership at the club more years ago than I wish to say."

The brim of her floppy hat brushed the top of Harold's head, but he didn't seem to notice.

"Such a terrible waste," she said, with a sad face. "Have you paid your respects to Martha Lee's parents?"

I shook my head. "No, not yet. Actually, I've never met her family."

She looked across the hall and into the parlor. If nothing else, her vision appeared to be good.

"There," she said. "That's Ethel, in the blue suit."

I followed her gaze and spotted a blond woman of medium height, maybe late fifties, standing among four or five other women. They didn't seem to be talking, but just standing around waiting for something to happen.

"And over there," my guide said, pointing at a group of men standing about ten feet from Marti's mother. "That's Edgar, standing in the middle."

The balding father of Marti Patton was deep in discussion with the others, and paying no attention to his wife.

"He seems busy," I said, knowing as the words came out that they would sound bad.

She seemed not to notice. "Well," she said behind a gloved hand, "at least he came to the funeral."

"What do you mean?" I said. "He's about to bury his daughter."

"Yes, of course. But he didn't attend the wedding. In fact, he wouldn't allow Ethel to attend, either. Actually," she said, behind the glove again, "None of us attended. It would have been disrespectful to the Harrisons, don't you know."

"Jesus," I said, softly. "Sorry. I guess I find that hard to believe."

"Young man," she said, "you aren't a Southerner by birth, are you?"

"No," I said, a bit defensively. "What difference does that make?"

She sighed. "For some people, some things simply cannot change. It just cannot happen."

"That's a shame."

"Yes," she said. "I suppose it is. Don't you think, Harold?"

✱   ✱   ✱   ✱

I followed my new friends as they snaked their way through the crowd toward the Harrisons, passing the closed casket containing the mutilated remains of the beautiful blond girl, aglow, the last time I had seen her, with anticipation of the birth of her first child. I watched as Rita Montague gave Ethel Harrison a small hug, and then she dragged Harold past the group of women toward Marti's father and his friends.

Ethel seemed to be in a constant fog. She showed no emotion, offered no thanks for the mourners' presence.

As I approached, she took my hand in a robotic move, and before I could offer condolences, she said, "Thank you for coming" in a small voice, and turned her attention to the person behind me.

As I approached Marti's father, I put out my hand. "I'm very sorry for your loss, Mr. Harrison."

He took my hand and shook it once and thanked me. That was it. He didn't ask me who I was or why I was there.

"I was wondering," I said, as he went back to his conversation. "I'm looking for the Patton family. I thought they might be here."

Edgar Harrison looked at me with cold eyes. "Well, I guess they had their own burying to deal with today," he said in a dismissive way. And, that quickly, I was no longer the point of his focus.

That pissed me off, and I decided to press the issue. "Oh, and I was wondering why no one here seems to give a damn that your daughter's marriage to my friend, Willie Patton, seems to have been wiped away?"

Harrison didn't react, but I heard my friend with the hat who was standing nearby with her comatose husband, give a small gasp. Almost immediately, I found myself staring up at the stony glare of one of Elmer Harrison's pals, who had positioned himself between me and Marti's father. He was huge, and had certainly played on the offensive line for some college or other some years back.

"Now, son," he said in a low but authoritative voice, "I don't think you want to be talkin' that way to a grieving father, now, do you?"

"No," I said, quietly. "Not to a grieving father," I turned, and walked away. I had made my point. This was not the time to push it. But I knew I would be seeing Edgar Harrison again. I could feel the cold eyes of Harrison and his friends on my back.

A low voice came over the loudspeaker announcing the start of services, and asked that we take our seats. I didn't think I needed, or could stand, to be around for the next step in this travesty.

I headed back to the front doors and went outside, glad to be back in the sunshine. Bobby Hemphill's Durango was parked a few spaces away. I went over and got in.

"Jesus, you look like hell." Bobby waved his hand in front of my face. "You okay, man?"

"Yeah. Let's just get outta' here."

"Sure," Bobby said. "Next stop, Nashville."

CHAPTER 8

▼

August 9, 2003

"Thomas? Can you hear me, Thomas?!" Abby said. "We're going home, sweetheart!"

"Sure we are, babe," I said, and her beautiful, chocolate-eyes were the last thing I saw before I passed out.

A crash of thunder jolted me out of a deep sleep and almost immediately, my cell phone, which I had set on "vibrate" at the funeral home, began to buzz against my chest. I shook off the fuzziness and took the phone out of my jacket breast pocket.

"Max?" I croaked, through a dry throat.

"Tommy? Where are you?"

I looked at Bobby, who was busy fighting the drenching rain that was overpowering the wiper blades. "Where are we?"

"Near Chattanooga."

"We're a couple hours north of Atlanta, Max. Rain's heavy, but we should reach Nashville on schedule."

"Good. Sorry I missed you at the funeral home. Something came up, but I finally caught up with the procession at the cemetery."

"Sorry I didn't wait," I said. "I needed to get out of there before I did something stupid." Which, I realized as I said it, I may have already done. Challenging Edgar Harrison like that had been foolish at best. I decided not to mention the incident to Max for now.

"I understand. They are a strange crowd, I know."

"Where are you now?"

"At the Patton wake, waiting for the services to start."

I'd had enough of funerals for the time being. "It's raining pretty hard, but we'll be in Nashville long before the meeting time."

"Okay," Max said. "Keep me informed. And be careful, Tommy."

"Sure, Max. Call you tomorrow."

Bobby looked at me questioningly.

"Nothing new," I said.

We rode in silence for a while, and I watched the windshield wipers push the heavy downpour aside, only to have the glass inundated again immediately. I reached behind Bobby's seat and pulled up the box of files from Max' office. I wasn't anxious to go through them again, but I was going to have to live with the crime scene photos they contained for a long time There was no sense in denying their existence.

Bobby drove on for about an hour, and slowly the rain slackened. He kept silent while I went through the paperwork.

I closed the file I had been studying, having compared it with information in other folders.

"I don't get it," I said. "I can't find any common thread." I tossed the box behind the seat again. "Why were these people targeted? We've got victims from every walk of life: different ages, financial conditions, careers, religious affiliations, some men black, some white, and the same with the women. There's no information that they might have known each other, We have crimes committed in Georgia, Virginia, South Carolina, Texas, Alabama, Arkansas, and Tennessee," I shook my head. "In every case, the only constant is that each couple was bi-racial, yet the crime scenes were nearly identical."

Bobby let me stew for awhile, then he said: "So how are going to play this tonight?"

"What?" I asked, my mind still on the files.

"The meeting with this Wiggins guy. What are we going to try to get out of him?"

"Oh," I said, trying to clear my head. "Well, Max wants us to see if there is any additional information Carl Lee has come up with. That's the first thing, I guess. After that, we'll split up and visit some of the relatives and friends of the victims, and see if there's any way to connect the murders."

"But if Wiggins had anything else, wouldn't he have told Max?"

"Hell, I don't know," I said. "Maybe, maybe not. He might have had a change of heart after Willie was murdered."

Bobby was quiet for awhile. "If it was me," he said, finally, "I think I would have run for cover. You know, figuring someone very dangerous was on to me. I mean, fear and self-preservation are reasonable responses when your best friend is killed, right?"

"I guess it all depends on whether Willie's murder scared him, or made him angry. Besides, he committed to meet with us, right? He could have just blown Max off if he was done with this thing."

"I guess," Bobby said. "But I still say he should want to save himself."

"Maybe. But maybe he wants justice more."

✱   ✱   ✱   ✱

We were about an hour out of Nashville and several hours short of our scheduled meeting time with Carl Lee Wiggins. The rain was long gone but had left a heavy humidity in the air.

I called Abby's cell and got her voice mail, but I caught up with her at her mom's house. I felt relief wash over me when I heard her voice. She and Maria were about to start their hunt for new school clothes for Abby's younger sister, Nina. At least she was safe. Of course, I had no real reason to be worried about her, but I kept thinking that the people in those files in the box behind Bobby's seat had gone to bed in their homes, feeling safe behind locked doors and windows. And they all died. Willie Patton died. Marti Patton died. Their unborn child died. How was it possible in 2003 that people vicious enough to kill them, especially in such a brutal way, could be running free in our society?

The truth was, I knew, that the fact that it was possible was not important. They were out there. They had to be stopped. I only wished I knew how to make that happen.

We drove along in silence for awhile, then Bobby said, "I've been thinking, Tommy."

I looked at him. "What about?"

"I mean, it seems pretty clear to me that no one person, or even a small group, is running around from state to state committing these crimes at random, right? These are serial killer crimes, but serial killers don't usually travel over long distances. They like to stay in a tightly controlled area, you know, familiar surroundings so they can feel safe, right? Its how they keep control of their actions and tease the law enforcement groups that are chasing them."

"That's a reasonable assumption."

"Okay, so if these crimes are all nearly the same, it makes sense to me that there still has to be a connection between the killers."

"True, but I can't figure out what that connection is though."

Bobby was quiet for a few minutes, then he said, "So maybe we should be looking for a large group or organization that is capable of multiple murders over a large geographical area."

"I follow you, Bobby, but I still don't know how we do that. I'm open to any suggestions."

"That's my point, Tommy. There are police and FBI by the thousands out there. Why aren't they chasing this thing? How are *we* supposed to find these bastards when there has to be all kinds of data on groups like this, and the people with that data aren't doing anything?"

I didn't know how to answer that. It had bothered me since the meeting in Max Howard's office. *"Why not bring the FBI in now, Max?"*

His answer had been that he wanted to build a solid case first. Jake Berger had agreed with Max.

"As much as I trust Jake Berger, I think his hands may be tied on this case," Max had said. There had been no reason given for that statement, and I had let it slide.

Bobby looked at me, awaiting an answer to his question. I had none. "We play this Max' way for now," I said, feeling the weight of my inexperience. "I'm not sure what else to do."

We rode the rest of the way to Nashville in silence. There were several hotels near the airport and we pulled off the Interstate and found a Fairfield Inn. I checked us in while Bobby gathered our bags and the file box.

We still had a long wait before we had to head to our meeting downtown. I told Bobby to rest up, and I headed across the street to an Exxon station to pick up a map of the Greater Nashville area.

I found my partner fast asleep when I returned to the room. I felt groggy enough to sleep myself, but instead I opened up the map and laid it out on the small, round table by the window. I took the slip of paper out of my wallet that contained the name and location of the bar where we would meet Carl Lee Wiggins. I found the area near downtown known as Music City. Notes on the map explained that this was the entertainment area of Nashville, with music museums, restaurants and bars featuring live bands specializing in country music and jazz.

According to Max Howard's note, Mo Kelly's Bar and Grill was on 14th Avenue South off Hawkins Street. Carl Lee would be expecting us at 11 p.m. I figured out our best route to the bar, and closed up the map. Fatigue was taking over, and my leg, which I had injured during that fateful first and last game at Ohio State, was cramping up from the long car ride.

I set the alarm for 10 p.m. and flopped on my bed. Bobby was snoring gently, and the TV was on but silent, and tuned to CNN Headline News. I watched the storylines across the bottom of the screen for a few minutes, never really concentrating on what they said.

Finally, I rolled over on my side, and drifted into a fitful sleep.

CHAPTER 9

▼

August 9, 2003, 10:50 P.M.
Nashville, Tennessee

A steamy mist was rising from the hot pavement, and light rain fell again as we pulled up across the street from *Mo Kelly's*. It was an old place with the last two letters of the neon sign blacked out. In the center of the brick front was a lone metal door that looked more like it was guarding a warehouse than a bar. Three small windows had lit signs advertising brands of beer. Otherwise, the street was dark and barren.

Just around the corner gas lights gave off a friendly glow, and a mix of live music escaped from doors left open to entice the tourists. Mo Kelly's definitely wasn't a tourist bar. This was likely to be where the locals hung out, and not the well-to-do locals.

We sat in the Durango and watched the door for a few minutes. No one went in or out.

At ten minutes after eleven, Bobby said, "Either he ain't comin' or he's already inside."

If he doesn't show, I thought to myself, *we may have lost him for good.* "Let's go find out."

We locked up the truck and walked across the street, the sound of our footsteps echoing in my ears. We stopped at the door and looked at each other.

"Actually," Bobby said, a half-smile on his face, "I always saw myself as a career 'kept man.' So tell me again how I wound up here?"

I opened the heavy door and we were plunged into an even darker atmosphere. There were ceiling-height wooden walls forming a kind of entrance hallway. About fifteen feet away, I could see the dim lights of the main room. We walked through the tunnel-like entrance, our sight slowly getting used to the dim light, and wound up facing a long bar at the back of the room. To the left was a jumble of tables, only five of which were in use. The whole place had the sour smell of years of spilled beer and cheap booze, and a million smoked cigarettes. These people were here to drink, not socialize.

"Nice," Bobby whispered in my ear. "Make a good place for a wedding reception, huh?"

I ignored his quip and headed towards the bar. We grabbed a couple of stools at the end of the bar and waited. The bartender, a giant black man of maybe six foot three or four with a bodybuilder's physique and a shiny bald head spotted us from the other end, where he was in deep conversation with a couple of customers. He gave us a full minute of a stony glare before coming over at a slow, deliberate pace.

He said nothing, but threw a couple of those cardboard coasters in front of us, and waited.

"A couple beers," I finally said.

He kept the glare trained on us but pulled two long-neck Buds out of an ice filled tub, flipped off the tops and put them, none to gently, on the coasters.

"You boys in the right place?" he said in a deep, gravelly voice.

"Just here for the floor show," I said, and took a pull on my beer. I kept my eyes trained on his, but I wasn't as comfortable doing the stare thing as he seemed to be.

He leaned forward and rested his hands on the bar. He leaned closer still, and the thickness of his arms was not lost on me.

"What you want?" he said, with the same steady, no-nonsense stare, as if he could look right into my brain.

"What makes you think we want anything more than a cold beer?"

Sasquatch backed up a little and reached under the bar where I felt sure his massive hands were caressing a weapon of some kind. There wasn't any reason to prolong our little game. We weren't here looking for trouble.

"We're looking for someone. We have a meeting scheduled for eleven tonight."

"And who might you be looking for?" he said, his hands still hidden from view.

I looked at Bobby and he nodded. "We need to find a guy named Carl Lee Wiggins. He's expecting us."

The bartender backed off a little and brought his empty hands up from under the bar, but he wasn't about to give away information.

"How I know that?"

"Don't expect you *would* know that. But the fact is he is expecting us, and we need to find him. Do you know him or not?"

He stood quietly for a few seconds sizing us up. "Where you come from?"

"What difference does that make?" I said. I could feel my frustration starting to build.

The bartender leaned in again. "You wanna' see Carl Lee, you tell me where you from. That plain enough?"

"All right," I said. "We'll play it your way. We're from Atlanta, and Carl Lee really is expecting us."

The man gave a sudden, gap-toothed grin. "See? That wasn't so hard, now was it?" He nodded over to his right. I could see that there saw a small area of tables back behind the tunnel wall we had entered through that was secluded from the rest of the barroom. At the back end of the area was a table deep in the shadows. A lone figure sat with his back against the outside wall and facing in towards the bar. A small red glow followed by a puff of blue smoke escaped from the shadowy face.

"You go on over," the bartender said. "I'll bring your drinks."

We slid off our stools and approached the figure sitting at the table. As I got closer, the form took shape. He was a black man, and appeared to be close to Willie Patton's age, which would put him in his mid-thirties. Even sitting down, I could tell he was a big man, not like our bald friend at the bar, but big just the same. He drew a deep drag on his cigarette as we stopped before him, and expelled the heavy smoke toward us.

"Mr. Wiggins?" I said, through the blue fog. "Carl Lee Wiggins?"

He studied us for a good half minute. "So you the boys Mr. Max sent to talk to me." It wasn't a question. His voice was deep and raspy, and sounded like he had smoked a lot of those cigarettes over the years. "You all don't look old enough to be involved in this kinda' shit," he said, not unkindly, and motioned to us to sit.

"Yeah, we came here on behalf of Max Howard," I said with a sigh, "and I'll tell you, Mr. Wiggins, I feel a lot older than I look."

He gave a slight chuckle, but there wasn't much humor in it.

The bartender was suddenly beside us. He put three beers on the table along with a full bottle of sour mash and three shot glasses. Wiggins poured the shots and immediately downed his.

"This here's Cletus Mackey. This is his place."

"*You're* Mo Kelly?" Bobby said, surprise in his voice.

Cletus gave a loud snort. "I look like a 'Mo Kelly' to you, boy? Hell, they been five, six owners since ol' Mo be around. But people know the name, so nobody ever did change it."

He nodded to Wiggins. "You jus' call, you be needin' anything, Carl Lee."

"He takes good care of me," Carl Lee said after Cletus left us. "He's a good friend," he added, quietly.

Carl Lee took the second shot down and followed it with a pull on his beer. He studied the both of us for a minute.

"You boys knew Willie?" he asked.

"Not very well, Mr. Wiggins. Only through our dealings with the firm," I said. "But Max was very fond of him, and we're very fond of Max. We want to help find out why this happened."

He nodded. "So what you gonna' do?"

I finally took a sip of the whiskey. I waited for the burn to dissipate. "It would help if we knew a little bit more about how this all started. Max wants us to try and establish some common thread of some kind among the different murders you investigated. It would be helpful to know how you got into this."

He leaned back. "Easy enough. My partner and me, we were the closest unit when a call came in about a double homicide about a mile from where we were patrolling. So we were the first unit at the scene."

"That would be the Smith-Meriweather crime scene, right?" I asked.

"Yeah, that's the one. Neighbor lady found the front door wide open, so she goes up to the house callin' for Nessie Smith."

He shook his head slowly. "Lord, I never seen nothin' like it. I seen murdered people before, but I ain't never seen *that* kinda' shit. I couldn't keep food down for days after that."

The pictures from that file flashed through my mind. It bothered me that I remembered them so clearly: Forty year old white dentist, Art Meriweather's genitals slashed from his body and nailed to the wall. The crude cross embedded in his chest. Nessie Smith, a twenty-two year old waitress, had been stabbed repeatedly, and that was only a small part of the degradation they had suffered. And those bloody signs and marks on the walls, like that number "11," with the letter "x" through it. What did they mean?

"Anyway," Wiggins said, "It made big news for a couple days like you would expect. But then, it all just kinda' went away, you know?"

"Went away, how?" Bobby asked.

"Nobody was even talkin' about it. I tried to ask about the investigation, and little by little I figured it out. There wasn't any. Not any kinda' real police work bein' done by anybody in my precinct anyway. At first I figured that maybe it got passed up the line because of the nature of the crime, but that wasn't it, either. Wasn't even in the newspaper, or on the TV no more."

"So what did you do then?" I asked.

"Hell, man, I stopped talkin' about it." Carl Lee finished his beer and held the bottle up where Cletus could see it. "Figured that was the smart thing to do. But when I was on duty at the precinct instead of out on patrol, I started runnin' through the national computer files to see if anything like this had happened before." He drank a shot and swallowed some of the fresh beer Cletus had delivered.

"So did you show your captain what you found?" Bobby asked.

"Never got a chance. One night, I was pullin' some copies of the information I'd found. Then, Eddie Wayne, one of the cops on duty that night, comes around and he's watchin' what I'm doin'. He's a white guy, but he's okay, you know. We were pretty friendly. But next thing I know, captain calls me in and tells me I don't need to be lookin' for this stuff. Says we got no business worryin' about out-of-state crimes and I should just do my job."

"Is that when you sent the files to Willie Patton?"

He shook his head. "Let things cool down for awhile first, you know? Pretend I lost interest. But people were lookin' at me a little different now. So I thought I better get this information to somebody who might have better luck with it. That's when I called Willie."

"You must have been talking with Max about this, too, right?"

"Some," Carl Lee said. "But mostly with Willie." He sat back again. "Mr. Max was the one who called to tell me about what happened."

He downed his third shot. Bobby and I waited.

"I killed Willie just as sure as if I put a bullet in his head."

I shook my head. "That's crazy Carl Lee. Nobody is blaming you for what happened to the Patton family."

"*I* blame me," he said, emphatically. "Don't much matter what anybody else thinks."

"Look," I said, not wanting to argue the point, "it's not up to me to change your way of thinking, but if that's how you feel, the best thing you can do is to help us find the killers. We've got to end this thing, Carl Lee."

"Meanin'?"

"Is there anything else you can tell us? Have you found out anything new that might help us?"

Wiggins sat back, his hand fingering the empty shot glass.

"Nothin' I can give you yet," he said, slowly.

"Yet? What do you mean, 'yet'?"

"What I said," Carl Lee answered. "I got some information, but I ain't ready to tell nobody about it."

"Jesus," Bobby said. "Don't you think we should know about any new information soon as possible?"

Carl Lee poured the shot, but didn't drink. "I'm still a cop. That means I don't go accusing anybody 'til I know something for sure. That's the way it's gonna' be."

He was dug in. We weren't going to get anything else from him tonight.

"Okay, Carl Lee," I said. "But sooner would be more helpful than later."

"So, what we do now," he asked.

"Bobby and I are going to visit some of the people close to the victims. See if we can put together some connection between all of the murders. We're going to need to reach you, Carl Lee. We should have some set time to speak if anything comes up. Can we get a home number?"

Wiggins was quiet for a moment. Then he said, "Don't go there much anymore. Not since my Gracie left."

"Sorry, I didn't know you were divorced."

Carl Lee Wiggins took the shot and sat back.

"Had us a boy," he said, quietly. "He was born with the sickle cell, you know?"

I nodded.

"He did good for awhile. Little smaller than the other kids his age, but we got by."

He was looking right at me, but he wasn't seeing me. He was off somewhere in his own private hell.

"Then he got the measles; them German kind. The doctor's said he would be okay, but two days later, the only word we hear out of their mouths was 'complications.' Grace, she stayed in the hospital with him day and night, I'd go there when I was off duty."

Carl Lee drank the rest of his beer. "I get there one night, late. My boy's all covered up with a white sheet. Gracie, she just sittin' there, holdin' his hand and singin' to him real soft." He sighed. "She took it real hard, you know? But I was worse," he said. "Started drinkin', and I wasn't much good to her no more. Just took off for days at a time. Nearly lost my job. We struggled along like that maybe six months, then I come home from a two day bender, and she leaves me a letter. Says she loves me, but she can't mourn for me and my boy both. Since then, I don't go home much anymore."

I didn't know what to say, so I just said: "Sorry."

He was coming back. "Funny thing," he said. "Some nights I just shows up where she's livin' now. She let's me in, makes me some dinner, and I end up sleepin' on her couch. I wake up in the mornin', she done covered me with a blanket. Through all of that, sometimes we don't even say a word."

"I can't even imagine how terrible it's been for you."

"Anyway," he said, with a sigh. "Cletus got a cot set up for me in the back room. I do some work for him; little carpentry, plumbing and such, and he let's me stay here. You need me, I got a separate phone line back there. First time you call me, leave me a number to call you back at 11 p.m. that night.

It's best you find some pay phone and don't use your cell or home numbers to call me."

"You really think that's necessary?" Bobby asked.

"Somebody found out I called Willie," Carl Lee said. "Don't want you to wind up dead, too."

CHAPTER 10

▼

August 10, 2003
Nashville, Tennessee

Bobby dropped me off in front of the Air Tran ticket entrance at the Nashville airport. Earlier that morning, we had packed up the files and put them in the back of the Durango, except for the two files that I was taking with me to Virginia. After I rented a car at the Richmond airport, my main job would be to visit with anyone I could get to talk to me about the Allen/Tenley murders. They were the teenage victims Max had told us about at his office. Then I would be driving down to Norfolk to do some checking on the Fairchild/Masters case.

Bobby was driving the Durango down to Montgomery, Alabama, then on to Birmingham to research two other cases. We planned to meet back home in a day or two, if all went well.

I purchased my ticket to Richmond, with a flight home from the Virginia Beach-Norfolk airport, and walked out to my gate to wait out the hour before take-off.

It gave me time to think about the conversation with Carl Lee Wiggins. Actually, I hadn't thought about much else since we had left the bar at about 1:15 a.m.

There was no doubt in my mind that Carl Lee was in danger. How much I wasn't sure, but in danger, just the same. It made me wonder about my safety and Bobby's as well. Someone knew that people in Atlanta were involved with Wiggins' investigation. Those same people either killed, or had Willie and Marti Patton killed. It wasn't reasonable to think they would stop watching Max Howard or anyone associated with his firm. They would want to know if he was going to press on with the work Willie had been doing.

I tried to put those thoughts out of my head for now, and concentrate on what I was going to do in Virginia. I quickly realized that I was going to have to play it by ear. It was the only way to go about the task at hand. I could stop at the newspaper, or at a library, and review any articles about the case, but what I really needed was to talk to people who knew the victims. Best to start with their families, and from the file I knew that the young basketball player had been raised by his maternal grandmother. It was as good a place as any to start, *if* she would talk to me.

The weather in Richmond was hot and sultry, and it took a long time for the A/C in the Ford I had rented to catch up.

I drove west from the airport to the neighborhood where Maurice Tenley had grown up. It was an older section of the city and appeared to be mostly blue collar. I drove around for awhile until I found the right street, and looked for the address listed in the file.

I found it and pulled up across the street from the Tenley home, and parked. It was a two story brick home, maybe forty or so years old, with a porch running the length of the first floor. Five stairs led up to the front porch, so I figured there was a basement.

The house looked to be in very good shape, and the front lawn, bordered by a spotless white picket fence, was well trimmed. Beds of colorful summer flowers dotted the grounds, some surrounding two beautiful old oak trees. Pride lived in this house.

The front door opened and an elderly black woman sporting a brightly colored summer dress and a wide brimmed hat came out of the house. She carried a broom and began sweeping the porch. Then she walked down the steps and began sweeping the concrete walkway that led to the front gate at the sidewalk.

I watched her for a few minutes. This would be Maurice's grandmother, Althea Tenley, age 74 and small, maybe five foot one or two. According to the file, she had been the one who had identified his body at the coroner's office. It gave me pause to think about the pain and horror I was about to ask her to relive. I could understand it if she refused to talk to me.

I turned off the engine and almost immediately began to feel the sweat roll down my back, as the car's interior quickly heated up. Opening the door I stepped out into the blistering sun and moisture-filled air and tossed the file onto the driver's seat. I didn't want to bring it anywhere near the woman.

I walked across the street and approached the gate. Mrs. Tenley was nearing the end of her task.

"It certainly is a hot one today," I said, in a neighborly voice.

The woman didn't look up but kept on with her sweeping.

"Are you selling something, young man?" she asked in a quiet, but authoritative voice.

"No, ma'am, I surely am not." I stopped in front of the gate.

"Are you a policeman, or maybe a reporter?" she asked.

"No," I said, simply.

"You don't work for one of those magazines that make up stories about aliens and such, do you?"

I smiled in spite of the gravity of the situation. "No, Mrs. Tenley. I'm not a writer."

She finally looked up at me. "But, you *are* here to talk to me about my grandson, are you not?"

It was almost as if she had been waiting for me....or someone...to come to see her.

"Yes, I am, and I'm sorry to bring all this up for you again, but I assure you it's important. I desperately need your help, ma'am."

She studied me for a minute. "Well, then, I expect you better come sit down on the porch. I've just made some fresh lemonade."

She turned back to the house and went gingerly up the front steps the way my grandmother used to when her arthritis was acting up.

"Make yourself comfortable," she nodded toward the table and chairs on the porch. "I'll get the lemonade."

"Thank you, ma'am," I said, gratefully.

I waited for her to return and took the tray with the pitcher and glasses from her, and put it on the table. There was a dish of sugar cookies in the center of the tray. She motioned me to sit, and poured the lemonade.

"You haven't told me your name, young man," she said.

"Thomas. Thomas Patrick."

She glanced at me. "You aren't from Richmond, are you, Mr. Patrick?"

"No, ma'am. I live in Atlanta."

"And you came all the way from Georgia just to see me?" She took a sip of her drink. "To talk about my Maurice?"

"That's the main reason I'm here, Mrs. Tenley."

She rocked gently in her chair. "It surely is hot," she said, quietly.

We sat without speaking for a little while.

Then she said: "Why would you come here to talk to me about Maurice and that poor young girl? I can't seem to get anyone in Richmond to talk with me. Why are you here, Mr. Patrick?"

I tried to figure the easiest way to discuss why I was there, but there simply was no easier way than the truth.

"Mrs. Tenley, I'm working with a law firm in Atlanta that is investigating a series of murders throughout the South that were almost identical to what happened to your grandson and his friend here in Richmond. I'm trying to establish some kind of tie-in…some similarity that will hopefully lead us to the perpetrators." I stopped to make sure she was following me. She was.

"What do you mean, almost identical?" she asked.

"Well," I said, slowly. "The victims were killed in the same manner. They were all mixed-race couples, and the crimes all took place under similar circumstances." I sighed. "What is puzzling is that there seems to be a great number of differences between the victims themselves."

She took a sip of the lemonade and rocked a little again. "You mean they were not all young couples?"

"Yes, ma'am. There were vast differences in ages, and finances. Some couples were married, some not." I shook my head. "I'm getting nowhere fast. I thought it might help to know more about Maurice and his friend…if it doesn't make you too uncomfortable to talk about it."

Althea Tenley sat back and was silent for almost a minute. I was about to speak, when she said: "I wanted Maurice to have a chance at a good life. His mother was my only child, you see, and she threw her life away." She nodded to herself, as if remembering.

"His daddy was a drug dealer, and he got Theresa hooked real good on heroin. He toyed with her a long time, Mr. Patrick. I guess she paid for the drugs with sex because she couldn't hold a job to make money. They were never married, of course, and he dropped her pretty fast when she turned up with child."

We drank some, and I felt the air wavy with heat and humidity so thick I could almost grab it, brush my damp face.

Mrs. Tenley went on: "She came to me for help when she was already six months gone. I took her back in, of course, and she tried real hard to get herself clean while she was here." She sighed deeply. "But she broke down a few times. Don't know where she got the drugs, but she did. I was surprised she didn't lose the child. Did you ever see a child born full of drugs, Mr. Patrick?"

"No." It was all I could think of to say.

"It is a terrible thing to behold. They didn't expect Maurice to live, but he did. He was a fighter, that little five-pound baby, and I wanted him to have a real life. My daughter abandoned the baby and left us about three months after we brought Maurice home from the hospital. I never saw her alive again. They found her dead in an alley not long after."

This lady had already endured more pain than anyone deserved in a lifetime. And now, the child she fought to save and raise was gone, too.

"I'm very sorry, ma'am. I wish it wasn't necessary to ask you about this."

She smiled a sad smile. "Don't trouble yourself, Mr. Patrick. I was born and grew up in a South not that much different than it was before the Civil War. I have become used to sorrow."

I let it all sit for a few minutes, then asked: "Ma'am, how well did you know Maurice's girl friend?"

"Sandy Allen," she said, sadly. "I never met Sandy before my grandson showed up with her to tell me about the baby. They loved each other. Oh, I know it was the wrong time for them. They were so young, and Maurice had a real good chance at a basketball scholarship to college. But there were real feelings between those children, Mr. Patrick. This was not some tawdry thing that just happened. Do you know her father turned me away from her funeral? I came to express my sorrow at their loss, and they turned me away. Of course, they never came to Maurice's wake." There was a tear slowly working its way down her cheek.

"I've troubled you enough, Mrs. Tenley." I knew I should ask her if there was any chance that Maurice might have been involved with drugs or something else that might have gotten him in with the wrong people, but I couldn't do it. Not after what had happened to her daughter. Besides, I couldn't imagine this woman allowing that to happen.

I got up to leave.

She gazed up at me. "Mr. Patrick, you never told me why you are interested in what happened to Maurice. So I must ask you. Why?"

I thought about how best to answer. She deserved to know.

"An acquaintance of mine," I said, "a black man, was killed the same way as Maurice. So were his wife, a white girl, and their unborn child."

She nodded, sadly. "So you want to stop whoever is doing these terrible things."

I shook my head. "Not just to stop them, Mrs. Tenley. I want to punish them."

Bobby Hemphill caught up with me by cell phone as I was passing Williamsburg, Virginia, on my way to Norfolk. He was on his way to Birmingham.

"I got nothing, Tommy," he said, and I could hear the frustration in his voice. "Those people couldn't be more normal. A black man, a bank manager, married to a white woman for twelve years. Three kids, church-goers, well-liked by their neighbors."

"Three kids?"

"Yeah," Bobby said. "How's that for luck? The kids were visiting their grandparents in Florida for vacation. God knows what would have happened if they had been home that night."

"You know exactly what would have happened to them, Bobby."

"Yeah, I guess."

I told him about my day. Great couple of investigators we were. We kicked around some ideas for a few more minutes, but the more we talked, the more desperate we sounded. Finally, we hung up, and I drove on towards Norfolk and my last chance to learn anything of use to us.

CHAPTER 11

▼

August 10, 2003
Norfolk, Virginia

She was stunning, to say the least. Marissa Fairchild stood just inside the door of her lavishly decorated office, arms folded across her chest. She was dressed in an emerald green skirt that I would have thought too short for a high-priced attorney, a matching jacket over a white blouse, her auburn hair cascading over her shoulders. Green stiletto heals capped the long, perfect legs. Her face was angelic, looking way younger than her forty- two years, but there was a pervading hard edge in her eyes.

I was seated in an arm chair at her desk, where I had been since I had bullied her receptionist into calling Ms. Fairchild, interrupting a "very important" meeting, to inform her of the very insistent "person" who wasn't going to leave until he saw her. After much consternation and many dirty looks, I had been escorted to Marissa Fairchild's private office, where I had now been waiting nearly forty-five minutes. I was in no mood to stand on formalities when she finally showed up, and remained seated, trying to keep the awe at her appearance from my face.

She studied me from the doorway for a minute.

"I'm sure," she finally said, in a steely voice, "that my secretary told you that it normally takes thirty days or more to get an appointment with me, Mr...," she looked down at my card in her hand, "Mr. Patrick. Nor is it acceptable for you to barge your way past office personnel or disrupt my meeting schedule."

I was quickly succumbing to a lack of sleep, disturbing confrontations, and borderline despair at the state of the investigation. The situation wasn't doing my patience any good.

"Yeah," I said from my seat. "I get the point. You're busy. But frankly, Ms. Fairchild, I don't much care."

She bristled noticeably, but she moved towards her desk. "Now listen, buster…," she said, and I interrupted.

"I am rather busy myself," I said, my voice rising a little in volume. "I need to talk to you about your husband's murder, and there isn't a lot of time."

She was standing behind the ornate mahogany desk now, her arms still folded across her chest.

"You've got ten minutes," she said, finally, seeming to calm down a little, but still trying to remain in control.

"Then we had better get started."

"I spent months working with the Norfolk police after Phillip was killed," she said, finally sitting down. "Your card says you are a private investigator from Atlanta. Just what are you investigating, and for whom, and why should I be talking to you?"

I decided to take a direct approach, ignoring her questions for now. "Ms. Fairchild, during the police investigation, did anyone mention to you the similarity of your husband's…circumstances, to those of several other crimes that had occurred in other cities over the last two years?"

Her face went blank for a moment, my words taking some of the stiffness out of her posture. Silence filled the room as I waited for her response.

"I don't understand," she said. "What do you mean, 'similar'?"

"Then I take it this was not discussed?"

She was getting a little curious now. "Please explain yourself, Mr. Patrick."

So I did, telling her what I knew without being as graphic as I could have been. When I finished, she sat quietly, looking not at me, but through me. I decided that it was time to show some compassion for her situation, hoping I could draw her out.

"Look, Ms. Fairchild, I know its rough having me show up like this. The last thing I want to do is force you to relive the pain and sorrow of such a tragic loss. I'm sure it is hard…" I suddenly realized that Marissa Fairchild was smiling. It was a humorless smile, but a smile just the same.

"Nice of you to offer condolences," she said, "but let me make it clear that if my husband's death caused me pain, and it most definitely has, it is because of the 'circumstances' under which he chose to get himself killed."

I was at a loss to offer a response, so I kept quiet.

"Phillip and I had a somewhat open marriage, Mr. Patrick. We both had money and shared the expenses of life, and our daughters were very fond of him. He could be quite charming." She seemed to be drifting away, but went on with her story in a strong voice.

"As a well-to-do, handsome man, he had every opportunity to satisfy his 'appetites' among our acquaintances. Don't get me wrong. I'm sorry he's gone, and, yes, this has been a painful situation. But the pain comes from the embarrassment he caused me and my daughters."

"I see," I said, feeling an embarrassment of my own.

"You're surprised to hear me speak this way? Don't be. The story is well known around Norfolk. I used to be a prosecutor before I became a partner here. I had some good friends in the police department, and they did their best to keep certain details out of the papers. But juicy stories have a way of getting out, don't they?"

I didn't answer, and we were quiet for a few moments.

"What reason did Phillip have for dying in the bed of a nineteen-year-old, poor, black waitress in a seedy motel? I can't answer that, and believe me, I've tried. So how are these other murders related?"

"I'm trying to figure that out," I said, no longer feeling the need to be gentle in my questioning. "Could your husband have been involved in anything illegal? Something that could have caused someone to kill him out of retribution?"

She seemed to think about that, taking no offense at the question.

"You mean drugs?" she asked, finally. "I won't say that Phillip might not have been a recreational user, but selling? Dealing with drug dealers?" She shook her head. "No, he didn't have the guts for the dangers involved in that, and he certainly didn't need the money."

"I understand the girl had a child," I said, trying a different tact. "Could your husband....."

"Have been the father? Believe me, you're not the first to consider that, either," she smiled that cool smile again. "According to the police, she came here from Columbia, South Carolina a while back, and the child was already over a year old. As far as I know, my husband had never been to Columbia."

"I see," I said, beginning to see the continuing brick wall in my investigation getting higher.

"Do you know where the child is now?"

"I believe the grandmother came here from South Carolina, and took the baby back there. Mr. Patrick, I just don't see how I can help you. Phillip is dead and I want my girls to get past this as quickly as possible."

"I suppose you're right." I sat there for a moment, trying to decide my next step.

"How long are you in town for?" Marissa Fairchild was looking at me with a different demeanor now.

"Sorry? What?"

"There are some great seafood restaurants over in Virginia Beach," she said, in a soft voice. "Maybe you would like to join me for dinner tonight?"

As I realized what she was suggesting, the last visage of Marissa Fairchild's attractiveness fell away. I stood to leave, suddenly anxious to be away from her.

"Maybe some other time," I said, knowing there wouldn't be one.

"Pity," she said in that sultry tone. "You don't know what you're missing."

"Yeah, I do," I said as I opened the office door. "And she's waiting for me in Atlanta."

✳   ✳   ✳   ✳

The way my luck was running, it came as no surprise that my flight back to Atlanta was going to be delayed for almost two hours. I was desperate to get away from Virginia, but there was nothing I could do but sit around and wait out at the gate.

I called Abby, but she wasn't home so I left her a message about my late arrival. I figured Bobby would be on his way back to Atlanta by now, and thought about calling him on his cell. Frankly, I really wasn't up to talking with him. What was the old saying about other people having it worse than you, no matter how bleak life seemed?

If Bobby had come up with anything important in Alabama, he would have called. Our investigation was going nowhere fast.

We finally took off and headed for home at about 9:45 p.m. I slept for most of the short trip, waking as the wheels bumpily touched down at Hartsfield Airport an hour later. My cabby dropped me off in front of Ireland's Own at 11:40.

I looked up at the windows of my little office/home. Abby would be up there, waiting for me.

Before going up, I walked a short block south of Pat's pub to the phone I had decided to use to contact Carl Lee Wiggins in Nashville. I hoped he wouldn't pick up, and he didn't, so I left a message that I would be at this phone tomorrow night at 11p.m. and hung up.

I picked up my bag, and headed home. I felt a little lighter with every step that brought me closer to Abby Barrett.

CHAPTER 12

─────────── ▼ ───────────

August 11, 2003
Atlanta, Georgia

I woke up the next morning to the smell of fresh strawberries. When I opened my eyes, Abby was sitting on the edge of the bed, smiling down at me. Her hair still was wet from her shower, the strawberry shampoo she liked to use still giving off a pleasant bouquet.

"Good morning, sleepy-head," she said, in her sweet voice, and the world seemed to be a little brighter.

"What time is it?" I croaked.

"Six," she answered. "The day's almost gone!"

"Who are you?" I said, in mock horror. "And how did you get in here, cruel woman?"

"Sorry," she laughed. "I just wanted to see you before I left for school. I need to work out some class schedule problems."

"I'm glad you did," I smiled, and took her hand in mine. "I really did miss you, you know? Just in case I forgot to mention it last night while you were taking advantage of me."

"Did you, now? I like it when you miss me. And who took advantage of whom, sir?"

She gave me a hug and a kiss.

"Will you be long?"

"A couple of hours or so. What about you?"

"I need to check in with Bobby, and probably meet up with Max."

"Bobby called last night. He spent the night at Sabine's place. He's going to call you around eight, unless you call him first. The number is by the phone." She got up from the bed, leaned over and gave me another kiss. "I'll see you later, Thomas, and you can tell me about your trip."

I was glad I didn't have to get into that discussion right away. I wasn't ready to relive it just yet.

*   *   *   *

I was eating one of the homemade banana muffins Abby's mom had sent home with her, when Bobby called.

"I figured you didn't have any more luck than I did or you would have called last night," he said.

"No luck is right. I'm just trying to get the taste of the last two days out of my mouth. You still at Sabine's place?"

"Yeah, but I'm getting ready to drop her off at the airport. She's traveling the next few days. You want to meet up?"

"I need to report to Max," I said. "Stay loose until I set something up with him and I'll meet you at his office."

"Okay. Did you talk with Carl Lee yet?"

"I left him a message to call me tonight. Bobby, we need his help. If he has any other information, we need to get it out of him."

"Don't I know it," he answered, and hung up.

*   *   *   *

Max Howard decided to meet us at Ireland's Own for an early lunch before the place got too busy, so I did a light workout on the heavy bag I keep hanging in the corner of my living room/office. I followed that up with the stretching exercises that the Cleveland sports clinic had suggested to keep the leg I had broken at Ohio State as limber as possible. My limp had gotten less noticeable, according to my brother, Pat, but *I* still know its there.

I showered, dressed, and went downstairs at 10:45 to get a table in the back room so that we would have some privacy until the place filled up. Bobby and Max arrived about a half hour later, and we settled down with a round of beers brought in by Pat.

We gave Max a run-down on the last few days, from our meeting with Carl Lee Wiggins through our visits to the relatives of some of the victims. It was unpleasant at the least to revisit my meetings with Mrs. Tenley and the Fairchild woman, but Max needed to hear it all. When we finished our reports, Max sat back and took another swig of beer. His legendary appetite had not returned, and our food remained pretty much untouched.

"It doesn't seem worthwhile to continue calling on the relatives and friends, does it?" Max said, finally.

I shrugged. "I don't think it will get us anywhere. There's definitely a connection between the crimes, Max. But I don't think it's on the victim side. What we can't get our arms around, is who is killing these people and why. What are they getting out of this? There are no robberies connected with the crimes that we can find, and we still have the most important part of the mystery, which is the bi-racial angle."

"So what do we do now?" Bobby asked.

"Good question," Max answered.

"Has Jake had any luck down at the precinct?"

"Nothing of consequence. In fact, he can't get anyone to even talk about it."

"That makes no sense to me," I said. "Its like every police force in the South has taken a vow of silence. Like there's a vast conspiracy or something."

We sat for awhile, a morose silence hanging over us like a cloud. Pat came in and sat down.

"You guys need anything?"

"Yeah," Bobby piped up. "We need help, and maybe another beer."

"The beer I can help with." Pat left us again.

"Max, we need to get Carl Lee to give us whatever other files he's got," I said. "It doesn't matter whether he's ready to or not. We need to see if there really are other angles to investigate."

"Can't force him," Max said. "Have you asked about this other information he says he's been collecting?"

"I haven't had a chance, but he's supposed to call me tonight."

$$\ast \quad \ast \quad \ast \quad \ast$$

At precisely 11 p.m., Bobby and I were waiting at the pay phone down the block from Ireland's Own. The phone rang and Carl Lee Wiggins' deep voice said, "That you?"

"It's me, Carl Lee. I'm glad to hear from you."

He got right down to business. "So you get anywhere?"

"Depends what you mean. Where we got to was enough information to decide we're at a dead end. There's no connection we can find among the victims."

"Couda' told you that."

There was no emotion in his voice, but his cavalier attitude got my juices flowing.

"Then why didn't you!" I barked. Bobby held up his hand, signaling me to calm down.

I tried.

"Look, Carl Lee, people are dead and the best case scenario is that more are going to die. We had to take a shot at a tie-in between the victims and we did that. We got nowhere, and we can't continue to keep going nowhere.

The cops aren't talking, so there's no help there." I took a breath and tried to relax. The message I needed to get through to Wiggins was clear, and wasn't going to change it just because I was in a bad mood, or because of the way I might say it.

"Carl Lee," I said, "I know you feel responsible for what happened to Willie and his wife, but no one could have known what would happen to them. But I wake up every day expecting that another murder might have happened while I slept. I don't think any of us wants that. There's no more time for games." I took a deep breath. "I need to know what you know. You said you had other information, and now is the time to give it to us."

There was a long silence on the other end of the phone. Time crept by and I thought he had hung up.

"Carl Lee?"

In a calm voice he said: "Not yet."

"Damn it, why not?! Look, you came to us, not the other way around! You sent information to Willie, and he and his family are dead." My frustration had to be evident to him. "Why the games, Carl Lee, why now?"

"This ain't no game," he said, calmly. "I know Willie's dead, and I know why." He was quiet again. "I got information, but I gotta' make sure its right. Can't be throwin' no names around on something this big if I ain't right. There's a meeting tomorrow night. I need to know what this person knows to be sure. I can't tell you nothin' 'til then. I gotta' be sure."

"Why?" I said. "This is bullshit, Carl Lee! Who are you meeting with, and why is this meeting so important?"

"I'll call you when I know for sure," he said with finality. "Two days."

The line went dead.

"Carl Lee?! Carl Lee?! *God damn it!*"

CHAPTER 13

▼

August 13, 2003, Evening
Atlanta, Georgia

I had tried to get Carl Lee Wiggins back immediately after he had hung up. I know he was there, but he wouldn't pick up. I spent a sleepless night, unable to figure out why it was necessary for him to play this stupid and dangerous game.

To me, it was pointless and unfeeling to put more lives at risk while we did this little dance with Wiggins, but as Max said when I had reported the conversation to him earlier in the morning, Carl Lee was holding all the cards. The question was, what cards were in his hand?

Now, Max and I were seated around the dinner table with Abby, her little sister, Nina, and Abby's beautiful and gracious mother, Maria Barrett. Normally, this would be a happy and relaxed gathering. I love Maria. Looking at her is like seeing Abby twenty-five years into the future, and I like what I see. Max and Maria have spent a lot of time together since the Cuban incident, when Max had helped get her through those awful days while I was frantically searching for her kidnapped daughter in an unfriendly country.

It was obvious to all of us that Max, a confirmed bachelor for all of his fifty- plus years, was in love with Maria and that she returned his feelings. That made both Abby and me very happy. They deserve happiness.

Tonight, Max and I are lousy company, both of us lost in our own thoughts, hardly tasting the wonderful Cuban specialties Maria has prepared.

"How do you like the antelope steak, Max?" Maria said.

"Huh?" Max said, as he picked at the roasted pork and plantains. "Oh, wonderful, Maria. As always, the dinner is wonderful."

Maria smiled at Abby and gave her a wink. Abby playfully nudged me in the side with her elbow.

"What color blouse am I wearing, Thomas? Don't look!"

I put down my fork. "I'm sorry ladies. I guess we're a little out of it tonight. Max and I are working on a very troublesome case, Maria. Its got us both a little preoccupied. And by the way, Abby is wearing a deep blue blouse and a white skirt." I said with a smile.

Abby smiled back. "Ahh, so you do pay attention to me."

"Always," I said, and returned her smile.

"Well, you are both forgiven," Maria said, and put her hand over Max'. "Try to relax for a little while."

Max looked at her as if she were an angel removing a heavy burden from his heart.

*   *   *   *

Two days. That's what Carl Lee had said. Two days before we would hear back from him and, hopefully, get information that would help us. All I had at the moment was a Nashville policeman who felt responsible for the death of his closest friend, and a need for absolution that would come with being responsible for ending this bloodbath.

Or would it?

Abby and I drove back to our little apartment above Ireland's Own about ten that night. I was still quiet and absorbed in the case but, at least for the remainder of the evening at Maria Barrett's home, Max and I had joined in the conversation, and we had all passed a pleasant time.

"Still thinking about Mr. Wiggins?" Abby asked.

"I can't seem to get through to him." I shook my head. "Why doesn't he understand that we're trying to help?"

"I think he does, Thomas. But for whatever reason, he feels he has to do this his way."

I nodded. "I know, or at least I think I know why, but it's foolish to go it on his own like this. I mean if there is some important meeting happening, why not let us be there?"

She reached over and touched my arm. "Let it go for now. After all, it's only two days."

*   *   *   *

The stiflingly hot wind that had blown in from the Gulf, crossing over the bayous and deep into the heart of New Orleans for the past several days showed no sign of letting up, and drenching the four men in their own sweat. They were sitting in the rusted-out Buick LeSabre, a fifteen year old wreck held together by several layers of old pain, and shod with four bald tires. Not that it mattered.

The stolen car, taken from the driveway of a ramshackle cottage down in bayou country, would be abandoned after tonight's work was done.

They were parked in an alleyway in the Garden District of the city, just a short distance from Bourbon Street. The District, an area of ancient houses that had found new life and respectability with the coming of the Yuppie money in the 80's and 90's, was deadly quiet at 2:45 a.m. The men in the car sat silently, ignoring each other's presence, except for the incessant smoking of one of the men in the back. They were white men, all wearing dark clothing. Beneath their dark shirts, each had a tattoo above their left breast of a crimson circle with the number "11" in black, and an "x" running through the number inside the circle.

The leader of the group sat in the front passenger seat. He checked his watch again for the tenth time in the last several minutes. It was approaching three in the morning. It was time to begin.

The leader opened the door, but with the interior lights removed from the cabin, it remained dark. The others followed suit. Soon the four were moving toward the rear door of a recently remodeled 1940's two- story Craftsman house.

The four stole up the steps to the rear door of the house, keeping a constant watch on the neighborhood, looking for the slightest movement. There was a continued silence. The leader checked his watch once more, and then signaled to one of the others to begin work on the lock.

It was picked within thirty seconds. Like most of the homes in the area under renovation, the doors and windows were old and sub par. The door popped open with a soft rustle and the men froze. They were told the owners, a prominent black attorney and his wife, a white woman, did not have a dog, but the four waited expectantly for the bark of a startled animal. It never came.

There were no human noises either. One by one the four moved quietly into the house. Inside, the stillness of the deep night lent an air of unreality to the situation made more so by the darkness. The last of the men stumbled slightly as he entered and the object in his hand, a crude cross of about two feet from top to the pointed bottom rapped against the door jamb. Again the four men froze, but again, nothing stirred inside the house.

"Upstairs," the leader whispered. "First door on the left."

Two of the men drew guns in case the owner was waiting for them with a weapon of his own, and they started up the stairs. At the top they stopped again, listening intently. The sound of snoring came from down the hallway, and the men relaxed. Moving forward again, the leader stopped at the closed door of the bedroom, then gently turned the knob and entered the room.

A moment later, the four were standing above the sleeping couple. At a signal from the leader, the man holding the wooden cross moved to stand directly over the still sleeping man, who was lying on his back. Two of the others moved around the bed to stand over the woman.

With his breath coming faster and heavier, the leader pulled a short handled sledge hammer from a holder on his belt, and raised it above his head. He nodded to the man with the cross who, with an answering nod, slammed the pointed end of the wood against the owner's chest as the leader drove the spiked end through the sleeping mans chest cavity.

The woman woke with a start at the noise and tried to sit up in the bed, but another of the intruders threw massive forearms around her head, and twisted hard and fast, grinding the vertebrae in her neck into jagged bits. She never heard her own scream.

The leader dropped the hammer and closed his eyes, a feeling of peace and satisfaction crossing over him. Slowly, he removed one of the gloves he wore, and dipped two fingers into the mass of blood seeping from the dead man's wound.

The leader made the sign of the cross, the blood dripping down his forehead.

"Eleven," he said, and the others followed suit.

"Eleven."

CHAPTER 14

▼

August 15, 2003, Dawn
Atlanta, Georgia

I was wide awake by 6 a.m. but in no hurry to get out of bed. Abby had the alarm set for 6:30 to get ready to drive to the Georgia Tech campus for her first class of the day, and I decided to just stay in bed 'til it went off. There was no good reason to chance waking her early.

The sun was already blooming in the east, and the high temperature for the day was expected to reach over one hundred again. I remembered, lying there, how I used to think the summers back home in Cleveland were hot. But they never seemed to go on and on the way they did here in Georgia. I thanked God for the A/C that fed off the big units serving the restaurant flooding our little apartment with cool, dry air.

This wasn't going to be a good day, I thought. First, Bobby Hemphill and I were going to meet to go over everything we knew about the case one more time. It wouldn't help, but there was always the chance, they had taught us in PI school that we may have glossed over some little tidbit that might not have seemed important before. I didn't think we'd find one, but I'm learning that a big part of this job is repetition- until, hopefully, some light bulb goes off in your head. At least there are two of us to go over stuff again and again instead of just me.

Then, I needed to chase down Carl Lee Wiggins and convince him to share whatever new information he had come up with. He was supposed to call that night at the latest, but I didn't see any benefit to waiting. I was trying very hard to understand Carl Lee. For someone who had put himself and his friends at risk, he was being bullheaded about how he was going about this. I didn't want to think about the innocent people who couldn't even fathom that they might be targeted by murderers.

It took a moment to register the sound of my cell phone ringing in the living room. I got out of bed as quietly as I could and closed the bedroom door behind me as I reached for the phone on the table next to the couch. I figured it was Bobby calling, but it did seem early for that. The lighted screen said *J. Berger.*

Jake was calling from the 14th Precinct.

"This can't be good news," I said into the mouthpiece.

"It's not, Tom," Berger said. "Sorry to call so early, but I thought you needed to know as soon as possible."

"Where?" I asked, not needing to ask "*what*" he was referring to.

"New Orleans. Down in the Garden District."

I could feel my blood rising to a boil. Another crime that might have been stopped, if Carl Lee wasn't playing fast and loose with this investigation. I knew as quickly as I thought it, that I was probably indulging in wishful thinking. But I had to blame someone for the helplessness coursing through me, and right now that was Carl Lee Wiggins.

"I thought you'd want to let our friend in Nashville know, in case he hadn't picked up the story yet."

"I'm not so sure how much of a 'friend' he is," I said, bitterly. "I take it the circumstances were the same?"

"Yeah. There's no question of a tie-in to the other crime scenes."

"What are the cops saying, Jake?"

"Nothing. Not a damned thing. I picked up a wire report of a double homicide, mixed race married couple. I called Max and he checked with an old friend in the prosecutor's office. If the guy was supposed to zip his lips, he hadn't got the message yet. Told Max everything, and it all fit."

We were quiet for a few moments while a hundred disjointed thoughts ran through our minds.

"Jake, I need to call Carl Lee. It's time for a come-to-Jesus meeting, and there's no sense waiting until he calls tonight. The bullshit's over."

"Call me later," Jake Berger replied, and the line went dead.

And that's the way it stayed the entire day. I called Carl Lee's phone a dozen or more times, leaving message after message, with no response. I was getting angrier and more frustrated as the day went on, and finally decided to break the protocol we had established and I called the phone at Cletus' bar. Again, I got a voice recording, giving me nothing more than the hours of operation of Mo Kelly's Bar.

That night at 10:30, I was standing at the pay phone down the street from Ireland's Own waiting for the call I was hoping would come from Nashville. A million tings that I wanted to say to Carl Lee Wiggins flowed through my fevered brain, but I knew I would not say any of them. This was not the time to unload on Carl Lee. I needed his cooperation, and I needed it now.

Jake and Max had called me in the late afternoon with additional details about the New Orleans murder scene. I could tell from the conversation, which recounted almost verbatim the details of nearly every one of the cases we were investigating, that Max was especially burdened by this last instance, as the Garden District was where he had grown up in his beloved New Orleans.

"Anything from our friend in Nashville?" Jake had asked.

"I can't reach him," I answered, frustration edged in my voice. "I've been trying all day. He should call tonight if he keeps to the schedule he set, to report on this secret meeting he wouldn't tell me about. I'm hoping the messages I've been leaving all day will force a response."

And here I was, standing at a pay phone in Buckhead, the hot, humid air of a Georgia night in August causing the sweat to course down my face and back, wishing that the phone would ring. And there I stood, for two hours. Nothing.

And that's the way it stayed the entire next day. My nerves were disintegrating and the anger I was feeling towards Carl Lee grew with every unreturned call I made. This wasn't making any sense. He had to have had his meeting with his unknown informant by now.

To top it off, Jake Berger continued to get the silent treatment from the New Orleans police department, and Max' friend in the prosecutor's office was suddenly nowhere to be found.

After dinner at Pat's place, I walked Abby back up to the apartment and grabbed my cell phone. I needed to hear from Nashville tonight, but it was only 9 p.m., and Carl Lee wouldn't be expecting me to be at the pay phone until eleven. I left the apartment and got out onto Peachtree Street, but the sidewalks were packed with locals and tourists, so I found a quieter side street and camped out just down from the corner. I took out my cell phone and dialed my parent's home in Cleveland.

I had a need to hear the calming voice of my mother, but I had an ulterior motive for the call. After a few minutes speaking with mom, and a dozen admonitions to be careful, I got my dad on the phone. Seamus Patrick had just retired from a long career with the Cleveland police. I didn't get into the meat of the case, not wanting to overly concern him, but I needed his advice.

"Why would several law enforcement agencies suppress information about a series of seemingly relates crimes, Dad?"

"There's no reason I can think of why they should, Thomas."

"But they are. I'm sure of it. Even Jake Berger can't get anything out of anybody." Dad had met Jake when I had been beaten up and hospitalized last year, and the folks had come down to Atlanta to see me.

"What you are describing is a conspiracy, Boyo. Not unheard of within a police department, especially if the police think they are fighting criminals that the courts can't, or refuse, to punish. But you said this is happening in several departments across state lines?"

"Yes, that is what I'm saying."

Dad was quiet for a while. "That, Thomas, I've never heard of."

I sighed. Dad had no answers, nor should I have expected him too. This was all too strange. After a little while, we said our goodbyes and hung up.

I checked the clock on my phone. Still an hour and a half 'til eleven. I didn't want to go back to the apartment, so I just walked, thinking a thousand thoughts and getting nowhere. At 11 p.m., I was standing at the pay phone as a light drizzle began to fall. I hardly noticed the rain, even though my clothes began to soak up the moisture, and rivulets of water began to course down the back of my neck and inside my shirt collar.

At midnight, I started calling the phone in the back room of Mo Kelly's Bar in Nashville, without getting an answer. Then I tried the bar's phone and got the same aggravating "hours of operation" message followed by the abrupt hang up.

At 2 a.m., soaked to the skin and totally despondent, I went home.

I awoke from a fitful sleep as Abby was getting ready to leave for classes at Tech, and after a kiss and a hug, she was gone. I took a shower and made some coffee, but my mind was on only one thing.

Deciding it was time to say to hell with protocol, I started calling the numbers in Nashville, this time from my cell, but with the same results.

I had had all I could take and, calling information to get the number of Carl Lee's precinct, I called the police department. On the third ring, a male voice answered.

"Ninth Precinct."

"Yes," I said. "Officer Wiggins, please. Carl Lee Wiggins."

There was a momentary stillness on the other end of the line.

"Are you a friend or family?" the voice said.

CHAPTER 15

▼

August 17, 2003

"He's dead, Max," I said, trying to keep the panic I was feeling from taking over my voice.

"What?! Who, Tommy?! Who's dead?!"

I could tell Max Howard knew the answer before I gave it to him, but I said, "Carl Lee, Max. Two days ago."

The silence on the other end of the line was deafening.

"The cops wouldn't tell me much other than that he was killed during a routine traffic stop at about 3 a.m. But we found the newspaper report and it said Wiggins stopped a suspicious vehicle in an old industrial part of town. They reported that the police said he radioed in the license plate and got out of his car. Supposedly, whoever was driving that vehicle shot him three times in the chest and took off." I let that sink in. "Paper said he was found by workers arriving in the area about five."

"Hold on, Tommy," Max said, and the line clicked over to "hold." A few moments later, he picked up again, with Jake Berger also on the line.

I went over what I had told Max again for Jake's benefit. We were all quiet for awhile.

"It's bullshit," Jake finally said.

"Sorry?"

"Cops say Carl Lee stops a suspicious car in a dead zone area at three in the morning. He radios in the tag information, and tells the dispatcher he's going to roust the occupant of the car, and no one checks on him again? Even two hours later? And why was he patrolling a dangerous area without a partner in the first place? It's bullshit, Tom. At the very least, the dispatcher would have called him back with the tag status, and that call would have been heard by Wiggins on his shoulder walky-talky, even if he was out of his car.

With no response from him, they would have had a backup unit there in a heartbeat. Besides, he probably would have called in backup himself, under the circumstances."

"Shit. I see your point."

"It was a setup?" Max asked.

"I'd bet on it," Jake answered. "They killed him, and they did it with the help of someone in the department."

"My God," Max said, in a half whisper. "What do we do now?"

"I'll see what else I can find out," Jake offered.

After a moment I said: "I'm going to Nashville. I have to try and find any other files Carl Lee had, and who he was supposed to be meeting with the other night." I sighed. "We might be finished without that information. I'll keep in touch."

We hung up, and I called Bobby Hemphill.

"Pack a bag," I told him when he answered. "We may be gone a few days."

*   *   *   *

We pulled up in front of Mo Kelly's at 7:45 p.m. The neon lights were off, and the front door was propped open. The sidewalk was covered with green tarps loaded with debris. Cletus Mackey appeared in the doorway carrying one of those industrial push brooms, and swept what I took to be broken glass onto the tarp.

Bobby and I jumped out of the Durango and hurried across the street.

Cletus looked up from his work. "Thought you two would show up." Fatigue and maybe sadness edged in his voice.

"What happened, Cletus?" I asked.

He propped the broom up against the outer wall of the bar.

"Had me some visitors, I guess. 'Thought it mighta' been you two." He turned and walked inside and we followed. The lights were on, and the damage to the place was readily visible. Bottles and glasses behind the bar were smashed and scattered everywhere. The stench of a mixture of cheap liquors and beer permeated the room. The tables and chairs were scattered and broken, as if some unstoppable force had slammed them into the walls. The juke box was lying on its side, the front glass broken and the back of the machine ripped open.

"Thought you done it," Cletus said, again.

"Why would we do this?" Bobby said, gesturing at the damage.

"Seen you talkin' with Carl Lee, figured you wanted somethin'." His face took on a sadness that was palpable. "But I guess you wouldn't come back here if you done it."

"We didn't wreck your place, Cletus," I said.

Bobby turned a table upright and found some chairs that were still useable. We got Cletus to sit down with us.

"What happened to Carl Lee?" I asked, softly.

He's dead," he answered just as softly. "What else I got to know?" He shook his head. "Don't know nothin' else."

Cletus ran a hand over the rough table top absentmindedly. "Say he was killed by some fuckin' punk he stopped in the middle of the night. Just a bad break, that's all. That's what the paper said." He barked a short, humorless laugh. "They don't know Carl Lee. He never would'a been that stupid."

I looked at Bobby. "So you don't believe this was an accident?"

Cletus looked at me, hard. "Carl Lee didn't have 'accidents'. He was a good cop."

I let it sit for awhile.

"He was buried this mornin'." Cletus' eyes were vacant, and he stared straight ahead. "Sons-a-bitches didn't even give him one of those special funerals for cops killed in the line a duty." He smiled that sad smile again. "Said the family wanted a private funeral. Shit, only family he had left was his wife, Gracie, and nobody asked her about nothin'." He shrugged. "At least they paid for the burial."

I sighed. "He was set up, Cletus. We're sure of it. But you're right," I waived my hand around the destroyed room. "Whoever did this was looking for something. We aren't sure what, but its information we have to get our hands on if we're going to have a chance of finding out who killed Carl Lee."

Cletus sat back in his chair, not saying anything.

"He was supposed to give us some files pertaining to an investigation he was working on with us." Still no response.

I tried again. "Did he give you anything to hold for him? Any papers he wanted to keep out of the hands of someone else, maybe?"

"Don't know nothin'."

"Cletus...."

"Said I don't know nothin'!" he said, more forcefully. "Carl Lee ain't tell me nothin'." His voice softened a little. "Said he was doin' something could get people hurt, and he don't want me involved. Said it was enough I let him stay here, you know?"

I was beginning to realize how much this friendship had meant to him.

I tried a different tack. "Did anyone else come in here looking for him?"

Cletus was quiet for a moment, as if trying to decide what he could tell me.

"No," he said, simply.

I sighed. "We need to see Carl Lee's room, Cletus. It's important."

He sat back in his chair, the distrustful look back on his face.

"Tell me one good reason I should trust you boys. I don't know you for shit." His eyes looked moist, and pain was evident in his face. "All I know is Carl Lee is dead, and I don't know why."

He was right, of course. He didn't know us, and he had lost a friend. His place had been ransacked, and I couldn't even give him any assurance that he wasn't personally in danger. If people were looking for Carl Lee's files at Mo Kelley's, how probable would it be for them to decide that Cletus might know something about the investigation? He could be the next to die if they felt threatened by him.

"I understand what you mean, and I don't know how to convince you to help us, Cletus. I can't tell you what this is all about, and you're better off not knowing. But someone else is looking for the information Carl Lee had, and they won't stop until they find it. Unless we stop them first, that is."

I let that sink in, and he seemed to be considering what to do.

"Cletus," I said, again, "we need to see Carl Lee's room."

Finally, he said, "Same shit gone on in there."

He got up slowly and we followed him back to the little room that I hoped against hope might hold the secret that could pull us out of the abyss.

*   *   *   *

He was right. The sparsely furnished room Carl Lee had used to escape from the realities of a dead baby boy and the failure of his marriage was a shambles. The bed was overturned, the thin mattress slashed and bleeding its cotton stuffing. A small overturned dresser lay amid the rubble, the drawers, wrenched from the metal locks that held them in place were ripped out and dumped.

A few pieces of clothing were tossed around amid broken dishes and glasses. My heart sank. If there had been files hidden in this room, they had most likely been found.

"There's a computer cord still in the wall," Bobby said, after pushing some clothes away with his foot.

"But no computer," I said. "Did he have one, Cletus?"

"Yeah. One of them laptop jobs. Maybe he had it with him, or maybe he took it to his house."

I knew that if he had it with him the night he died, it was gone for sure. His house? Carl Lee said he rarely went there anymore. Would he leave a computer with important documents on it where he couldn't watch it? Maybe. Not likely.

"You know, we've been thinking about 'files' like they were a bunch of folders stuffed with papers." Bobby picked up the end of the computer cord. It had been yanked from the laptop, and had a broken tip. "We may be looking for a little round disk," he said, waving the end of the cord.

I nodded. "If we are, he may have hidden it somewhere else." A glimmer of hope started to rise.

"But that stuff would be on the hard drive," Bobby looked skeptical. "The bad guys would have it now."

"Yeah, but they're not out of the woods without the disk."

But did a disk exist? Was it hidden somewhere? Were there other copies? I had to hold on to that possibility, otherwise we were at a dead end.

"Cletus, I need the address of Carl Lee's house."

CHAPTER 16

▼

August 18, 2003
Nashville, Tennessee

Bobby yawned and pushed himself up in the passenger seat of the Durango.

"What time is it?" he asked, sleepily.

"A little past Midnight."

He looked at me with distrust. *"How* little?"

I smiled. "About two hours."

"Jeez," he griped. "Don't we do anything during the daytime?"

"I don't really care to have someone see us ransacking the house of a dead policeman. Bad for our image."

We turned right onto the street where Carl Lee's house was located. I squinted at the paper Cletus had given me with the address and checked the house numbers that I could make out.

"You really think we're going to find anything?" Bobby asked.

"I hope so. But it's a long shot."

"The first files Carl Lee sent Willie and Max were paper files," he went on. "Why do you think he switched to a computer disk for this batch of information?"

I shrugged. "We don't know that he did. We're just guessing, and that's the only thing we do know for sure. Besides, there *may* be paper files too, and he *might* have also transferred the information to several disks."

I looked at Bobby, and he said what I was thinking. "We may never find any of them."

We drove down the dark street slowly, catching a house number on a mail box here and there. The street was deserted, but several cars were parked along the right side of the road.

"That should be it," I said, finally. We were at mid-block, and the house on the left side of the road was pitch black inside. No porch or security light was on outside. I pulled up to the curb at the first empty spot I could find, not wanting to park in the driveway. That put the Wiggins house just ahead of us.

I let out a breath, and felt a slight shiver go up my spine. I wanted to be anywhere but here.

"How do we get in?" Bobby asked.

"We may have to break a window," I said. "Can't be helped."

"Hope there's no alarm set in there," he said.

"Thanks," I said. "Something else for me to worry about."

"Hey, don't shoot the messenger. After all, I'll be the one sharing a cell with you."

"Grab those two flashlights in the glove compartment," I said. "We better not put on any lights inside." I looked over the two story house, probably about forty years old, with a detached garage in the back. The front porch was up one level, so there was probably a basement.

Like the house in Richmond, where a grandmother mourned the loss of her grandson.

I shook the thought out of my head, and we started to get out of the Durango, when I felt Bobby's hand grip my arm.

"What was that?" he said, quietly.

"Huh? What was what?"

"That."

He was pointing out the window towards the house.

I I followed his gaze and watched intently until I saw what he had seen. A flash of light through a window on the main level of the house. We sat motionless and utterly silent, watching. There it was again, this time illuminating a section of wall within the house on the second level. Then another flash, back on the first floor.

We sat, dumbstruck.

Someone, maybe several people, were in Carl Lee Wiggin's house. In the dark. Looking for the same thing we were looking for, and we had almost walked right in on them.

Now flashes of light were everywhere. There were at least three, maybe four people in the house.

Finally, Bobby said, "Should we call the cops?"

I thought for a second.

"I don't think we better trust the cops. Besides, what do we tell them we're doing out here at 2 a.m.?"

He shrugged. "We could make it an anonymous call. Maybe convince them it's a neighbor calling."

"No, Bobby. This might be a chance for us to find out who is behind all this. The cops might blow our cover. These guys don't know who we are or that we're also looking for Carl Lee's files." I shook my head. "No, no cops. The best thing is that they're still looking, so they probably didn't find anything at Mo Kelly's."

I reached over to the glove compartment and took out my .38. Bobby was wearing his in a holster under his left arm. He took it out and looked at the weapon.

"I was hoping I wouldn't have to use this thing again," he said, quietly. The last time was that day on an island off the Cuban coast, when he fired a slug into the back of the head of a man who was choking the life out of me. Neither of us wanted to think about that right now. Or ever.

"How you want to play this?" he asked, coming back from his memories.

My lack of experience was hounding me again. Here I was, putting Bobby at risk on a guess once again.

"Smart thing would probably be to stay right here, then follow them when they leave. But at this time of night? They would pick up the tail pretty quickly, and we would probably lose them. If they find what they're looking for in there, well, we could lose our chance for sure."

I could feel the prickly nerve endings at the base of my skull kick in, and my breath came a little faster. "We gotta' go in, Bobby."

"I was afraid you were going to say that," he sighed. "I really wanted to see Venice before I died."

I switched off the Durango's inside lights so that they wouldn't illuminate when we opened the doors, and we got out. "Let's check the windows in the basement," I said, in a near whisper. "I haven't seen any flashes of light down there yet."

Bobby nodded his understanding.

We crossed the street and moved slowly up the driveway of the Wiggins home. The flashlights inside the house continued to move around, and as we got closer, the sound of furniture being tossed around was evident. Whoever was in there wasn't worried about leaving the place intact.

We flattened ourselves against the house and moved slowly towards the first of the basement windows, which looked big enough for us to squeeze through. I bent down to the pane of glass. I didn't want to use the flashlight, but it was impossible to make out anything in the dark interior through the dirty window.

I pushed gently against the bottom of the window, but it didn't give. I gestured to Bobby to move to the second window, about fifteen feet away, and he followed my actions, but that one wouldn't open either. I followed him around to the back of the house. The yard was so dark I could hardly see the gun in my hand as I pointed it ahead of me.

Bobby signaled that there were two more basement windows up ahead.

I shook my head. "No good," I whispered. "I'm betting they're all going to be locked. Let's try the back porch door."

The noise inside the house grew louder as we inched our way up the porch stairs. I could feel the perspiration on my forehead and running down my back. Whether it was from the humidity or fear was, for the moment, unimportant. I dragged my shirtsleeve across my eyes to clear the sweat from my vision.

I felt rather than heard Bobby come up behind me, and motioned him to the side of the door. There was a screen door, and I pulled it open as gently as I could. Then, reaching forward, I gripped the knob of the wooden door and tried to open it slowly and quietly. The door was locked tight.

Suddenly, behind us the loud squeaking of the garage door, some thirty feet away, broke the silence of the night.

"Hey!" A husky voice, full of surprise and indignation said. "What the fuck?!"

There were no windows in the garage, and we had never seen the flashlight that surely had been in use inside.

Another stupid mistake! I thought, as the vicious spit of a bullet from a silenced weapon splintered the door frame. I had gotten us trapped between the man in the garage and those in the house.

Another spit, and I felt the sting of splinters from the new hole that appeared inches from my face.

"Shit!" Bobby swore.

I could feel my heart racing. I couldn't think of anything else to do to get us out of the line of fire but to smash up against the door and force our way in, hoping the killers in the house weren't standing on the other side. The lock broke on the second try and we were in. Through the midnight darkness of the small space, we could barely see the end of the small hallway leading into the main part of the house. With the hot, moist air of an enclosed space that had been super- heated for days in ninety plus degree weather, it was stifling, but at least we were inside.

Bobby turned and got off a shot towards the garage, the noise from his weapon vibrating off the walls of the small space. I scoped the room ahead of us as best I could. If anyone suddenly appeared, I could at least get off the first round.

Swearing came from the garage again, and two more holes appeared in the door. Now there were voices, and more than one set of shoes clomping down the stairs from the second floor.

I did the only thing I could think of to maybe keep us from coming under fire from multiple sources.

"Come on, let's get em'! You guys get around the front!" I yelled, and fired the .38 twice into the darkness ahead of me. Bobby got off a second shot at the garage without a return of fire from whoever was out there.

The pounding on the steps died out and there was a sudden silence, as if indecision had struck the men on the other side of the wall ahead of me. I hit Bobby in the shoulder and signaled to remind him we were each down to four bullets. He nodded, and peered out around the door jamb toward the garage. A sudden shaft of light from a window at the house behind the Wiggins' place threw some light on the yard.

There was a crash ahead of me, and I heard wood breaking. Then there was a thin rush of wind brushing against my face from deep inside the house, and I knew the front door had been kicked open.

Bobby looked at me and I saw, through the darkness, a look of relief on his face.

"I think he's gone," he whispered.

"Yeah," I said, not sure whether to feel relief or disappointment. "I think they all are."

In the distance I could hear the first wailings of a police siren. Now more lights came on next door. The neighbors must have reported our gunshots.

"We better get out of here," I said, moving past Bobby and out onto the porch towards the steps. "We'll have to forget searching the house for now."

He sighed, and followed me down the steps.

"I may just get to see Venice after all," he said, as we headed for our car.

$$\ast \quad \ast \quad \ast \quad \ast$$

'Are you sure you two are okay?" Max Howard said into the phone, and I could hear the concern in his voice.

"We're fine, Max, I swear," I said.

There was no reason to explain why I was sitting on the uncomfortable bed in our motel room pressing a towel packed with ice against the cuts from glass shards all over my face. Bobby was sound asleep on the other bed. I was learning that he could sleep through just about anything.

I had told Max everything that had gone on at Carl Lee's, as well as what had happened at Mo Kelly's.

"I missed a chance at grabbing one of these guys. It could have turned this whole mess around." My disappointment was evident in my voice.

"You coulda' got killed, too," Max said.

"I know. We both know the risks, Max. We're trying not to do anything foolish. But we almost walked right in on those guys tonight."

"I take it you didn't contact the police?"

"Hell, we almost got caught by them," I said. "We thought it best not to hang around to answer questions."

"Good choice. I'll let Jake know what happened. Tommy, this might get a lot worse, now that you've had contact with these people."

"I know," I answered, quietly.

"I've put you at tremendous risk, son," he said. Doubt and fear for our safety was on his mind.

"I'm right where I want to be, Max." I said, trying to sound strong, and he cleared his throat.

"What are you gonna' do now?" he asked.

I had thought about that, and I had an idea, but our recent close call made me cautious.

"I need to sleep for awhile, Max. I need to think about the next step before I commit to any kind of plan."

We hung up, and I caught two hours of restless sleep.

At 6 a.m., I called the apartment. Abby didn't answer, and I figured she was in the shower. I rang back in fifteen minutes, and she picked up.

"How's it going up there?" she asked.

"Okay," I said. I didn't want to worry her any more than necessary. She knew what had happened to Carl Lee, and I knew she was already worried about me and Bobby.

"Will you be there awhile?"

"A few days, babe," I said, trying to sound as normal as possible, but able to hear the concern in my own voice.

Abby didn't push it. I knew she wouldn't.

"Call me tonight?" she asked.

"You bet," I replied, already looking forward to the sound of her voice.

CHAPTER 17

———————— ▼ ————————

August 19, 2003
Nashville, Tennessee

While Bobby slept away on the other bed. I used the time to think about what to do next. I was starting to feel a little jealous about his ability to sleep anywhere, anytime. I would have to find a way to get even with him some day.

I got up and went to the closet-sized bathroom and ran a hot shower. I stood under the beads of water and let the sting penetrate my shoulders until I began to relax. Finally, the fatigue lifted, and I began to think more clearly about my new plan.

Besides Cletus Mackey, there was only one person I could think of who might know something about Carl Lee and his files, and, maybe, who he was supposed to be meeting with the night he was killed. Since Cletus either didn't know, or wasn't going to tell us if he did know anything, we had to take a different tack and we needed to do it right away.

And that meant we had to find Gracie Wiggins, Carl Lee's estranged wife. Certainly Cletus would know where she was, but I thought it best to keep him out of this for right now. His distrust of Bobby and me might make him pass on his caution to Mrs. Wiggins, and I needed her cooperation in the worst way. So I decided to let my fingers do the walking, and I got dressed and went through the dresser drawers until I found a ratty looking phone book.

Bobby finally poked his head out from between the pillows and gave me a sleepy look.

"Ordering a pizza, I hope," he said.

"At 7:30 in the morning? Don't think so."

"Call the concierge," he said, as he sat up and yawned. "I need a massage."

"Wrong again."

"So what are you looking for, Tommy?"

"This," I said, finding the listing. It was the first thing that had gone right so far. Carl Lee's estranged wife had listed herself in the phone book at her sister's address.

"Grace Wiggins." Bobby took the book from me and copied down the address and phone number on he pad on the little table between the beds. "Think she knows anything? I mean, they were separated, right?"

"You heard Carl Lee, Bobby. Those people were having a bad time, but they loved each other."

He nodded. "They were pretty lucky, in a strange way."

"Thinking about Sabine?"

He smiled. "All the time." He was serious again. "You think those guys found anything at the house?"

"I don't think so, but we can't be sure. The more I think about it, it's hard to believe Carl Lee would leave sensitive information some place where he wouldn't be around to guard it." I sat up against the headboard. "That's why I thought it was more likely to be at Cletus' place. But those people are still looking, so I guess they didn't find anything there, either."

"You think his wife has the files?"

I shook my head. "I don't know. Would he put her in that kind of danger? It's only a matter of time before somebody on the other side thinks of that possibility. If they're hidden where she is living, I doubt she knows it."

Bobby got up and headed for the bathroom.

"Then we better be the first to check it out," he said.

We found the street where Grace Wiggins was now living. It was just a few blocks from the house she had shared with Carl Lee. Bobby pulled up across from the address we had found in the phone book. The house could have been designed by the same architect that had done the home she had shared with her husband. And, at nine in the morning, it looked deserted.

"Maybe she works," Bobby said.

We sat and watched for a while, but no one entered or exited the house. No lights could be seen through the thin curtains. There was no car in the driveway.

We stayed in the car and watched for Grace Wiggins to return.

"We could call," Bobby finally said, after about an hour. "Maybe she's got an answering machine. She could get back to us when she gets home."

I shook my head. "I'm afraid she won't call back. Even more afraid she might disappear."

"Why would she do that?"

"I don't really know," I said, "but things haven't been going well enough to take any chances. Cletus might have spoken with her and told her we've been nosing around, asking questions. If she does know anything, it might spook her."

He shrugged. "I guess that makes sense. But I'm sure getting hungry."

I laughed. "So what's new about that?"

I was about to give up for the time being, and started to turn the car key. There was a Burger King a couple of blocks away, and I figured it couldn't hurt to grab one of those thousand calorie breakfast sandwiches and a cup of coffee while we waited.

I saw it then: a slight movement of the curtain in a front window; a cat maybe, or a dog; sitting at a window awaiting the return of its owner?

"You see that?"

Bobby's eyes came alive, and he sat, motionless, watching the house with me.

"There!" he said, pointing. "At the side window."

I saw it, too: another slight movement, not the quick movements of a pet. We were being watched.

"What do you think?" Bobby asked.

I shrugged. "Whoever's in that house wants us to think the place is empty, but are they hiding from us, or are they hiding from someone else?" I looked at him. "Or are they setting a trap for us?"

He let out a breath. "The guys from last night?"

"Maybe."

"I'd sure like that sandwich right now," Bobby said, and I saw him touch the weapon in the holster inside his jacket. "You really think those guys knew we were coming here, and showed up to set a trap for us?"

I shrugged. "One way to find out," I said, and opened the door and got out of the car. I was halfway across the street when Bobby caught up with me.

"Don't suppose I can talk you out of this?" he said, keeping pace with me.

"Gonna' have to check it out sooner or later," I answered.

∗   ∗   ∗   ∗

"Mrs. Wiggins?" I called out again as I knocked on the door. "Ma'am? My name is Thomas Patrick. I'm from Atlanta, and my friend and I need to speak with you, please."

There was no response from inside the house, but I could swear I felt the presence of a body on the other side of the door. I only hoped it wasn't holding a gun.

"Sorry to trouble you like this, Mrs. Wiggins, but I need to talk to you about Carl Lee."

Again there was silence. I decided to try a different tack.

"Gracie," I said, softly, using the nickname Carl Lee had used for his wife that night at the bar. "Gracie, I was a friend of Willie Patton and his wife. Carl Lee was helping us find out who killed them. Cletus at Mo Kelly's saw us meet with your husband, Gracie. I believe he will tell you that you should speak with us." I had no idea if that was true.

We waited quietly for a while. There didn't seem to be anything else to say.

After a few minutes, the door opened slightly. I could hear labored breathing on the other side, as if the person standing against it expected us to push our way in.

I didn't want to spook her, but I said, as softly as I could and still be heard, "Gracie, Carl Lee told us about your son. He told us why he didn't go home much anymore."

There was a sob on the other side of the door, and after a moment it opened a little more, then more again, until we were face to face with Grace Wiggins.

She was a slight woman, maybe five foot four or five, Her skin was coffee-cream colored, her face pleasant but carrying a pall of sadness. Finally, she stood back from the doorway.

"Carl Lee told you about all that?" she said, softly. "You best come in. My husband didn't trust many people enough to tell them about that."

Bobby followed me in, and we found ourselves in a small living room furnished with old, but neat, furniture.

"This is my sister's place. I been here since I left our home."

I caught the wording she used. She had left the house and the sadness and memories it contained, but not Carl Lee.

I introduced Bobby as she motioned us to the couch, and took a seat in an arm chair for herself.

"We're very sorry about your loss, ma'am," I said, and Bobby nodded. "And I know this is a terrible time to trouble you, but believe me, it is critically important, or we wouldn't have come."

She offered us coffee but I declined. I didn't want to let her out of the room now that we had her attention.

"You say you knew Willie?"

I nodded. "He worked for an attorney who is our friend and employer," I answered.

She shook her head, slowly. "My husband loved Willie. They grew up together."

"I know."

"Carl Lee took Willie getting killed real bad, you know?"

"Yes," I said. "We all did. The man he worked for asked us to find out why this happened to the Patton family. Carl Lee was helping us do that."

I looked for any recognition in her eyes, but she sat motionless, waiting.

I looked at Bobby, and he nodded, and I decided to take the plunge.

"Mrs. Wiggins, did Carl Lee talk to you about what he was doing?"

"Doing? You mean, about Willie?"

"Well…yes. But there was a lot more to what he was doing than that, I'm afraid."

"We didn't speak to each other much," she said, and the sadness was back on her face. "I don't think I know what you mean."

I told her. I told her what was happening in Nashville, and Richmond, and New Orleans. I told her how Carl Lee had come onto the similar murders and how he had given that information to Willie Patton. She sat still as I talked, as if frozen to her chair.

"So that's why Carl Lee said he was the cause of Willie's death," she said, finally.

There was a tear running down her cheek, but she made no move to wipe it away.

"Then he told you about all this?" I asked, hopefully.

She shook her head. "No, but, my husband….drank sometimes, Mr. Patrick. He came here late some nights, and he wouldn't say much to me, but sometimes after he fell asleep, he would talk out loud, like he was dreaming, you know?"

I remembered Carl Lee's description of his late night visits to his wife.

"He had some bad dreams. He would talk to Willie in his sleep, and I heard him saying he was sorry, that it was 'all his fault.' But I never knew why he would say that."

I nodded. "I know he felt responsible. But he wasn't. I promise you that, ma'am."

She seemed to relax a little.

"He felt responsible for our son's death, too," she said. "Carl Lee was a very sad man, and I couldn't help him no more." The tears came again. "That's why I left."

We sat in silence for a long while.

Finally, she said, "All those people getting killed. Who would do such a terrible thing?"

"We don't know, ma'am," I answered, honestly, "but, we think it's the same people who killed Carl Lee."

She looked me dead in the eye.

"I knew it. I knew it wasn't some 'random act' like the police have been saying. Carl Lee was a good policeman, Mr. Patrick." She was becoming angry, or maybe the anger that had been beneath the surface of this gentle woman's soul was finally coming out.

"We don't believe their story, either. Neither does Cletus."

After a minute, she said, "I want to know who killed my husband."

"So do we," I said. "We want to stop these people before anyone else dies."

I told her about the meeting Carl Lee was supposed to be having with an informant. "Do you know who that could have been?" I asked.

She shook her head. "He never talked much about his work. Especially this last year, or so."

"Mrs. Wiggins," I said, "did Carl Lee leave any papers here? Some files, maybe, or some computer disks?"

She thought for a minute. "I don't think so. If he did, he didn't tell me about it."

I was disappointed, and I m sure it showed, but I really would have been surprised if Carl Lee had left information with two defenseless women, knowing somebody could come looking for it.

"Did you ask Cletus? Carl Lee stayed at his place most nights."

I didn't want to tell her what had happened at Mo Kelly's, but I knew I had to tell her about the incident at her home. If the police were to contact her about the break-in, I didn't want her to be blindsided.

"Yes," I said. "It wasn't left there, either." And I told her about the house.

"What had my husband gotten himself into?" she said, shaking her head sadly.

"He was trying to stop this, Mrs. Wiggins. He had the best of intentions, but he's gone now, and we need o find out what he knew."

Another solitary tear rolled down her cheek.

"I don't know how to help you," she said, simply, and I knew she was right.

Another dead end, it seemed. I sighed, and we stood to leave. "I'm so sorry we had to trouble you."

She remained seated. "I could look around," she said. "Or, you are welcome to look."

"Maybe later," I said. "I don't want to bother you anymore right now."

She rose and we walked toward the door.

"If you think of anything, my numbers are on the card."

She shook hands with both of us, and opened the door. I was halfway out, following Bobby, when she stopped us.

"Mr. Patrick," she said. "There is one place you might want to look for these files you mentioned."

I felt a slight tingling sensation.

"Where, ma'am? Where should we look?"

"Wait," she said, and left the room.

Bobby and I stood there, hoping against hope that there was something tangible that could come out of this.

When Grace Wiggins returned a few minutes later, she was carrying a folded piece of paper.

"Carl Lee didn't know I knew about this," she said, a wistful smile on her face. "I found a bill of sale for a camp site and an old trailer that a friend of his had kept on it for weekend fishing trips, on a lake about two hours from here. He would go up there alone, sometimes even for just a few hours, but I know he was going up there more often since I left."

She handed me the paper. "These are the directions, and the number of the camp site," she said. "I guess you could look there, but I don't have a key to the trailer."

"Thank you," I said. "We'll check it out."

We started out again, but I turned to her.

"I hate saying this," I said, "but we just don't know who we can trust, including the police. If they contact you about the break- in at the house, which they should, maybe it would be best…."

She took my hand, again, in both of hers. "You were never here. But please, you find out who killed Carl Lee for me, Mr. Patrick."

I nodded. "We will, I promise," I said, and hoped I wasn't lying to her.

CHAPTER 18

▼

August 20, 2003
Evening, Tims Ford Lake,
North of Chattanooga, Tennessee

It was after ten and we were still about twenty miles outside the small town of Mansford, Tennessee, on the southern side of Tims Ford Lake.

Bobby was driving and I was attempting to read the directions Grace Wiggins had provided us with, in the dim light through tired eyes. We had already seen signs for camp grounds around the lake, each designated by large colored dots; red, blue, white, which delineated the different locations. That gave us the answer to the green dot on Carl Lee's bill of sale. I kept an eye out for a sign locating the area we were looking for, but my mind was wandering back over everything that had transpired over the last few days.

It was while thinking about the mistakes that had cost Carl Lee Wiggins his life on that dark street when it came to me: a possible answer to one of the many mysteries we faced.

"I'll be damned," I said, more to myself than aloud, but Bobby heard me anyway.

"What?" he asked.

"That's how it happened," I said, softly.

"How what happened, Tommy? What are you mumbling about?"

I was quiet for a second, then said: "I think I know how Carl Lee was killed."

"We already know that, don't we?" Bobby said.

"Let me try something out on you. Cletus and Grace Wiggins made a point of telling us that Carl Lee was a good and careful cop. When I told Jake Berger about the details of Carl Lee's death, he immediately knew it had been a set up."

He shrugged. "Well, it was, right?"

"Yeah," I said. "But maybe not the way we thought. Jake wanted to know why Carl Lee was patrolling alone that night. Why didn't the precinct follow up on his arrest call, leaving him all alone out there for hours? And why was an experienced cop willing to approach a car in the middle of the night in a bad part of town without backup?"

Bobby looked at me, expectantly.

"So what are you getting at?"

"I don't think the precinct even knew he was out there. I think Carl Lee went there to meet his informant."

"The guy in the car?" he said, surprise in his voice. "Jesus. His informant was the shooter?"

I shook my head.

"Not necessarily, But I think that's who he was expecting to be in that car. God knows, it could have been anybody."

"So the informant set him up, huh?"

"Again, not necessarily. If someone found out about that meeting, they might have grabbed the informant and sent someone else out there to kill Carl Lee."

Bobby sighed. "So the poor bastard thinks he's meeting a guy who is going to help him, and winds up walking into a trap. He never had a chance."

"It's just a theory," I said.

"Maybe, but it answers a lot of questions if you're right. But why the story by the police department? Why all the lies about what happened?"

"They had to tell the press something. Somebody was bound to ask questions about a dead cop sooner or later. This way, it just looks like a sloppy cop made a bad choice and paid the price."

"We gotta' find the guy who Carl Lee was supposed to be meeting," Bobby said. "But where the hell would he be now?"

"Maybe," I said, ruefully, "we should check the Nashville morgue."

✳   ✳   ✳   ✳

"There," I said, pointing through the dim light. "The sign for the green campground."

"How do we find the right trailer?"

I looked at the slip of paper Grace Wiggins had given me.

"Should be number 23. There must be a marker for each site."

Bobby turned onto the narrow dirt road, and the night seemed to get even darker. He yawned, and I knew just how he felt. It had been a long day, and it wasn't over yet, but I had thought that we would be better off searching the trailer late at night rather than in daylight. For all we knew, there might not be anyone around, but it was better not to take a chance.

The dusty road wound around for about a quarter of a mile, finally widening into a large, flat area. We seemed to be on a point surrounded by shoreline, and there were some other trailers and campers set at different angles around the grounds. Either they were unoccupied, or everyone was asleep. We found small posts in front of each camp site, along with what appeared to be a water pipe connection and an electrical box at each location.

"That's it, over there, number 23," Bobby said, pointing off to the left. Luckily, there were no units on the adjoining lots.

"Pull over there, and cut the lights," I said, and we came to a stop alongside Carl Lee's trailer.

We sat for awhile with the engine off, but no lights came on, and no doors opened. It looked like most, if not all, of the trailers were here for daytime and weekend use.

"Okay, grab a flashlights and let's take a look." Bobby opened the glove compartment to get the lights. "Wait," I said, as he went to close it again. I'm not sure why, but I felt the need to take the .Smith and Wesson .38 out of the glove compartment, and stuck it in the waistband of my slacks. I wondered if I would ever get used to the need to have the weapon nearby.

The hot August night air felt damp and uncomfortable as we got out of the Durango. Immediately, the night was filled with the sounds of tree frogs and other nocturnal insects. I motioned to Bobby to unlatch the rear door. I found a tire iron and a screwdriver, and he pushed the door back down and closed it as quietly as possible. There were no human noises to be heard but the crunching sound our shoes made on the gravel covering the ground as we made our way over to the door of the beat up old trailer. As I expected, the door was locked.

"Here," I whispered to Bobby, "hold this." I handed him the tire iron and pushed the flat tip of the screwdriver into the frame of the door, just above the lock. I twisted the head of the tool, and pried outward. The lock popped and snapped like one of those hard pretzels my father likes so much with his Guinness, A gush of hot air thick with the smell of musty fabrics and spoiled food escaped from inside.

Bobby caught the door as it sung out from the frame. "That was easy."

"Thing's pretty rusty," I whispered back.

I pushed the door open further and peered into the dark interior of the trailer. The fetid air within poured out, but not a sound escaped from inside. I handed Bobby the screwdriver and snapped on my flashlight, pointing the narrow beam up inside the trailer. Stepping up inside into the dark space, I quickly flashed the light up and down the interior. All was quiet, and

Bobby followed me inside. He closed the door the hot, humid air engulfing us immediately. I felt the sweat start to form on my forehead and down my back.

Everything was a disheveled mess with beer cans, liquor bottles, and fast food wrappers holding remnants of food, on the counter and in the sink. The small refrigerator was open, the power off. Clothing and fishing gear were spread over the whole interior, but it didn't appear that any searchers had tossed the place. The whole effect was of a lonely hideout, where Carl Lee Wiggins had come to try to escape his sadness.

"Doesn't look like he'd been here for awhile," Bobby said, softly.

"Hard to tell," I said.

"Man, it stinks in here."

"Crack open a couple windows," I said. "We better leave the door closed."

Bobby did, and we began to survey the task before us.

"Where the hell do we start?" he said.

"Anywhere. Look for disks, or for any piece of paper. Check everything." I pointed my flashlight at the cushions on the small couch. "If any of those look like they've been opened and put back together, tear them apart. I'll start in the bedroom."

*   *   *   *

A half hour later, soaked in sweat and already steeling myself against another futile search result, I worked my way back through the narrow hallway from the bedroom to help Bobby finish searching the rest of the trailer's dark interior. There was little breeze coming through the small vent-like windows and I was feeling a little claustrophobic. I could hear Bobby's breath coming in deep pulls, as if he were trying to extract pure oxygen from the damp, stale air.

Bobby glanced up from his work. "Anything?"

"No," I answered. "You?"

He stopped searching through the kitchenette drawers and he pointed his flashlight at me.

"Nope. You know," he said, "we might be kidding ourselves, Tommy. Maybe Carl Lee didn't have any other information. Or maybe he was going to get it from the informant the night he was killed." He shrugged. "Maybe this is all bullshit."

I gave that a minute to sink in, but I couldn't get myself to believe it.

"I don't think so. He was too involved in this. There was too much at stake, what with Willie getting killed and all. No, there's something somewhere that we're missing. We better keep looking."

And that's what we were doing when the first "punching" sound followed by the angry buzz of a mad bumble bee; a kind of "zzzzz," rang past my ear. It was followed in rapid succession by several more matching bursts, and I felt Bobby grabbing at me and pushing me down hard onto the floor.

"Jesus!" he yelled, and I realized immediately that someone was firing into the cabin of the trailer-- and that they were using armor piercing bullets.

There were more bullets smashing through the thin walls, and windows exploded. I felt like I was deep in the middle of a hive of stinging, flying insects. But I never heard the blast of a weapon outside. *They ust be musing silencers,* I thought. But who were they?

"Stay down!" I hissed, as Bobby drew his .38 from its shoulder holster, and struggled to stand up. "Just fire a couple shots up through the window. Maybe we can keep them off us for a few minutes."

More shots, all seeming to come from the same direction zipped just over our heads.

"Stay here and keep them busy!" I got to my knees and made my way back through the hallway to the bedroom.

There were two small windows high up on the walls, but no door to the outside. I could hear Bobby scrambling back towards me. He continued to fire off a couple of shots every minute or so just to let our assailants know we weren't dead yet. His efforts were always followed by a spray of slugs tearing through the trailer.

"I'm almost out of ammunition," he said. I was struck by how calm he was.

"I've got a clip," I said. "We better save what we've got left for when they charge us."

Another series of shots dug into the thin walls of the trailer, this time going farther down the hallway towards where we were lying. Bobby looked at me through the darkness. "They're gonna' start working on the rest of this place."

"Yeah," I answered. "I know."

It quieted down for awhile.

"Here," I said, handing him my gun. "Fire off a few rounds up front again."

Bobby crawled forward into the kitchen area again, and the .38 boomed in the small space. I looked around for anything we could use for weapons once we got into a hand-to-hand showdown with whoever was trying to kill us.

I started to move forward to where I figured we would make our stand, still looking for anything we could use, when I opened the door of what I thought was a closet, hoping against hope that Carl Lee had left some weapon here. It turned out to be the toilet. Except there wasn't any toilet mounted inside.

I felt a little rush of damp air against my face. Pointing my flashlight downward and masking the beam of light as best I could, I saw the gaping hole, maybe two feet wide, through the floor. Beyond the hole was darkness, but I knew the ground was down there.

"Bobby!" I called out as quietly as I could and still get his attention. "Get over here!"

I heard him scuffle back towards where I lay. I pointed at the hole.

"Alice in Wonderland," he said, following my gaze. "Let's get out of this casket."

"Feet first," I said. "And be quiet as possible. Stay flat on the ground, okay? Here, let me have my gun."

Bobby slithered around and dropped his legs through the hole. In a second, he was gone. I fired three shots from the .38, and followed him out through our escape hatch.

Once out, I lay on the ground next to Bobby. The open area under the trailer was blocked off by cheap, cross-hatched white fencing, so we couldn't see out very well, but no one could see us either. The air was stifling and sweat was pouring down my face. My hands felt like I had just put them under running water, then caked them with dirt, and I had to fight to hold onto my gun.

Upstairs, another swarm of bees zipped through the rapidly disintegrating trailer.

"Stay here," I whispered, and crawled toward the rear of the space. Through the fencing, I could see the sparkle of moonlight playing off the lake. For the time being, the shooters were sticking to the front of the trailer. We looked to be about ten feet from the lake. It was a lousy chance to take, but we had no choice.

I motioned to Bobby and he crawled over to me. "Stay low and follow me," I whispered.

I pulled the fencing away from the trailer floor, and, taking a deep breath, I crawled out from underneath and pulled myself toward the water's edge. I could hear Bobby pushing the fence back into place as he followed me. Luck was with us, and we moved unseen from the place where the shooters were. I guessed that they had to be getting antsy by now, and I expected them to rush the trailer soon.

There was a drop of about two feet near the edge of the lake. We rolled down onto a little beach of hard packed sand, and then scrambled into the lake. The water was warm, but felt cool on my hot skin. I could feel the small, lapping waves washing the dirt and sweat from my face and arms. Trying to make as little noise as possible, we pushed off into the lake, flipped over onto our backs in order to see our enemy if they suddenly appeared, and worked our way ten, then twenty, then thirty yards out into the dark water.

"Keep your head down," I whispered to Bobby, and paddled as best I could, keeping my arms below the surface, and fighting the urge to turn over and swim for it.

Now we could see the flashing muzzles of the automatic weapons firing another round into the trailer. I estimated we had worked our way about fifty yards from the little beach when, finally, the interior of the trailer exploded in flashing lights as the gunmen stormed the place. We kept moving farther out into the lake, praying for a chance to get another ten yards away. And then another ten.

Almost immediately, the grounds around the trailer were lit with flashlight beams. I could hear cursing, and we could see at least four men running around outside. They covered the grounds in every direction before turning their lights out onto the lake. We were a good distance out by then, and as the beams followed outward, we slowly dropped beneath the surface without causing a ripple.

As the lights played away from the surface above us, I came up slowly, again only up to my neck, and shook the streaming water from my face, and saw Bobby do the same. Under water, we continued to move our arms like crazed turtles and kicked slowly. With every foot farther away from shore, I felt a little safer.

Suddenly, we could see the flashlights go dark, and the headlights of a car came on. The car began to move backwards very quickly, then rushed forward down the dirt road, and was gone in a flash. I sighed with relief, and thought about how many of my nine lives I'd used up.

The explosion was startling and blinding, as Bobby's Durango ignited in a fireball, rising off the ground and slamming back down again. The multicolored flames danced on the water before us. I looked over at Bobby in shocked disbelief.

He stared back at me, his eyes wide as saucers.

"They blew up my truck! Holy shit!" he said, awestruck. "I think that was a bit much, don't you?!"

I looked at him, sure that he was going into shock, but suddenly he began to laugh, although, I thought, a bit hysterically. And then we were both laughing with relief.

On another spit of land about a hundred yards away, lights were popping on in trailers and cabins and we heard doors slamming open. We had been lucky that our camp ground had turned out to be deserted; otherwise someone would have died for sure. I turned to my partner and pointed off towards the campers behind us.

"We better get out of here before someone calls the cops," I said.

"Anywhere in particular you'd like to go?" he replied. "Bermuda, maybe?"

I looked around for a dark area along the shore. "Somewhere not so crowded."

There was an area maybe half a mile away lying between two camp grounds.

"Over there." I pointed. And we started a leisurely swim towards the distant shore.

CHAPTER 19

▼

August 20, 2003, Early Morning
Tims Ford Lake, Tennessee

Tired and soaked to the skin, we stumbled onto a deserted two-lane about a half mile off the lake. As I had feared, our cell phones were dead, but we found a working pay phone on the road in front of a closed gas station. I made a collect call to my not-to-happy brother, and he was on his way to pick us up. We huddled in the shadows behind the building.

Bobby had quickly displayed his rather annoying talent for being able to sleep anywhere, under any circumstances, and had passed out, looking perfectly comfortable, on an old picnic table. As for me, sleep wasn't happening.

This thing we were involved in now possessed a life of its own, and had, once again, nearly consumed ours. How had we allowed our enemies to find us and trail us all the way to the lake? Was Grace Wiggins okay? Had someone followed us to her house and forced her to tell them where we were going? But then, no one even knew we were in Nashville, or so we had thought. That old fear came back; that we were in over our heads, out of our league. And suddenly, I was feeling like the lives of a lot of people were at risk because I couldn't get a handle on this job.

I tried to take stock of where we were, and the picture wasn't pretty. The latest murders in New Orleans; Carl Lee was dead and we may have put Grace Wiggins in danger. The other files Carl Lee supposedly had were still missing and most certainly gone for good, if they had been in the trailer; and many very bad people were trying very hard to kill us.

It was about 2:30 a.m., and despite my concerns, I was starting to doze off from pure exhaustion when I heard the sound of a big engine roaring down the road just east of the gas station. It was the first vehicle we had heard in hours, and I had a sudden fear that the people who had tried to kill us had found us again. But as the vehicle came into view, the driver flashed the headlights several times in rapid succession, and the massive body of the Chevy Suburban was suddenly visible. I knew Pat had found us.

The SUV pulled up in front of the station and the lights went off. I nudged Bobby awake, and we ran up front to meet Pat.

The front passenger door of the truck swung open, and my sister-in-law, C.J., hopped down from the cab. I thought: how could anyone look that good at this time of the morning? She looked great, and she looked pretty darn mad, too.

"Yankee Tom," she said, in her best "mommy" voice. "You and that brother of mine are gonna' make a drinker out of me yet!"

I could feel Bobby shrink back and move behind me.

"Now, sis...," he said, in a defensive but petulant voice.

"Don't you 'now, sis' me, Bobby Hemphill! You boys have scared another wrinkle onto my forehead, and that is something no self respecting Southern girl is gonna' put up with!"

I knew she was yelling more from relief than anger, but she was loud just the same.

Pat was standing on the other side of the Chevy, watching with amusement and enjoying himself a little too much.

I looked over at him for help, but he just smiled that same smile he always had when I got in trouble with mom when we were kids.

"Hey, I've been listening to her for three hours, and I haven't even done anything wrong. It's your turn now, boys."

"We were just doing our jobs, sis," I said, in a placating voice. "You can't be mad at us for that."

"Yeah," Bobby said, in a near whisper, "We're the ones got shot at, you know."

"You're not helping," I said, through clenched teeth.

C.J. wasn't listening anyway. "You two just get your sorry butts in this truck."

I climbed into the rear seat. Bobby followed, keeping a wary eye on his sister in case she decided to smack him on the head.

"Oh, you just wait 'til Momma, hears about this, Bobby!" she said, and I couldn't help but laugh.

*   *   *   *

By the time we started back to Atlanta, I had already decided I didn't want to call Abby and worry her. I knew that by the time we reached the city, she would be getting ready for the day's classes, so we had Pat and C.J. drop us at the stately Hemphill home on East Paces Ferry Rd., in the heart of Buckhead instead of at my place.

After a hot shower and some much needed food, Bobby went up to his room to crash for a few hours. I set up shop in his dad's study, plopping into a deep, cherry red colored chair. The air in the room was rich with the comforting smells of oiled wood, pipe tobacco, and old leather, and I dozed off for awhile, but couldn't stay asleep for very long. I couldn't seem to shut my mind to all that was happening and, so far, my pitiful efforts to do anything about it.

I awoke with a start, momentarily confused about where I was, but the night's activities quickly came back to me. I rubbed my tired eyes and settled back into the overstuffed chair. The room was still dark, as the heavy curtains blocking out the early rising sun, and eerily quiet. By now, back in the little apartment I shared with Abby, I would be hearing the clatter from Pat's kitchen below as his crew started to prepare for the lunch crowd. It would be another hot, sultry day in my adopted city and I was in no hurry for the new day to start.

Bobby's dad is a big-time Atlanta corporate attorney. Their relationship hasn't always been a good one, mostly because my partner had been more than a little rebellious in his youth. His father is an old line Southerner, whose life is steeped in the social traditions of the region- at least as envisioned by the wealthy families who have been entrenched here for generations. But things had settled down between father and son with Bobby's recent maturity, and I could see a grudging acceptance and, I think, a good bit of family pride in how he had handled himself since Cuba, as well.

I'd apparently had all the rest I was going to get, so I borrowed a few sheets of white Xerox paper from Mr. Hemphill's desk and a pen. Returning to the comfortable chair, I sketched out the symbols that had been found painted in blood on the walls of the murder scenes. I had done this a hundred times before, but I still couldn't figure out how they translated into clues to the identities of the killers, or if they even did.

I reached over and swung the floor lamp next to the chair a little to bring the full force of its light onto the paper. I stared again at what I had drawn: the "x" with the number "eleven" written across the middle; then the cross with the circle connecting the four ends. And then there was a new one that we had found in the photos taken at the New Orleans house: a crudely drawn five- point star, again with the number "eleven" scrawled in the center.

I was getting nowhere, but I took a clean sheet and drew the symbols again, as if the repetition was going to magically transform my ignorance into a sudden and complete understanding.

I was working on my third sheet of paper when there was a quiet knock on the door, and Robert Hemphill Sr., came into the study. I grabbed the papers off the floor and got up, but he put his hand up.

"Stay there, Thomas. Just checking to see if everything is all right."

"Yes, sir," I said. "Thanks for letting me stay here last night."

"Anytime."

He smiled, a curious look crossing his face. I could see the strong resemblance to his son.

"I take it you two had a bit of an adventure up in Tennessee."

I felt a little like a schoolboy in his presence. "I guess C.J. kind of gave you a breakdown on what happened."

He smiled again. "That girl never could keep a secret." He became a little more serious. "She's worried about you guys."

"I know."

He sat down in the matching chair across from mine.

"You know. C.J. never would give up on Bobby. She always said she saw something in him." He shook his head. "Just give him time, she'd say. I'm glad she was right."

I sighed. "She was more than right, sir. He saved my life."

We were quiet for awhile, and then Mr. Hemphill leaned forward in his chair.

"What's that you've got there?" he said, pointing at the papers in my hand.

"Just some sketches of symbols we found at the different crime scenes. They're our main proof that the perpetrators are somehow tied together. But we haven't been able to figure out what they mean."

"You mind if I take a look?" he said, holding out a hand.

"No, of course not. I've been staring at them for days now and I'm getting nowhere fast."

Robert Hemphill studied the crude drawings while I waited. I could feel the exhaustion starting to overtake me again. I concentrated on watching him.

"Nobody we know has seen those markings before," I said. "Our contact at police headquarters has searched their files for gang symbolism matches, but he struck out, too. Max Howard has been working on political extremist groups, but nothing has turned up. It's hard to believe a bunch of unrelated crazies are all using these independently, but we're running out of ways to tie them together."

"I don't think you'll find anything that way." He got up from the chair. "Hold on a minute." He went over to one of the massive walls of books.

I waited while he ran through the titles, wondering what he was getting at. When he finally returned he was carrying an old, worn-looking book bound in dark leather. Sitting again, he thumbed through the pages. A slightly musty smell began to permeate the room.

Robert Hemphill found what he was looking for. Leaning forward in his chair, he turned the book around and handed it to me.

Like the sudden gust of a chilling breeze, I felt a tingling sensation against my skin, and a rush of blood to my brain made me feel faint. I found myself staring at the very symbols I had been drawing over and over for weeks, but now in defined, perfectly symmetrical, clearly recognizable shapes.

The star with the "11" was there, and the cross with the perfect circle connecting the arms. The "x" was there, too, with the number eleven inscribed in its center. But it wasn't an "x." I could see that clearly now. It was shaped like an "x," but widely banded, with stars emblazoned within. It was a cross, but a different type of cross. One that I had seen before.

I tore my eyes from the pages and looked questioningly at Bobby's dad.

"How...?" I started to say, but he held up his hand.

"This is the South, Thomas," he said with a smile. "There are a lot of us who have studied the minutia of the most important events in our family histories."

He pointed at the book.

"Those are symbols, all right, but you won't find them in police records. At least not very recent ones, that is. Those are Klan symbols."

"Klan?" I said, dumbstruck. "You mean..."

He nodded. "Ku Klux Klan markings, from a very long time ago."

I shook my head. "But I don't understand. Why would somebody be leaving KKK symbols at murder scenes? It doesn't make sense."

There was a knock at the door, and Bobby stuck his head into the room. "You up? Oh, hey Dad," he said, but neither of us responded, and he came over to where we were sitting.

"I'll tell you what is even stranger," his father said, quietly. "Those particular symbols were used by a very small offshoot of the Klan. Not many people were even aware of its existence."

"What are you guys talking about?" Bobby said.

I handed him the open book.

"What does that mean, exactly?" I asked.

Mr. Hemphill sat back in his chair.

"This group was known as the 'Klan of the Gold Circle,'" he said. "It was a small group, or 'klavern' as they were known. Still are, actually."

"Still are?" I said. But I let that go for now. "I thought the Klan was just the Klan."

Mr. Hemphill got up to fetch his pipe and tobacco pouch from his desk.

"You are essentially right," he said, when he returned. "But there were scattered klaverns, some made up of hotheads and misfits who were never part of the Klan as a whole, for one reason or another. The Klan survived by secrecy, and the leadership shied away from those who were too demonstrative about their leanings, unless they could use them to their benefit that is." He took the book from his son, and tapped a finger on the open pages.

"This one, though, had a very special purpose; one that was kept secret even from other Klan groups for many years."

"Why?" Bobby asked. "What was so special about this one?"

"Well, it's a long story, and much of it may be rooted in myths and falsehoods," Robert Hemphill began, "but a lot of people believe to this day that there is at least a good bit of truth to the legends."

"What legends?" I sat forward, hanging on his ever word.

"In 1865, as the Confederacy was collapsing in on itself, the government planned and executed an escape, code named, 'Grey Phoenix,' from the capital city of Richmond, Virginia," he said. "The Union forces had the city virtually surrounded, but somehow President Jefferson Davis and his cabinet and their families got away before Richmond fell. The plan was to operate as a government in exile, and continue the war as best they could. Davis always assumed, and maybe it was wishful thinking, that if he could continue to disrupt the Federal government in Washington for an extended period, he could force an eventual negotiation favorable to the South. Even more amazing was their ability to elude the Yankee army for weeks before finally being taken as prisoners. That much of the story we know is true."

This was an interesting history lesson, but I wasn't making a connection. "But..."

He held up a hand. "Hold on," he said. "I'm getting to that. So the Confederate government was in captivity, and the war was essentially over. But there was one thing missing."

"What? " Bobby said, "What was missing?"

His dad smiled. "About Twenty million dollars, maybe more, in gold. It was the remaining treasury of the Confederate States of America."

I whistled. "That's a lot of money. Why would they surrender with that kind of cash?"

"It was in gold bars, actually. But that's not very much money when you're fighting a war, even back then." He sighed. "Besides, those with level heads knew it was a lost cause. The North had the manpower, the factories to produce war materials. And then there was the British."

"The British?" I asked. "What about them?"

"Well," he said, "up until 1863, the South had been waltzed around by the British government, and fully expected them to come into the war on the Southern side, much like the French did with the American colonies during the Revolutionary War. That all ended after Gettysburg, where the South's defeat was so complete that the British decided the North would surely win the war. On top of that, four pro-slavery states, including Kentucky, Maryland, and others had stayed in the Union. Take that and the fact that the western counties of Virginia basically seceded from the South and were admitted to the Union as West Virginia in 1863, and you wind up with European countries that were unsure that the Confederacy would hang together for very long. All that left Davis with no chance for a European alliance. Soon the Union navy bottled up what was left of the Confederate war and merchant ships in foreign ports. It strangled the South, which was desperate for nearly every commodity."

He finally lit this pipe and the rich, aromatic aroma filled the room. "After that, and a few more military disasters, it was all pretty much decided."

I felt a little let down.

"So that was the end of it?"

He shook his head. "Not exactly. As unrealistic as it might have been, President Davis actually believed they could elude the Yankee army and somehow reach a safe haven from where the war could have been continued. Some historians believe he was aiming for Mexico, where we know he was offered asylum by the government there. Others think it more likely he was taking his people to some island in the Caribbean."

"Doesn't sound like they were being very realistic," I mused.

"Some dreams die harder than others," he said. "These were very proud people."

"Yeah," Bobby said, impatiently. "But, what about the gold?"

"That's just it," his father said. "What about the gold? Davis obviously intended to use it to finance his continuing war plans. Somehow, Davis was able to hide the gold before he was captured. He never told the Yankees where it was hidden. It was never found, of course, but the stories set off a hysterical search which lasted well into the early years of the 1900's, that resembled the California Gold Rush or the Black Hills gold hysteria. That's where the Klan of the Gold Circle comes into the picture."

"How do you mean?" I asked.

"They were formed to keep others from the money by passing off bogus information. Although it has never been proven that they knew where the gold was, and most scholars don't think they did, they kept others from finding it. They even 'salted' areas of forests and other places, burying gold Confederate coins to throw the searchers off the trail. In the mean time, they went on looking for it themselves."

I sat back.

"Okay. So now I understand who they were, and what they were, and that they had all these secret symbols. But why are these markings showing up all over the South at murder scenes now?"

Robert Hemphill Sr. struck a match and refreshed the glowing embers in the bowl of his pipe.

"I don't know, Thomas," he said. "But maybe they're not done looking yet."

CHAPTER 20

▼

August 20, 2003
Atlanta, Georgia

"Could he have been serious, Max?"

I was stretched out on my old couch in the apartment above Ireland's own, talking on the phone with Max Howard about the events of the last few days….and my conversation with Robert Hemphill.

Bobby had borrowed my truck and was off meeting with Jake Berger, who had suggested filing a "stolen" vehicle report on the Durango.

"No sense answering questions for a bunch of Tennessee cops if we can avoid it," Jake had said. "I'll date the report for the day before the vehicle was destroyed. No big deal."

"No big deal?! They blew up my truck!" Bobby had retorted, in mock horror. We both knew we were lucky to be alive. The guys who had trailed us to the lake weren't playing games.

"Hey, at least you weren't in it," Jake said.

"He's got you there," I laughed.

Now I was trying to get Max to help me make sense of the conversation with Bobby's dad. I still had no idea how we had been tracked from Nashville to the trailer, or how it had been discovered that we were in Nashville to begin with. But at least I had been able to check in with Grace Wiggins. She was safe, for now at least, and had not had any visitors showing up to ask about us.

I heard Max sigh. "Far be it from me to question Robert Hemphill about anything pertaining to the Civil War era, Tommy. The guy is known throughout the South as an expert on the subject."

"Yeah, but can he really believe this 'Gold Circle' group still exists?"

"You'd be surprised how many people would swear on their life that the Klan has been gone for a hundred years. They're nowhere near as prevalent or powerful as they once were, to be sure, but every once in a while they stick their heads out of whatever hole they been hiding in just to let you know they're still around."

"Okay, so maybe there is some hidden treasury of the Confederacy out there, though I don't see how it wouldn't have been found by now. And maybe somebody out there is still looking for it. But, for the life of me, I can't figure how that ties in to the murders of bi-racial couples all over the South."

"I don't know the answer to that," Max said. "But what I do know is that I've put you boys in harm's way once too often, Tommy. Maybe it's time to pull you off of this case before someone gets hurt bad."

I could hear the strain in Max Howard's voice. He was genuinely worried about me and Bobby, but we had come too far to stop now. He needed us, just as we had once needed him.

"Sorry, Max, but this is too personal now. Besides, no one knows all the ins and outs like we do. No one else will ever have the chance to talk with Carl Lee like we did." I let that sink in. "We may have put Grace Wiggins at risk, and we need to protect her. We won't quit now, Max."

There was a dead silence on the line.

"All right, son," Max finally said, and for all the worry that I knew was in his heart, there was a sense of relief in his voice. "We'll play it out, but please be careful."

"We will, Max," I said, and I wondered if I would ever learn enough to keep that promise.

*   *   *   *

Abby and I met Bobby and Sabine Metaine for dinner at Sam's, a local hangout a couple blocks south of Ireland's Own, at 7 p.m. Sabine had just completed two days of flying and they had come straight from the airport, where Bobby had picked her up. They were a round behind us, but Bobby got them caught up in a hurry with a Desert Pear Martini for Sabine and a Sam Adams for himself. It made me feel good to see them together, and it was obvious they *were* together. They hadn't let go of each other's hand since they had arrived. Abby noticed it too, and gave my hand a squeeze. It was the first time in days that I felt relaxed and safely within the zone of my real life- the life that always included Abby.

A waiter went by with a tray of sizzling steaks, the aroma settling down over our table like a comforting blanket.

"Umm, I'm starving," Abby said.

"Me too," Sabine giggled. "Six cities in two days and I never left the airports. I've been existing on cafeteria food."

Bobby smiled. "Then we came to the right place. Best steaks in the city."

We ordered another round.

"Did Bobby tell you the news?" Sabine asked. "I've got a week's vacation coming up, and I asked him to come home with me." She gave him a big smile.

"Hey," he said. "I haven't asked the 'boss' for time off yet."

"Works for me if it'll get you out of my hair for a while," I said, in mock seriousness. "Please take him with you. He's not worth much when you're not around anyway."

"Barbados," Abby said, dreamily. "Sounds fabulous."

"Well, don't get any ideas, babe. With Romeo out of town, one of us has to work," I said.

As always, I had finally confided in Abby, telling her about Tennessee. I told her all of it, trying to play down the near disaster at the lake, but she saw through me. She always did, but she never shows the fear I'm sure she feels. Abby knows it would worry me even more if she showed her concern. We ordered dinner and were just talking as old friends do, when Sabine asked about our trip. Bobby's face showed a momentary panic, which I knew she had noticed.

"Something happened, didn't it?" she said in a quiet voice, her eyes searching our faces. "Bobby?"

He put on a carefree look. "It was nothing, honey, just the usual, you know."

Sabine looked at me. "The 'usual,' huh? Is that why you're driving a rental, Bobby? Come on, guys,. "what happened up there?"

I tried to look away, but her stare held my eyes.

"She deserves to know, Thomas," Abby encouraged. "She and Bobby are in a relationship, and she deserves to know, right?"

Sabine touched Bobby's face. "I'm a lot stronger than you think, mister. I care for you, in case you've forgotten. You can tell me what's going on."

And so we did. Slowly, calmly, trying not to over emphasize the fear we had felt, or the true danger we had been in. As I think about it now, there seemed to be a release of tension in Bobby brought on by being able to finally talk about all we had been through, as if the keeping of this information from someone he was in love with had become a burden almost too great to bear.

I waited for the expected gush of concern, or maybe even anger from Sabine, but it never came. She listened in silence without any display of emotion, reminding me of my own good fortune in having Abby, and the serenity and calm she brought to our lives every day. I had come to imagine that it had been our brush with death in Cuba that had steeled her against the dangers of the business I had chosen, but now I was beginning to understand that her inner strength had been a long time thing; far beyond the time I had known her. Sabine seemed to have it too.

When we finished our story, Bobby looked at Sabine like a child who had been caught being naughty, and was waiting for a scolding.

Finally, she said, "So, what kind of car are you going to get now?"

Bobby looked at her like he hadn't understood the question, and Sabine chuckled.

"Did you two think I was going to fall apart over this?" she asked, looking at both of us. "I'm worried about you, just like Abby is," she said. "But I know what you do, and I know why you do it, you know? I'll probably never like it, but I do understand it. Just be careful, okay? Protect yourselves." She gave his arm a squeeze, and kissed him on the cheek. I felt Abby's hand tighten in mine.

I raised my hand. "I vote for a Hummer," I said. "Preferably something with an anti-tank gun mounted on the roof!"

∗   ∗   ∗   ∗

We left the restaurant about an hour later, stepping from the cool air conditioning out into the hot, thick air of Atlanta in August. A light drizzle was falling, which bothered none of us and we decided to walk the few blocks back to Ireland's Own, where Bobby had left his rental car. The rain was cooling and Abby snuggled up against me. We walked close to the buildings along the sidewalk to catch an occasional awning over some of the storefronts.

It was about 10 p.m., and Peachtree Street was crowded with people as usual. The parade of traffic inched its way through Buckhead. I could hear Bobby and Sabine behind us, talking animatedly, enjoying the others nearness.

Abby turned to look up at me, the rain making her beautiful face glow, even in the dim light.

That was when I heard the sound.

It was unfamiliar to me at first, a kind of "spitting" sound, repeating over and over. But I had heard it before, and it came to me like a sudden, debilitating kick in the gut. I had heard it at the lake.

Just as suddenly, the windows of the store we were passing exploded into a million razor-like shards. My face erupted in spouts of warm blood as bullets ripped into walls, and the fragments of brick pelted us.

"Abby! Get down!" I heard myself yelling as I pushed her to the ground, and threw myself on top of her body.

The night was filled with the sounds of screaming, people crying out in fear and pain, car horns bleating, and the throaty roar of a powerful, screaming engine, and above it all, the unrelenting spit of the silenced automatic weapon. The cries of injured pedestrians rose to a crescendo, and the weapon blasted on for what seemed an eternity, but I didn't dare to look away from Abby. I pressed myself even tighter against her.

She didn't utter a sound, didn't move. I prayed she was okay, and cursed myself at the same time for having left my own gun in a drawer back at the apartment.

Then, as suddenly as it had started, the firing stopped and the vehicle was gone, but the wailing of the wounded and the screams of people crying out for help was like a dead weight on me, pushing me down toward the ground, and I was afraid to look up at the carnage around me.

"Thomas?!" It was Abby, pushing up from underneath me. "Thomas? You're bleeding." She touched the blood on my face.

"I'm okay," I said, taking her hand. "Are you hurt, Abby?!"

She shook her head, rain cascading down her face, "No. No, I don't think so."

I hugged her tightly to me, unwilling to let go.

Then she said, quietly, "Oh, God. Oh, God, no."

I looked down to reassure her again, but she wasn't looking at me. I forced myself to follow her gaze. All around us there were bodies, some moving painfully and some, I knew, would never move again. Some of the uninjured were trying to help, but others stared dumbly at the scene around them, unable to react.

But Abby was looking at Bobby Hemphill. He was on his knees, cradling Sabine Metaine's head in his lap. He was stroking her cheek and speaking softly to her. I heard him say that she would be okay and that he would take care of her. But Sabine was not okay. The side of her head above her left ear was a mass of blood and torn tissue. Abby was suddenly behind Bobby, speaking softly in his ear while she stroked his face gently.

"You have to put her down, Bobby," she said, as I broke from my own shock and crawled over to them. "It will be all right for you to put her down. I promise."

Bobby looked up at Abby, a mixture of rain and tears running down his face. I gently took Sabine from him, and laid her down on the ground. My partner sat back and hugged his knees hard against his chest. I don't think he even knew what had happened. But I did, and I knew that the cries around me would never be out of my mind.

In the distance, I could hear many sirens coming toward us, and I forced myself to think.

"Abby," I said, taking her hands in mine and helping her to her feet. "Abby, get to Ireland's Own, get Pat. Tell him to call C.J. and get her down here. I want Bobby out of here as soon as possible. Tell Pat to come here as quick as he can, and we'll try to get Bobby back to our place, okay?"

She nodded.

"Then you go up to the apartment, lock the door, and stay there until we get back."

CHAPTER 21

▼

August 24, 2003
Atlanta, Georgia

We held a one night wake for Sabine so that her friends and co-workers from the airline that were stationed in Atlanta could say their goodbyes before her body was shipped back to Barbados for burial. Bobby had barely said a word since the attack on Peachtree Street by the still unknown assailants. I had kept a close eye on Abby, concerned that the trauma of our experience might catch up with her. But in that stoic, seemingly imperturbable way that I had come to expect from her, she seemed to be coping with the situation much better than I was. I couldn't shake the feeling that people were dead because of our investigation...or worse, my incompetence. People I had never known....or would ever know, were dead, and it was Bobby and me that were supposed to be. Abby was safe, but how many more times could I put her in harm's way and still be able to say that?

I still had Abby, but the woman Bobby Hemphill had loved was gone. The anger that I felt for the senseless loss of her life was deep and suffocating, but it would have to wait. Now was the time to support Bobby, and let myself grieve for his loss.

Throughout the evening of the wake, Bobby sat in a deep leather chair just a few feet from the pearl colored casket, just staring at the lifeless form it held. He said nothing, as if the shock of her dying in his arms on a busy Atlanta street was the last thing he could remember, and that the time since then, when my brother, and I had taken him from that scene of carnage and brought him to my apartment above Ireland's Own, was just a blur of unconnected thoughts and actions. I couldn't help but think back to another wake, another beautiful young woman, cut down in the prime of her life at a time of happiness and expectancy, as a child grew inside her. Snuffed out in a moment of mindless, senseless violence. And I vowed not to forget or forgive what had happened to Sabine...., or Marti Patton. I saw again in my mind's eye, the smug, almost unfeeling face of her father, and I knew then that this thing would never be over until vengeance had run its course.

Abby and I were standing near my partner when I saw his parents walk into the parlor. Robert Hemphill, Sr., this proud and learned man, seemed ill at ease as he stood silently nearby, watching his son. After a few minutes, he walked slowly over to where Bobby sat, putting a tentative hand on his shoulder, and spoke softly to him.

"I'm very sorry about that girl, Bobby. Very sorry." He stood there, his hand still on the shoulder of the son he loved, but had had such a disjointed and uncomfortable relationship with for so many years.

Then, Bobby leaned over, his head resting against his father's leg. And the tears finally came.

$$\ast \quad \ast \quad \ast \quad \ast$$

I didn't think it was a good idea. I was afraid Bobby would be walking into a situation full of guilt, recrimination, and, hate, and that the remorse he felt would turn into a sense of self- loathing. But he had made up his mind that he would accompany Sabine's body back to her island home, and the family that now had to bury her. He would not be dissuaded, so I was relieved when C.J. declared that she would go with him.

"He won't get closure if he doesn't do this," she had told me the night before the flight. "So he has to go, but not alone."

I dropped them off at the International Terminal at Hartsfield at eight on the morning of the 24th and, after an uncomfortable goodbye, was heading back to Buckhead, when my cell phone rang, jarring me back from the constant retread of unhappy thoughts flooding through my tired mind. Jake Berger was on the other end, and he didn't waste time.

"Where are you?"

"On I-85 heading back to Buckhead. What's up, Jake?" I was dreading the announcement of some new murder scene.

"Then you're only ten minutes from here," he said. "I need you to swing by the precinct."

"Okay, but..."

He interrupted me. "I want you to meet one of the guys we think tried to kill you."

I could feel my blood turn cold; a mixed feeling of rage tinged with a cold- sweat fear growing in me. In my mind I heard the spit of the automatic weapon and the screams of pain again. I could feel Abby's ridged body pinned under me. I saw Sabine Metaine, her lifeless form cradled in Bobby's arms.

"You caught him?" I said, in a cautious tone.

"Maybe," Jake answered. "He fits the description we got from several people at the scene and I think it's a good bet. But for the record….maybe."

A few minutes later, I pulled into a parking space in the 14th Precinct lot in Midtown and went looking for Jake Berger. He was waiting for me in the lobby.

"Coffee?"

I shook my head. He turned and led me back through a doorway and down a long, pea-green painted hallway. Jake stopped in front of a windowless door.

"He's in there?" I asked, feeling an uncomfortable pressure building in my chest.

"Viewing room. One-way glass between us and our friend." He pushed open the door and I followed him into the small, dimly lit room. A big glass window separated us from where the prisoner was seated in an adjacent room of about the same size.

There was a table and three chairs in the other room. No other furniture. Seated at the table was a lone figure. He was maybe late thirties, early forties; a biker type, sporting long, unkempt hair and a beard, a sleeveless denim vest hung over his shirtless, muscular torso. He was covered in tattoos, some too faded to distinguish, and a purplish scar ran down the right side of his evil looking face. He seemed to be shrouded in a cocoon of indifference to the situation he was in. I stood in front of the one-way window and stared at this monster. I couldn't help but wonder if he had any understanding of the carnage he had wreaked on dozens of lives…or if he was even capable of caring. I saw again the haunted look on the face of Bobby Hemphill, on that hot, rainy night.

"There were two of them," I said, softly to Jake Berger.

"Yeah. We don't know where the other guy is." Jake sighed. "Thomas, he might not be one of the people we're looking for, you know."

"Who is he?" I asked, ignoring the possibility. I wanted this to be him.

"No ID. Says we should call him 'Rebel,' but I doubt that's what's on his birth certificate We're running prints. I've got an officer down at Grady Memorial getting stitches."

I looked at him, questioningly.

"He really didn't want to give us a set of prints, but we eventually convinced him to do so."

I pulled over one of the cheap plastic chairs from against the wall and sat down, heavily. My eyes never left the face of Jake's prisoner. "Where'd you find him?"

Jake shrugged. "Pure dumb luck. His '93 Chevy broke down on the I-75, and a county sheriff's cruiser stopped to help him. He was liquored up and had an open bottle of bourbon in the car. No ID, no registration. So the cop called it in and the dispatcher caught the similarity in his car and the description of the one used in the attack that we had posted. From there it only took three cruisers full of deputies to bring his ass in."

I was surprised. "They didn't keep him themselves?"

Jake smiled. "Professional courtesy. We had him within an hour."

I was still watching the man in the other room. He was leaning back in his chair, smoking, blowing smoke rings, as if he hadn't a care in the world.

"What about the other guy?"

Jake shrugged. "Like I said, he was all alone. Right now, all we have on the other guy is a theory."

I looked at him. "Theory? What kind of theory?"

He sat down on the other plastic chair. "If this is one of our guys, then maybe he was brought in from out of town and was hooked up with some local familiar with Atlanta. Makes sense he'd be needing help finding his way around...and finding you. Afterwards, he drops off his pal and heads out of town."

I was starting to feel the anger grow again. "You keep saying 'if,' Jake, and 'maybe.' Is he one of them or not?!"

Jake didn't say anything.

I shook my head. "This is bullshit! You know he is, so why the games?"

He gave me a stern look. "No, I don't!" he said, forcefully. "And neither do you, since you never saw the perps." Jake sighed, and his voice softened. "Look, Tom. We've got a thirty second crime committed on a dark street. We've got no prints from the scene, no weapon, and no motive we can tie this guy to." He let that sink in. "And, if we don't come up with something quick, this tub of shit is out of here tomorrow."

"Can't you hold him longer? What about him assaulting your officer?"

"If we try to hold him on that, he'll lawyer up and post bail. He'll disappear in a heartbeat. We might not be so lucky finding him again."

I could feel the bile rising in my throat. "That's fucking great," I said, as I rose and headed for the door. "Tell that to Bobby when he gets back from burying his girl." As I turned the knob, I looked back at Jake Berger. "Tell me, Jake," I said. "Why the hell did you even bother to call me down here if you weren't going to hold this animal?"

He sat back, his head resting against the wall. "Because I have nothing on him, and when he leaves here at ten a.m. tomorrow, I can't harass him... or follow him. Even if there were a chance he could lead me to whoever hired him to try to kill you."

I shook my head, slowly. "This isn't fair, Jake."

"No," he said in a hushed voice. "No, it's not."

I gave him one last long look, walked out and closed the door behind me.

CHAPTER 22

──────────── ▼ ────────────

August 24, 2003
Washington, D.C.

The cab pulled up to the curb in front of Lafayette Park on Pennsylvania Avenue, directly across the street from the White House, and jolted to a stop. The rear door opened and a portly man in his mid-seventy's, and supporting himself with a cane, exited gingerly from the vehicle, feeling the arthritic stiffness in his hips. His name was Arthur Ellis, and he was serving his sixth term as a U.S. senator from the State of Tennessee.

Ellis gazed across the street at the president's home as the cab pulled away. He could feel the August heat and humidity, a scourge to the Nation's capital, attacking his skin, the prickly feeling on his scalp under the shock of wavy white hair causing rivulets of sweat starting to form and roll down the back of his neck . But his agitated state, well hidden from public view as befits a Southern gentleman, was caused by reasons other than the weather. He grasped the cane in his arthritic fingers and balanced himself to step down from the curb. Congress was in recess for the month, and he could have been home in his beloved state, nursing the ill feelings he held for his fellow legislators and their latest round of misguided laws. No, he thought, there were more important things to take care of right now. Time was short. At seventy- six years of age, and in failing health, the senator knew this could be his last term in Congress. After years of pushing his private agenda, and having little success, he had realized that a change in tactics would be necessary. So changes had been made, and success was, he felt, within his grasp. But mistakes were being made as well; mistakes that could sabotage the Noble Cause. They had to stop, and that was the reason for his visit today.

Ellis crossed Pennsylvania Avenue and walked westward across the front of the White House. The flag staff atop the roof was bare. No American flag fluttered from the top of the pole. The president was not in residence. Probably at the ranch in Crawford, Texas, he thought, not that the dirt brown, brush filled wasteland deserved the term. Ellis had been there before along with other Republican legislators, for bar-b-ques and fund raisers. He found the place to be devoid of charm and grace, unlike his beloved "Hartsdale," the great plantation near Nashville, which had passed to the Ellis family one hundred twenty years ago from the Geary family of Pulaski, Tennessee, by way of the marriage of Geary's daughter to the Senator's ancestor, Alton Henry Ellis. Southerner or not, he thought, the country was better off when the president was out of Washington and tucked away in Texas, where he could do the least harm.

He stopped and gazed up at the ornate but worn edifice of the Old Executive Office Building at the western edge of the White House, which still housed senior congressional members as well as the private office of the Vice-President and other White House staff, and gave himself time to catch his breath. The warm, moist air was taking its toll on his strength, and he yearned once again for the cooling breezes of the foothills of Tennessee.

He entered the building via the entrance reserved for congressmen and other government personnel and, following a few others who seemed less than pleased to be on duty on this summer's day, eventually flashed his Member of Congress credentials at the security desk. It was a necessary procedure in these dangerous times, but the wait in line played havoc with his knees. Once at the head of the line, he was quickly recognized and passed through the metal detector. Moments later he was on his way to the third floor in the decrepit elevator, thankful, at least, for the air conditioning.

The third floor hallway was predictably quiet, and his cane made a tapping noise on the marble floors that echoed in his ears as he sought out the office door of Congressman Gerald W. Greenway, of the Tenth Congressional District, and the Biloxi Greenways, of the Great State of Mississippi. Ellis stopped in front of the congressman's door and listened for a moment. He could hear muted conversation- a phone call in progress, perhaps. He used his shoulder and pushed against the heavy door.

The woman behind the desk looked up at Ellis as he entered, and offered him a smile- one practiced over many years- crossed her heavily made-up face. She was in her early fifties, and plump, but well dressed and very practiced at her craft.

"Why, good morning to you, Senator," she gushed, with just enough enthusiasm and Southern charm. "I didn't know we were expecting you this fine day."

"Ms. Purdy, you are indeed a pleasant sight, as usual," Ellis gushed back, as he gave her a slight salute. "I thought I might stop by to say hello to my dear friend, the Congressman, since it appears we are both resigned to spending our holiday in the city, if he could spare me a few minutes of his valuable time, that is."

"I'm sure he will be glad to see you, Senator. Let me tell him you're here."
She picked up the phone, pushed a button, and after a moment said a few quiet words. "Go right in, Senator. I'll bring some coffee."

Ellis gave her a little bow and stepped through the door into Gerald Greenway's private office.

Behind the ornate desk framed between an American flag and the Mississippi standard, sat the congressman, a thin, sandy haired man who was obviously not as pleased to see the senator as his secretary had been. His face was drawn and looked as if he had not slept very well, which he hadn't, and he didn't smile as he offered Ellis a chair.

"Arthur, to what do we owe this honor?"

Ellis took the chair and felt his tired muscles relax a little. "I didn't know I needed a special reason to visit you, Gerald," he said, as he laid the came across the front of Greenway's desk.

There was a knock on the door, and the two men spent a few uncomfortable moments in silence, while Ms. Purdy served the coffee and then left them alone again.

"We both know you don't do anything without a reason, Arthur," Greenway said, with a slight edge in his voice.

Ellis sighed, and took a sip of the coffee. "All right, Gerald. Since you appear to be in no mood for small talk, suppose you tell me whose brilliant idea it was to send those two idiots to Atlanta?"

The congressman bristled a little, but spoke calmly. "Someone panicked," he said, looking uncomfortable.

"And who, pray tell, might that have been?"

Greenway was sure Ellis already knew the answer, and he wasn't about to take the bait.

"What does it matter?" he said, testily. Then, in a calmer voice, "They were getting too close. After the incident at the lake, too many of our people were getting worried."

Senator Ellis shifted slightly in his chair as the pain in his hip ignited again.

"Understandable, Gerald. And there are professionals to handle such things. But sending those two clowns to kill those detectives was a stupid idea at best." He shook his head. "They shot ten people, and didn't touch their intended targets." Ellis drank some more coffee, letting Greenway stew. "And now, one of them is in jail."

"We wanted it to look like a random act of violence," Greenway said, defensively, "not like some gangland execution, Arthur."

"It didn't quite work out that way, did it?" Ellis pushed. "That was stupid, Gerald. You will bring down the police, and probably the Feds on us."

Now the congressman was getting chastised, and he didn't like it. He shook his head. "That won't happen," he said, with more confidence than he felt. But he'd had enough of Ellis' tone. "One of our people in Atlanta is an attorney. He assures me our man will be out today, since they have nothing to hold him on. And," he added, "I took care of the Fed situation."

"I hope so," Ellis said, "for your own protection."

Fuck you, you old bastard, Greenway thought. But Ellis was a powerful man, and a leader of the Cause. Still, it was time to throw this back on him.

"It's being handled, Arthur. Besides, you have much more to worry about than this!"

"Oh?" Ellis said, calmly. "And what should I be worried about, if not this mess you've created Gerald?"

Greenway sat back in his chair. "Our boys are doing their jobs," he said, "but they are wondering when you are going to do yours."

Ellis drank the last of his coffee, and made a slow show of pouring more. "And, what job would that be?"

"Stop playing games, Arthur," Greenway said, his voice rising slightly. "We can't move forward without the money. They want to know when it will be distributed. I don't have any answers for them, Arthur. Do you?"

Ellis winced slightly as the pain in his hips intensified. "We are getting close. We will have our funds soon." He wasn't about to tell Greenway that the last clues had led to another futile search to locate the gold.

"When, Arthur?" Greenway said, not letting go just yet. It felt good to have something on the old man.

"Soon," Senator Ellis said, again.

"That would be a very good idea, Arthur," Congressman Greenway said. "A very good idea."

I wasn't about to take the chance that Charles Murphy, as we now knew the biker's name to be, might be released before 10 a.m., as Jake Berger had said, so I was parked across the street from the main entrance to the 14th Precinct at eight. I was driving Pat's big Chevy SUV, in case Murphy knew what kind of vehicle I drove. I took a pull on the thermos of hot coffee and a bite of the Krispy Krème donut that my brother had tossed into a bag and left on the seat for me. But my attention was on the door of the building, and I hardly noticed what I was eating. Neither Pat nor Abby had been thrilled by my intention to follow the man who had killed Sabine Metaine and the others just a few days ago, but Pat was much more insistent, suggesting that I at least let him come along. But I wasn't about to put anyone else in danger's path. As usual, Abby knew I had to do this, and, like it or not, she didn't try to change my mind.

Jake had arranged for Murphy's car to be impounded two blocks west of the precinct, assuring that he would leave the jail on foot so that I would be sure to pick up his trail without trouble. I felt a slight tingle of excitement as the release time approached, as I saw this as a chance to be led to those behind the horrible events of the last few months, as well as revulsion deep in my gut that this murderer would soon be walking the streets in freedom. I had promised myself throughout the night while I lay awake thinking about today, that I would not let him stay free for long.

At 10:20 a.m., two police officers trotted up the steps of the 14th Precinct and through the door. Charles Murphy walked out before the door had a chance to close and hurried down to the sidewalk. I felt a cold sweat on my forehead, my hand going instinctively to the butt of the .38 under my arm. It would be so easy to gun him down right here on Peachtree Street, just as he had done to those people less than two miles away from here on that fateful night, I knew I could do it with a clear conscience, and more than a little satisfaction. While it might be justice and closure for the dead and wounded of that night, I knew that it would not bring an end to the murders we were investigating. I knew Murphy alone wasn't responsible for all that misery. Maybe he hadn't committed any of the other crimes. But he was responsible for what had happened in Atlanta, and for that, he had to pay.

Murphy stood on the sidewalk and looked up and down Peachtree, as if he had expected someone to be waiting for him. His partner who had eluded the cops after the shooting? Could I be that lucky? He stood there for maybe ten minutes, and I still half expected him to head for the impound lot some ten blocks away. Most people released from police custody, for whatever reason, wasted no time in getting as far away from jail as possible. But Charles Murphy wasn't in a hurry. He showed no sign of fear. I could feel my anger rising to an even higher intensity.

I slumped down a little in my seat and kept my eyes riveted on Murphy. About ten minutes later, a Black Lincoln Town Car slid slowly past me, as if the driver was looking for a parking space. Instead, it cruised to a stop across from the police building. Charles Murphy stepped off the curb and darted across Peachtree. He got in on the passenger side, and the Town Car slowly moved out into the traffic. I started the engine on Pat's SUV, and pulled out, about five cars behind Murphy's car. We drove down the road a few blocks, then the Lincoln pulled sharply towards the curb and parked in front of a small mom-and-pop restaurant. Over the doorway, a sign said: "Breakfast 24 Hours a Day" in faded red letters. I was still several cars behind, but was able to pull into the only other parking spot, which left me about sixty or seventy feet from the Lincoln's rear bumper.

Neither Murphy nor the driver exited the car. I was too far back to see them through the tinted windows, but I had to figure they were having a conversation. I reached behind the passenger seat and, luckily, found one of the Falcon's team caps on the floor that my brother always kept around.

Pulling the hat on and down low on my forehead, I stepped out of the truck and walked around behind, then out onto the sidewalk. There was a *USA Today* newspaper box along the curb in front of the restaurant. I walked as casually as I could to the box, praying that I would find the seventy-five cents in change in my pocket that I would need for the paper.

For once luck was riding with me. I dumped the change into the machine and pulled open the door. Grabbing a copy of the paper, I quickly flipped to the Sports section and opened it up to the second page, hoping I looked like a workman scanning baseball scores before moving on. I took a quick look at the Lincoln. Murphy was still inside, but now that I could see the occupants of the car, I could tell they were having a heated discussion. But the A/C must have been on, because as hot as it was becoming, the windows were closed, and I couldn't hear their conversation.

This was taking too long. I was going to have to move on soon. I glanced at the license plate. It was a Georgia plate. I started to repeat the number over and over in my head. "GHN 2836"

When I was sure I had burned it into my memory, I closed up the paper, grabbed the other sections I had laid on the top of the box, and walked into the restaurant. Only one table was occupied, and two people were at the counter. I stood back a few feet from the window, but had a clear view of the Lincoln.

"Anyplace you want," the fry cook behind the counter called out. "Mister?" he said, when I didn't respond. "You want something?"

"Coffee to go," I said, without taking my eyes off the car. "Large, sugar, no cream."

He filled my order and put the coffee down next to the register. I hurriedly paid and stepped back to the window. Charles Murphy was getting out of the car. The window dropped down and the driver pushed a white envelope out. Murphy took it, and the Lincoln pulled away from the curb. Murphy stood there, watching the big car drive away, then he turned and walked to the impound garage.

CHAPTER 23

▼ ─────────────

I was back in the SUV when Murphy pulled out of the garage twenty minutes later, turned right heading for the north-bound on ramp of I-75/85. I followed him up the ramp and allowed him to get comfortably ahead of me, but not so far that I might lose sight of him. It was going to be a long ride, and it's pretty easy to spot a tail if you're looking for one. Every fifteen minutes or so, I would drop back, almost out of sight for a while.

Twenty miles south of the Tennessee border, Murphy pulled off the interstate and into a combination gas station/ McDonalds. I had to fight the urge to follow him in, but I pulled into a Burger King restaurant across the street, and watched while he filled up and went through the drive thru. A little while later, he abruptly drove off the interstate again. I was about a hundred yards behind and starting to get a sinking feeling in the pit of my stomach. Had he finally figured me out? I thought better of following him, and drove past the interchange to the next exit, about three miles north. I pulled off the highway, crossed over the roadway at the bottom of the exit ramp, and then halfway up the on ramp to head north, from where I could see cars heading north, but far enough down the ramp that I could not be easily seen by the drivers as they passed by. I sat there, for about ten minutes wondering if I had overplayed my hand, and waited, hopefully, for Murphy to pass me again. Just when I was about to admit to myself that I had lost him, I saw his beat up vehicle pass by the interchange. He was driving well beyond the speed limit, making it even clearer that he was attempting to lose a tail.

I had to force myself not to floor the accelerator and counted to twenty before heading back onto the Interstate. Murphy's car was almost out of sight, and I gradually increased my speed until I was about three hundred yards behind him, easing in between two trailer trucks.

Outside Chattanooga, we got on I-24 heading west. Things stayed pretty much the same with our little game of hide and seek, which I was hoping

Charles Murphy wasn't aware of. We were on a course which appeared to be taking us toward Nashville until, with a burst of speed and a last second maneuver that almost caused a major accident, Murphy spun out of the inside lane and, with tires shrieking so loudly that I could hear the noise from a hundred yards behind, he threw his car down an off ramp.

My heart sank. I knew he had made me. There was no reason to continue our little game, and I barely got over in the midst of traffic in time to catch the exit. When I reached the bottom of the ramp, Murphy's car was nearly out of sight. I slammed Pat's SUV into a tight right turn and set off in pursuit. Luckily, we were in a rural area and there was little traffic, and I was able to keep Murphy in view most of the time. I looked at the speedometer. We were doing over eighty on a two lane, winding road when we hit an area of old, rundown buildings, and he made a sharp left at a crossroads in the center of the town.

I followed, and within a couple of hundred yards we were back in the vacant landscape of the Tennessee countryside. About a mile further down the road, I lost sight of him around a bend, but a cloud of dust shot up into the air ahead of me and as I hit the brakes and rounded the curve in the road, I came to a dirt path heading east. Murphy was leaving a heavy cloud of dirt behind him as he sped away from me.

I made the turn and slammed down on the gas again. I was getting madder by the moment. Firstly, at myself for having been spotted out on the Interstate, but mostly because I was fearful that this murdering bastard might get away from me, and I knew I might lose any chance of finding out who had sent him to kill me and Bobby Hemphill.

As we hit a "Y" in the road, Murphy swerved right and thundered up the gravel driveway of what looked like a farmhouse, spewing rocks and a cloud of grey dust into the air. Skidding to a stop, Murphy jumped out of the car and ran up rickety steps to the porch, kicked in the door and disappeared inside.

I was barely out of my truck before I drew my .38 and, feeling rage overtake me, I hurried up the steps, threw myself against the door, and pushed into the house. The house had been closed up tight; shades covered the windows, and it was nearly pitch dark. There was the musty, damp odor of a house that had been sweltering in summer heat, with no cooling air having penetrated inside for a long time.

I backed up against a wall in the entranceway, and tried to calm down and get control of my breathing. Feeling the droplets of sweat beginning to course down my forehead, I swept the moisture from my eyes. I stood stock still, and listened. There wasn't a sound to be heard, and I couldn't even begin to guess where Charles Murphy was hiding.

Then the loud "BANG" of a door being kicked open, and a flash of light shot through the darkness from the other end of the house. *He's gone out the back door!* I thought, and began to work my way quickly through the house.

I could see more light, and I knew I was near the rear entrance. Suddenly, as I started to run toward the light, I felt, more than heard, a presence behind me.

Before I could spin around, I felt the rope go tight around my neck, and I was slammed backwards against a hard body. I could feel Murphy's breath on the back of my neck as he strained to keep control of me as I bucked and tried to kick his legs. I dropped my gun and grabbed at the tightening rope, but I couldn't get my fingers between the rope and my neck. I could feel the pressure increasing, and I started to gasp for air. I tried to push back, hoping to slam Murphy against a wall and break his grip, but he was incredibly strong, and I couldn't budge him. Bursts of light shot through my tightly closed eyes as I struggled against him, but I was getting weaker. I couldn't breathe, and I felt my muscles beginning to ache as I strained, unable to get oxygen into my lungs.

I knew I was dying. I couldn't help myself as I slid to the ground on both knees. Voices boomed in my head, and I thought I could hear my name being called. *Abby's calling me,* I thought.

As I felt myself slipping into darkness, I was suddenly thrown forward, my face hitting the ground hard. I felt blood explode from my nose and lips. But there was something else, too. The tightness around my throat was gone. I gasped for air and found I could finally get some.

I tried to swallow, and did, but the pain was intense.

I breathed in the stinking hot air and tried to turn over. Then, I heard my name again, this time louder, and more clearly, as rough hands grabbed my arms and swung me over onto my back. I choked on blood and coughed, spasmodically.

"Tommy! Tom, are you okay?!"

I looked up into the dusky space above me through painful eyes laced with grit and tears. "Pat?" I croaked.

"Jesus, Tommy," my brother said, "look at you! Hold on for a minute," he got to his feet. "Stay down there."

"I can handle that," I heard myself say, in a raspy voice.

Pat's face disappeared for a few minutes, and I lay back, feeling the weakness in my muscles starting to slowly recede. Then he was back.

"Here, kid," he said, and held soft tissues gently against my bloodied lips.

Finally, after a few minutes, I was breathing more normally.

"I think he's okay, now," Pat said "Let's get him sitting up."

"Who....?" I said, realizing he was not alone. I looked up to my left, and there was the beet-red, sweaty face of a very worried looking Max Howard.

Max put his hand under my arm as Pat did the same on the other side.

"Tommy," Max said, with a sigh, as they gently lifted me to a sitting position. "Son, you are gonna' make a drinkin' man outta' me yet!"

"Yeah," I said, quietly, out of swollen lips. "I hear that a lot, lately."

CHAPTER 24

▼

Pat had gone to check the back door.

"I didn't see him anywhere," Pat had reported. "But there's an old barn and some outbuildings about fifty yards from here. I'm gonna' go check them out."

"No! You could get trapped out there. Besides, he knows those buildings and where he could hide. Don't do that, Pat." In my heart, I knew Murphy was long gone.

We had waited awhile until I felt stronger. Then we had got out of the farmhouse and away from the scene of my latest near- death experience, before either the police or Murphy and some of his friends could show up. Now I was stretched out in the back seat of Pat's truck, holding a Burger King soda cup full of melting ice against my bruised face. There wasn't anything available to sooth my bruised ego. Pat was behind the wheel and we were parked outside the National Car Rental building at the Chattanooga airport. Max was inside, returning the car they had used to follow me to Tennessee.

I was feeling pretty depressed about my utter lack of control when faced with the opportunity to corner Murphy, and I was sure my actions had pushed back the investigation, maybe beyond recovery. I sat up and leaned over the front seat.

"Why the hell did you follow me, Pat? You shouldn't have done that."

"Hey, somebody had to be around to save your ass, hotshot."

"Pat, cut the bullshit. Why did you follow me?!"

Pat turned sideways in his seat and looked at me. "Because you wouldn't let me go with you in the first place."

"I didn't want you to," I said, with what belligerence I could still muster.

"Yeah, I know. That's why I did it."

"I'm not one your kids, Pat."

"Hell, I know that!" he laughed. "My kids have more common sense than you do!"

"Cute," I replied, still trying, but failing badly, to be in control. Then I said, quietly, "I didn't want you to come because I didn't want you to be in danger. You got a family, you know? What if something happened to you?"

Pat looked at me, and there was no lightness in the way he spoke. "You're family too, Tommy. You think it would be any easier on us if something happened to *you*? That would destroy our folks, you know. Ma expected me to watch out for you, when she sent you down to Atlanta."

He smiled. "You think I want her mad at me?"

I was quiet for a while. I knew he was right.

"You gonna' call Abby?"

I shook my head. "I don't want to scare her. We'll be home soon enough." I looked at Pat. "How did I screw this up so bad?"

"Back when I was making my living trying to sack quarterbacks for the Falcons," Pat said, "the guys on the defensive line had a saying: the best rush is a team rush."

"How sweet!" I said, sarcastically, but my lips hurt too much for me to sound very convincing. "Just what the hell does that mean?"

"What it means, you moron," he said, with big- brotherly exasperation, "is that when the right side defensive end rushes alone, the QB can go up the middle, or go to his left, and get away. When the left side defensive end rushes alone, the QB can go up the middle, or to his right. If the middle linebacker rushes alone…., well, you get the picture,"

"Yeah, so?"

"So," Pat said, "you don't do by yourself what should be done as a team."

"Is that your way of telling me I should have called for backup?"

"Yup."

"And you couldn't have told me that without one of your stupid football analogies?"

"Life's lessons are best learned by example, grasshopper," Pat said, with the look of a pride- filled teacher on has face.

"I don't know what C.J. ever saw in you," I said, with mock disgust.

"By the way, C.J. called last night. Said it's been tough on Bobby, but Sabine's family has been terrific to him. They'll be coming home day after tomorrow. Their flight's due in around 7 p.m."

"Damn. Don't tell him about this. He'll blame himself for not being with me."

"Oh, right," Pat laughed. "All he has to do is look at you and I think he'll figure it out."

"Well, that won't be a problem, since I don't intend to ever leave my apartment again. How'd you ever get Max involved with this?"

Pat was serious this time. "He insisted on coming," he said. "The man cares about you, Tommy. He knows he put you in danger when he got you involved, and he's worried sick. Besides, it's been a long time since Max and I have just been lawyer and client. He has no family, no one he cares about but the people who work for him, and us. We *are* his family."

I knew that was the truth.

"He's the best," I said.

'Yeah," Pat said, as Max Howard came out of the building and headed toward us. "So, do him a favor, and live through this mess, okay?"

✳   ✳   ✳   ✳

We were about an hour out of Atlanta, and I was dozing in the back seat when I heard Max tell Pat he was going to check in with his office. I heard him ask the receptionist to transfer his call to Coral Mae, his right hand. Then, in my near-fog state, I heard the familiar tones of my own cell, and instinctively reached for the phone, but it wasn't in my pocket. I had left it on the seat of the SUV, and it had probably been thrown to the floor during my high speed chase of Charles Murphy.

I saw my brother reach down, and he came up with the phone, tossing it into the back seat.

It was Jake Berger's number on the call screen.

"Hello," I said, trying to sound like I was fully alert, which I wasn't.

"You sound God awful," Jake said.

"I have been better," I said.

"You'll have to tell me about it someday. In the meantime, I've got a make on that license plate you called in earlier."

I perked up. "What do you have, Jake?"

Max was on the line talking with Coral Mae, and I turned up the volume on my phone so I could hear Jake better.

"Car's registered to a Benton Fielding. Give you the address when you return from wherever you are that I don't want to know about," Jake said, with a chuckle. "But he's an attorney, according to the phone book, with an office in Midtown."

I made a mental note of the name. "Benton Fielding, right, I've got it."

I heard Max say, loudly, "Hold on, Coral Mae!" He turned in his seat, and said, "What did you say, Tommy?"

"Huh?"

Max had a look of surprise on his face.

"Hold on, Jake" I said.

"Coral Mae," Max said, into his phone. "I need to call you back." He hung up.

"You said, Benton Fielding. What about him?"

"He's the guy that was driving Murphy around this morning. What is it, Max? You know this guy?"

Max was thinking. "Yeah, I know him," he said, finally. "He's a big time corporate lawyer."

"Seems weird that a corporate type would be representing a criminal defendant," Pat mused.

"That doesn't bother me half as much as the fact," Max said, "that he's a partner in the same firm as Edgar Harrison."

I felt a cold numbness course up my spine. What, in God's name would the father of Marti Patton have to do with the people who probably killed his daughter? "Are you sure, Max?"

"Dead sure," he said.

CHAPTER 25

▼

August 25, 2003, 1:00 A.M.
Atlanta, Georgia

I was lying on my back, wide awake, on our bed in the little apartment above Ireland's Own. Abby was nestled up against me, her hand resting on my chest. The small lamp on the end table next to me gave the room it's only light. I looked at her. She was watching me with loving, protective eyes. I gave her a weak smile.

"I'm okay, babe," I said.

"You sure I can't get you some more ice?"

"I'm fine, really."

However, my mind wouldn't shut down and let me enjoy being with her. I had begun to believe I was making some sense of all the bits and pieces of this puzzle we were involved in, and then this connection--or whatever it really is--to Edgar Harrison's law firm pops up. I knew one thing for sure: this was too crazy to be just a coincidence.

Abby slid up against the headboard and ran her fingers through my hair.

"What do you think it all means?" she wondered.

"What?"

"This lawyer, Fielding? What's his connection to all this?"

I love that about Abby. I had told her the truth about what had happened, just like always, and I know she is worried about me. I know this latest episode has scared her, but she's not going to let me dwell on what happened, or what might have been.

"Well," she said. "Isn't it possible he represented this Murphy before?"

I shook my head. "No. His firm doesn't have a criminal defense group. Never done any work like that, according to Max. They're strictly big ticket corporate types." I sighed. "Besides, even if they did, they would never have anything to do with scum like Murphy. They would be handling white- collar stuff."

I sat up beside her, and she took my hand.

"If garbage like Charles Murphy get arrested and charged, they're assigned a public defender at best. "Of course, now that I've lost him, we may never get a chance to nail him again."

"Maybe it's as simple as someone hiring Fielding just to get Murphy out of jail?"

"I don't think so," I said. "Besides, a criminal attorney would have done it with no questions asked."

"So what *is* the connection?"

"I'll be damned if I can figure it out, Abby. Is he involved with this group of maniacs? Is his firm? Is Elmer Harrison involved? I can't believe he would be. But it makes no sense for guys like that to get involved unless they had something to gain...or protect."

She sighed. "What's the next step, then?"

"I wish I knew."

We sat there together in silence for a few minutes. "Bobby and C.J. are coming home soon." I said. "Maybe he can think of a way to find Murphy and his friends."

"Don't worry," Abby said, with complete confidence. "You can find them. You're a great detective, you know."

I laughed. "And you know that how?"

"Well," she said, as she reached across me and turned off the light. "After all, you found me, didn't you?"

✱   ✱   ✱   ✱

Later, while Abby slept, I lay awake unable to shut down my thoughts. There were so many questions, and so few answers. I glanced at the clock. It was just past three in the morning. No sounds came up the stairway from Ireland's Own, no heavy traffic noises from Peachtree Street. The world seemed at rest, but as long as the murderers of so many innocent people were moving freely among us, I faced many sleepless nights. And the face that haunted me belonged to Charles Murphy.

Abby would be getting up for her classes at Tech in a few hours, and I was afraid my tossing and turning would wake her, so I got out of bed and padded quietly out to the living room. I stood at the window overlooking a nearly deserted Peachtree, but I wasn't really seeing the landscape of Buckhead spread out before me. I was looking inward, trying to recap the day: what went right, what went wrong. It wasn't a pretty picture.

There had to be answers. The problem was finding them quickly. I knew, very deep in my heart, that the murders weren't over. The calls from Jake Berger would keep coming. Montgomery? Jacksonville? Dallas? Savannah? Somewhere out there, people were going to die.

First things first, I thought to myself. There were questions about today that might lead to answers tomorrow, but I had to answer for my own actions, first.

Up until Murphy had shot off the interstate in a rural section of Tennessee, I was pretty sure he was unaware that he was being followed. But things had taken too many strange twists and turns after that.

I went over to my little desk and grabbed a legal pad and a pen. I drew a line down the center of the top page of the pad and marked one side "Questions," and the other side "Possible Answers."

I sat down, and began to write. Question: Why did Murphy get off at that particular exit? Question: why did he take that particular turn at the fork in the road, and drive into that particular property? Question: how did he know the property was abandoned? Question: how was he able to get around in the farmhouse in the dark so easily? Question: how, after abandoning his car in the driveway, was he able to disappear so easily in the open fields behind the house?

The "Answers" column was conspicuous in its emptiness. But, the more I thought about it, the more questions continued to come to me, as my subconscious started to let loose of some of the details that I had forgotten.

There was something. What was it? Something that seemed strange to me at the time. I replayed the events of the day again and again, but just couldn't pull it back from the recesses of my memory.

And then, I did. At about 6 a.m., possibly because I was too tired to think about immediate things, I remembered what had seemed so strange to me.

I grabbed the phone and dialed Max Howard's cell.

"Sorry to call so early. Max," I said, when he answered. "Hope I didn't wale you."

"No," he answered. "Don't sleep much anymore. What's up, Tommy?"

I collected my thoughts. "Max, do you remember just before we got out of the farmhouse, you brought me some ice to put on my lip?"

"Sure. You were swollen up pretty good."

"Yes, but where did you get the ice?"

"Where? Well, from Burger King," he replied. "We had some drinks in the car from when we got off the freeway to follow Murphy after you had to pass by him. Why?"

"Do you remember what you said to me when you brought me the ice? Because I swear I remember you saying that there wasn't any ice in the fridge in the kitchen. Am I right?"

Max said, "Yeah, that's right. There wasn't any ice. But why is that important?"

"Because, you said that there wasn't any ice. You didn't say the refrigerator was *off*, or that there wasn't any power."

Max was quiet for a minute.

"Damn! You're right, Tommy. The light wasn't on, but the air in the fridge was running, and it was plenty cold! That means the place wasn't abandoned. We just never thought to turn on a dang light."

"So," I said. "That means Murphy was leading me there on purpose. But, why? If he was looking to trap me, why go somewhere like that? Unless…"

"Unless what?"

"Did Murphy use a phone back at the interchange when you followed him?"

Max was quiet for a few seconds. "I guess he could have. He went into one of those gas station/ Burger Kings. That's when we got the drinks from the drive-thru. There surely were phones inside."

It was beginning to make sense. "I'm betting that he was calling ahead, trying to get some of his pals to meet him at the farm house to help trap me."

"I think you're right, Tommy. Let me talk to Jake. Maybe he knows someone up there he can trust that might be able to take another look around the place."

"Call me back, Max."

I hung up. As I turned to go get dressed, Abby was standing in the bedroom doorway, wrapped in a towel, fresh from her shower.

"You heard?"

She nodded. "Thomas," she said, thoughtfully. "Was the house furnished?"

"Furnished?" I asked. "Well, we were only in the living room and kitchen," I said. "But, yeah, I guess it was. Why?"

"How was it furnished?" she questioned.

"How?" I thought for a moment. "Old stuff, old couch against the wall." I searched my memory.

Lots of chairs. Those cheap folding ones."

"In the living room?"

"Yeah," I said. "What are you getting at, Abby?"

"How were they arranged?"

"Arranged? Mostly against the wall, as I remember," I said. "There must have been twenty or more."

She smiled. "That wasn't somebody's residence, Thomas. That was a meeting place."

★   ★   ★   ★

Washington, D.C.
Grand Hotel Dinning Room
7:00 P.M.

Arthur Ellis was incensed. He had received the call moments before a dinner meeting with a major contributor to his campaign fund, and now he was struggling to keep his mind on his dinner companion's conversation. The near-constant pain in his joints was flaring up again, but he dare not reach for the vile of strong pain pills in his pocket. He had learned long ago, that you could never show weakness of any kind when you were soliciting funds from your constituents. But the pain, and the worrisome call he had received from Nashville took his attention away.

"Are you all right, Senator?" his companion was saying.

"Humm?" Ellis said, realizing that the man was watching him closely. "Oh, yes, Richard," he said. "Sorry, my friend. There's something I need to handle for the majority whip, and it hasn't been done. Would you please excuse me for a minute? I need to check on that."

"Of course, Arthur. Would you like to use my phone? I know you don't carry one."

"Old habits die hard," Ellis forced a smile. "No, I'm afraid I must do this privately."

Ellis left the dining room and found a pay phone booth in the hall off the dining room, and dialed the private office number of Congressman Gerald Greenway. He knew the Congressman never left his office before eight p.m., and on cue, Greenway answered on the third ring.

"How could you let this happen?" Ellis blurted into the phone when he heard Greenway's voice.

The Congressman had obviously been expecting the call. "I will not discuss this now, Arthur, he said, stopping the Senator cold. "Not over an open line," he said, caution in his voice.

Ellis was exasperated by the calmness in Greenway's voice. "You cannot push me off on this, Gerald!" he said.

"I'm busy, Arthur. I have a dinner engagement in an hour."

"Dinner!" Ellis exclaimed, fighting the urge to scream out the word. He fought to calm himself. "Is it possible you do not understand how close you have brought us to disaster?"

"Nonsense," Greenway said, calmly. "Now, excuse me, Arthur, I said I'm busy."

Ellis felt desperation rising. "Wait! We must discuss this right now!"

"No," Greenway said. "Not over the phone." Again, there was a warning in his tone. He could sense Ellis losing control. It worried him, but gave him a touch of pleasure at the same time.

The Senator tried a different tack. "Then we have to meet right now."

"I told you, I have a dinner meeting in an hour."

Ellis was nearly pleading now. "You can spare a few minutes, Gerald. Please!"

Greenway let him hang for nearly a minute, and Ellis began to fear that he had hung up.

"Twenty minutes. The usually place," the Congressman said, quietly.

"Yes," Ellis let out a breath. "The usual place."

He hung up, and went back to the dining room to make his excuses. Five minutes later, he was hailing a cab.

Senator Arthur Ellis sat on the concrete bench across the reflecting pool from the Jefferson Memorial. There were still a large number of tourists around the monument, but few were walking near where he sat waiting impatiently. Congressman Greenway was ten minutes late, and Ellis felt the fear growing again. Greenway was going to stand him up. The younger man had been acting on his own initiative far too often of late. This ridiculous obsession with the Atlanta detectives was becoming a dangerous game.

Ellis felt the drip of sweat sliding down his brow as the humid August air engulfed him like a heavy blanket. Greenway needed to be put in his place; to be reigned in. His ego wasn't important, only the Cause. Ellis heard the footsteps then, and turned to face the Congressman.

"Arthur," the Greenway said, quietly, as he sat down. "I am very short on time. What is it you want?"

"What I want, Gerald, is an explanation! Recent events have gotten out of control, and you are putting our Cause in jeopardy."

"Nonsense," Greenway said, quietly. "That problem is being corrected. In any case, it is you who is causing the problems."

"What are you talking about?!" Ellis shot back, through clenched teeth. "I'm not the one who sent those fools to Atlanta! I'm not the one…"

"Quiet!" Greenway shot back, then stopped to let a family of visitors walk by. "I told you, that is being handled. Listen, Arthur. You are the one who set the rules for our people. You wanted this foolish 'initiation' arrangement. What kind of clientele did you think that was going to buy us?"

Greenway gave him a disgusted look.

"Listen to me, Senator," he whispered. "Within the next two weeks, there will be at least three more 'incidents', which means there will be three more groups looking *for the money they were promised. Right now, all the groups that are in place are already buying people and influence in their respective states, and they're using their own money to do it. But they expect us to deliver what we promised, and soon."*

Greenway stopped again as more tourists passed by. "Believe me, Arthur, if we don't deliver, you and I are going to wind up dead!"

Ellis felt the sweat running down his brow. "What are you talking about, Gerald?! Our friends will wait until we are prepared to pay them. These men are patriots like..."

The Congressman grunted a laugh. "Arthur, you are such a fool," he said, with distain.

"Gerald...," Ellis started, but Greenway cut him off, and moved within inches of Ellis' face.

"Now, you listen to me! Those men are not patriots, Arthur. They are businessmen, and illegitimate businessmen at that, willing to commit murder without hesitation, in order to accomplish their aims! They don't care about this great Cause of yours. They are taking our money because they will use it to make more money, by controlling the districts assigned to them! For that, they will deliver you your precious new Confederacy. But you had better get it through your head that they will not wait much longer. And our lives are at stake, Arthur. You had better believe that!"

Ellis was stunned by the vicious tone in Greenway's voice, but the words stung even more. Was it possible Greenway didn't understand how sacred the Cause was to everyone involved?

"Where is the gold, Arthur?" Greenway asked, quietly, a moment later. He was deadly serious in what he had said, but rational enough to know he still needed the Senator.

"I have the map," Ellis said, suddenly wary of the Congressman, and needing to keep his answer simple. "And we are working on all the marked locations. But there are several of them, and it takes time."

Greenway shook his head, slowly. "We don't even know if the map is real."

"Of course it's real, Gerald! That document has been passed down to generations of true believers, just for this moment in history. Naturally, you could not expect those who made it to make it too simple and risk the treasure of the Confederacy being found by the undeserving!"

Gerald Greenway looked into Arthur Ellis' eyes one last time. "Find it, Arthur," he said, calmly. "Do it soon, or we will do it for you."

Ellis started to protest Greenway's words, but the Congressman stood and walked into the dense summer night.

CHAPTER 26

───────────── ▼ ─────────────

August 26, 2003, Morning
Atlanta, Georgia

Abby and I spent a quiet night having dinner with her mom, Maria, and were back at the apartment by 9 p.m. I was still sore from my run-in with Charles Murphy, but otherwise healed. The red marks on my neck remained, and I caught Abby watching me intently a couple of times during the evening. But, true to form, neither she nor Maria voiced their concern. For my own part, I tried to keep up a reasonably carefree demeanor. I wasn't kidding anybody.

At 7 a.m. this morning, Abby reluctantly left for her classes after assuring herself as best she could, that I wasn't suicidal. I was just out of the shower, when Max called and asked me, without explaining why, to hustle down to his office.

I arrived a little after eight, and Max was waiting to usher me into the conference room. Coffee and donuts were on the big table, and Jake Berger was standing over the speaker phone. He nodded to me, and spoke into the phone.

"We're all here now," he said, and then looked at me. "For purposes of brevity, and plausible deniability on your part, if it should come to that, I'm not going to introduce you to the man on the other end. Suffice it to say, we served in the Gulf War together, and he is trained in special ops. That satisfactory to you, Tom?"

I looked at Max, questioningly, but he only nodded.

"Okay, sure," I said, and took a seat across from where Jake stood.

"Go ahead," Jake said.

The man on the other end of the line spoke. His voice was military, and commanding. He wasn't waiting for questions.

"At 0200 hours this morning," the voice said, "four operatives with me in charge were deposited by a fifth man about a half mile from the target."

I looked at Max, and he mouthed the word, "farmhouse."

"We worked our way through the surrounding fields to a position in the wooded area about sixty yards from the target. We set up an observation post with night vision equipment, and watched for approximately ninety minutes. No vehicles were on site when we arrived, and none appeared during that time period," the voice went on.

So this is what Max had in mind when he mentioned asking Jake Berger to have someone check out the farmhouse in Tennessee. I wondered if he had done this to keep me from going back there.

"At 0330 hours, I sent a team of two operatives up to the house. They entered from the rear door." the voice went on. "They found the place empty, and I entered with my other man. We went through all the rooms, including three bedrooms upstairs that were set up with several cots each, but it appears that no one has stayed there recently. We did find a three day old *USA Today*, and a couple old gun magazines."

"So it looks like we've got ourselves a meeting, or even a safe house location," Jake said.

"I'd say so," his friend went on.

"Any idea where this Murphy fellow hid outside after we showed up?" Max said. "He disappeared in a flash."

"My guess is he never left," came over the line.

"What?" I said, surprised at the statement. "I don't understand. What are you getting at?"

"When we checked out the first level, we found a pantry closet in the kitchen."

"So?" I said. "What? Are you telling me he was hiding in the pantry?"

"Not exactly," the voice said. "The pantry was only two feet deep. But the interior was a false front. It slid back into the wall, exposing a stairway which led to a small basement room."

"Jesus," Max said. "That possibility never crossed my mind."

"We figure this Murphy threw open the rear door to make you think he was escaping into the fields and woods back there, then slipped into the kitchen, slid back the false wall of shelves in the pantry, and hid out down in the basement until you left the premises. After he was sure you were gone, it would have been a simple thing to get in his car and drive away."

We sat in silence for a full minute before the voice went on. "I found some pamphlets in the basement you need to see. Give me an address, and I'll send you down some."

"Pamphlets?" Max said.

"You've got yourselves a group of guys that don't know the Civil War is over, Jake. Some group called 'The Eleven,' whatever that means."

Berger looked at Max, then me.

"We thought it might be something like that," he said, and gave his friend a mailing address where he could send the pamphlets by overnight.

"At 0500 hours, we moved back into the woods, and packed up. But we left two operatives in place with photographic and night vision equipment."

"Good," Jake said. "Maybe we'll get lucky and pick up the faces and license numbers of any visitors."

"We already did," the voice stated. "No more than twenty minutes after we left the target. That's what is so strange."

"Strange?" I heard myself say.

"Yeah," the voice said. "There were two guys. They were County Sheriff Department personnel and they arrived in a squad car, in full uniform. They just walked in, using a key they appeared to have brought with them, and twenty minutes later, they came out carrying a box. It was the same box we found in the safe room. They knew exactly what they were doing, Jake."

We sat there in stunned silence.

Finally, Max said, "If the cops are involved with these guys......." The thought went unfinished, but we all understood what he was thinking.

The voice spoke again, "I don't know what you've got yourselves into, Jake, but you better be very careful."

*   *   *   *

After Jake's friend had promised to send the pictures of the two county cops with the pamphlets found in the farmhouse, we ended the phone call. The three of us sat there, lost in our own thoughts, each trying to decide the best course of action.

After awhile, Jake said, "Are we really surprised about this? After every incident, we've had near silence from law enforcement in every town. The Nashville cops pretty much buried the true facts of Carl Lee Wiggins' death along with his body. There's almost no information available from police sources or the internet on a series of multiple murders." He shook his head. "I didn't want to believe this thing was so widespread, but the truth has been right there in front of us, and we had better stop kidding ourselves."

"Isn't this even more reason to get the Feds involved?" I said. "Isn't it time we told them what we've been doing, and got some help?"

Max shook his head, sadly. "If we can't trust the police, how can we trust the Feds?"

"Max," I pleaded, softly, "we can't handle this."

"I can't, Tommy," he said. "I owe it to Willie Patton's family to make sure no one gets away with this! I'll understand if you want out, but I can't do that."

I think he knew in his heart that I would never do that to him, but I said so anyway.

"I'm in as long as you are, Max. I guess I just don't know what to do next."

Jake said: "We do what we've been doing, and wait for a break. If the time comes when we have to bring the FBI in, we'll make that determination then." He sighed. "Maybe we'll get something out of these pamphlets."

"I think we all know what those things are going to say," Max said, disgustedly. "Just a lot of hate garbage, written by a bunch of delusional clowns."

"True," I said, quietly, "but those 'clowns' are responsible for a lot of deaths." I sighed. 'Anyway, we might get an idea about what this 'Eleven' stuff is all about."

"I think I've got that figured out, now," Max said. "Bobby was right about the murders all happening in the South, although I don't think we were really convinced that was the case back when we first started this. But the new cases since then all happened down here as well."

I was beginning to see where he was going with this, and it all fit, especially after my conversation with Bobby Hemphill's father.

"There were eleven states in the original Confederacy," I said, softly.

"Yes," Max said, "there were."

$$* \quad * \quad * \quad *$$

"What, in God's name, is this all about, Max?'

We were alone in the conference room, the meeting over and Jake Berger was on his way back to his office. A melancholy had settled over us, and I knew we were still hitting brick walls in this investigation.

"Are we really supposed to believe there is some sinister, one hundred forty year old society of wacko's out there killing innocent people in the name of some long-dead ideals? What kind of people come up with something like this? What can they be trying to achieve?" I felt completely stymied by the latest information we had just been listening to. Cops involved with killers on a scale this large? Could that be possible?

"If we knew what the aim was we might be able to formulate a realistic answer to those questions, Tommy," Max said. "But I'll be damned if I can figure out what they, whoever 'they' are, are up to."

"Well, I guess we need to see what this stuff is that Jake's friend is shipping to us."

"Good a place to start as any, even though it doesn't seem like much," Max said. "Like you say, maybe there will be something of value there."

I glanced at my watch. Still several long hours before Bobby and C.J. would be landing at Hartsfield. I suddenly felt tired from lack of sleep, and an overwhelming sense of frustration.

"What do you want to do?" Max asked.

I tried to give him a smile. "Just like Jake says. We keep on doing what we're doing."

He nodded, but I could see it in his eyes: a sense of purpose, and, I thought, relief that he wasn't going it alone.

My cell phone broke the silence.

"Hello."

"Mr. Patrick? Mr. Thomas Patrick?" The female voice was soft and steady, and sounded of culture and refinement.

"Yes, this is Thomas Patrick. Who is this?"

The voice hesitated for a moment.

"You don't know me, sir." Again, a hesitation. "But you visited my sister a few days ago. Do you remember?"

There had only been one person that Bobby and I had met with recently. I felt an involuntary moment of fear. "Yes, of course," I said, quickly, afraid to ask. "Is she okay? What's happened to her?"

"She is fine, Mr. Patrick. Scared, but otherwise, fine." The voice didn't offer a name. "I don't like seeing her scared." she said, simply.

"Yes," I said. "I know, and I'm truly sorry about that. It's my fault."

"I know you were doing what you had to do," she said, and her voice softened. "But I wanted you to know the cost of all this."

"People are dying," I said, quietly. "I wish to God it wasn't happening, and I wish your family could have been spared all of this, but it's real, ma'am. Honestly, I don't know if I can stop it, but I have to try."

The voice was silent for a while, as if trying to gauge my sincerity. Then: "My sister asked me to call you from my workplace Mr. Patrick. She is afraid to use the phone at home."

"If there's anything I can...."

"We found something," the voice said, and I felt the nerves along my spine fire. I let her talk.

"The police came to the house to tell us about the break-in at her home, just like you said they would. They asked a lot of questions about Carl Lee and my sister, and even questioned me about their relationship, and how often she had seen him in the days before he was killed."

"I was concerned they might do that," I said. I was anxious to know what they had found, but I didn't want to push her. "I hope they weren't too rough on the two of you."

"They said they were investigating the break-in," she said. "But they were asking too many questions unrelated to anything that had happened. I said Carl Lee's dead, so why are you asking about things that don't matter anymore. That's when they finally left, but since then, we've seen strange cars parked nearby for hours at a time."

I had been afraid of that. I was surprised that her house hadn't been ransacked like the Wiggin's house before now. Maybe they hadn't known where Grace Wiggins was living, until I had led them right to her. There wasn't much I could say.

"Anyway," she went on, "we went to the house to get it cleaned up and get the door fixed. It was while we were cleaning up that we found the key."

I felt my heart skip a beat. "Key?"

"Yes. It had been buried in the soil of a plant that had been knocked over the night of the break-in. My sister had never seen it before, but I knew right away what it was."

"Ma'am," I said, trying to keep the excitement I was felling welling up in me at bay. "This might be very important. What was the key used for?"

"I work in a bank, Mr. Patrick. I see these keys every day. It was a key to a safe- deposit box. I especially knew this key, because I recognized it as one of ours."

"My God. And your sister didn't know about the box?"

"No sir," she answered. "I checked the records myself, and Carl Lee had not put her on the list for access."

"But wouldn't the bank have notified the authorities about the box after Carl Lee died?"

"Yes, but it takes time before these things work their way through the system. And, anyway, somebody has to be watching out for these things. This time, they didn't."

Finally, I thought, we might have caught a break.

"What did you do with the key, ma'am?"

"Yesterday, during the time the assistant who handles the safe-deposit boxes was at lunch, I took the bank's key and the one we found, matched up the box number from the files and went to empty the box." She sighed "I would never have thought to do something like that under any other circumstance, Mr. Patrick."

It was as if she was apologizing for breaking bank rules.

"You did the right thing, ma'am," I told her, quietly. "What was in the box?"

She hesitated, but only for a moment. "There were only four sheets of paper. Standard letter size, but for copying things. Tracing paper, I guess you would call it. You could see through the paper."

I was mystified. "Tracing paper? Was there anything on the sheets?"

"Yes. It appeared to be a tracing of a map of some kind. The sheets had been put over what I believe was a map, but it only showed a long line, maybe a road, connecting several city names, then extending farther to a spot where the letters 'C.I.' appears."

"A road," I mused. "Were the pages you found attached to each other?"

"No," she said, "but if you put them next to each other in a certain way, they did appear to be a continuation of the line. It was like one sheet had not been enough to cover what was on the original."

"You said there are city names?"

"Yes: Richmond, Danville, Atlanta, and a few others."

"Is there anything else on the sheets?" I said, hopefully.

She thought about it. "Only some 'x' s along the line. Several of them actually. Oh, and a 'star'-shaped symbol, next to the word 'Ir'ville,' or something like that." She seemed to be thinking. "And a few numbers and other markings, but I have no idea what they mean."

"Nothing else you can decipher?"

"No. There was one thing, though," she said. "There is a group of letters and numbers at the top of one page. Wait, I wrote them down."

I heard papers being shuffled.

"Here it is: PJDNBF465. Does that mean anything to you?"

"No," I said, disappointedly. "It doesn't. Ma'am, where are the pages you found, now?"

"I sent them to the address on your card by Federal Express this morning," she said. "You should have them tomorrow."

"Good," I said. "Thank you for your help."

"I also got rid of any evidence of the box belonging to Carl Lee."

"I think that was a good idea."

There was a silence on the other end of the line for nearly a minute, then, Grace Wiggin's sister spoke.

"Mr. Patrick, I know it would break my sister's heart, but I have to know. The questions the police asked….was Carl Lee…. dirty?" She asked the question with concern, and trepidation.

"No, ma'am," I replied. "He was one of the good guys."

CHAPTER 27

$\blacktriangledown$

Abby was the first to spot C.J. as she came out of the Jamaica Air terminal. We were parked along the curb about thirty yards from the door, and she walked over to us. C.J. gave us both a big smile and a hug.

"Where's Bobby?"

"Getting the luggage. She and Abby got into the rear of Pat's Suburban. "It was just coming up."

I was afraid to ask, but I got in behind the wheel, and turning to her asked: "How's he doing?"

She gave a small shrug. "I don't think I really understood how hard this was on him until the day of the funeral," she said. "I've never seen Bobby so despondent. But he got through it, with the help of a lot of wonderful people. Sabine's mom was fantastic. She really took him to her heart."

I was relieved to hear that, and for a moment I wasn't thinking about the problems we were facing.

"You've had an interesting week," my sister-in-law said, slyly, and it all came back to me. "Patrick filled me in on the phone last night about what happened to you."

My heart sank. "I wish he hadn't told you while you were away. I didn't want you to worry. Does Bobby know?"

"No, I thought it best not to put anything else on him last night. Leaving Barbados was going to be hard enough."

"Yeah. I've got to find a way to keep him out of this for awhile. Give him a chance to get back on his feet."

C.J. shook her head.

"Don't do that, Thomas," she said, seriously. "Bobby needs to get back into this thing you're doing and help you. The sooner, the better."

"She's right," Abby said. "It won't do him any good to wallow in the pain of losing Sabine, as well as feeling useless to you." She gave me a knowing smile. "Thomas, do you remember how you felt when I was in Cuba, and you didn't know how you would find me...or *if* you would find me?"

"I'll never forget it," I said, and meant it.

I saw Bobby come out of the terminal, and blew the horn. He saw us and started over, and I got out to help him stow their luggage.

He looked a little worn out, which didn't surprise me, but otherwise he seemed okay. We put the bags in the back, and he gave me a wan smile and a hug, and I was suddenly struck with how glad I was to see him. He poked his head through Abby's open window, and gave her a kiss, and we climbed back into the truck.

"Glad you're back," I said.

"Yeah, me too," he sighed. "I feel like I've been away a very long time."

We pulled out into traffic and made our way to the on-ramp of I-85, and headed back to Buckhead. We rode in an uncomfortable silence for awhile, then Bobby said: "What's been happening here?"

I had been dreading the question. "Pretty quiet, right now," I said.

"Uh huh," Bobby said, as he cupped my chin with his left hand and turned my still lumpy, and slightly discolored face towards him.

"You wanna' tell me about *that*?" he said, with a knowing smile.

I heard Abby chuckle.

"No," I said, sheepishly.

And then, I did.

*   *   *   *

I pitched in at Ireland's Own for the night so that Pat could join Bobby, C.J., and the kids for dinner at her parent's home. We were busy until nearly closing time, so I was able to avoid thinking about everything that had happened over the last few days, for a little while. Business slowed down about 1:00 a.m., and I headed upstairs, thinking that I was tired enough to sleep for a week. But two hours later, I was still awake, sitting in my ratty old chair in our little living room overlooking a quiet Peachtree Street.

Abby was sound asleep, only a few hours away from waking to get ready for the final day of classes for the week, so I was all alone to ruminate once again on the events that were overtaking my life.

The thoughts that went through my head centered on the two packages being delivered by overnight in the morning. One, the package from Jake Berger's friend, would be delivered to him, so I would have to wait to hear from him on its contents. But the other, from Grace Wiggin's sister, would arrive downstairs around 10 a.m. I kept vacillating between the excitement and hope for the arrival of useful information, and the fear of crushing disappointment. But at least there was, for a few hours, something to look forward to which might be helpful. I could be thankful at least, that for now, Carl Lee's wife had not been threatened---or worse, however, I knew that this was no guarantee of her long term safety. She was still in danger. Frankly I was amazed no attempt had been made to search her house already. It was for sure, though, that they were being watched. If anyone found out that these women had found something, however inconsequential that "something" turned out to be, I felt sure the people looking for Carl Lee's files would press them to their utter limits.

Bobby was back, and that was good. I knew C.J. and Abby were right about his needing to get his life back to normal as soon as possible. I also knew that it would help me to have someone with whom I could share the burden of all that was happening.

I had finally dozed off in my chair sometime after 4 a.m., and probably would have slept a long time if Abby hadn't woke me up at seven, and forced me to go to bed for awhile, but I couldn't go back to sleep and somehow, in my fatigue- induced stupor, I made it to the shower, where I stood under the hot water for what must have been twenty minutes. When I had dried off, I went back into the bedroom, there was a steaming cup of coffee sitting on my nightstand, and Abby was gone. Beside the cup of coffee, there was a note in Abby's handwriting. It said: "breathe, just breathe." I smiled for what seemed like the first time in days. Her mom, Maria, had once told me that when Abby was away from us, being held for ransom in Cuba, and she didn't know what to do to relieve the horrible tension, she would find a quiet place, to sit alone, and just breathe, deeply, and slowly. This simple act of gaining control of herself and her emotions helped to put everything in perspective. Abby was telling me to do the same.

Had I lost perspective? Maybe. Could I regain control of myself and my emotions? I honestly didn't have a clue. I was sure of only one thing: nothing I had done up 'til now had stopped one innocent person from dying. Willie Patton and his wife, Marti, and their unborn child were dead. And Carl Lee. And Sabine Metaine, not to mention the innocent people who had been strolling down Peachtree when we were attacked. Even worse, I know the death count could have been higher. I nearly lost Bobby and Abby the night Sabine died, and I had put Grace Wiggins and her sister in danger. And what might have happened if my brother and Max had showed up to save me in a farmhouse outside Chattanooga, and walked into a trap set by Charles Murphy and his friends?

Yet, try as I might, I couldn't think of anything I could have done that might have changed what had happened. And I still didn't have any idea of what to do next. My whole plan was to hope that information on its way to me would help me find the right direction.

It was deathly quiet in the apartment, and I wished I had spent time with Abby instead of in the shower. It was always a lonely place when she wasn't around but now it seemed even worse, with so much on my mind, and no one to share it with.

It would be at least another two hours before FedEx dropped off the package from Grace Wiggins' sister. I decided to try and get rid of some of the pent-up anxiety I was feeling, so I threw on some sweats, strapped on a pair of training gloves, and started to throw some light punches at the hanging bag I had brought with me from Cleveland. Finally, I started to feel the light line of sweat forming on my forehead, and I increased the power and speed of my punches. The bag swung back and forth as I increased the intensity of my workout a little more. I felt the sting of sweat rolling down my back, and on my face and arms. It felt good, like they always tell you exercise is supposed to feel, but rarely does.

I kept up the pace for another twenty minutes, then brought myself down slowly to my original pace. The bag moved less, and then to an almost stand-still position. I grabbed the bag with both arms, pulling it tight against my chest, and breathed deeply a few times. I was standing there, eyes shut, holding onto the bag, when I heard my cell phone ring. I grabbed a towel from the chair near the hanging bag, tossed it over my shoulder, and went to the bedroom to fetch it.

"Yeah, Jake?" I said, into the phone quickly, recognizing his number on the lit screen.

"You been out jogging?" he said. "You sound out of breath."

"Just a little hand-eye training, while I've been trying to keep my head from exploding,"

He chuckled. "Know the feeling."

"What have you got?" I said, hopefully.

"We've got two county cops with undistinguishable faces, but we can read the cruiser number clearly. Should be easy to find out who was using that car at that time of the morning. My friend will put a tail on them for the next few days. See what we get out of that."

"How about the stake-out?"

"Still in place, but no new visitors," Jake said. "They'll keep watching, but I doubt old Charlie Murphy's going to be showing up there for awhile."

I knew he was right. "He's the key, isn't he?"

"Would make it a lot easier," Jake said, with a sigh. "At least we know who he is. Could be he might lead us to someone higher up in the food chain."

"You don't sound hopeful," I said.

"No, I'm not."

"What about the pamphlet?" I said.

"A little more enlightening, if you're interested in hysterical, inaccurate, hate- filled recruiting information."

"Recruiting?"

"Yup," he said. "Max was right. These guys are trying to put together the Confederacy again, at least in principle, if you can believe that. Looks like they believe blacks are the root cause of all our problems and, according to this crap, they were much happier when they were pickin' cotton and dancing. And these guys don't like Hispanics or the Federal Government much, either."

"So, 'The Eleven' really does stand for the Confederate states, huh?" I sighed. "This is nuts, Jake."

"Yeah, but a lot of problems have been caused throughout the world by nut jobs."

"So what are they after, Jake?" I said. "They can't really believe they can convince several million Americans to secede from the Union again, can they?"

"Don't ever discount what a bunch of zealots can believe they can do, Tom." He warned. "At the very least, they can damage a lot of innocent people."

"But what do they accomplish with these senseless killings?"

He was quiet for a moment. "I don't know," he said, finally.

A thought hit me. One I really didn't want to even consider.

"Jake, what if we're wrong?"

"What do you mean?"

"What if these bozos are just that? What if they're just a bunch of idiots, and the shooting on Peachtree was a random act of drug or alcohol induced violence?" I said. "What if they have nothing to do with all these murders?"

"Then," Jake Burger said, "we've been wasting our time chasing the wrong people. But I just don't think so." Frankly, Tom, I don't think you believe that's possible, either."

The apartment phone rang. "Hold on, Jake," I said, into the cell and answered the other phone.

"Tommy," my brother, Pat, said, without preamble. "You're package is here."

✴   ✴   ✴   ✴

Jake promised to meet me at Pat's restaurant after he had called Max and asked him to join us. I called Bobby's line at the Hemphill residence. He answered on the first ring. It didn't surprise me. I figured he wasn't sleeping very well these days. With everyone on their way over, I headed down to Ireland's Own to pick up the overnight envelope from Grace Wiggins' sister, subconsciously breathing a sigh of relief that it had gotten here without incident. Nothing could have happened to it after it was in FedEx's possession, but I had worried about it anyway.

Pat was waiting for me at the bar, and handed over the thin envelope. It didn't look big enough to contain anything of real importance, but I tried not to think in those terms. The smallest piece of paper might hold the answers to all our problems. Or not. I told him that everyone was on their way over.

"I'll watch for them," Pat said. "Why don't you take the back room? I shouldn't need to seat anyone back there 'til noon or so. I'll send back some coffee, and send Robbie out for some donuts."

I was on my second cup of coffee when Bobby showed up. He took a cup and then flipped on one of the ceiling-mounted TVs, switching the channel to the CNN weather report. The sound was turned down, but the weather map, showing a big number "96" pasted over the Atlanta area, said it all.

"That's nearly two weeks straight in the mid- nineties," he said. "Tell me again why I used to like this kind of heat."

Max came through the door. "Bobby!" he said, with genuine affection, and gave him a big bear hug. "Good to see you, son."

"You, too, Max," Bobby said. "You, too."

We sat down to wait for Jake Berger. I had decided to wait to open the package from Nashville until we were all together, and the FedEx envelope lay in front of me, with each of us wondering what we would find inside.

Ten minutes later, Jake came through the door. "What's the good word?" he said, with a tired smile.

"We got *Krispy Kremes* coming," I said.

"Then it's gonna' be a good day."

I poured everyone coffee, and we sat around the table. "Might as well get started," I said, pulling the tab opener on the FedEx package, and then carefully removing several sheets of flimsy-eight-and-a-half by eleven tracing paper. There was also a sheet of stationery from a bank, which I supposed was the one where the safe deposit box had been found.

"What is it?" Bobby asked.

"Pretty much the same explanation Grace Wiggins' sister gave me over the phone. I guess she was afraid she might not get to talk to me before the package arrived." I put the letter down, and laid out the remaining pages. "Let's see what we've got here."

As the letter said, each page was numbered at the top, one through four. The long line was there, and I was able to match it up into a continuing trail across the four sheets of paper. The symbols Grace's sister had mentioned where there, as well. We crowded around the crude drawing, each of us trying to guess what significance it held.

"What do you think?" Max said.

"Damned if I know," I said. "But it definitely looks like an overlay of a map. Don't have an idea what it signifies, though."

"Up here, on top," Jake said. "Says 'Richmond.' Let's consider that to be Virginia's Richmond, which seems like a good bet to me, especially with 'Danville' being listed below that. This squiggly thing crossing the line could signify the Dan River." His finger followed the main line downward. "Atlanta, here seems right, but the Interstate doesn't connect these towns the way this drawing shows it."

Bobby said, "What's this 'W.C.,' farther down here mean? And, 'Ir'ville'?"

"I don't know," Max said. "But this 'C.I.' deal looks like it could mean Cumberland Island, on the Georgia coast. But Jake's right: there's no highway connecting all these places like this shows."

Pat came in with the donuts and a fresh pot of coffee.

"Can we get some copies of this stuff?" I asked.

"Sure," he said. "I'll have Robbie do it right away. Four enough?"

"Great," I said. "And, do you happen to have a state map in your office?"

"Might have one in the car," Pat said. "I'll check."

Five minutes later, we were pouring over the only map Pat had found in his Suburban. It was one of those Southeastern States maps, mostly showing the major Interstate and State routes connecting the major cities in the region. We tried matching up the tracings. "Scales off," I said. "And there is no connection by Interstate the way these sheets show."

"Not much help on this 'W.C.', C.I., or 'Ir'ville,'" Max said.

"We need some state maps," I said, "something with more detail. I can pick some up at Barnes & Noble this afternoon."

"What's this mean?" Bobby said pointing to the top of the page marked 'one.'

PJDNBF465," I said, reading it off. "No idea. And I can't figure out what these 'x' marking along the road, or whatever it is, mean, either."

Max sighed with disappointment. "So what we've got is a map with a whole lot of stuff we can't decipher. Hell, this thing might be a directional map on how to get to the coast, and nothing more."

"And Carl Lee hid something that meaningless in a secretly held safe-deposit box? Didn't even tell his wife about it? I don't think so. Besides, Wiggins lived in Nashville, not Richmond."

Just then, Jake's cell phone rang. "Hold on," he said, and flipped open the phone. "Berger. Yeah, Marcus, what'd you get?" He signaled silently for a pad and grabbed a pen from his coat pocket. "Go ahead."

He hung up a few minutes later, and turned to us.

"Got the names of the county cops up in Chattanooga that showed up at the farmhouse," he said, and referred to his notes. "Hackley, Tyler, and Meeks, Bertram; both been with the county sheriff's office about five years. Hackley's a sergeant, Meeks' a deputy. And," he added, "get this: both have had charges filed against them in individual cases, for violations of civil rights; which is to say, they both were charged with beating suspects under arrest for various crimes."

"Let me guess," Max said. "The victims were black?"

"They were. Even got the beatings on tape, but the charges were dropped," Jake said.

"What do we do about them now?" I asked.

"The boys will follow them for now and see who they might meet up with." Jake tossed the pad on the table, and sat down, heavily. "Let's face it. If our cop friends don't meet up with our old pal, Charles Murphy, we aren't going to be able to tie them to much. They'll just say the farmhouse is some kind of clubhouse or something. We didn't even obtain the pamphlet legally with a search warrant." Jake reached inside his sport coat. "By the way, here's some reading for you, if you can stomach it." He threw some of the pamphlets sent from Chattanooga onto the table. "Not much there, though."

"So," I said, quietly. "It still comes down to Murphy, right? We need to find him."

"Make things a lot easier," Jake replied. "At least we know him, and can follow him. But, other than knowing he's from Nashville, we don't have much to go on. We don't even know if the guy that was with him during the attack on Peachtree Street is from Atlanta, or somewhere else, altogether." He picked up a couple of the tracing paper sheets. "Frankly, I don't know if we can get anywhere with this stuff. Keep trying to make sense out of them, but we don't have much of anything without Murphy."

That sick feeling in the pit of my stomach was back. I had been the one who lost him. I knew that no one was blaming me, but I knew it was true. "We have to find him. Simple as that. We'll have to go to Nashville right away, and see if we can pick up his trail. Okay with you, Bobby?"

I turned to him, but he wasn't paying attention to us. He stared into space, and I thought that Jake's mention of the Peachtree incident might have upset him.

"Bobby?" I said, again, but he wasn't listening. Instead, he got up slowly, and walked over to the silent TV hanging from the ceiling nearby. He stared at the screen, which showed a reporter standing outside, in front of an old four-story brick building. The words, "BREAKING NEWS," and "NASHVILLE" were printed on the screen below the woman, who was speaking into a microphone.

Bobby reached up and raised the volume, and the woman's voice flooded out into the room.

"*....And the police spokesman said that the gunman led them on a wild chase, which started when they were alerted by an anonymous phone call to a home invasion and a suspected attempt to kidnap a child living there., and wound up in this industrial area on the south side of the city. The high-speed car chase ended at about three a.m., when the suspect crashed his 1997 sedan into a telephone pole. He then took off on foot, and wound up attempting to hide inside the building behind me. During the ensuing gun battle, the suspect fired several shots at the officers who had been chasing him, until he was shot to death resisting arrest, when police stormed the building, at about 3:45. No officers were wounded.*"

"*That report from our Deborah Urbanic, live from the Southside Industrial Park where, incidentally, a Nashville police officer, Carl Lee Wiggins, was killed by an unknown assailant, during a routine traffic stop, just eleven days ago.*" the studio anchor said. "*Once again, a suspect in a home invasion was killed by Nashville police early this morning, The gunman, identified as one Charles Murphy, had a police record, including three arrests in the Nashville area. He is said to have been a native of Memphis, and was forty-one years of age. We'll have more on that story as it comes in... Moving on....*"

Bobby reached up, and lowered the volume, until the room was silent again.

Turning to us, he said: "Found 'im."

CHAPTER 28

▼

August 27, 2003, Morning

The stunned silence in the room was defining.

Finally, I said, quietly, "That's the same area where Carl Lee was killed."

Max stood up and walked, nervously, away from the table.

"My God," he said in a shocked tone. "They killed him. They killed their own man, because they knew he was your only lead, Tommy, and they knew you would keep coming after him."

"They did more than that," Jake said.

I fought the bile at the back of my throat. "What do you mean?"

Jake sighed, and leaned back in his chair. "They're sending you a message. Two messages, actually. One, they control at least some of the area police, and they can make them do what they want. Two, by killing Murphy where they murdered Wiggins, they want us to know that the two deaths are related, and they don't care who knows it. In other words, they are ruthless, unafraid…, and they think they're unstoppable."

"This is not good," Bobby said.

"No, it's not. But it's all we've got," I said.

"Which may be nothing," he answered, glumly.

"So what do we do now?" Max said.

We thought about that for awhile. The shock of Murphy's murder hung like a heavy curtain around the room. Only the muted sounds of lunch patrons starting to fill Ireland's Own broke the silence.

"Maybe we could roust those cops and sweat them," Bobby said, hopefully. "Maybe we could get something out of them."

Jake shook his head. "Not without the Feds, we couldn't. And I still don't think we can go to them yet. Besides, if we got nothing from the county cops, we'd have shown our hand without tangible results. Could push the guys we want deeper into the weeds."

"Jake's right," I agreed. "We've got to try and make some sense out of the map tracings. Right now, we don't have anything else."

"But how do we do that, Tommy?" Max said. "We been trying to do that, and so far, we've got nothing out of it."

"I know, Max." I said. "Look, let me pick up some Virginia and Georgia maps and play with this for a little while. In the mean time, we wait to see if Jake's operatives come up with anything. But Bobby and me, we head to Nashville no later than day after tomorrow."

*   *   *   *

After the meeting broke up and Bobby headed to Barnes & Noble up the street, I went upstairs to wait for him to return. It was only noon, but the day had already officially become a disaster. Another piece of the puzzle was off the board, and it had been the most important piece we had.

"Thomas?" I heard Abby say, as I walked into the apartment.

"It's me," I called back, suddenly feeling a little less desperate. She came out of the bedroom and gave me a hug.

"I didn't expect to see you until tonight," she said.

I gave her a long kiss. "Didn't expect to finish the meeting so soon. Bobby will be here in a little while. We need to do some work on the stuff I got this morning from Grace Wiggins."

She pulled back a little, and said: "Any good news there?"

I handed her the envelope. "Not much I'm afraid, or at least not that we can see."

Abby took my hand and we walked over to the couch. She took the four sheets of tracing paper and the letter of explanation out and looked at them for a minute, then handed them to me.

"Tell me what you see," she said.

"Well, it's definitely a map, but it just looks like something someone compiled to show the relationship of several towns to each other. We can't figure why Carl Lee would have secreted it away. It looks too innocent to have been in a safe deposit box."

"I guess that wouldn't make much sense," she said. "If that is really what it is, I mean. But, it isn't."

I looked at her. "What do you mean, Abby?"

"I mean that you're right. It wouldn't make sense for something that simple to be hidden away, therefore, it's *not* that simple." She pursed her lips. "So, what is it?"

She was right, of course. It wasn't that simple. Every gas station, book store, and drug store, for that matter, carries maps. No one would need to do a tracing, unless there was a special purpose or need.

"Mr. Wiggins drew this, right?" Abby asked.

"We assume so. At the very least, he's the one who found it and put it in the safe deposit box."

"Then, this must be a part of the investigation he was conducting, right? It has to be at least part of the information that he admitted having, but had been unwilling to share with you before he was killed."

There was a knock on the door, and I called out to Bobby to come in. He gave Abby a hug, and then we gathered around the little table where we ate our meals, and he opened the foldout maps of Virginia and Georgia. Abby brought the tracings over and we started with the Virginia map.

"Here's Danville," Bobby said, pointing out the small city along the Dan River, in southern Virginia.

I pulled over the Georgia map, located Atlanta, which lay off the line on the tracing, but was clearly marked, and moved my finger down I-75, toward the Florida state line.

"Look!" Bobby said, excitedly, as he followed my hand down the map. "'Irwinville!' That's got to be the 'Ir'ville' on the tracing, right?"

"I think so," I said, "and here's Washington County right by it. That could be the 'W.C.'"

"Then the line curves to the east, and that's got to lead to Cumberland Island, just like Max said."

"Makes sense, but something doesn't seem right. Damned if I can figure out what it is, though."

We all stared at the tracing, trying to understand what was making me so uncomfortable

about our analysis, besides the fact that we still didn't know the significance of the drawings from Nashville.

It was Abby, standing beside me, so close that I could smell the strawberry fragrance of her shampoo, who saw it first.

"It's the scale, Thomas," she said, suddenly.

"What do you mean?" Bobby said.

"Look at the state maps," she said. "Look at the locations of the marked towns, and the distances between them."

"Yeah" I said, intrigued. "What does that tell you, Abby?"

"Now look at the tracings, Thomas," she said, pulling the four sheets over the map of Georgia. "No city is exactly where it should be, if the tracing were done over a standardized, published map."

I was beginning to see what she meant. "I'll be damned," I said.

"I don't get it," Bobby said. "What does that mean?"

"It means," I said, "one of two things: either the tracing isn't a tracing at all, but just a free-hand drawing, or it was traced over a map from a very long time ago, when maps weren't exactly accurate."

"Damn," Bobby said. "You mean a map that could be a century old?"

"Or more," I said, and my excitement began to grow. "Bobby, call your father, and ask him if he would have some time for us this evening."

"My Dad?"

"Yeah," I said. "Your Dad."

✳   ✳   ✳   ✳

We had been sitting in the cocoon-like comfort of Robert Hemphill's study for over an hour, while I told him what had transpired over the last week, including the cops at the farmhouse, the pamphlets found there, and the tracings. While I talked, Mr. Hemphill walked around the room, silently taking it all in.

"My God, Thomas," he said, when I had finished. "This investigation has gotten too dangerous. That poor girl," he said, looking at his son, concern in his eyes, "and we almost lost Bobby. Then you narrowly escape death at the hands of a maniac." He sat down across from me, in the other big red chair.

"Now you tell me that whoever is responsible for this madness killed their own man, just to keep you at bay."

"Yes, sir," I said. "I know what you mean, but we simply can't stop now."

He sighed, and looked at me, a bit sadly. "Yes, I know." He leaned forward in the chair. "And you're sure the attorney who met this Murphy fellow was Benton Fielding?"

"I've never seen Fielding, but the car is registered to him, according to Jake Berger."

He shook his head, "I can't see what the relationship would be, especially after what happened to Edgar's daughter," he said, speaking of Marti Patton. "But that's a question for a different day. Suppose we take a look at the tracings."

I laid out the four sheets on the big, ornate desk, and arranged them so that the pages flowed correctly. Mr. Hemphill studied the tracings for what seemed like a long time. Then he unfolded the two maps of Virginia and Georgia.

"I see what you mean about the inaccuracy of the distances between the marked towns on the new maps and the old. But they're not so off that they would preclude these tracings coming from an old map."

"But they could also just be rough hand drawings for some purpose unrelated to what we're doing?" Bobby asked.

His father thought for a minute, then sat down. "I don't think so," he replied, "for two reasons. First, the 'x's marked along the line from Danville to this spot south of Irwinville are here for a reason, and are probably fairly accurate distance-wise," he said. Then he stopped and stared at the tracings again, then the Georgia map.

"Yeah," Bobby said, "but you said there were two reasons. What's the other?"

"The other reason," Mr. Hemphill said, "is that I think I know what these tracings were meant to tell somebody."

I sat forward in my chair. "What?! What do they mean?"

"Hold on a minute," he said, as he got up, and went to one of the walls stacked with book shelves.

Bobby looked at me and shrugged his shoulders, as if to say, *What's he up to?*

Finally, Mr. Hemphill drew a large book from a shelf, and brought it to the desk. He rifled through the pages for a minute, then slapped the open page, with satisfaction. "I thought so," he said.

"What is it, Dad?" Bobby said, impatiently.

He turned the book so that we could see the page. It was a map, not unlike the tracings we had been studying.

"Do you remember my telling you about the Confederate treasury that was lost, and the Klan of the Gold Circle?"

"Yes. Why?"

"This star shaped symbol below the town of Irwinville," he said. "I think this marks the location of a little crossroads village called, Ocilla. He grabbed the Georgia map. "See?" he pointed to a spot near Irwinville. "Right there, which corresponds to the location where your tracings show the line heading east towards the coast."

"Yeah, I see it," I said. "But what's the significance?"

"When Jeff Davis' government left Richmond, we know they went by rail to Danville, Virginia. From there, they used wagons to travel through Georgia."

"Dad, I don't get..."

"Hold on Bobby. I know this will take a minute or two, but I'm trying to arrange my thoughts so it all makes some sense."

"Go ahead, sir," I said.

"Historians agree that during the trip south, Davis planned a way to throw off the Union troops he knew would be chasing him. Remember, he was carrying the life's blood of the Confederacy in gold. Some of those scholars think he met up with a residual force of cavalry, and made it appear that they took the treasure from him, and headed for Mexico to wait for Davis, and to continue raids into the United States."

"I remember that," I said.

"Others are adamant, and I agree, that Davis intended to go to the Caribbean, not Mexico, and that, in any case, he would never have let the gold out of his possession." He sat back in his chair, and lit his pipe. The blue smoke, smelling sweetly of cherries, and fine brandy filled the room. "But it would make sense that he would need an alternate plan to hide the gold if capture seemed imminent."

"Sure," Bobby said. "But what's that got to do with this drawing?"

"Well, if you might need to hide a fortune in gold, and if you believed that you would never be able to retrieve it yourself, wouldn't you want a way to at least guide your successor to the hiding place, without being too obvious, that is?"

"Okay," I said, sitting forward in my chair, wondering where this was all going. "I can buy that. So, what are you thinking?"

Mr. Hemphill leaned over the map again.

"This village," he said, pointing to Ocilla. "This is where Jefferson Davis was finally captured. He was taken to Union headquarters in Irwinville, where he was questioned by General Grant, himself."

I felt a shock of excitement. "You know that for certain, sir?"

He nodded, "I do," he said. "That's why there are no 'x's after Ocilla. That was as far as Davis and his people got. And," he added, "that's why there are no 'x's between Richmond and Danville, since they were traveling by train at that point. I think it is fair to assume that he met up with his cavalry decoys south of Atlanta, and north of Washington County."

"I'll be damned," I said. "But who would this map be sent to? How do we find out who might have received it?"

He smiled. "Whoever traced this map gave us a good clue," he said.

"They did?" Bobby said. "What is it?"

"See the notation at the top of this page?" he said, pointing to the page marked 'one.' PJDNBF465."

"But what does it mean?" I asked.

"I think the 'PJD' means the original came from President Jefferson Davis, and he was captured in April of 1865. That's the '465.' I think the 'NBF' refers to Nathan Bedford Forrest, one of the last surviving Confederate generals still fighting at that time. I think he was the decoy, being that he was a cavalry officer, and was known to be operating in Alabama during March and April of '65. He could have met Davis in Georgia."

"Incredible," I said, quietly.

"There's one other thing," Bobby's father said. "Forrest was a founder of the Ku Klux Klan. If he got the map from Davis, he may have eventually given it to this Klan of the Gold Circle."

"What about these 'x's? What are they supposed to signify?" Bobby asked.

"I'd guess they are possible burial or hiding spots, but that's a guess. The original of this map had to be more specific, or at least contain clues beyond what is on your tracings, I don't see how you could find anything from just these drawings."

"So what does this all mean?" Bobby asked. "And why wouldn't whoever had a chance to make these tracings taken the other clues off the original, too?"

"I don't know, but overall, I think it means," Robert Hemphill said, "that you may have found proof that the treasure was hidden in Georgia, never went near Mexico, and that someone may be looking for it as we speak."

"It means something else, too," I said. "It means someone has the original map. But who?"

CHAPTER 29

▼

August 27, 2003, Evening
Atlanta, Georgia

Abby and I were sitting on the couch having coffee and some apple dumplings she had brought back from her mom's.

"I'm going to be with C.J. tomorrow morning," she said. "She's going over to Sabine's apartment to help pack up her things to send home to Barbados. I told her I'd like to help."

"Hum," I nodded. "Bobby's probably got some things over there."

"Yes," Abby said, "I know. He wanted to come with us, but C.J. thought he shouldn't. The pain is still too fresh, don't you think?'

"Yes. He hasn't said a word about Sabine, or the funeral, or anything for that matter, since he got back," I said. "I'm a little worried about him."

"Give him some time," she said. "He'll come around."

I shook my head. "I'm not so sure, Abby," I said. "You should have seen his face when we saw the report on Murphy's death. It was almost like the chance for revenge had been taken from him."

We sat quietly for awhile. I thought about the day's events, trying to piece it all together. We were getting somewhere at last, or so it seemed, and I felt a small sense of relief following our meeting with Robert Hemphill. That feeling lasted exactly eight hours. That's when the call I had been dreading came. My cell rang, the noise breaking into the silent room. I fought the urge to ignore the call, but I reluctantly got up from the couch, and retrieved the cell from the bedroom. It was Jake Berger's cell number on the screen. I tentatively said "hello," but there was a hesitation on the other end of the line. I knew instinctively why Jake was calling, and I felt sick to my stomach.

"Where?" I asked, as I sat down heavily on the edge of the bed.

"Houston," Jake said, "and Jackson, Mississippi."

"Two?" I said. "In one day?"

"Yeah," he sighed. "This thing's starting to escalate, Tom. I don't know if I believe we can stop it anymore." I could relate to the helplessness I heard in his voice. "Look, I know it's getting late, but I think we should meet for a few minutes, if you can break away."

I glanced at the alarm clock on the dresser. Ireland's Own would be fairly quiet now. "Sure, when can you be here?"

"I'm on my way. Be there in ten."

I arranged to meet him downstairs in the same room where we had heard the news about Charles Murphy. I had a feeling that Jake wanted to speak privately, I decided not to call Bobby for the time being. I could fill him in later, if necessary.

"Are you going out?" Abby asked, when I came back into the living room.

"Jake needs to see me for a few minutes, babe. I won't be long."

She looked at me with those deep brown eyes, as if she was studying me, but she didn't press me for details. I smiled as best I could, which I knew by now didn't fool her at all.

I kissed Abby, and she gave me a warm smile. "I'll be back soon."

My head was spinning, and I felt completely out of control of the situation. There were things so fundamental to this case that continued to elude me. Now there were more deaths to deal with. It was time for some answers. I closed the door behind me, and went downstairs to wait for Jake.

*   *   *   *

As I had expected, the back dining room of Ireland's Own was empty, and I was pouring a cup of coffee when Jake came in and sat down heavily across from me. He looked exhausted.

"Quite a day we're having, huh?" he said, with a sigh, as he loosened his tie.

"I'm not believing this, Jake," I said. "Things can't possibly get any worse."

"Maybe not, but I'm not betting against it."

We drank coffee in silence for a few moments, and then he said: "Let's lay out what we do know for sure. We've had two murder scenes to add to our little list today. Two states, four more dead. This should pretty much do away with any lingering doubts about all these crimes being committed by the same people."

"But they've got to be part of the same organization." I said.

"Yeah, I agree. But that just makes it worse." Jake replied. "Means we're up against a very large and powerful group. The fact that the new murders also happened in the South removes any doubt about this 'Confederacy' angle, at least in my mind."

"I don't know," I said. "Sometimes that whole idea still seems too crazy to believe."

Jake scratched his chin, and yawned. "I think that for the time being, it's the best theory we have, even if the true purpose of these people is unclear. As far as the pattern of the murders, we know that, subject to any past crimes we haven't tied into this yet, there have now been two instances in Alabama, Texas, Virginia, South Carolina, and Tennessee. Why two in each state? What's the significance of that number? And why do all the murders seem to take place in the biggest cities in each of those states? For those questions, we have no answers. Then there's been one case each in Louisiana, Mississippi, Arkansas, and Georgia...."

"Georgia," I interrupted, "if the Patton's were part of the plan. Killing Willie and his family might have been an attempt to hide what was going on elsewhere, by stopping his investigation."

"Okay," Jake said, "but for the moment, let's include them in the pattern. Which means that if we are correct, we can expect additional crimes in those states which have had only one crime to date."

"That leaves Florida and North Carolina as the only former Confederate states where no murders have occurred yet." I said. "But that leaves at least eight more murders that we can expect. Jake, that's sixteen people!"

"Yeah," he said, as he poured more coffee into our cups. "But the only thing we know for sure is that a local attorney who shouldn't be anywhere near this case, met with Murphy, and that isn't much."

"And now, Murphy's dead, too," I said, with a touch of rising anger in my voice.

"It's all we know," Jake said, again.

"You left out a couple things, Jake," I said. "Willie and his family are dead, Carl Lee's dead, and his wife may be in harm's way, Sabine is dead. Abby, Bobby, and I came close to dying with her. Cops are involved on the side of the bad guys, someone apparently wants to bring back the Civil War, and we have no idea how large a conspiracy we're facing! We can't control this thing Jake! It's too big, too spread out, and we have no idea who we should be trying to protect out there!"

I stopped, realizing he knew all this. But it wasn't his fault, either.

"I know how you feel...."

I held up my hand to stop him.

"It's too much, Jake. It's time for you to level with me. Why aren't we talking to the Feds? This makes no sense. I know you and Max are worried about the local cops that might be involved in some way, but why aren't we talking to the Feds?"

He leaned back in his chair, and was silent for a full minute, as if trying to decide what to say, but the look on his face said he had expected my question. "Okay," he said, and sat forward.

"In '85, there was a series of killings here in Atlanta. Three young girls, all in their twenties, the murders spaced out over two months. The M.O. was the same in every case....they were out partying late at night, never reached home, and were all found strangled, sexually molested, wrapped in blankets, and left at construction sites around the downtown area, where they would easily be found the next morning.

"After the third murder, the cops arrested a young black man who was living on the street. Turns out he was a Viet Nam vet, badly wounded in the head, and probably suffered some brain damage."

He drank some of the coffee. I waited for him to continue.

"Max took the case, because no one else would. The evidence against the guy was extremely circumstantial. The investigation was shoddy at best, the victims were probably killed somewhere else then transported to the sites where they were found. Hell, the guy didn't even have a car! So Max thought the defense was strong for an acquittal. The case probably should have never reached a courtroom.

"The lead prosecutor was a guy named John Saxbee. Young, like Max, but a very well connected country club type. He was in a hurry to make a name for himself, and he had the public on his side, because the crimes were so horrific...and the girls were white."

"The guy was arrested because he was black?" I asked.

"Maybe, or maybe he was just 'convenient.' Didn't really matter, He was the perp, far as Saxbee was concerned, and he threw the book at the guy. He gave Max a rough time all through discovery, and Max was convinced the prosecution was literally manufacturing evidence against his client. Saxbee tried the case on TV damn near every day before it ever went to trial, and the Judge blocked every motion Max made to keep it out of the media. Thing finally goes to court, and Max brings in two top flight head doctors that had evaluated the defendant. They both swore this guy was no threat, couldn't have done the deeds, and probably didn't even realize what was happening to him...the whole works. Max finds three witnesses who say they saw this guy far from the scenes of the crimes." Jake let out a hollow sound. "Judge throws all of it out. Max' client gets life, no parole."

"Jesus," I said, quietly.

"Gotta' remember," he said. "Even in the Eighties, this wasn't a great place to get justice if you were a black charged with killing a white person."

He shook his head. "Anyway, it gets worse. Max appeals the verdict, and after some time, people start listening a little, because a similar murder took place two months after the conviction. By this time, Saxbee's a hero, and there's a full-fledged media blitz from the prosecutor's office saying the newest crime wasn't the same as the first three, and Max' guy is guilty. But Max keeps after it because he knows the whole thing is racially motivated."

The coffee was cold, but Jake slugged down the dregs from his cup as if he didn't even taste it.

"Did he get the new trial?"

"Yeah, but it didn't matter. Two days before he was to appear in court for a trial scheduling session, they found Max' client, beat to a pulp and hanging from a pipe in the laundry facility. Called it a suicide, for Christ's sake."

I let out a breath. "Doesn't sound like something you do to yourself when you're about to get a new trial."

Jake leaned closer. "You've noticed that where the murders have happened the local cops haven't exactly been working overtime to solve these cases," he said. "Hell, the crime gets reported, mostly because the press gets wind of it, but within days, the story fades away. And one thing's for sure, Tom: The info on these cases is readily available to the FBI, and they aren't even looking into them."

"Yeah, but…."

"Tom," Jake interrupted. "John Saxbee is the head of the FBI Southeast Regional office here in Atlanta now. He oversees all the state offices in this area of the country. Anything we send to Washington will come back to him for follow-up first. Max doesn't want to give them any chance to bury this investigation, because if Saxbee reports to Washington that there's nothing to it, it dies right there. If we can get some hard evidence, he won't be able to sweep it under the rug."

"How'd you find out about all this?"

Jake smiled a tired smile. "Let's just say Max and I have had a few beers together over the years."

"Why didn't Max just tell me about this?"

He shrugged. "Don't know, but I suspect he feels responsible for that guy not getting a fair shake in '79, although he probably knows that's not the case. But whatever his reasons for handling things this way, I'm prepared to back him."

"Me, too, "I said.

We sat for awhile in silence, out of words, and mentally exhausted. The TV's surrounding us were silent, and only faint noises from the kitchen clean-up crew invaded the quiet.

"Don't know about you," Jake said, "but I'm ready to call it a day."

"Yeah," I said, getting up to leave. "Let's talk tomorrow."

"You still planning on going to Nashville?"

"No." I said. "The more I think about it, the more I'm beginning to think that's a dead end. I think these guys want us to waste our time in Nashville. Frankly, we're wasting our time anyway, since all we're doing is reacting after something happens, instead of *making* something happen."

Jake Berger sat down again. "What are you saying, Tom?"

"We need to get inside whatever organization these people have put together. We know that what's happening isn't being accomplished by just a few crazy bastards. We need to get inside where we have a chance to disrupt things, and find out who the leaders are."

He nodded, slowly. "So what are you suggesting?"

"Your operatives….they still up near Chattanooga?"

He nodded. "Still watching the farmhouse, but it's been quiet."

"So," I said. "How would they feel about kidnapping a couple of county cops?"

Jake gave me a steady look, and I wasn't sure he understood my meaning. Then he pulled his cell phone from his pocket, and said, "Oh, what the hell. Let's find out, shall we?"

CHAPTER 30

▼

"I suppose you guys have given this a lot of thought," the voice came back across the line from the motel outside Chattanooga.

We were still in the backroom of the restaurant, which was now closed. Pat had kept his staff out of the room, so we were using the speaker on Jake's cell phone. Jake looked at me, and gave me a wink.

"Yeah, of course," he said. "We discussed it for the better part of two minutes before calling you."

The voice said, seriously: "You know you're changing the game plan here, Jake."

"Tom's right," he answered. "We have to get inside this thing. The playing field is way too big, and the other team has too many players in too many places. We simply can't react fast enough."

"Just making sure you understand the ramifications of doing this."

I rubbed my eyes, and tried to concentrate on what the operative in Tennessee was implying, but fatigue and impatience were irritating me. I was much too tired to accept the need to debate the plan. "Can we do it?" I asked, an edge in my voice. "Can we do it, and are you willing to be a part of this?"

Jake was watching me intently, but said nothing.

The voice was silent for a minute, then: "It can be done. Anything *can* be done. The question is *should* it be done. As for my team...no, we aren't afraid to be involved, if that's what you're asking. But I insist on knowing if you understand the ramifications of the action you are proposing."

I sighed, and tried to calm myself. "I understand the criminal implications," I said. "But I don't see any other way."

"Maybe there isn't any other way, but I still want to make sure you really want to do this, because there won't be any turning back afterwards." The voice went quiet for awhile. "Are you sure there will be enough benefit from

questioning these guys? Because the cleanup is going to make things....
awkward for you, at best."

I glanced at Jake, but he was staring at the phone which was lying on the
table between us.

"I don't get it," I said. "What do you mean?"

"Look," the voice said. "We will probably have to grab these guys at night
after their shift is over. That means we'll have most of the night to work on
them. But what do we do in the morning? As I see it, you're going to have
three choices, and they all stink."

"I just want to ask them…"

"No," he cut in. "You're not going to *ask* them anything. You're going to
interrogate them. There's a big difference. Interrogations can get messy. What
I want to know is what are you going to do with them in the morning? Like
I said, you've got three lousy choices."

"What are you thinking," Jake said.

"One, you let them go. But I don't see how that's a good situation for you.
Two, we stash them away somewhere 'til we don't need them anymore. But I
guarantee you, come two-three hours into their next shift, *somebody's* gonna'
be looking for those guys. If the lookers are legitimate cops, they might think
their buddies are off on a bender or something, but if they're part of this same
gang, they'll put the pieces together pretty quick. They might disappear on
you; or worse, they might come looking for you. Either way, your investigation
is probably screwed."

Jake said: "That's what you meant by deciding if what information we
can get is worth the risk?"

"Yeah," the voice said, simply.

"You said there are three choices," I said, fully expecting to dislike what
I was about to hear. The voice didn't hesitate.

"Three, you make them disappear…permanently."

I closed my eyes. Had it come to this? Had *I* come to this?

"People will still look for these guys, but they'll never find them. At least
they won't be able to identify you, though."

I sat back in my chair and thought about it for awhile.

"I'm not prepared to decide about that right now," I said, finally. "But I
still think we have to do this."

Jake gave me a nod, but said nothing.

"Look," the voice said, "we've been trailing these guys for some time now.
Give us the rest of tomorrow to track them. I'll get back to you when we have
a plan. That will give you some time to think, and also to come up with what
you want to ask them if we go forward."

I felt a little relief in being able to put off a decision for a few hours.

"Okay," I said. "We can be there in a few hours once you decide to move on them. I'll be ready to question them."

"That's not a good idea, either," the voice said.

"What?"

"If you're not prepared to dispose of the threat these guys represent to us if they were to get free, it's best they don't see you or hear your voice. Besides….," the voice hesitated for a moment, "you're too emotionally involved. If you insist on being here during the interrogation, maybe we can set you up in another room; tie you in electronically so you can listen in. And, you will have to give me your word that you will let us handle this, and that you will not interfere in any way."

I started to protest, but in my heart I knew he was right. If there were a chance I was going to meet up with any of these guys in the future, I had to stay away from them now. If I was honest with myself, I frankly didn't know if I could be physically…or mentally, involved in what I knew would have to be done to the deputies. "Okay," I agreed, reluctantly. "It's your show."

"One more thing, Jake," the voice said, "you're out of it for now. The law enforcement community is too small, and you could jeopardize your career. Not to mention, your involvement could taint a case against these guys for jurisdictional reasons. Give my name and number to your friend, but you and I don't talk again on this one."

"He's right, Jake." I said.

Jake gave me a long look, and I knew he was worried, but he said: "Okay. We play it your way."

"I'll be in touch," the voice said, and the line went dead.

$$\ast \quad \ast \quad \ast \quad \ast$$

11 P.M.
Washington, D.C.

Congressman Gerald Greenway put down the voluminous document he was reading. He rubbed his eyes, tired from several hours of poring over the report of the Appropriations Committee he chaired. He toyed with the idea of taking the papers, and several other documents needing his attention, home to complete in his den, but he would have to deal with Elaine's griping about his long hours. He decided to stay a while longer.

Greenway reopened the thick report folder and began to read again. Outside his private office, he heard the outer door open. He had been alone, having sent his staff home around 8:30 p.m. The janitorial crew, he thought, and went on reading.

Moments later, the door to his private office opened, and a tall man stood in the doorway, wearing the uniform of the Congressional janitorial staff, and holding a plastic bucket, a cloth hanging out over its side.

"You can go ahead and start out there," Greenway said. "I'll be leaving in a few minutes."

The man didn't move. He stood there, his face hidden by the backlighting of the bright lights in the outer office, but Greenway could see the starkly white, bald head, the man's physique nearly filling the doorway.

Greenway put down the report again. Another Hispanic who can't speak English, he thought, with a sigh. "I said, you may start out there," he said, again, with a dismissive wave toward the outer room.

Instead, the man took two steps into the office and closed the door, quietly. The Congressman, startled by the action, stopped reading.

"What the….." he started, but the man dropped the bucket, which made a loud noise that startled Greenway even more. The man moved forward toward the Congressman, and stopped just behind the guest chairs sitting in front of Greenway's desk.

"I have a message for you, Congressman," the man said, in a deep, penetrating voice.

The Congressman felt a slight spark race up the nerves in his spine. He sat back in his chair. "Who are you?" he said. "What is it you want?"

The man stepped forward again, and stood in front of the Congressman. His face was nondescript, except for his eyes, which were black as coal, and dead looking. He sat down across from Greenway, tenting his fingers in front of his lips, and spoke, softly. "As I said, I have a message for you."

"A message? Usually, people who wish to talk to me call me on the phone."

"I doubt you would wish to have this conversation over the phone. My employers in Baton Rouge have suggested we have a little talk…," the man said.

Greenway felt a stab of fear deep in his gut. "Now, wait a minute," he said. "You agreed you were never to come here…."

The man held up his hand. "My employers agreed that they would never come here, Congressman. They do not feel that such a prohibition excluded sending a representative to see you." He spoke quietly, without fear, without a concern for a breach of protocol.

"This is unacceptable," Greenway said, but there was no bluster in his voice.

"Probably," the man agreed, "but we shall have to live with that."

Greenway felt a sudden urge to be done with this; to get it over with as quickly as possible.

"What is your message," he asked.

"Very well," the man said, matter-of-factly. "Evidently, the small talk is over."
He leaned forward in his chair, and Greenway involuntarily pushed his weight
tighter against the back of his own chair.

"My employers are operating in Louisiana. They have successfully completed
the first requirements of their....shall we say, franchise agreement...some time ago.
Since then, they have been moving forward with great speed on the second phase
of the agreement: buying, if you will, the cooperation of local law enforcement
personnel, and politicians. Quite an expensive proposition, as you might expect, but
extremely important to our little enterprise. Wouldn't you say, Congressman?"

Gerald Greenway felt a stabbing fear. Was this man an FBI agent? Did they
know about the plan? Was this a trap? There was no time to decide what to say
or not say. He didn't answer.

"And you see," the man continued, "my employers have put at risk a very large
sum of their own capital in order to meet your timetable." He wagged a finger at
Greenway. "That was not the agreement, Congressman, and they want the money
that was promised them. Now."

"Now just a minute," Greenway said, and his voice sounded a little shrill,
and reedy. "Your people are well aware that my responsibilities to our enterprise,
as you call it, are strictly organizational. There are others who are responsible for
supplying you with the funds."

"Ah," the man said, "but that statement presupposed that my employers make
a distinction between you and these 'others' you mentioned, or that they accept any
delineation of responsibilities on your part. I assure you, they do not."

Greenway felt the panic rising again. "But…"

The man rose from the chair suddenly, and Greenway's chair backed away
from the desk a little as he recoiled from the motion.

"Congressman," the man said, and his voice had a sudden edge to it. "In a very
short time, my employers are going to make an effort to recover their expenditures,
as well as a suitable profit. They will use every method at their disposal, including
forwarding information to the FBI detailing your involvement in this business."
He leaned forward, resting his powerful looking hands on the desk. "And you
should truly believe me when I say 'all' methods."

Greenway tried desperately to stand his ground. "I do not enjoy being
threatened," he said, trying hard to speak with authority. "I'm sure you know
there are security guards on every floor of this building! I need only to push this
button," he said, resting his finger on a small box attached to the phone, "and there
will be several armed guards here in thirty seconds."

The man smiled, and stood back off the desk, seemingly unfazed by the
veiled threat. "You are making two assumptions, Congressman. One, that any
number of guards would be enough to stop me, and two, that I have any fear of

dying. Neither is correct."He smiled again, and held out his hands, palms turned upward. "Besides, why would you assume I have intentions of harming you?"

His black eyes moved from Greenway's face to a picture frame sitting on the desk. He picked it up and looked at the portrait of three young children, arm in arm, running across a white sand beach. "Beautiful," he said, once again flashing the grotesque smile. "Grandchildren, I suspect? Such fun at that age, eh?"

Greenway felt stinging sweat at the crown of his scalp.

The man stopped smiling, and his stare became stony. He laid the picture frame gently on the desk, face down. "The money, Congressman, and soon, or you and I will certainly need to speak again." He turned and walked toward the door. He stopped, and looked at Greenway. "And Congressman, I wouldn't push that button. It would be a shame to get some innocent security guards killed for no good reason. It wouldn't change a thing, you know."

Greenway's eyes never left the man's huge frame, until he disappeared through the office door.

A minute later, sure that he was alone again, Congressman Gerald Greenway fumbled with the phone, dialing the cell number of Senator Arthur Ellis. The phone rang, but the only voice Greenway heard was the senator's voice mail greeting.

Three hours later, Ellis still had not answered.

✻　✻　✻　✻

August 28, 2003, 10:30 P.M.

They took Bertram Meeks twenty-two hours and fifteen minutes after Jake and I had hung up from our conversation with the operative in Chattanooga. It happened at his home, and it wasn't hard. Deputy Meeks lived alone, and he liked to have several drinks at a place called, *Eddie's Bar and Grill.* Then, more often than not, he would fall asleep on the stained brown couch in his living room. Sergeant Tyler Hackley wasn't much more difficult. Seems he is going through a nasty divorce, and rarely went home anymore. They took him just outside the residence of one Sadie Forsythe, a plump, 40ish woman; herself recently divorced, and generally regarded as Hackley's new main squeeze. As I understood it, both gentlemen were sleeping soundly, under the influence of a very strong, and liberally administered sedative, awaiting our arrival.

Bobby and I were in his new Durango, which had replaced the one that had become a charred wreck up on the lake. We were about twenty miles from the farmhouse where I had last encountered the recently deceased Charles Murphy. The leader of Jake Berger's little Black Ops team, who I now knew by the name of Terry Morgan, had arranged to take the deputies there for interrogation, since no other members of the gang had shown up there since the Murphy affair. We had been instructed to drive past the farmhouse about a hundred yards to a dirt road that led back into the woods where the team had set up their observation post. From there, a team member would meet us and escort us to the farmhouse. I dialed the number Jake had given me. The leader of the Ops team answered on the first ring, without greeting.

"Where are you?" he asked.

"About twenty minutes to a half hour out," I responded.

"Good. In about fifteen minutes, I'll send one of my men to the observation post in the woods. The dirt road was used as an entrance to the pasture area. There's a gate up by the roadway, but it will be unlocked. Head up to the wooded area about a hundred fifty yards from the entrance. He'll meet you there."

The line went dead.

"Talkative guy," Bobby said.

A little while later, we reached the "Y" in the road, then passed the farmhouse. The place was dark inside and out. Bobby slowed down, but the gate to the dirt road was readily visible. He turned into the entrance and stopped.

"Kill your lights," I said. "Use your fog lamps only." I wasn't sure we had to be that careful, since we hadn't passed a car on the road in the last three miles, but Bobby did as I asked, and I jumped out to open the gate.

He pulled forward, and I closed the gate again. We moved on up the road at a snail's pace, the tires crunching on the loose gravel spread over the road, the woods a distant shadow. The fog lights, mounted low on the bumper of the Durango, gave off just enough light for us to keep moving, as the gravel gave out and we found ourselves driving on hard- packed dirt. We crossed a hundred yards of open pasture. I glanced behind us a few times, but never saw the lights of another vehicle.

Up ahead, the tree line of the wooded area loomed like an even darker shadow. I felt the urge to tell Bobby to stop, as I felt the need to check for a trap ahead.

Suddenly, out of the center of the dark mass, a thin beam of light from what I figured was one of those high intensity pen flashlights cut through the darkness. Bobby instinctively slowed down even more, but I motioned him forward. As we approached the first of the trees, the light penetrated our windshield, then motioned downward. We moved toward the light, and as we got to within ten yards of it, the light went out. Bobby stopped and turned off the engine, and we got out.

"Hold it right there, gentlemen," a voice said.

We stopped, and I peered into the darkness. The voice came from up ahead, but its owner was totally invisible. I willed my eyes to adjust to the darkness after having stared at the powerful light, but the night engulfed us. I could feel the sweat on my back, the air heavy with moisture and heat, now that we were out of the air conditioned cabin of the Durango.

The light flashed again as it was pointed at my face. I squinted, but could see nothing.

"You're Thomas?" the ghost said.

"Yes, I'm Thomas, Thomas Patrick." I answered.

"Who is that with you?"

I held my hand up to shield my eyes, but still saw nothing. "This is Bobby Hemphill, my partner," I said.

The light moved toward Bobby, then back to me.

"Who are you expecting to meet here?" the voice said.

"Don't you know?" I said, feeling the irritation growing. "I thought…"

"Who are you expecting to meet here?" the voice repeated, as if I hadn't spoken.

"Terry," I said, "Terry Morgan. Jake Berger sent us."

The light went out, and in the dark quiet, I heard the release of a hammer from a hand gun that had obviously been pointed at us the whole time. I heard the crunch of boots on twigs and stones, and we were finally face-to-face with a massive figure, dressed totally in black, his face daubed with camouflage paint.

"Sorry about that, Mr. Patrick. Can't be too careful right now."

I relaxed a little. "Sure," I said. "Where is everybody?" I asked. Ours was the only vehicle parked amid the trees.

"Up at the house. The vehicles are all hidden in the barn. Follow me. I'll get you over to the house so we can get started," he said. "Grounds pretty rutted, so be careful where you step." He turned and headed through the stand of trees toward what I knew was the most important meeting we would be having in this investigation, and I hoped we would not be disappointed again.

CHAPTER 31

▼

August 28, 2003, 11:25 P.M.
The Farmhouse

The bucketful of ice cold water hit Bertram Meeks full force in the face and chest. The deputy, who had been kept in a sedated condition, came awake with a shuddering gasp, as the water poured into his open mouth. He gagged and coughed repeatedly, trying desperately to catch his breath, but the second bucketful thrown with considerably more force, caught him in mid-gasp and I thought he would surely drown.

After a lot of talking, Bobby and I had been allowed to witness the interrogation in the living room, which was lined with chairs just as it had been the day Charles Murphy had almost killed me. We had promised not to interrupt Terry Morgan just as he had insisted when Jake and I had spoken with him. We were in the room now, the two if us, with Morgan and one of his men. If I had taken the time to imagine what a Black Ops member would look like, I would have imagined Terry Morgan. About six-one, stocky but powerful, close cut hair, and extremely confident. They were still dressed in their Black Ops gear, but like Bobby and me, now their faces were also covered with black hoods, only their eyes visible. Bobby and I were tucked back in a corner of the room, which had been darkened to near blackness. The only light came from a beam of a high intensity bulb aimed directly into the face of Bertram Meeks. Hackley, who was tied to a chair like Meeks, was still unconscious.

Meeks shook his head to rid his eyes of the streaming water and strained against the tape holding him to the chair. He began to realize he was tightly bound as he shook off the sedative, and his eyes flitted open and shut as the beam of light bore into his face. Morgan slapped him hard twice, and Meeks was fully awake.

"Wha.., what the hell?! Jesus!"

Morgan cut the beam of light off, and pointed a pen light up at his own face. The result must have looked like a horror show to the frightened deputy. Morgan slapped him again as he gave off a startled cry.

"Huuh…"

"Be quiet, Bertram," Morgan said, in a tone dripping danger, and Meeks tried to suppress his fear, as a whimper escaped from his trembling mouth.

"Better," Morgan said, as the man went silent. "Someone hasn't been working and playing well with others, so I have a few questions I need to ask you, Bertram, and I don't want to hear you make a sound, other than to answer those questions."

"Who are you?!" the deputy blurted out. "Who the fuck.…"

Morgan pulled a 9- millimeter automatic from the holster at his waist and in one fluid motion, placed the barrel firmly against Meeks' forehead, and pulled the trigger. The loud metallic click caught me by surprise, but the effect on Meeks was startling. His eyes nearly bulged out of his head, and he screamed, once, twice, and then stopped in mid-scream as he realized he wasn't dead.

"Do I have to explain the program to you again?" Morgan said, threateningly. Then he shined the light from his flashlight on the face of the comatose figure of Sergeant Hackley, propped up in the chair a few feet from Meeks'. "I'm going to get answers from one of you, and I highly recommend that you take this opportunity to sing like a bird."

I heard an audible gasp escape from the swollen lips of the deputy as he stared at Hackley, then he shook his head "yes," and stared up at the black eyes of his inquisitor like a dog awaiting his master's command.

The farmhouse was closed up tight as a drum, so that no light or noise would escape into the hot Tennessee night, and the air in the house was dank with moisture and heat, and stank of mold and rot. Sweat poured down my face under the heavy hood, and my breathing was labored as I sucked in the humid, gamy air. I glanced at Bobby. He sat there in a trance-like state, seemingly unmoved by the scene playing out in front of us.

Morgan motioned to the other member of his team, a tall, heavily built man, who had been utterly silent since they had brought Meeks around. He doused Hackley with a bucket of cold water. Like Meeks, it took a second hit before he came fully awake, but unlike Meeks, the sergeant showed no fear and was utterly calm as he took in the situation.

"Took you assholes long enough," he sputtered, as water dripped down his face.

Morgan said, "Long enough for what?"

Hackley eyed the black figure in front of him. "To find us," he said, bitterly. "You think we didn't know you was lookin' for us? You think an organization like ours wouldn't know what you was doin'? But it won't do you fuckin' Feds no good. Your mistake was grabbin' me and Bert, cause we ain't gonna' tell you nothin'."

Morgan fingered the butt of the 9- millimeter, and stared at Hackley. "Who is 'us', Tyson?"

"Fuck you!" Hackley spat out. "That ain't your business nohow! You tell 'em, Bert! You tell 'em they're wastin' their time."

Hackley laughed a sour, mirthless laugh. "And your time is runnin' out," he said, quietly.

" Oh? Well, in that case....," Morgan said, and his partner slipped around behind Meeks, and suddenly, there was a thick nylon cord looped around the deputy's neck. The Ops man pulled back sharply on the cord, and Meeks' eyes bulged out from his head. I felt a sharp spike jolt down my spine, but Bobby sat frozen, unable to tear his eyes from Meeks' face.

"Stop!" Meeks struggled to suck air into his closing windpipe as the rope tightened. "I'll tell you what you want! Just please stop!"

Hackley fought against the tape holding him to the chair. "Shut the fuck up, Bert! They ain't, gonna' kill you, but I will if you don't shut up!"

The rope around Meeks' neck got tighter, and I thought he might faint, but suddenly the pressure was off, and the Ops man moved away from him. Meeks gasped for air, and tears rolled down his cheeks. The air in the room was so stifling I thought I might faint myself.

The sergeant continued to strain against his bonds, and sputtered at Meeks. "Bert! You hear me, boy?! You keep your mouth shut, or you're gonna' be sorry!"

Morgan ignored Hackley and bent his face down to within inches of Meeks'. "Bertram," he said, in a soothing tone. "We understand each other, right? I'm going to ask you some questions, and you are going to give me answers. You understand what will happen next if you do not cooperate fully, don't you?"

"Bert! I'm warnin' you....!" Hackley was nearly screaming with rage.

"Fuck you, Ty!" Meeks spat back. "I ain't dyin' for this bullshit! I didn't sign up for this shit!"

Morgan grabbed Meeks' chin, "Bert! Tell me we understand each other."

Meeks forced his head up and down against the pressure of Morgan's grip.

"Son- of- a- bitch!" Hackley was purple with hatred.

Morgan gave a slight nod to his partner. The uppercut came out of nowhere, and lifted the sergeant and his chair a good three inches off the floor. The rear leg of the chair snapped off with a sharp crack as it slammed back down to earth, and the chair and its occupant teetered and fell away. Hackley never felt his head bounce off the floor.

Meeks stared down at the inert figure. "Shit!" he said, softly.

Morgan's partner took a small recorder out of a pack strapped around his waist, and placed it on a chair that he pulled over and put in front of the deputy, and pushed the "record" button.

"Okay, Bertram," Morgan said. "Let's play '*Twenty Questions*'."

* * * *

Meeks looked at Morgan in utter astonishment. "How do you know that stuff?" he said. "That's supposed to be secret!"

"Are we forgetting who is asking the questions?"

"Okay, okay!" the deputy cried out, his voice wavering, "Okay! Jesus!"

"Now," Morgan said, calmly, "let's go through this one more time, then we're going to play 'fill in the blanks'." He stood over the frightened man and said: "You and your friend here belong to a secret organization operating in the South. We know this organization is attempting to band White Supremacists inside former Confederate states together for some reason. We know a Klan group known at the Gold Circle is somehow involved with this craziness, and that a huge amount of money is involved as well. You with me so far?"

Meeks nodded; sweat nearly blinding him as it dripped from his hairline and down his face.

"And," Morgan said. "We know a lot of innocent people, blacks and whites, have been murdered in very nasty ways in their homes. That a cop in Nashville was killed in the middle of the night because he was on to your little scheme. We know you and your buddy there," he nodded toward Hackley, "are responsible for some of those murders."

"No!" Meeks shouted, suddenly sounding more afraid of the words he was hearing than the ghostly apparition delivering them. "No, no, now you wait just a minute! I didn't kill nobody! I swear it!" He was visibly shaken. "And Ty, there…," he said, nodding at the lump on the floor. "He's an asshole sure enough, but he never killed nobody either!" Meeks was practically begging Morgan to believe him.

Morgan turned away from the sweating, fearful deputy, and gave me a quick nod. We both had been pretty sure neither of these guys had what it took to be killers, but had agreed that we needed to make them believe we were going to stick them with these crimes, to force them to defend themselves by naming others as the culprits.

Morgan turned back to Meeks and drew his weapon again. He pointed it into the deputy's face. "Don't lie to me, Bertram," he said, his tone dripping with malice. "We know your record! We know what you've done!"

But the pitiful man was fighting for his life now.

"No, man, I swear it! Okay, so I don't like those people. I gotta' right! I mean, they gotta' be kept in their place, you know? But that don't mean we killed anybody! We didn't do that stuff!"

Morgan made him wait awhile, then lowered his weapon, pulled a chair from a nearby wall and sat down in front of Meeks.

"Convince me," he said, quietly.

Meeks looked startled by the change in Morgan's tone.

"What?"

"Convince me, Bert. Tell me why you don't deserve to die right now. You have five minutes."

"Jesus Christ!" Meeks blurted. "Can I have some water, for Christ's sake?! It's hot as hell in here."

"Four minutes, fifty seconds," Morgan said.

"All right, all right! Jesus. What do you want to know?"

Morgan leaned closer to the sweating deputy. "Tell me about the organization. Everything, Bertram," he said.

"The organization?" Meeks said, questioningly. "I don't know that much about it."

"Don't give me that," Morgan said, gruffly. "Tell me what you know. Now you've got four minutes."

"Okay!" Panic was edging into the deputy's voice again. I was beginning to fear we were about to be disappointed again.

"Ahh..., there's these guys, this Gold Circle group you said you know about. They're some kind of KKK group...call themselves a...a klavern, or something like that. They got this crazy idea about the old Confederacy, like you said, but it ain't about seceding from the United States like in the Civil War. They know they can't do that." Meeks stopped and swallowed hard. "Please, give me some water."

"Soon, Bertram," Morgan said, "Keep talking. You want water; you tell me something I don't know."

Meeks coughed a dry cough. "The thing is, they think that if they control a bunch of politicians and law enforcement, they can make things like they were....you know, change laws, put blacks in their place, maybe even go back to segregation in schools, that kind of shit."

Morgan gave a dismissive laugh. "That's bullshit, Bert! Segregation is against federal law! You better get serious!"

"I am, man! I swear. I know it sounds crazy," he calmed down a little. "I never said they weren't crazy, but that's what they talk about."

"Go on," Morgan prodded.

"Yeah, yeah. So they hold like this contest, you know? They start talkin' to these mob guys, and gang leaders, that kind of people. They tell 'em that they will let them control areas in these old Confederate states. All they got to do is arrange the cooperation of the politicians and as many high- placed cops and judges, and such, and they get to control gambling, girls, all kinds of stuff. Then they kick back some of their profits to the Klan." He coughed again. "Please…"

Morgan nodded to his partner, and the silent man left the room. Morgan let Meeks rest for a few minutes until his partner returned with a bottle of water. He held it to Meeks' mouth, and the deputy drank greedily. The Ops agent abruptly pulled the bottle from Meeks' lips, and the deputy nearly knocked over his chair reaching forward for the bottle. But he was like a trained monkey now, knowing what was expected of him in order that he might get more of the water.

Meeks licked his lips furiously, trying to capture the liquid dripping down his chin. "I know what you're thinkin'," he said to Morgan. "This shit sounds crazy, right? I'll tell you what's crazy!" He let out a sharp, barking laugh. "How's about makin' murder into an initiation?!"

He laughed again, but there was fear in the sound. "You believe that? These guys want in; they got to kill somebody who's involved with some nigger!? They got to prove to a bunch of weird bastards that they're against… what you call it….the 'destruction' of the white race, or some shit like that." Meeks shook his head. "The sheriff, he thought that was hilarious, you know? An *initiation,* for Christ's sake!"

I felt the cold bile of hatred and disgust rising in my throat. I tried to take a deep breath, but the hot, stale air trapped under the hood gagged me. It wasn't possible. *An initiation,* Meeks had used that word. Twice. All those people had died horrible deaths for an initiation into a club of lunatics? Had we reached that point of depravity? Suddenly, realizing that there was this kind of insanity and cruelty in the world, I was anxious to talk to Abby, to get her on the phone and know she was all right. I fought the urge to run out of the room and call her, but it was backed up by a strong feeling of hate and resolve as well. I had to find a way to stop this before anyone else died. I knew at that moment that I would be capable of anything, if it meant stopping the killing.

The Patton family, Carl Lee, faceless others I would never know.... Sabine.

I felt rather than saw Bobby Hemphill rise silently from his chair, his hand reaching for the .38 in the holster under his arm. I knew that if I didn't react quickly, Bertram Meeks was going to die in a matter of seconds. I put my hand firmly on his arm. "Not yet," I whispered through the hood soaked with my sweat. "Not now. Not him alone. He isn't worth it."

It took a good thirty seconds, but Bobby finally relaxed his arm, and slid slowly back into the chair.

Terry Morgan wasn't letting up on the deputy. "What's the sheriff got to do with all this?"

"Jesus," Meeks said, urgently. "I gotta' pee, bad!"

"The sheriff, Bert," Morgan prodded. "Concentrate!"

"Ahh," Meeks stammered. "He's their man down here. You know, he's supposed to keep the guys they buy in line. For that he gets a cut, you know? That's how me and Ty got involved. We help the sheriff and he gives us a cut of his share."

"If you're telling the truth...," Morgan said.

"I am, man! Honest to God!"

"If you are telling the truth," Morgan repeated, "all this takes a lot of money. Where's it coming from?"

Meeks was panting with thirst and fear. "That's what this Gold Circle thing is all about," he said. "They're supposed to supply the seed money to put all this in play. From what I hear, they really think this is some crusade or something, and that we are all dedicated to it."

He barked a laugh that turned into a dry cough. "Shit, man, I just wanted to make a few bucks 'til this damn thing came down on 'em." He was softly sobbing now. "Christ," he said, more to himself than to Morgan. "I never thought all this killing stuff was gonna' happen! It was all about money to me, you know?"

Morgan got up and stood over the crying deputy. Then, he walked slowly over to where Bobby and I were sitting in stunned silence.

"He's done, I think," he whispered. "He's a nobody in this thing," he looked back at Meeks. "I think he's just realized that."

"That's it?" Bobby said. "That's it? That's all we get?"

Morgan shrugged. "Maybe we let him sit for awhile," he said. "Might get something else, but he's done for now."

I nodded, slowly.

Morgan turned back to Meeks, and walked toward him. I remember thinking: *Meeks thinks he's going to die now.*

"What am I going to do with you, Bertram?" Morgan said.

"Jesus!" Meeks said, pleadingly. "Please! Just let me outta' here. I'll disappear, man! I got no reason to stay around here!"

"Can't do that, Bert," Morgan said. "I got him to deal with, too." He nodded toward the lumpy form of the sergeant, still out cold on the floor.

"Hey," Meeks said, "You can't leave me with him! He'll kill me for sure for this and if he don't, he'll sure as hell tell them at the meeting, and they'll do it for him! Either way, I'm a dead man if I stay around here."

Morgan stopped dead in his tracks. "Meeting? What meeting?"

"The induction meeting...that's what they call it. It's our turn."

Morgan sat back down. "Tell me about it."

"You know, everybody that gets tied up with one of the main groups gotta' go to one of these meetings to, you know, swear they're on board with the program. All secret stuff. Sheriff says we gotta' wear them sheets or robes or whatever, and hoods, and they make you take an oath and listen to a lot of mumbo jumbo. Then they burn this cross like in the movies."

Morgan held the water bottle up to Meeks' parched lips, and he drank, deeply. "The sheriff says these guys really believe you're like them after you say this oath." He shook his head. "Dumb bastards."

"When is this meeting?"

"Gotta' be there by eight tomorrow night. Me and Ty are off duty 'til after we get back."

"Sheriff going to be there?" Morgan asked.

"Uh uh," Meeks said. "He's been. Now we gotta' go 'cause we work for him, you know?"

Morgan sat back in his chair.

"I gotta' pee, bad," Meeks said again.

"So how many people do you know who are going to this meeting, Bert?"

Meeks was trying hard to control his bladder.

"Don't know nobody who's going to be there. You gotta' show up wearing the hood after you go through the checkpoint and show some ID."

"Where is this meeting being held?"

"Some farm or something like that. I got directions," Meeks said, squirming against the bonds holding him to the chair. "In my car, with the robes, and hoods, and stuff."

Morgan stood up. "You've been a good boy, Bertram," he said. "Why don't you take a little rest?"

He hit Meeks' jaw as hard as I have ever seen someone get hit. The chair went over hard. Meeks didn't move, but a stream of urine flowed down his leg to form a puddle around him.

Morgan pulled the hood from his head. "Guess he really did have to go," he said. "We need to talk."

I nodded. I took off my hood, and even the hot air in the room felt cool against my skin. I looked over at the two inert forms on the floor.

"Glad you're not mad at me," I said.

Morgan shrugged, casually. "Hell, I'm not mad at anybody."

CHAPTER 32

▼

August 29, 2003, 2:20 A.M.
The Farmhouse

"It's the only way, Max," I said into the cell phone. "We've talked it through, and we all agree that it's the only way."

We were standing on the rear porch of the farmhouse; Bobby, Morgan, and I. The hot August night air was an improvement over the stifling heat inside the house. In the darkness, I could just see two of Terry Morgan's shadow warriors making their way toward the old barn, the comatose body of Sergeant Tyson Hackley between them, his feet dragging along the dry dirt lane.

"I don't like this, Tommy," Max was saying, earnestly. "I don't like this one bit. I feel like we're delivering you into the hands of the devil himself!" "Hear him out, Max," I heard Jake Berger say. We had patched him in on the call, knowing Max would put up a strong resistance to the idea.

"Look," I said. "I know this is dangerous, but we all agreed the other night that we needed to get inside this group in order to have a chance to stop them, and now we have a way in. Max, they killed all those people like they were swatting flies. They killed them like it was one big fraternity prank, and they're not done yet."

I let that sink in, and waited for a reply. I knew Jake would agree, but Max Howard needed to know that I was going to do this, and that the decision was mine. If things went wrong, I didn't want Max to feel like Bobby and I were being forced to do this.

Max was agitated. "You want to walk into a Klan meeting, pretending to be those two cops you're holdin', and I'm not supposed to worry?"

"I didn't say that, Max." I said, soothingly. "You know me. I'm no cowboy. I know I'm putting Bobby at risk as well, and I don't do this kind of thing to get my jollies. Just think about the opportunity that's dropped into our laps, Max. This may be our only real chance to find out who's behind this, right?" He didn't answer, and I knew he would grudgingly agree in time.

Jake cut in. "Where is this place, Tom, and what's the plan?"

"Best we can tell from the directions Meeks had in his car, the meeting place is about an hour from here, near Pulaski, Tennessee. Looks like it might be in a valley in the foothills of the Appalachian Mountains. The instructions give the name of what we think is some restaurant or diner, and the contact is a guy named Enos. We're supposed to stop there and have him check our ID's, then he'll send us on to the location," I said. "Must be a pretty rural area up through there."

"Then what?"

"Then we put on the Klan gear, show up and see what happens, I guess. Not exactly very scientific, I know. Frankly, we just don't know what comes next." I wished I could say something to ease Max' concerns, but I didn't want to lie to him. "Morgan and two of his guys will leave before us and recon the area. They will try and find someplace they can watch from, or at least be near in case we need help, but we won't know where they are for sure," I told them. "We'll try and signal them by cell if things look dicey. We should be okay, though. Your guys here have an Identa-kit with them, Jake. We're going to put our pictures on the badge folders our deputy friends had on them. Height and weight info is close enough that I don't think anyone will look close enough to know we aren't them."

"That's if Meeks didn't lie to you about not knowing anyone else at the meeting," Max reminded me.

"True," I agreed. "We probably will have one more go at him in the morning, but I think he understands what will happen to him if he doesn't level with us."

"What are you going to do with those guys?" Jake asked.

"Right now they're locked up in a couple of horse stalls in the old barn." I said. "Two of Morgan's team will stay here with them."

"But what about afterwards?" Max asked. "Sooner or later you will have to decide what to do with them."

"We thought about that," I said. "I agree with Bobby. After we get away from the meeting place, it really doesn't matter if we let them go. It's not like the Klan doesn't already know who we are. After all, they did send Murphy and his pal after us."

I heard Max sigh with resignation.

"I guess I'm outvoted," he said. "Believe me, I understand what y'all are sayin, I just don't much like it, for sure."

"We'll be careful, Max," I said. "I promise. One other thing, though. I need to let Abby know where I am, and that we're all right. She'll be worried if I don't contact her. But I don't want to worry her more than necessary."

"Leave that to me," Max said. "I'll see that Abby and Maria are informed that you're safe, in the gentlest way I can."

"Thanks," I said, gratefully.

"Just don't make me a liar, son."

✶   ✶   ✶   ✶

Later, utterly exhausted and emotionally spent, Bobby and I were trying to get some rest on the cots upstairs, but the hot, humid air in the closed up room left us awake, bathed in sweat.

I lay there, staring up into the darkness, thinking a million disjointed thoughts and wondering if our plan to infiltrate the Klan meeting would be doomed before it began.

I heard Bobby tossing around on the uncomfortable bed, then he was still for a long time, and I thought he had finally fallen asleep.

"I could have killed that bastard tonight," he said, in a near whisper. "I could have put a bullet into his brain, and never given it a second thought."

I didn't say anything. I knew what he had been thinking. I knew what *I* had been thinking.

"I could see myself," he went on. "I could see myself, walking towards Meeks, taking my gun out, putting the barrel between his eyes and pulling the trigger. I could see it, but I didn't do it."

I rose up on my elbow and looked over at him. He was barely visible in the darkness.

"It wouldn't have ended this, Bobby," I said. "You know it wouldn't have ended this thing. Morgan's right: these guys, they're just hoodlums; petty crooks looking for a payday. It doesn't excuse anything, I know, but we're after bigger fish than them."

He was quiet for awhile, and I lay back down.

"I keep seeing her face, you know? I keep seeing her face, and I hear her asking me why I didn't protect her." His voice was steady, but lifeless.

"It's not your fault," I said, but in my heart I knew exactly what was eating at Bobby Hemphill. It was the same feeling of helplessness and inadequacy I had felt when Abby was missing. It is with me even now; that certain knowledge that we can never really protect those we love, but that we will always try.

"We'll stop them," I said. "For Sabine, for Carl Lee, for all of them. I promise you."

*   *   *   *

2:25 A.M.
Columbus, Georgia

He almost missed it.

Master Sergeant DeWayne Kennerly was on a three day pass from his duties as a Drill Instructor at the Ft Benning Army base outside Columbus, in southwestern Georgia. That meant coming home to the small, fifty- year old, two story house he owned with his girlfriend. After two tours of duty in Germany, the tall, solidly built soldier had been assigned to recruitment and eventually training facilities back in the States. That was his job now, and he had been stationed near Columbus the past two years.

That's where he had met the slim, willowy blond waitress, who was working at a nearby bar frequented by servicemen. She was the one who now shared his life, at least when he was off duty. She was sleeping fitfully next to him, turned on her side, with a pillow propped under her widening belly, to help support the weight of the baby growing inside her.

Kennerly couldn't sleep. The hot, moist air permeated every inch of the small bedroom. His taut, dark brown body glistened with sweat, the sheets around him cloying and uncomfortable. He looked over at her. She lay with her back to him, but her cascading blond hair brushed up against him, and he could smell the dewy freshness of her. He turned on his side, slowly, so as not to wake her, but the trickles of sweat sliding down his shaved head, and the thick air made it impossible to fall asleep.

The Master Sergeant slid out of bed and went to the small bathroom that split the two bedrooms of the little house- theirs, and the one that would soon serve as a nursery. He closed the door and stood above the sink, splashing cool water over his face, his neck, and shoulders. He stood there for maybe five minutes before he shut off the water, and toweled himself dry.

And that was how he almost missed it.

The "tinkling" sound of breaking glass, the click of the lock as it released the latch on the front door.

His senses, honed by his military training, took over. Kennerly looked over at the girl, went quickly but silently to the chest of drawers near the window, and took his Army sidearm from the holster hanging over the frame of the mirror. He went to the girl, and gently put his hand over her mouth. She awoke with a start, her eyes wide and questioning.

Kennerly put his finger to his lips, pointed at the door, then downward with his finger, as if to say, someone's in the house.

The girl sat up against the headboard, her hand supporting her belly. She was quiet, steady. It had been one of the things that drew him to her...the way she handled the occasional rowdy soldier.

They both heard the creaking of the steps as weight pushed up on them, and Kennerly moved quietly to the bedroom door, and cracked it open an inch. In the deep shadows, he could see three figures nearing the top of the landing. He waited a moment longer, until they were bunched together, maybe twenty feet away, cocked the .45 he held in his right hand, and opened the door another foot.

"Freeze, motherfuckers!" he yelled at the top of his voice.

He heard a loud "Fuck!" and a shot boomed out in the hallway, and a large caliber bullet punched into the bedroom door, six inches from Kennerly's face, throwing splinters into his cheek. The girl screamed out, a long, shrill, penetrating sound of fear, and the Master Sergeant fired two rapid, accurate shots into the dark hallway.

There was a loud cry of pain, and Kennerly fired again, and then bodies were falling down the stairs. The sharp cracks of the railing breaking and falling with the intruders filled the air.

Kennerly threw open the bedroom door and moved down the hallway, his gun trained out in front of him. From down below, there were screams of pain and the flailing sounds of men scrambling over each other. The front door slammed open against the wall, and Simpson pumped two more shots down into the well of the stairway. There was the sound of a grunt, and another body falling, then the sound of running feet. Then silence.

The patrolmen who were the first to arrive at the little house were cordoning off an area outside with crime scene tape to hold back the growing number of neighbors who had been awakened by the gunshots, when Sergeant Harvey Trembley, a grizzled veteran of the Columbus Homicide Squad showed up. He parked in front of the house, went up the porch stairs, and climbed over the body of a white male, who looked to be in his thirties, and stepped into the front entrance. Kennerly was there, dressed only in pajama bottoms, shirtless, his bald head glistening with sweat.

Trembley, in his forties, short, but powerfully built, surveyed the scene. He looked up at the top of the stairs. The girl was there, barefoot, wrapped in a sheet, her blond hair tumbling down around her face.

"Trouble?" Tremblay said, casually. He didn't expect an answer, and didn't get one.

The cop went back to the body at the door, gave the patrolman another minute to take more pictures, then nodded to a second officer, who carefully rolled the body over just far enough for Tremblay to study the face for a minute. The sergeant squinted hard, straining to see the dead man's features through the blood that was already hardening against his face. He shook his head, and the officer let the body down again. Trembley went over to the second body that lay on its stomach, about ten feet away. He inspected the tattoos that ran the length of the body's arms then motioned to the officer, and they repeated the turning process on the second body. This time, when the body was rolled over, Trembley whistled a low whistle, and knelt down beside the dead man. Underneath him, there was a wooden stake-like weapon. Two crossed sticks, with a sharply pointed end. A few feet away, he saw a hammer with a hatchet face on one end, instead of that nail puller most hammers have. Then he noticed a black mark just inside the shirt collar of the dead man, and took a pen out of his jacket pocket. He lifted the top of the collar a few inches. The tattoo, the number "11"encased in a circle, was prominent and looked new.

"What the hell?" he said, in a near whisper.

Thrembley stood and went over to where Kennerly was standing, silently watching the cops work. In the distance, another siren was wailing in the distance, probably the M.E. on his way here with the "meat wagon," the sergeant thought.

"Officer outside says you think there was more of 'em," he said to Kennerly. Kennerly nodded, slowly. "Saw three," he said, quietly.

Trembley nodded. He looked up at the girl again. She stood there like a statue, fingers to her lips, eyes shocked- looking, and blank.

The cop nodded again. "They're not carrying any identification. You recognize either of them?" he asked

Kennerly was quiet for a minute, staring straight into Trembley's eyes. Finally he said, "Yeah," and shifted his eyes towards the second body. Then he looked up at the girl, a look Trembley could not read on his face.

"Her brother," he said, almost in a whisper.

✳   ✳   ✳   ✳

Later, Trembley pulled up outside a dingy, all night diner where he often stopped for coffee. He turned off the engine, and sat thinking for a moment. Then he looked at his watch, shrugged, and took out his cell phone, and dialed a number in Atlanta.

Chapter 33

▼

August 29, 2003, Dawn

I hardly recognized Terry Morgan and the Ops Team members who would be traveling with him to the valley near Pulaski, where they would be trying to protect Bobby and me. They were all dressed in casual civilian clothes, but I knew that the vehicle that they had brought up from the barn and parked close behind the farmhouse, that they were loading now would be outfitted with every weapon and device they might need for the job ahead. They also looked well- rested and clean shaven. I on the other hand, couldn't imagine feeling any worse than I did at that moment. Bobby was still upstairs sleeping, but I hadn't been able to shut down my brain and relax.

Morgan looked up from packing a large bag with equipment. "Coffee and donuts inside," he said, nodding towards the kitchen window.

"You baked?" I said, with a smile.

"Yeah," he chuckled. "Right after I prepared the *Coq-a-vin*. Give me a few minutes, and then we'll talk."

I choked down a donut quickly, finding that I was much hungrier than I would have thought, and had grabbed a second one when Morgan came in from the porch.

"You look beat," he replied, eyeing me closely.

"I'm okay," I said, pouring more coffee.

"You should get some sleep. You're going to need your wits about you tonight." He poured a cup for himself. "Plenty of time before you need to leave."

"Maybe later," I said. 'Right now I need to concentrate on what we're going to do next."

Morgan let it sit for a minute. Then he said: "How's your friend doing?"

"Huh?" I said, surprised by the question.

"He looked pretty shook up last night," Morgan said. "How's he holding up?"

I looked at him. He was studying me closely, as if trying to read something in my eyes. I shrugged. "Bobby's had a rough time," I said. "Losing his girl like that..." I didn't finish the thought.

"I don't mean to tell you your business. But if he's not right," Morgan shrugged, as if to ask me to excuse the word, then he said: "If he can't handle what goes on up there, or the crap he hears, he could get you both killed."

"You don't pull any punches," I said, quietly.

"Can't afford to, Tom." He nodded towards the window. "Everything we do puts those guys out there at risk, but that's the business we're in. We can handle the danger because we expect it every moment we're on assignment." Morgan drank some of the coffee. "But each of us knows exactly how the others will react in every circumstance. Your friend," he said. "For him, it's personal. That's not good."

I gave him a steady look. "It's personal for both of us," I said, softly. A year ago, I would have had the same doubts about Bobby Hemphill. He was a lost soul trying to find his inner strength, as well as a reason to exist. But that was before he fired a bullet into the head of a crazed Cuban gunman who was trying to choke the life out of me. Now I had no doubt I would trust him with my life.

"I know what you're saying," I said to Terry Morgan. "Bobby's okay. He'll do what he needs to do."

Morgan nodded. "Okay," he shrugged. "Let's plan this picnic."

*   *   *   *

We were poring over a map of Tennessee when Bobby joined us in the kitchen. It was still very early, and the heat expected to continue throughout the day was still to come. The few clouds outlined by the light of the slowly rising sun appeared to hold no rain that might relieve the summer discomfort we had grown to expect nearly every day of the month. Bobby looked the way I felt, but he waived off the offer of coffee, and took a seat at the table with us.

"I figure it should take you about an hour to an hour and a half to reach the restaurant they are using as a checkpoint," Terry Morgan was saying. "So you don't have to leave here for several hours. Frankly, the later you reach the checkpoint, the less likely anyone will be paying much attention to the ID.s we made for you using the Polaroid photos we took last night, and the sheriff's badge holders we got from our friendly deputies. You're Meeks," he said to Bobby, "and you fit Hackley the best, size-wise," he told me.

"What about those guys?" I said.

"They came around early this morning," Morgan said. "We let them use the old toilet down in the barn, and gave them some food." He gave a small smile. "Funny thing about that food, though. Seemed to make them sleepy again. They're tied up again and sharing a horse stall. Don't worry, they'll be okay, and of no threat to you."

"What are you going to do?" I asked.

"We'll leave here within the hour, I want to take our time and try and find the best place to set up an observation post before it gets dark," he said. "And since we don't know the area at all, or the lay of the land, we'll probably need as much time as we can get."

"What if you can't find a good spot?" Bobby asked.

Morgan pointed to a spot on the map just north of the town of Pulaski. "Best we can figure, we think the location you're going to is an old plantation site north of town in a valley surrounded by low-lying hills. According to the aerial photos we got off the internet last night, it looks like a good possibility that there will be ample sites to choose from that will give us good cover, but put us close by."

"But will you be able to see us?" I asked.

"Probably not, especially with those hoods you'll be wearing," he said. "That's why we want to make sure we can hear you."

"Hear us? How?" Bobby asked.

Morgan reached down into a leather equipment bag sitting on the floor next to him. He pulled out a small pouch, opened it, and took out two small devices that looked like those Bluetooth ear pieces cell phone uses used, but they were about half the size.

"Hook this over your ear and put the earpiece into your ear canal when you put the hoods on," he said. "They give us a range of almost a half mile. We can talk to you, and this," he pointed to a small oval on the main body of the device with pinpoint holes in it, "will pick up your voice if you need to call for help. This is the on-off switch."

He pointed to another spot on the map. "If we're right about the location of the meeting site, then it looks like the checkpoint is about five miles from a dirt road that goes back about a mile to the valley entrance. There is a second spot, a kind of staging area I'd call it, located on the dirt road where you're supposed to put on the Klan garb before driving on to the meeting."

"That's a little theatrical, isn't it?" Bobby said.

Morgan nodded. "That's what the Klan is all about," he said. "They control their members with secrecy, mysticism, and symbols. There's a copy of all this info on the front seat of Hackley's pickup. I figure that's the best vehicle for you to use. It's the newer of the deputy's cars and the most powerful."

"What about weapons?" I said. Bobby nodded, and I knew that had been on his mind, too.

Morgan sat back in his chair. "Chances are you won't be allowed to take firearms onto the site," he said. "But I think that the way we handle that possibility is, you take the deputy's guns with you in open sight. If you are questioned about that, you simply say that you're cops, and that you always carry weapons. If they take them away...so be it. We could try to hide other guns somewhere in the pickup, but if you're searched and they're found, that will look suspicious."

"I can see that." I said. "Don't much like it, but I think you're right."

"Oh," Morgan said, "and don't take your cell phones. They're traceable. I think you should carry the phones Meeks and Hackley had, but keep them turned off. In other words, you can also look suspicious by *not* having things like phones, since everybody carries them these days. I think, though, that they'll probably confiscate them anyway. They're not going to like people making phone calls from a secret meeting."

We both nodded our agreement.

"What do we do once we're in?" Bobby inquired.

"Absolutely nothing," Morgan said. "Just go along with the flow: listen, observe, and get lost in the crowd as much as possible. You'll be there overnight and put up in tents, from what we got from Meeks' sheet of instructions, so if anything critical is said, or if you see anything we should know about quickly, you can get clear of everybody later and speak into the mike on your ear bud. *But* don't take any overt risk. Worse that happens; we'll debrief you after you're out of there tomorrow."

"Doesn't seem like nearly enough," Bobby said, ruefully, and I knew that anger and hate were simmering just below the line of reason. Terry Morgan saw it too.

"You can't end this thing tomorrow, Mr. Hemphill," he said, quietly. "It will just be the beginning of the end. Trying to make it more than that could lead you to disaster."

We sat there for a minute, the silence hanging like a curtain over us. Then without a word, Bobby got up from the table and walked out of the room.

Morgan gave me a long look, and then without saying what I knew he was thinking, he folded up the map of Tennessee, handed it to me and stood up.

"If you have no further questions," he said, "I need to get ready to leave."

He walked out of the kitchen, leaving me there to ponder the enormity of the choices I had made.

*   *   *   *

Bobby was sitting on his cot when I went up to change and gather my few belongings. He sat hunched over, his hands clasped before him, his head down.

I sat across from him on the other cot, but he remained silentl, as if I wasn't there.

But I couldn't. I had heard Terry Morgan loud and clear. "Look, Bobby…"

He held up his hand to stop me.

"I won't lie to you, Tommy," he said, quietly. "I feel like I'm being eaten up from the inside out. This thing with Sabine….," he stopped for a minute as if trying to find the words. He looked up at me, and his eyes were clear and steady. "I feel worse now than I did when it first happened. I can't shake the feeling that her death was my fault."

"I know," I said. "It wasn't, Bobby. I won't try and tell you that there is a reason why these things happen, some cosmic plan or some crap like that. Sabine and all the others died because there is pure evil in this world. The same kind of greed, hate, inhumanity, whatever you want to call it, that would make a father like Richard Barrett nearly end the life of the daughter he had raised. And it has to be cut out like a cancer."

"I know that in my heart," he said. "But it hurts so much sometimes." He shook his head. "I won't let you down, Tommy. I can do whatever I need to do to make sure I don't let you down."

I looked deep into his eyes. My heart felt heavy and sad for him, but he held my gaze steadily.

"I never even gave it a thought," I told him.

CHAPTER 34

▼

August 29, 2003, 5:00 P.M.
The Valley

"….And the good news is that the oppressive heat that has plagued most of the Southeast for the better part of the month may finally be letting up, at least for a few days," the weatherman on the radio was reporting. *"But the bad news is that the much needed rain showers which will start showing up over Middle Tennessee during the next few hours are expected to change over to potentially severe thunder storms by late night or early morning. Those storms will last into your rush hour tomorrow, and may very well produce some strong lightning, and even hail, before they move on. That's your forecast from the folks here at your Severe Weather Team. Stay tuned for further bulletins on the hour. Back to you, Mary…"*

I switched off the radio of Tyson Hackley's '02 Ford 150 pickup and glanced at my watch. If Terry Morgan had estimated correctly, we should be hitting the eastern outskirts of Pulaski in about a half hour.

Pure exhaustion had finally allowed me and Bobby to get a few hours of sleep after Morgan and his two men had left the farmhouse. They were somewhere up ahead of us now, hopefully finding a good observation location near where we were to meet our "fellow" Klansmen. Bobby was driving, and had remained quiet and reclusive in his thoughts, not that I couldn't guess what he was thinking. We were about to walk into the wolf's lair, and either begin to unravel this secret society of criminals, or meet a fate which it would do us no earthly good to contemplate.

About four, I had called Max to give him the word that we were on our way, and that the plan was in motion. I'm pretty sure he had been hoping that overnight we would have come to our senses and given up this crazy idea. However, he was supportive, didn't argue any further, seemingly resigned to anxious hours of waiting for word that we were safely away from the meeting place.

After we had hung up, Bobby got our few pieces of gear stowed in the truck. I wanted desperately to talk to Abby, but at the same time was afraid to hear worry in her voice. I couldn't afford to let caution and fear control my emotion or my actions over the next twenty-four hours. But the need to speak to her was too strong, and I finally called her cell.

"I'm glad for called, Thomas," her soothing voice came over the phone. "I know what you're doing. Dear Max called me last night and told me about it. He's so worried about you, you know. I could hear it in his voice, even though he tried to make it sound as though everything was fine."

"Everything will be okay, Abby," I said.

"Yes, I know," she sighed. "I am scared for you, Thomas. I know you are too, but there really aren't any other choices, are there?"

"I knew you would understand, and if there was another way, I swear I wouldn't make you worry like this."

"I know. Just promise me...."

"I promise," I said, quickly, before she could finish. I didn't want her to hear me say: *"I promise I'll come back safely,"* because I couldn't make that promise, when there was a chance that I would break it.

✳   ✳   ✳   ✳

By 6 p.m., we were winding our way through Pulaski, crossing from East College Street to West College Street, in the center of town. I took out the sheet of directions and instructions that Bertram Meeks had in his car, and checked for the next road we needed to find.

"Columbia Highway," I said. "It should be coming up very soon. We need to head north."

"There it is," Bobby said, almost immediately. He turned right and we headed out of town about a mile to a fork in the road. At the corner by the right hand fork stood an old, clapboard structure. It appeared to have been a residence at some point in its long history. At least two, one story additions had been added, to it since then. The lot was not grassed, but was paved with crushed stone and a beat up sign post on the street held an old, rusting sign that said, "Enos'." There were no cars parked in front.

"That's it," I said, and a shiver went up my spine. This was it: our first test, and our last, if somehow word had gotten out about us.

Bobby pulled off the road onto the property. The soft crunch of our tires on the stones filled the cab of the truck. A woman sat on a chair near the entrance to the diner under a small awning, to protect herself from the sun. She appeared to be in her late forties or early fifties. She was a plump, blousy former blond, from the looks of her now- graying, unkempt hair. She wore a hard life on her face.

Bobby pulled up and stopped, but kept the engine running. I looked around, but the place seemed deserted except for the woman. I got out of the truck feeling as if a thousand eyes were on me, but I saw no one else around, and approached her. She watched me with a distrustful gaze waiting for me to speak first, as I stopped about ten feet from her.

I nodded to her. "We're looking for Enos," I said, matter-of-factly. "He around?"

She kept her eyes glued to my face. "Who wants 'im?" she asked. Her voice had a distinctive drawl, and her face was drawn and deeply lined, but her stare was rock- hard and penetrating.

"I was told...."

"Who wants 'im?" she said again.

"Names Hackley," I said. "I was told to..."

"Who's your friend?" she said, finally glancing around me to squint at the windshield of the pickup.

"That's Bert Meeks," I said. "Look..."

She reached into the breast pocket of the discolored, man's shirt she was wearing. It was then that I noticed it. A tattoo on her forearm: a black circle with the number "eleven" at its center. I tried to show no recognition or surprise, as if it were perfectly reasonable to find someone adorned with that symbol here.

The woman took a folded sheet of paper from the pocket, and glanced at it for several seconds. Apparently satisfied by what she saw, she said: "Wait here," and pushed herself up out of the chair. She disappeared through the front door of the diner.

I stood there, exposed to the hot August sun, half expecting a fusillade of bullets to erupt from the building. A minute later, a large, bearded man, wearing clothes similar to our lady friend, came out of the door. His massive, bare arms hanging from sleeves rolled up to his shoulders were covered with tattoos. All the symbols were there: the cross, the "eleven" in the circle, a Confederate flag. There was no doubt in my mind that he was armed, and very dangerous.

"You're Enos?" I asked.

He walked over to me and, ignoring my question, looked over at Bobby, who was still sitting in the truck, with the engine still running. The man still didn't say anything, but reached out with his right hand, palm up.

I looked back at Bobby and nodded. I saw him reach into his shirt pocket, and then he was holding his black badge folder out the window. I took out my own, and handed it to the man known as Enos.

He opened the folder, and over the next minute looked from the photo to my face and back again, several times. Enos handed me back the folder, and then, while keeping an eye on me, went over and took Bobby's ID. He went through the same motions.

After want seemed like a lifetime, he handed Bobby back the folder and came back to me. "Five miles up the road," he said, flashing a thumb toward the right- handed fork in the road. "Look for a small cross by the edge of a dirt road. Painted gold," he added. "Turn left, go to a second gold cross. Stop there and put on your robes."

I nodded my understanding. I could tell from the intensity with which he watched me that he still didn't trust us.

"Stop again when you get to the stone pillars," he said. "Wait there. And don't talk to nobody! Y'all got that?"

I nodded again.

He turned and walked into the diner without another word. A moment later, the woman returned, took her seat at the front door, and watched us in silence.

I got back in the truck, and Bobby took us up the fork in the road towards our rendezvous with the Klan of the Gold Circle. To the west, I could see the clouds moving slowly eastward taking on a deepening grey hue as they slid across the path of the sun.

The gold painted cross was right where Enos had said it would be, but it would have been easy to miss if we hadn't been looking for it. It stood just two feet high at the edge of the road, and was surrounded by tall beds of weeds and dead grass. Bobby took the turn and we headed down the dirt road toward the spot where we would don the hated robes and hoods lying folded on the rear seat.

Above us, the clouds continued to roll in, and the respite from the blistering sun was a welcomed relief, though the discomfort from the heat was the least of my concerns at the moment. We could still be driving into a trap. Not having access to our phones, and not wanting to use the deputy's phones to call Terry Morgan to make sure nothing had gone wrong, was disconcerting at best. We couldn't be sure that Morgan and his men had arrived safely, and were watching out for us. The closer we got, the more I doubted my sanity for hatching this plan.

It was too late to worry about any of that. We were committed, and with every turn of the tires on the dusty, rutted road, we were moving closer to the center of the evil that had dogged us for nearly a month.

It was hard to tell if we were actually in a valley. If this had once been cultivated plantation land as Terry Morgan had said, it was now heavily overgrown and wooded, with limited visibility in every direction except along the path of the road. After a time, we reached a small clearing, and found the second gold cross. Bobby pulled over and we got out and put on the robes and hoods.

"Don't forget your earpiece," I said, as he pulled the robe over his head.

"It gives me the willies just to put this thing on," he cringed. I knew how he felt. It wasn't hard to imagine the horror the mere appearance of these clothes had brought to so many for over a hundred years. Now, to end a new reign of terror, we had to wear those same symbols of hate and death.

As we got back into Hackley's pickup and started forward again, the first loud splats of huge raindrops hit the windshield. A minute later, we were in a light but steady shower. Bobby put the wipers on, and the headlights, as he sky darkened, moving us into almost total darkness in the narrow, confined area of the roadway.

"So that Enos guy said we'd be met at some pillars or something like that?" Bobby asked, as we moved another mile up the road.

"Yeah. Gotta' be an entrance to the valley, or at least the meeting grounds." We kept moving as the rain started to fall faster and stronger. The road began to quickly turn muddy as the ruts turned to brown colored puddles. We had squinted our way through another mile of rain when Bobby said: "There! That must be what he was talking about."

Up ahead, two shadowy stone pillars, maybe three feet square and eight or nine feet high flanked the roadway about fifty feet ahead of us.

"Stop up there," I said.

"I just thought of something," Bobby said, as he rolled the truck to a stop. "If anyone asks us who we work for, we don't even know that sheriff guy's name."

He was right, but as it turned out, we weren't going to have time to worry about that. Two ghostly figures appeared from behind a stand of trees along the roadside. Each was dressed as we were, except for a blood-red cross with a golden circle connecting the four points which was centered on the chest of their robes. Behind them, I could make out a camouflage- painted tent that must have been where they had been waiting. Each was carrying a shotgun. As one approached us, one hung back, his weapon not pointed at us, but at the ready, and the other motioned to us to get out of the truck.

"Oh, shit," Bobby said, softly, and I wondered if we had been sent into a trap from which we had no way out. I moved my hand slightly toward the holster sitting on the seat between us, but thought better of it. Any quick movement on my part would certainly bring a lot of buckshot raining down on us. We climbed down from the cab, trying not to look like we were about to bolt, and I moved over to the driver's side, next to Bobby. The man closest to us used the barrel of his shotgun to motion to us to lift our robes up. We did, and he circled us slowly, checking for weapons. Then he moved to the open door, and peered into the truck. The cell phones and the two holsters with our .38's were up front in plain view as we had planned.

"What's this shit!" the man said, gruffly, holding up one of the holsters. His companion swung his weapon toward my chest.

"What?" I said, with as much innocence as I could muster under the circumstances.

"Them guns, that's what!" With his companion's shotgun still trained on us, he began to systematically search the pickup; under the seats, the glove box- anywhere another weapon might be hidden. Bobby gave me a look, as if to say, *Morgan was right.*

"Hey, man," I said. "We're sheriff's deputies. Just part of the job, you know? Nobody said nothin' about not bringin' our weapons." I shrugged. "Sorry."

He finished his search, and seemed to soften just a little. "Well, they ain't allowed. Y'all gonna' hafta' leave 'em with us 'til y'all leave. Phones, too."

"Yeah, sure," I said, trying my best to look innocent.

The rain started to come down a little harder again, and they were quickly losing interest in us.

"Two mile up the road," the man said. "Leave the truck with the keys in it, and walk in. The path's clear enough."

We both nodded, and without another word climbed back into the cab of the pickup, and Bobby started the engine.

"Anyone else need to change their underwear?" he said, and we moved on.

✳   ✳   ✳   ✳

We parked Sergeant Hackley's pickup in a small clearing at the end of the roadway, about a half mile from the last checkpoint. Bobby cut the engine and we got out slowly, listening for any hostile sounds, but the air was quiet except for the soft tapping of raindrops that were falling from the trees above us. Steam rose from the forest floor, creating a low- lying fog around us. It was beginning to feel like one of those Sherlock Holmes mystery movies from the Thirties, but I reminded myself that the situation was deadly serious. Bobby looked at me and I nodded toward a narrow pathway that led north from the clearing. If we took the path, we'd be in an even smaller area in which to maneuver, with no weapons, and not even the pickup to protect us.

We had no choice. But I held up my hand as he started for the path's entrance. This might be the last chance to try and establish contact with the Ops team before we found ourselves surrounded by Klan members.

"Terry?" I said, the words rattling around inside the hood. "Can you hear me, Terry?" I waited a few moments, and tried once again.

Nothing. Bobby looked at me, questioningly. I shook my head, and tried once more. He came up close to me. "Where the hell are they?"

I shrugged. "We can't just stand here," I said, quietly. "We might be being watched."

We started down the path. The air had cooled some from the rain that had all but stopped now, but the steamy heat that rose from the ground was suffocating. Bobby sidled up close to me as we walked.

"What if Morgan can't hear us? These trees might be cutting off our signal," he said softly. "You think he'll move closer and try to get a visual on us?"

"I don't know," I replied. "It's possible there are guards posted all over these woods. He might not be able to get close enough without being discovered."

"That's comforting," he whispered back.

"Could have lied to you," I said.

"I could have lived with that."

CHAPTER 35

───────────── ▼ ─────────────

August 29, 2003, 6:45 P.M.

About fifty feet ahead of us, the neck of the pathway appeared to widen. We sped up a little and kept moving forward, anxious to be out of the confined area, yet, admittedly, uneasy about what lay beyond. As we neared the end, I could see the wide space on the other side. This had to be, at long last, the meeting grounds. The wolf's lair.

Suddenly, we were confronted once again by the massive, white cloaked figure of a hooded Klan member, accompanied by the ever-present shotgun at the ready.

"Y'all together?" he said.

"Yeah," I answered, and we showed our ID's again.

"Tent marked number three," he said, pointing off to the right. "Y'all 'cn take off yer hoods 'til the ceremony since y'all know each other. But keep covered up when you go outside."

I stole a glance around the guard. The field was wide open, about forty to forty-five yards square. Off to the right there was a double line of tents, with mesh windows and a flap for a door that would hold two or three cots each. A much larger tent sat at the front of the two columns, like a commanding officer in front of his troops. I figured that was where the leader of this nightmare would be staying. At the very center of the clearing, a huge wooded cross stood nearly twenty feet into the dimming light of a cloudy sky.

"What's that?" I heard Bobby say. I followed his gaze to a small rise on the western edge of the open area, where long, wispy strands of smoke curled up from a large pit.

The guard shook his head. "Well, that's the damn food, son! Wha'd y'all think it was?!"

"Food?" I said.

"Yep. Some roasted venison and pig," the man said, and I could visualize him smacking his lips under that damned hood. "Plenty 'a good Tennessee sour mash and beer to wash it down, too." He was much more relaxed than our past inquisitors, and I guessed that he figured that if we had gotten this far, we must be okay.

I tried to give off a small laugh. "Pretty hard to eat with these on," I said, tugging at the bottom of my hood.

"Y'all 'cn take 'em off after y'all take the pledge," he answered. "Part of the Brotherhood then."

I nodded, and thought to myself: *I hope Meeks was right about everybody being strangers.*

"They gonna' ring the assembly bell at eight. That's when the Leader will call us to the Cross," our guide said. "Y'all come runnin', hear?"

I nodded and we headed off toward the tent. The sun had disappeared behind rainclouds, and the air was thickening with the smell of cooking meat, and I suddenly realized that we had not eaten in a long time. There were about twenty-five or thirty hooded Klansmen and, I supposed, Klansmen-to-be, milling around the grounds; some working, and some getting adjusted to their surroundings. The whole effect was like an armed camp in wartime. I motioned to Bobby, and we walked over to where the large tent stood. Straining to hear as we went by, I wasn't able to pick up any conversation coming from inside.

Our tent was in the second row behind the large one. We stood in front of it watching, without, I hoped, appearing to be watching.

"Now what do we do?" Bobby said. "And who the hell is this 'Leader'?"

"*Not so loud, gentlemen.*" The voice had come through the earpiece in my right ear, and I almost jumped off the ground. "*Get inside,*" it said.

We scrambled into the tent and dropped the flap covering the opening. There were two cots inside and a small camp table with a Coleman gas lamp sitting on it. I sat down and put my hand over my ear to hear better.

"Morgan?" I felt an immediate relief. "Thank God. Where've you been?"

"*Let me do the talking,*" he replied. "*You might be heard through the tent, so keep it down if you say something. We got a visual on you once you got into the open, but couldn't get a signal while you were deep in the woods. So try and stay in the clear as much as possible.*"

"So you're close by?" I said in a near whisper.

"*Close enough, but we might have to pull back if they put any sentries into the woods tonight.*"

"Have you recognized anyone? This guy they call the Leader?"

"Negative. *These boys like those hoods. A few years ago, they'd have called him the Grand Wizard, or Grand Dragon. We haven't seen him yet.*"

"We'll keep our eyes open," I told him. "One of the guards said we'll be taking the hoods off after whatever this ceremony they have planned is. Maybe we can draw somebody over to where you can get a picture or something."

"*We'll take care of that,*" Morgan said. "*Just do what they tell you and remember to stay close to groups of them so you don't stick out. Listen for instructions. Keep your ears open and keep quiet whenever possible.*"

"Morgan," I said, "the sheriff. It might come up. What's his name?"

"*That's my fault,*" he said, apologetically. "*It's Stevens. Melvin Stevens. He's fifty-one, and he's been the sheriff for six years,*"

"Got it," I said. I tried to think of a way to extend the conversation, reluctant to cut ourselves off from our lifeline.

After a few seconds, Morgan said: "*Anything else?*"

I looked over to Bobby, who had been following our conversation through his own earpiece. He shrugged.

"Yeah," he said, quietly. "Do you recommend the venison or the pig?"

At exactly 8 p.m., the sound of a bell rang through the camp, one note then silence, then the same note again. I threw back the flap on our tent, and we stepped out into the night. The wind had picked up a little, and had freshened with the coolness of the front that was now crossing the Tennessee hills from the west. But the air was damp, and the sky above, though dark, showed heavy white patches of fast moving clouds floating by. The perimeter of the meeting grounds was lit by flaming torches. Several more torches surrounded the cross standing like a monolith in the middle of a growing group of white-clad figures. It was like a gathering of ghosts, which seemed to me appropriate, since this specter of our past should have been dead and buried a long time ago.

"Here goes," Bobby whispered, and we headed off to join the party.

There were about fifty to sixty hooded figures gathered before the big cross. The number of newcomers to the cause, signified by the lack of the image of the cross and circle on the chests of their robes, seemed to greatly outnumber the veteran Klansmen. I guessed that this ritual was being run by only a small contingent of the total Klan of the Gold Circle. The important question was whether the upper echelons of the organization were present. Those were the people we wanted to identify.

"Stay close," I said to Bobby, and he nodded.

Klansmen, now without weapons, began to form us into two lines, one behind the other, facing the cross. There were about forty of us in this new group. Like us, most were looking around, wondering what was coming next. Veterans moved among us telling us to face forward and keep quiet. Over the next minute or so, order came over the clearing, and we stood silently.

The bell rang again; once, twice, then silence. There was a sudden commotion behind us, and I could hear footsteps- maybe three or four men-moving toward us. Among our ranks, you could have heard a pin drop. And then we saw them.

Five men, one in the center and the others boxed around him, came into view. They were dressed like the veterans, except that the man in the middle was dressed in a flowing robe of bright gold, a red cross with a black connecting circle stamped in the center of his chest. He was shorter than his guards, and moved slowly, with them in lockstep. He was bent over a little, and shuffled as he walked.

As they passed in front of us, I thought: *this is one of them. This is one of the leaders and perpetrators of all this misery.* I wanted to lunge out at him, rip the gold-colored hood from his head and strangle him here and now. Even more so, I was afraid that Bobby would do just that. I felt a dizzying hatred welling up in me, but I shut my eyes and held my place.

The small group moved to the front of our formation. The Leader stood before the wooden cross, the others, each carrying a Confederate flag; the "Stars and Bars," with its red field, and the Cross of St. Andrew and white stars, that had led the Rebel forces in battle, and that had also struck terror into the hearts of runaway slaves as they were chased down by brutal Home Guard Southern troops, moved slightly farther away from him. He raised his arms in the air, his eyes looking up to the heavens, as if asking some God to bear witness to his majesty.

As he started to speak, I heard a low rumble of distant thunder, and a flash of lightning went off behind the nearby hills.

"Brothers!" he said in a loud, but slightly quavering voice. "We come here this night to stand before our sacred symbol, the Christian cross, to affirm our dedication to the principles of our society. We come here tonight to affirm that we will, through all means necessary, return our beloved way of life to our homeland!"

I stole a look around. The lines of men listened in rapt attention. I thought back to what Bertram Meeks had said: that this was a money play for most of these guys; that the dream of a new Confederacy was in the minds of the die-hard Klansmen only. But these men were listening. They were either good actors, or True Believers.

"We come here tonight," the Leader went on, "to stand on hallowed ground. For it was on this very spot nearly one hundred thirty-five years ago, that the Knights of the Ku Klux Klan were born! It was in this sacred valley, surrounded by our beloved homeland, which had been drenched in Southern blood by the invaders from the North, where our ancestors, my own grandfather's father..."

"Say it!" my mind was screaming. *"Say the name of your bastard ancestor, so that we can track you!"*

"...and that great soldier of the Cause, General Nathan Bedford Forrest, vowed vengeance against those who had stolen our heritage!"

Again the distant rumble of thunder rippled through the valley. The wind freshened into quick, cool gusts and even then I could feel the sweat that ran down my face. I fought the urge to tear off the robe and hood, so that I could let the cooling air wash over me and somehow rid me of the words I was hearing.

"The Negro has been told," the Leader sang out, his voice growing in volume as he spoke, "that he is your equal! He runs rampant through your schools! He violates your homes! He murders your women!" He paused, as if to let the horrors of his pronouncements take hold.

"And now, his brown brothers from south of our borders have joined him in this great assault against our Southern states! They take your jobs! They ruin your neighborhoods! They assault your children. They assault your wives! And all the while Washington does nothing to stem the rising tide! But not all of Washington is sitting by and watching the destruction of our country. You have friends there! You have friends in many places! *We* are your friends!" He wagged his finger at the lines of initiates before him. "And through all the years, only our sacred society has stood between your wives and daughters and the colored hoards."

He raised his arms skyward again, and lightning flashed in the distance, like some staged pyrotechnics meant to emphasize his rant.

"The time has come! We have the resources and the will to take back our homeland!" He lowered his arms, then pointed at us, his gaze and gesture moving down the length of our line. "And your job will be to enforce the wishes of our leadership. Your job will be to keep the coloreds in their place! To punish the criminals until they dare not commit another crime! To destroy anyone who violates the white woman....and to punish any white man who consorts with the Negro woman! Such white people are no better than the Negroes they cohabitate with!"

My knees felt weak. I turned my eyes to look at Bobby Hemphill. He was standing there, stiff and rock-like, but his eyes were closed.

"We shall not allow the mongrelization of the white race! And *you* will be the instrument of our revenge!" He moved forward a little with halting steps, and his shoulders sagged as if he was getting tired. Behind him, one of his guards pulled a torch from the ground, and moved closer to the looming cross.

"Now my Brothers," the Leader said. "Come forth and take the oath! Come forth and be baptized in the fire of our resolve! Raise your fists to the God of our faith! Today, we begin the journey to take back our homeland!"

All around me, the arms rose towards the sky. Bobby's rose, then mine. But I don't remember a word of the oath the others were repeating in loud voices. I couldn't think of anything but the need to be away from this place; to be back in Atlanta, where I would find Abby and take her far away to a place where this kind of hatred, this filth, could never find us again. And I feared in my heart that no such place existed.

There was a sudden blistering heat against my face, and I watched in fascination as the great cross erupted in flames. It seemed to sear the fabric of the hood and robe against me, and I felt a sticky sweat explode all over my body. Yet I couldn't tear my eyes from the blaze. All around us, the members of the Gold Circle were chanting: "*Deo Vindice! Deo Vindice!* With God as our Vindicator!"

The next thing that I remember was Bobby, his hand clamped tightly on my arm, moving me away from the men massed around the cross. The Leader had disappeared, as if he had evaporated in the heat of the fire. Already the solemn gathering was turning into a party; with newly-admitted Klansmen congratulating each other; high-fiving and whooping as if there team had just scored a touchdown, as they moved toward the food and alcohol. Bobby pushed me gently in the other direction until we were back inside our tent. He sat me down and closed the window and door flaps.

"You okay?" he asked me.

I pulled the hood from my head and took a few deep breaths to calm myself. "Yeah," I said as I wiped sweat from my eyes with my sleeve. "I'm fine."

"We've got a problem," he said, softly. "Hitler and his homeboys went back to the big tent. If we can't get them to come out and party with the gang, Morgan's not going to get any pictures to ID."

I shrugged. "If I'd have had a gun it wouldn't have made a difference. I would have shot that sick son of a bitch here and now."

"Maybe we can figure out who that guy was without getting a picture. You heard him say he had a relative here when the Klan was formed, right?"

I shook my head. "I don't know. There could have been a hundred guys here. We don't have that kind of time."

He sighed. "So what do we do now?"

I thought about it for a few seconds. "We go out and help those assholes get stinkin' drunk, then we sneak around and see what we can find out." I pushed the earpiece tighter into my ear. "Morgan?" I said, quietly. "Did you hear that?"

Static crackled in my ear. *"I heard."*

Rebel yells filled the increasingly thick night air over the next several hours. The beer and whiskey flowed as the Klansmen celebrated their induction. A light, misty rain had started to fall around midnight, but no one seemed to notice. Bobby and I were able to stay on the outskirts of the melee, but the golden robe of the Leader never returned, and we heard no information that would help us.

As the party wore down, we returned to the tent and waited for the last of the Klansmen to turn in. It was past 2 a.m. before the camp was completely silent. We were sitting on the cots quietly planning our next move, when we heard raised voices coming from somewhere up ahead. I went to the tent flap and pushed it aside a little, and listened. Someone was moving around out there, and they weren't being careful about the noise they were making.

"Somebody just went into the big tent," I whispered to Bobby as he came up beside me. We could hear voices being raised, but the words were not clear.

I grabbed my hood and pulled it on. Then I motioned to Bobby. "Give me your earpiece," I said, and he handed it over.

"What are you....," he started, but I put a finger to my lips.

"Stay close. I'm going to see if we can catch what their saying." I took a look around, but no one else seemed to have notice anything. So I stepped out as silently as I could with Bobby close behind. We came up behind the Leader's tent. The heated words being spoken inside were still a little jumbled, but I got as close to the window as possible. The flap on the inside of the tent window was down, but not zipped in place, leaving a small opening through which the low light of a camp lantern showed through. I took the earpiece I had gotten from Bobby, and trying very hard to not touch the tent material with my hand, I managed to put the bug into the mesh of the window so that it rested in the opening. Immediately, my own earpiece crackled with the voices of whoever was inside.

Slowly, we backed away, checking constantly to see if anyone had come out and spotted us, but we saw nobody, and got back to our tent safely.

*   *   *   *

"I will remind you, Gerald," the voice I recognized as the Leader's said, sounding like a teacher speaking to an unruly student. "Not to speak to me that way. Must I remind you that we are standing on hallowed ground?"

"Oh, *fuck* your hallowed ground, Arthur!" The speaker was unknown to me, but his tone was commanding.

I could only hope that Terry Morgan was getting all of this, and that he might know who these men were.

"What is it?" Bobby asked, as I put my finger quickly to my lips.

"You purposely ignored my calls for two days," the visitor snapped, angrily. "And I will not accept that! Just what the hell were you thinking? God damn you, Arthur, you won't do that again!"

"You forget yourself, sir!" the Leader's voice was indignant.

'And *you* forget that my ancestors founded the Klan right along with yours! But while you wage your holy war, I'm left to deal with these animals you brought into your Cause!" There was a silence for a moment, then the visitor's voice went on softly, but the bug picked it up clearly. "That man's visit was a direct threat, Arthur, and you refuse to understand that. You hold our lives in your hands if you do not produce that gold. My God! He threatened my grandchildren for Christ's sake!"

"Now, Gerald," the Leader's voice was mollifying, but his visitor was having none of it.

"Don't give me that 'now, Gerald,' crap. He's coming back, and soon. And when he does, I'm pointing him right at you!"

"That will not be necessary. We are almost there, Gerald. The problem will be solved any moment now." The Leader's voice sounded excited and confident.

"Why?" the visitor asked, curiously. "What's happened?"

"We know the location now," the Leader responded gleefully. "I'm sure of it."

"Bullshit! I've heard that all before. You've dug up half the South and haven't found anything," the visitor said, but his tone had changed. Now he was trying to extract information rather than bully.

"No, no Gerald! I'm sure of it now. We have checked every one of the marked spots on the map, and we are down to the final one. And it's so logical! Inspired, even."

I thought: *the map*! It had to be the original of the map Grace Wiggins' sister had sent to me.

"What in God's name are you talking about, Arthur?"

"It's in Irwinville," he said. "A mile north of Irwinville, actually. It *has* to be! Near the very spot where our great president, Jefferson Davis, was captured by the Northern rabble!"

"I don't understand...,"

"The monument! There's a museum and monument near where Davis was captured! He hid the gold before surrendering. It makes so much sense."

The visitor seemed to be considering this information. The silence coming from the Leader's tent was broken by the sound of more thunder, moving ever closer to the valley. The light rain was intensifying, and heavy drops of water began to strike our tent. I pushed the earpiece tighter against my ear and strained to hear.

After a moment, the visitor said: "It doesn't sound like such a sure thing to me. Surely the Union troops would have found the gold?"

"They wouldn't have even looked for it!" the Leader said, dismissively. "They thought the gold was on its way to Mexico. Besides, the Blue Bellies were just ignorant conscripts."

More silence. Then: "You said this place is a monument?"

"A state park," the Leader said.

"And how will you find the right spot? There will be people there, Arthur. For God's sake, they aren't just going to let you tear the place apart!"

The Leader sounded indignant. "Give me some credit, Gerald. The park is closed from 2 p.m. on Sundays until Tuesday morning. Sunday is two days from now. I already have my men on the way there. And anyway, the town is very small, and the site is away from prying eyes. We will find it!"

"You had better," the visitor said. "Because we are nearly out of time, Arthur."

CHAPTER 36

▼

August 30, 2003, Near Dawn
The Valley

Between the utter mental exhaustion and the soft tap of raindrops on our tent, we had both given in to sleep, falling across our hard cots fully clothed. I had dropped off while wondering whether we had accomplished anything with our foray into the heart of the devil. The Leader's identity was still a mystery to us. As for his visitor- someone he was obviously involved with in a big way- we didn't know his identity, either. I had seen enough of the kind of men the Gold Circle had recruited to know that we could deal the organization a real blow if we could cut off the head of the snake. These people were simple, brutal automatons. Guns for hire, like Meeks and Hackley. But that might not stop the criminal leaders appointed to power in the states where the crimes had taken place. Or would take place.

No, the only real answer was to cut off the funds they so desperately wanted, and needed, to continue their reign of terror.

But how to do it? That's when I fell asleep.

I awoke suddenly to the sound of shouting, but Bobby was asleep and hadn't heard it. That's when I realized it was coming through the earpiece still wedged against my ear.

"Tom! Tom, wake up!" the voice was saying. It sounded of urgency and fear.

"Terry?" I said softly. "I hear you, Terry. What's going on?"

"Thank God! Tom, you need to move! You need to get out of there right now."

"Huh," I said, trying to fend off the fog that clouded my mind. "What is it? What are you talk…"

"There's no time to explain. Get Bobby and get out of the camp. You've got maybe five minutes before all hell's going to break loose!"

I reached over and shook Bobby awake. He gave me a puzzled look, seemed to catch the urgency of the conversation he couldn't hear, and rolled to a sitting position.

"The truck...," I started.

"Forget the truck! You'll never get to it. Get moving." Morgan said into my ear. *"Get out of those clothes and head east into the woods. Keep going east toward the Columbia Highway. Do it now."*

Bobby was at the door of the tent, listening intently, and I could hear people stirring nearby. He looked at me, and said: "I think we need to get out of here, Tommy."

I tore at the robe, pulling it up over my head. Bobby did the same. "Okay, Terry," I said. "We're moving out." I took a quick look around, saw no one, but heard excited voices nearby, and the sound was growing.

We stole out of the tent, turned left and quickly ran toward the tree line, thirty feet away. I had no sooner crossed into the woods, barely able to see the terrain before me in the pre-dawn darkness, when I heard someone shout: "There they are!" And almost simultaneously, two shots rang out, and the bark of a nearby tree exploded.

"Shit!" I heard Bobby yell, as we plunged forward on ground soaked and slippery from the rain. The ground was uneven and I found myself sliding down into shallow ditches, then needing to scramble up the other side. Behind us, the sound of Rebel yells and cursing coming from several Klansmen echoed in my ears as they chased us into the woods. More shot, badly aimed and sporadic, passed nearby, and we kept moving as best we could. I heard Bobby close behind me, but I had to keep my eyes glued to the ground in front of me. Even then, I almost went down several times.

My face was being whipped by low hanging, barely visible branches. I took a particularly heavy hit as more bullets surrounded us, and felt the sting on my forehead. Blood trickled down my face, blurring the vision of my left eye as it mixed with the rain. I could taste the salty blood as it flowed across my lips and into my open mouth as I ran.

I heard Bobby behind me. "Split up!" he yelled. 'We're too close!" I saw him moving away from me to the left as I dodged trees.

"No!" I yelled back, but he was already thirty yards away. I had no choice but to plunge on. Behind me, footfalls moving through the wet, tangled brush were coming closer. I could hear the heavy breathing, and then two more shots rang out. Tree bark fragments, like shards of glass, slammed into my face. My ankle buckled momentarily as I stepped into a hole, and the pain shot up my leg. I was able to keep my balance and stay upright, but I knew it was a matter of time before they had me. I gasped for air, my mouth and throat drying more with every rush of oxygen I sucked in.

Suddenly, up ahead maybe twenty yards, a shadow of a figure rose up from the ground, and I thought I saw a weapon come up to draw a bead on me. *This is it. They've got me,* I thought.

Then, with a force I had not felt since my playing days, I was hit with a driving tackle just above my right hip by someone I never saw, and my feet went out from under me. I was slammed to the ground, and felt the wind gush from my aching lungs.

At the same time, I heard the spit of a silenced semi-automatic weapon, and large caliber ammunition flew past me just inches away. I heard the "thunk" of the bullets striking something heavy, and the grunt of their victim as he went down. I heard two more shots and more grunts, then silence.

I took a deep breath and shoved back against the weight pinning me to the ground, and tried to get to my feet.

"Stop!" the voice said, urgently. "Tom, stop it! It's me, Terry."

The realization finally struck me. I was in the hands of the Ops team. But I pulled away from Terry Morgan, and tried to run back toward where the two dead Klansmen lay, looking like broken dolls in their white robes.

Morgan grabbed me again. "Tom, we need to get you out of here, now."

I fought against his grip.

"No!" I shouted. "No, wait! Where's Bobby?!"

Behind us, on the bloody trail leading back toward the meeting ground, there was only the falling raindrops to break the silence.

CHAPTER 37

─────────────── ▼ ───────────────

4:20 A.M.

"What the hell happened?" I said.

I was sitting in the back seat of the Ops team's SUV. Morgan and the man who had shot the two Klansmen who had almost caught me were sitting up front. The doors were closed, but the engine was off.

After I had calmed down enough to get my wits about me, Morgan had led me another half mile or so eastward to a small clearing where the team had set up their base camp. I was pressing a towel against the cut above my left eyebrow, which continued to leak blood.

"Sorry, Tom," Morgan said. "As it is, we were lucky to get word when we did. Another few minutes would have been too late."

"Too late for what? What the hell happened?!" I said, my patience nearly gone.

Morgan turned to face me. "It was Hackley. We let him and Meeks use the john in the barn. Somewhere in there he found a sharp piece of a can or something. Anyway, he used it to cut through the nylon rope he was tied up with and got out through a broken panel in the outside wall of the horse stall."

"Jesus Christ," I said, quietly.

"Before he got away," Morgan said, "he cut Meeks' throat from ear to ear, while he slept."

"God damn it, when did this happen?"

"About two, we think. It took him a little time to get to his sheriff buddy, but he must have known how to reach somebody in the camp. Our guy discovered what happened during a scheduled check on the barn."

I wanted to yell at somebody. I wanted to ask Morgan how he could let this happen. But I didn't say what I was thinking. It wasn't important now. I needed to find Bobby Hemphill, and nothing else mattered.

I heard a buzzing sound, and Morgan touched the earpiece of his headset. "Go," he said, softly, and listened intently for a minute.

"We'll wait for you at the staging area," he responded into the mike wand that floated in front of his mouth. Then he turned back to me. "There's no sign of your friend. My guy says they're breaking camp as quick as they can and are leaving the meeting grounds. He didn't see any sign of Bobby in the camp."

"We have to go back," I pleaded. "I can't leave here without him!"

Morgan shook his head. "No."

"No?! What do you mean, no?!"

"There are more than sixty half drunk, half crazed Klansmen in that valley, Tom," he said. "That's not the way to get your friend back alive. You have to trust me on this, Tom."

I couldn't talk. I could hardly swallow. My mind wouldn't wrap itself around all this. "I can't leave him here, Terry." I said, quietly.

He didn't say anything for a minute, and then he said: "Let's go talk to this guy, Enos. Maybe he'll know where they might take him."

✳   ✳   ✳   ✳

A little before 5 a.m., we parked Morgan's SUV in a field about two hundred yards from Enos' diner and moved along the road to the property. There was no movement, and the windows were dark and there was a heavy stillness in the air around us. We crossed to the door, and Morgan put his ear against the wood. He shook his head. No noise inside. He motioned to one of his men, who moved to the door and bent down to inspect the lock. He took a pick from his pocket, and in seconds, the lock popped open. He held the door open just an inch from the jamb until we got into position, then pushed it open slowly. A dim light spilled into the room as we entered, I carried a Glock .9 mm handgun Morgan had given me, while the others entered still carrying their silenced semis. We fanned out immediately, Morgan and the others out front, with me slightly behind. I could make out a few tables and chairs scattered around the room, and a bar center-right at the back of the room. A door with a window in the top half was next to the bar, and probably led to a kitchen. The stink of bad food and spilled beer, never properly cleaned up, and the stale smell of thousands of cigarettes filled my nostrils. A stairway to the far left led up into darkness.

I stepped forward close to Terry Morgan's ear and said: "Maybe he doesn't live here...."

Morgan put his finger to his lips. He stood stock-still and we followed suit. Then I heard it: a slight movement, Then another. I couldn't get a bead on it. Then came the unmistakable sound of a shotgun being cocked, and suddenly Morgan turned and shoved me down hard to the ground, and he and the others ducked down and rolled away from the light seeping through the doorway with a precision of a drill team.

I caught sight of the huge figure that loomed up from behind the bar as the shotgun discharged, shattering the top half of the door behind me. Enos cocked the gun again as Morgan came up into a crouch and fired back. Enos slammed backwards into the bottles and glasses on the ledge behind the bar as the bullets hit him, and disappeared from sight. All three of the Ops team members were instantly up, surveying the room with their weapons at the ready.

'Clear!" the man to the left shouted.

"Clear!" came from the right.

Morgan was already in motion, sliding over the bar to drop down next to the wounded man. I struggled to my feet and followed him. He was standing over Enos, who lay propped up against the wall where he had fallen. Two spreading florets of blood were centered in the middle of his chest. His labored breathing was the only sound in the suddenly silent room.

Morgan crouched down and pressed two fingers against the man's neck to check his pulse. He looked up at me and gave me a look that said Enos was dying.

"Where's our friend," he said, holding Enos' chin up so that he could look into his eyes.

Enos looked up at him, a bloody smile crossing his face. "In hell," he spit out. His breathing came in gasps as he tried to laugh. But it escaped from his mouth as a gurgle that turned to a cough, as blood ran down his chin. And then, an ominous silence filled the room again.

"Shit!" Morgan said as he stood up. "The son of a bitch knew we were coming." He nodded to one of his ghost- men, a man who had risked his life to help me, yet whose name I still didn't know, and he left us to keep watch at the front door. If Enos had been warned, we could be facing more armed Klansmen at any time. I was standing there, looking down at the pitiful excuse for a human being, when I heard the shotgun discharge, the buckshot slamming into the bar top a foot from my face.

The old woman from the rocking chair stood mid-way down the steps at the far side of the room. She looked at us as she tried to cock the weapon again. I saw her eyes settle on the limp figure of the dead man. A wailing sound, a mixture of hate and fear and sorrow, escaped from her lips. She fired again, this time at Morgan, but he had ducked down behind the bar.

I rose from a crouch, my brain screaming with indignation and a hate of my own that had been building for so long. It had hidden in my soul, but now it exploded in a rage. I raised my weapon, extended both arms and squeezed the trigger. I shot her three times in the chest. The wailing shut off like a spigot, and she hung in the air for what seemed like a lifetime. Then she went over the banister, carrying it with her, and crashed to the floor.

I stood there, immobilized, my .9 mm still pointing at the spot where she had stood. Then I felt the light grip on my arm, as Terry Morgan gently took the weapon from my hand.

"Its okay," he was saying, softly. "Let go, Tom."

I felt myself take a breath and exhale. My arms dropped to my side, but I still stood there, unmoving.

*   *   *   *

I'm not sure how I got back into the SUV, or when we left Enos' for the last time. I know I was confused, and in a state unresponsive to the situation we found ourselves in. My mind was criss-crossing over the events of the last twenty-four hours in no certain order, but at the crux of every thought was the fact that we had left Bobby Hemphill behind to an uncertain fate. Enos had said with his dying breath, that Bobby was "in hell." But I didn't believe that, and neither did Terry Morgan.

"If they have him, he's worth more alive than dead," he had said to me on the way to the diner where Enos had been waiting to surprise us. "They can ransom him, or at least demand we stay out of their business if we want to see him again."

This analysis was way too clinical for me. 'He's my friend, for God's sake! He's my responsibility, and I should have gone back for him!" I said angrily.

Morgan turned and looked at me from the front seat.

"I don't mean to minimize the situation," he said, softly. "Let's see what this Enos knows."

But if he had known anything, he hadn't told us before he died.

*   *   *   *

The sharp ring of Terry Morgan's phone shocked me like cold water thrown in a drunk's face. He spoke and listened for a couple of minutes, then hung up.

"We sent a transcript of the conversation between those Klansmen that you picked up, as well as that speech their leader gave before they started to party, to Jake," he said. "He's running it all through the data base, and later he'll try voice recognition after we get him the tapes we made off your mike."

"I need to talk to Jake and Max Howard," I said. "I need to tell them about Bobby. They can't possibly argue against bringing in the Feds now."

Morgan looked straight ahead. "Not my call."

I couldn't see how it would even be open for discussion at this point. "What the hell else can we do?! His life is in danger! If he's wandering around out there, we need to find him. If those bastards have him, we've got to get the Feds in there to get him out! How can you be so noncommittal about that?"

He continued to stare out the windshield. "I can't afford to get emotionally involved, Tom. Not my job. I don't make policy. I don't have the luxury of second guessing."

"Luxury," I said. And words failed me. Anger stoked by fear, and failure left me feeling numb, and brain dead. "I need to tell Max right now."

Terry Morgan turned to look at me. "He already knows."

CHAPTER 38

▼

August 30, 2003 10:20 A.M.
Atlanta

After that, everything was a blur. We stopped at the farmhouse where Morgan's men were cleaning up the mess made by Hackley. One of the Ops team members brought Bobby's Durango up to the woods near the roadway, and Terry Morgan took the wheel. I climbed into the passenger seat, and we started back to Atlanta. I must have slept most of the way, remembering only Morgan waking me and following me up to my apartment above Ireland's Own.

Now Abby and I were sitting on the old couch in our little living room, waiting for Jake Berger and Max Howard to arrive. Morgan was gone. I played over and over again in my mind the reasons why it was time to stop this game and call in the pros. I needed no one to convince me that this thing had gotten too big for me. Bobby was gone. No one had approached us with any word of his location or condition, and I had to consider the possibility that he was dead.

Abby touched the bandage covering the stitches above my eye, with her cool, gentle fingers.

"Thomas?"

"Hmm?"

"Are you all right? You haven't said a word to me in an hour."

"Sorry, Abby," I said. "I'm sorry. I just can't get my head clear, I guess. I did this all wrong. I should never have let Morgan leave the valley without Bobby."

My brother Pat and C.J. were at the Hemphill house with Bobby's parents. I could just imagine the scene there right now. I should be there with them. I should have been there to apologize to Mrs. Hemphill for putting her son at risk.

"They don't blame you, you know," Abby said, seeming to know what I was thinking.

I looked into her chocolate eyes. "Who else is there to blame? I hatched this crazy plan, and Bobby had no choice but to follow me into that nest of snakes."

She shook her head. "Bobby would follow you anywhere, I know. But he would tell you if he thought you were wrong first, wouldn't he? And he didn't, did he?"

"You don't understand, Abby. You should have seen him. He feels he was the cause of Sabine's death, just like I feel responsible for what's happened to him. All he needed was a plan, right or wrong, smart or stupid. It wouldn't have mattered, and he was ready to follow it. I gave him that plan."

She was silent for awhile. "I think you may have given him a chance for redemption. Even though what happened wasn't his fault, he thought he needed to do something to avenge Sabine."

"But we didn't accomplished a thing," I said, ruefully.

There was a soft knock at the door, and Jake Berger came in. He stood at the door and said, "Abby," with a nod in her direction.

"Hello, Jake," she said with a smile.

He closed the door and looked at me for a minute. "How you doin', sport?"

"Been better," I said.

He walked over to us and raised my chin with his hand, and studied my face.

"Had a gash like that a long time ago. Same spot," he commented. "Bleed like crazy and scar up, too. I got some cream at home that will help make the scar fade after you heal up."

"I'm not worried about scars, Jake."

"Yeah," he said with a sigh. "I know you're not." He sat down in the chair across from us. Abby seemed to sense that he wanted to speak to me alone.

"I'll get some coffee ready," she said, and left us. Jake sat there watching me, not saying anything.

"Where's Max?" I asked.

"He'll be along pretty soon," he said. We sat in silence some more.

Finally, Jake said: "There was another attempted murder last night, in Columbus, near the army base."

It was the last thing I needed to hear, and I covered my eyes with my hand.

"Army sergeant, on leave. Black man, staying at a house he owns with his girl...a pregnant white girl," he said.

And so it goes on, I thought, and then I stopped, and looked at him. "Wait, you said *attempted* murder, I think. Did you mean to say that?"

He nodded. "There were at least three of them," he said. "I guess they never thought he would hear them break in. Two of them never made it back out of the house."

"Could it have just been a similar situation, or a copycat murder?"

"Uh, uh," he said. "Same props, same tattoos on the corpses. A stake and a hatchet with a hammer head on one end."

How'd you find out so fast?" I asked.

"It's called 'exceptional police work,'" he replied with a smile. "I've been getting the word around to cops I know and trust. Detective from Columbus Homicide named Trembley was on the scene. Recognized the deal right away and called me."

"He killed two of 'em," I said, with a touch of satisfaction. "Guess they picked on the wrong people, huh?"

"Actually, they knew exactly who they were going after," Jake said. "One of the dead guys was the girl's brother."

"We shall not allow the mongrelization of the white race! Deo Vindice!"

*   *   *   *

Max Howard and Terry Morgan arrived about ten minutes later. I was already on my feet and ready to plead my case for calling the FBI, but Max motioned to me to sit down. "We'll get to all that in a little while, Tommy."

I couldn't imagine what could be more important, but I took a seat and tried to hide my impatience.

"Let's talk about what we do know," Max said. "We just had a scan run on the voices on the tape of the conversation you recorded at the Klan meeting. Unfortunately, we couldn't match up any names to the voices, but we were able to figure out that the dialect of the head guy is eastern Tennessee, and the second speaker has an accent typical of the Deep South; maybe coastal Alabama, or the Mississippi Delta region."

"That may be of interest down the line, Max," I said as impatience got the best of me. "Right now, all I care about is getting Bobby back safely."

"I know that, Tom," he said, softly. "Us, too."

I was back on my feet again. "So what are we doing about that?" I wanted to know. "Have you called the Feds yet?"

Max looked at Jake, then at me. "We can't do that, son. Not yet."

"Max!" I said, my voice rising. "I don't believe this! What the hell are you waiting for? You know I can't get to him, Max. You know that! What is it, that Saxbee guy you don't trust? There has to be somebody we can go to, if you don't want to contact that guy."

"He's part of the reason, and that's for sure, but not all of it, Tommy. You remember when the head honcho was givin' his big speech? Do you remember what he said about Washington; how those Klan people had friends in Washington?"

I tried to concentrate on what he was saying. "Yeah...I guess so. He did say they had friends in Washington. What's your point, Max?"

"The point is, we have reason to believe that some very high up people are involved in this. Maybe they're higher-ups in the FBI, maybe not. But how high would we have to go to reach somebody who isn't tainted by this thing?"

I felt like I was living a bad dream. "You can't honestly believe the whole U.S. government is involved?"

"Never said that," Max said, as he shook his head. "But where are the people who *are* involved hiding? Truth is, it appears somebody is protecting these Klan people."

I could feel defeat seeping into my heart. "What do we do, Max?" I said, softly. "What do we do for Bobby?"

Jake Berger spoke up. "According to the tape, somebody is going to be at the Jefferson Davis memorial south of Atlanta tomorrow night, and they think they're going to be retrieving the Confederate gold. We need to be there, too."

"To do what, Jake? Kill more people?" I said with exasperation. "Is that the answer?"

"I was thinking more along the lines that if we can get our hands on the gold, we'll have a bargaining chip for getting Bobby back."

I sighed. "If there's anything to get back," I said. Jake ignored my comment, and turned to Terry Morgan, who had been silent since arriving with Max.

"Can it be done?" Jake asked him.

"Maybe," he answered, slowly. "But there are a few things that bother me." We waited silently for him to go on. "I checked out this memorial park on Google. Thing's about eighteen acres. If these guys don't know exactly where to look, it could take a month of Sundays to find the gold. Nobody's going to get away with that."

Max said: "You heard the tape, son. That's where they're goin', so they must know exactly where to look, right?"

"You've seen the map, Max," I said. "There's nothing that specific on it by a long shot."

No one said anything for a few minutes, then Max Howard shrugged his shoulders. "It's all we got."

* * * *

We made plans to leave early the next morning. Abby had a late morning class at Georgia Tech that I had to convince her not to miss. Terry Morgan went to contact his team, and Max and Jake headed back to their offices. I was nursing a tequila and orange juice on the couch in the living room. There was a soft knock at the door, which I figured would be Pat coming to check on his baby brother. I yelled "come in," and the door opened. Bobby's father stood in the doorway, and I nearly knocked over my drink getting to my feet. I felt suddenly embarrassed.

"Mr. Hemphill," I stammered. "Sorry, sir, I wasn't expecting...."

"I'm the one who should apologize, coming by unannounced, Tom."

"No, sir. You're always welcome here." I motioned to the old chair. "Would you like to sit down? Can I get you...."

He held up his hand. "I can only stay a minute."

We stood a few feet from each other. I was hardly able to look into his eyes.

"I think I know how you're feeling, Thomas," he said. "I just wanted to stop by and tell you that...well, no matter what happens, I think you and Bobby did the right thing going into that Klan meeting."

I started to speak, but he raised his hand again.

"Ever since that girl died, Bobby hasn't been the same. I think he had to try and do this with you. I think I would have done the same thing."

My legs felt weak below me, and I sat down.

"What is it Mel Gibson said in that movie?" he smiled wanly. "'I've long feared that the sins of my past would return to haunt me,' I think it was, or something like that." He shook his head, slowly. "We Southerners have a lot to atone for, Tom. But if the public knew about all of this, I'm sure there'd be a lot more on your side than against you."

He turned and walked to the door. "You be careful, son," he said, and walked out.

Hot tears ran down my face as I listened to his footsteps fade on the stairs.

CHAPTER 39

▼

August 31, 2003 2:20 P.M.
Irwinville, Georgia

We made the trip from Atlanta in just under three hours, traveling in my brother's big Chevy Suburban so that we could travel together. Pat had insisted on coming with us, which I had reluctantly agreed to, but only after he had promised to wait back at the interstate until we called him to come get us.

We arrived well in advance of the afternoon closing time of the park, and after checking out the road pattern and the nearby buildings, we drove back to a service plaza eleven miles away at I-75, and took a room in a dingy motel on the property that was meant to service truckers needing a cheap place to crash for a few hours during long hauls. Then we sent Pat back to the Davis memorial, where, posing as a tourist, he picked up a copy of the pamphlet showing the entire property.

"As you can see," Terry Morgan said, "we're dealing with about eighteen acres. Most of the memorial and historic displays are centered at the museum, here." He pointed to the great white plantation-styled building a hundred yards off the highway. "It's obviously very visible from the road."

Our team, including Jake Berger, Morgan and three of his Black Ops team members that had been close enough to Atlanta to join us before we had left for Irwinville, took turns familiarizing ourselves with the layout. We were all dressed in dark clothing: jeans, dark tees, but the Ops team had foregone their military garb.

"The rest of the park is mostly picnic areas and walking trails," Morgan told us. "It's not likely these guys are going to just walk up the front entrance drive, so my best guess is that they are going to come in overland and get set up in the wooded area, away from the road. That's exactly what we're going to do, too."

"What if they're already in place?" I asked. Morgan gave me a look that said, *I thought about that, too.*

"Then we better hope they don't have more people than we do." Then he added, "But I bet they will." Morgan motioned to one of his men who produced an eight by ten aerial with the Jefferson Davis Memorial State Park centered in the image.

"This is the latest intel-sat photo at four hundred feet per inch, so we're covering about a quarter mile east and west of the park, and even further to the north and south." He pointed to a large contiguous parcel on the north side. "The land around here is pretty flat. I think Pat should drive across this field and insert us here." He pointed to the northwest corner of the parkland. "There're no houses nearby, so we should be able to get in there undetected."

"Then what?" I asked.

"We'll walk in like this," he said, using a red felt tip pen to trace three parallel lines into the park, each stopping within sight of the museum, yet deep enough in the woods to see anyone else moving in that direction.

"Two men here, two here, and you and I over here, Tom." I didn't have to be told that I was the least experienced at this kind of operation, and Morgan was right to have me sticking by his side. "Ideally, we want to sit back and let these guys dig up the gold, then step in and take them down," he continued. "But we have to consider the probability that they are most likely to be heavily armed, or have armed back-up with them for protection. If it comes to that, and the shooting starts, we need to make sure we take some of them alive. You two," he said, pointing to Jake and one of the Ops team member. "You're Team Two. You guys," he pointed to his other team members, are Team Three. We're Team One. If you spot anybody, just say your team number into your headset mike wand. Everyone else converge on that location, unless you spot additional people near your own location. Keep the talking to a minimum."

"I wonder how they expect to get that much gold out of here in such a short time," Jake said. "We're talking some heavy shit."

Terry Morgan shrugged. "We have to assume they will have some trucks standing by, or maybe they just intend to find it, rebury it and remove it over time. But that leaves open the chance of someone stumbling onto the burial site. They'd be foolish to chance that."

"We would never be able to remove it, even with their trucks," Jake said.

"We don't need to remove it," I said quietly. "We just need to stop them from taking it." I glanced at my watch. "The park closes in about an hour. Park staff will probably be out of there a half hour or so later. When do we go?"

"Right now," Morgan said.

"Terry," I said. "What if there're some guards or rangers or whatever on site during the time the park is closed? We could be putting more innocent people at risk."

"Yeah, but I don't think the bad guys would be trying this without knowing if the place is guarded," he answered. "Besides, it's a pretty rural park. I think it would be unguarded. In any case, we have no choice but to proceed as planned."

We separated at the drop-off point and moved into the woods, stretching out until each of our teams were about seventy or eighty yards apart. I stayed behind Morgan, letting him take the point position, and tried to scan the areas to our right and left. There were no signs of movement, and a deathly quiet surrounded us. We reached our position just inside the tree line to the southwest of the museum building. From there we had an open view of the lawns around the building, yet enough cover to be invisible to anyone approaching from the roadway. Morgan motioned me down next to him behind some heavy brush.

"You okay?" he asked.

"Yeah," I said, not feeling as confident as I tried to sound. I was harboring the hope that they would have Bobby Hemphill with them when they showed up. But I knew in my heart that they wouldn't, and I feared we would lose ground in finding him if things went badly. This was an enemy who showed no mercy. Morgan glanced at his watch as the last car in the parking lot, just visible at the front of the museum, drove down the long driveway to the road entrance. There, it stopped and the driver got out, closed the gate behind him, and then drove away. We were alone.

"One in place," he said quietly. Through my headset, with the earpiece tight against my ear, I heard: "Two in place," then "Three in place." Then silence again.

And that's the way it stayed for nearly three hours.

"This is Two, come in One." It took me a minute to register the voice coming in over the headset, but Terry Morgan answered immediately.

"One, over."

"This is Two," the voice went on. "Eight bogeys passing between Two and Three. Armed with automatics. Look like suppressed Mac 10's. Heading forward toward the clearing, over."

"Copy," Morgan whispered.

"Bogeys passing Three, in full view now, over," came next.

"Copy. Hold your positions. One, over." He motioned to me to slide further to the right, and as I did, he followed. Then we picked up the first sounds of the Klansmen heading our way. I pulled the Glock from its holster, hoping I wouldn't have to use it. Morgan slid closer to me. "Mac 10's with silencers," he said. "Nasty. You can empty a 30 round clip of .9 mm shells in about three seconds. They mean business."

Now they were in view. They wore black clothes like us, and moved through the woods with a confident sense of purpose. I could make out faces now, and wondered if these animals had been at the meeting ground, too. But these guys weren't acting like the untrained louts we had run into there. I felt a rush that was part excitement, and part fear. This was a chance to get some hard information, and maybe an upper hand, if we didn't screw up.

My weapon lay in my hand, as my finger slid along the trigger guard. Morgan reached over and put his hand on my forearm, as if to say, "steady." Klansmen, bogeys, murderers. I didn't care what they were called. These men had killed innocent people. And they had Bobby. They were barely forty feet away now. I just wanted to end this, and I fought the urge to jump them.

Suddenly, as they reached the edge of the clearing lying between us and the museum, their leader held up a hand, and they stopped. He made a fanning motion, and they spread out in front of us in a silent movement into a line, and dropped to the ground. They were about thirty-five yards from the empty building.

They didn't move. My nerves were raw, and my skin itched from the sweat that coursed around under my dark clothing as the heat of the day began to fade. Twenty minutes passed, and still no movement from the eight Klansmen.

Terry Morgan looked at me, as if to say, "What the hell?" then he said, "This is One. All Teams, to my position, over."

"Two moving, over."

"Three moving, over."

He looked at me and, covering his mike wand whispered: "These guys aren't here to dig for treasure."

"Protection?"

"For who? Where are the diggers? Who or what are they waiting for?" I was at a loss.

The others reached us quickly, sweating and breathing hard. Jake leaned over us to take a look.

"I don't get it," he said.

The sun had fallen well below the tree tops behind us now, and true dusk was upon us. Still the Klansmen didn't move, and another half hour passed. The dial on my watch read, 7:10.

"This is makin' no sense at all," Morgan said. "Team Two, work your way over to a position behind the northern end of their line. Team Three move...."

I grabbed his arm. "Wait! Something's happening." The bogey team leader was up on his knees, then upright. Signaling his men to hold their positions, he moved quickly forward in a crouch toward the museum. He slipped up against the rear of the building, then, after waiting about a minute, pumped his arm upward, and the rest of the Klansmen were on their feet and moving to his position. They spread out along the wall, crouched down and waited, weapons at the ready. Nothing happened. Only silence came from inside the museum.

Daylight was fading quickly, but I thought I saw the Klan leader put a phone or walky-talky to his ear. Was he finally calling in the treasure hunters? Was the gold hidden inside the museum?

There was an interminable wait as we watched the leader for a sign that the next phase of their operation was about to begin. Five minutes later, he was still talking.

"Somebody's confused about something," Jake said.

"Big time," Terry Morgan said.

"What do you mean by that, Jake?" I asked.

"They already wasted too much time to have any real chance to search, especially with the light nearly gone. Whoever they're waiting for is long overdue."

"He's moving!" Morgan said. We watched as the leader moved to the south side of the building, looked around, then motioned to his team to follow.

"He must be going in." I said, excitement building again. I could feel every nerve firing.

But he wasn't. A moment later, two big, dark colored vehicles that looked to be Ford Explorers pulled up sharply in front of the park entrance. Suddenly I was back on the *Autopista* highway in Cuba, dodging two Explorers just like these, full of people trying to kill Abby, and Bobby, and me. I shook off the memory of that nightmare. The Klansmen were up and running toward the SUV's, and in less than a minute, were climbing into them.

I was up on my feet. "What do we do?!" I yelled, no longer worried about being heard by our armed enemy.

Morgan stood up. "Nothing," he said quietly.

"Nothing?! Jesus! Nothing?!" I shouted. I looked back at the two vehicles, but they were already quickly moving away down the deserted road. "Terry, for God's sake!" I said, forlornly.

"We can't catch them," he said, shaking his head. "Even if we could, I'm not going to risk getting someone killed for nothing."

"Nothing?! They have Bobby, for Christ's sake!"

"He's right, Tom," Jake broke in. "They don't have the gold, and these guys don't have Bobby. I doubt they have any idea who Bobby is. They were professionals. I think they were hired guns doing a job. The job wasn't panning out, so they cut their chance of losses and got outta' here."

My disappointment was evident. I didn't know what else to say.

"We should get out of here," Morgan said. "You might as well call your brother and have him meet us."

I had turned my phone off, but had kept it with me so that I could reach Pat when we were ready for extraction. I turned it on and waited for the power bars to come up. But before I could punch in the number of Pat's line, the phone rang loudly, breaking the silence of the woods.

"Pat?" I said. There was a long silence on the other end.

Then a voice I didn't recognize said: "Are you starting to get the picture, Mr. Patrick?"

I glanced up at Jake. "What?" I said into the phone. "Who is this?"

"It was a ruse, Mr. Patrick; a trick of sorts," the voice went on. "Don't feel too badly. It was not meant to fool *you*, but someone else. Sometimes we get caught up in the deceit of others though, don't we?" The voice was cultured, educated, but I didn't understand the words.

"Who is this?!" I said, more urgently, and Jake gave me a questioning look. "What are you saying?"

"Listen carefully, Mr. Patrick. No one is coming there to retrieve the Treasury of the Confederacy. It simply is not there, you see. I know this for a fact, and so does the man who uttered the words that made you go there."

"I don't......"

"Listen!" The voice said more forcefully, and then resumed a quiet tone. Jake moved next to me, and I tilted the phone slightly so that he could hear. "The man you seek is going after the treasure. He will be in place to make his grab for it tomorrow evening, after dark. We require your attendance and assistance to make sure that doesn't happen."

"You're talking crazy," I said frantically. "I don't understand. Who are you, and why should I want to help you?"

"Why indeed," the voice said gently. "Never-the-less, you *will* help us. By the way, your Abby Barrett is a lovely young lady. So cultured and kind. She has agreed to accompany us to the place where we will await your arrival."

I broke out in a cold sweat. The nightmare was back again, vivid and terrifying.

"Be assured, we have no interest in harming your young lady," the voice went on. "But you will have to come to us. You should return home as soon as possible. There will be a brown envelope under your door with instructions which you should familiarize yourself with quickly, as there are travel plans to make. Please come alone, Mr. Patrick. In fact, I insist."

"Wait!" I shouted into the phone. "What are you doin?! Why are you involving...." But the line had gone dead. Frantically, I punched in the code for caller ID, but the incoming number had been blocked. I looked up at Jake.

"They've got Abby," I said.

CHAPTER 40

—————— ▼ ——————

11:45 P.M.

The instructions were right where the voice on the phone had said they would be.

After a harrowing trip back to Atlanta, which included a maddening half hour delay sitting still on the Interstate while tow trucks cleared an accident near Macon, I had run up to the apartment to find the flat brown envelope under my door. I had run through the place and found no signs of a struggle, but Abby was not there. I calmed myself as much as possible, thinking I would call Maria Barrett, and prayed that I might find her there. But I was worried about frightening Abby's mom, and bringing back those dreaded memories of Cuba again. Besides, I knew in my heart that this was no joke, no put-up job. They had her. I was sure of it.

I tried to keep my emotions bottled up as Jake, Terry Morgan, Pat, and Max sat in the empty rear room of Ireland's Own, and studied the contents of the envelope. "Memphis?" Max said as he read the single sheet of white paper. "Does this mean the gold's in Memphis?"

"Abby must be there," I said. "That's all I care about. Why else would they want me to meet them there?"

He looked at me, sympathetically. "We'll get her back, son. I promise you that."

I shook my head. "Not 'we,' Max. Me. They said to come alone, and that's how we're going to do it."

"Now, Tom...."

"This isn't open to discussion," I said. I had never talked to Max Howard with anything but the deepest respect, but Abby was not going to be the pawn in this thing. I wasn't going to lose her, not for this.

Terry Morgan took the paper from Max' hand. "I know this place," he said. "This Jefferson Davis monument at First and Union Street where you're supposed to make contact with the kidnappers. That's in the Confederate Park along the Mississippi River."

"You mean like the one in Irwinville?" Jake asked.

"Kinda', but it's an urban park, not very big; some statues, a museum, river walk; that type of thing, but it's just off I-40 along the river. As I remember, there's not much cover. It's a pretty open space, so we should be able to see Tom at all times. That Mud Island Riverboat museum," he pointed at a small island just off the river's bank, "is right across from the park. We might be able to get a sight line...."

"You guys aren't listening!" I said. "I'm going alone." The room fell silent. Then Pat gave me a long steady look; the kind that passes wordlessly between people who know each other's heart, and said: "It's Tommy's show. He says he's going alone, then he's going alone."

Jake sighed. "Okay, Tom," was all he said. And I thanked him silently. "Your instructions are pretty simple, but lets go over this one more time. You're to arrive at the park at midnight and go directly to the Davis memorial. The statue is located here, just about a hundred feet or so from the riverbank. Then," he said, slowly, "You wait."

"Okay," I said. "I've got it, but now I need to figure out how to get there without being tracked. Whoever called me today seems to know exactly where I am at all times. If I can get there earlier, I can have a chance to scout around and get the lay of the land in case we need a way out fast."

We were silent for a while, and then Jake said: "Jimmy Winston. He still have access to that Bell Jet Ranger?"

Morgan gave him a knowing smile. "Twenty-four/seven," he said. "Good idea, Jake. I'll get him on the phone and brief him."

"Who is this guy?" I asked.

"Top notch 'copter pilot. A good friend we can trust to do exactly what we need done, when we need it done," Jake said. "He can get you to Memphis fast and be available to you as long as you need him, and we can hook you up to the 'copter radio with one of Terry's super-duper earpiece mikes. At least then we can monitor your progress. Okay?"

I nodded. "But he stays out of the way, right?" I said, warily.

"Yes."

"What about a weapon?" Pat said. "There's nothing in the instructions about him showing up without a weapon, right?"

"Right," Jake said. "They know there's no way they could guarantee against that anyway, so you should take that Glock and a couple ammo clips.

Since you won't have to take a plane, we don't have to worry about you being stopped by security."

"But won't we have to file a flight plan and leave from an airport?"

"Not if you know where the riding stables are on the Lake Lanier Islands," Terry Morgan said, as he rejoined us.

"I do," I said.

"Good. Jimmy can meet us there at the big open field near the entrance to the corrals at 6 p.m. tomorrow," he said. "And," he looked at Jake. "You remember Arnie Peevy? He still lives just across the Mississippi River about ten miles from I-40. Jimmy will arrange to land on his farm, and they'll have a car for Tom to use, so we won't have to set up a rental. Arnie still flies that old bi-plane he restored, so he's got aviation gas on site for the 'copter."

I stood up. "Okay, then. We're all set, right?"

Jake nodded, But Max remained silent, his demeanor worried and unsure. I went to him and put a hand on his shoulder, and he looked up at me.

"How about Tuesday morning?" I said. "*Jimmy's Bayou* on Peachtree for beignets?"

He smiled back. "You're on," he said.

✱   ✱   ✱   ✱

September 1, 2003

The night was interminable. I couldn't close my eyes as I lay fully clothed on our bed in the little apartment that seemed empty and desolate without Abby.

The next morning was even worse as I faced many hours of waiting before I could meet this Jimmy Winston. At four, I took a cab to Max' office, but instead of going into the office building, I took the elevator to the third level of the parking garage. There, Max was waiting for me with his assistant, Coral Mae's, car.

"This should get us outta' here unnoticed," he said. "We should get to the islands by five, five-fifteen."

"Then we better get going," I said, slumping down in the passenger seat.

We reached the islands out in the middle of the huge expanse of Lake Lanier, about thirty-five miles north of Atlanta, via the Holiday Road causeway, right on time. By a quarter to six, Max had parked near the open field. The stables were closed for the night, so we were alone. We waited in the car. My nerves had already taken a big hit, what with worrying about Abby, and Bobby, and the long wait for this rendezvous with my pilot for the trip to Memphis. I felt a thin layer of sweat forming on my face, and it was hard to sit still.

I was the first to hear the whipping sound of the chopper blades approaching. We got out of the car and caught sight of the Jet Ranger as it circled and came in to drop gently to the ground just a few feet away. The blades slowed but the engine did not shut down. Max and I ran up to the side of the chopper, and the pilot opened his door. We got close and he shouted down: "You Patrick?"

"Yes!" I shouted back. "Thomas Patrick. Terry sent us...."

"I know all about it, son. Let's get a move-on."

I turned to Max, and he gave me a quick hug. "Good luck, Tommy," he said, and stepped away as I popped the rear door and climbed in. I slammed the door and strapped on my harness.

Winston turned and tapped his earphones, and pointed to another pair lying on the other rear seat. "Gonna' get noisy as hell in here," he said, as I put them on and plugged into the chopper's intercom. "Ready?"

I gave him a thumbs up, and we lifted off, reached a hundred feet, and rolled to the northwest over the lake. I looked back and watched as Max stood by the car and watched us fade away.

CHAPTER 41

▼

8:30 P.M.
Memphis, Tennessee

Winston crossed over the downtown area of Memphis just after sunset. The Confederate Park was off to the port side, and, in the bright light of the new moon, I could see the criss-cross of walkways wandering through the parkland. He banked left about a mile past the place where I hoped to find Abby, and approached the park from the Mississippi River side.

"You okay with that?" he said, over the headset. "We better not pass by again, or it might look like we're casing the joint to anybody who might be watching."

I gave him a thumbs up. He was right. There were still a few people visible at the park, especially along Union Street, but it was still early, and I wasn't due back here for three and a half hours. By then, the place would be deserted... at least by innocent people. We banked right, crossed the Mississippi, and entered Arkansas air space. Ten minutes later, in almost complete darkness, Jimmy Winston dropped the Jet Ranger neatly and gently onto an empty field, and cut the engine.

"You've done this before," I said as we jumped down from the cabin and shook hands for the first time. He was about six feet tall and very thin, with one of those little tufts of hair under his lower lip.

"Just a few times for the Navy," he said.

"Don't let that guy fool you with that modesty crap," a voice said from the other side of the chopper. A man I took to be Arnie Peevy, short, bearded, in his sixties and fit, wearing a University of Arkansas ball cap came around to join us, and the two men laughed and hugged.

"This guy pulled more downed pilots outta' the sea off the old *John F. Kennedy* than anyone in the history of the U.S. Navy, including my sorry ass….twice!" He turned serious. "Son, I hear you got troubles. You couldn't have a better man on your side, and that's a fact."

"I appreciate that, Mr. Peevy. In fact, I'm grateful for all your help. But I have to do this alone. I don't want anybody else in harm's way, and I'm afraid they'll hurt the girl if I don't do exactly what they want me to do."

Peevy gave me an appraising look, and then he said: "Okay, son. I respect that. But you just remember, it looks like you could be goin' up against some bad critters, and me and this here 'ol dog are ready to help if you change your mind. Now, come on up to the house. You got time to eat, and I got a wife dyin' to cook."

I added Jimmy Winston's phone number to my speed dial of my cell phone, and made arrangements as to two different locations where he could meet me after I had Abby, including a landing directly at the Confederate Park if it became necessary to make a quick get-a-way. Arnie Peevy gave me a map showing me the best places to park the car and get unseen onto the grounds.

"You should be okay," Peevy had said. "Downtown will be pretty much deserted that time of night. Memphis ain't exactly Chicago."

As I crossed over I-40, I saw that the park, off to my right, was in darkness. Union Street was quiet, and I was able to find the first parking area that Arnie had marked, about an eighth of a mile from my destination, without trouble. Heading west on foot a short distance, I came to the east bank of the Mississippi, turned north, and a few minutes later, found myself at the southern edge of the park. I got low to the ground and listened. Nothing; just the sound of the river lapping against the shoreline as a barge passed by. I stood up, but before moving on, I took the Glock .9 mm out of the shoulder holster inside my light windbreaker, and tucked it into the waistband of my jeans.

When I reached the ring of bushes encircling the Davis monument, I dropped to the ground and stayed as still as possible. There wasn't anyone around that I could see, so I got up into a crouch and approached the statue. The first shot, a muffled round from a silenced pistol, smacked into the granite, spraying me with shrapnel from the stone. I had just enough time to think: *You fool,* before a second shot slashed the right sleeve of my windbreaker, and I felt the stinging pain as my flesh tore away.

I dropped the Glock, and as I tried to grab it, a voice boomed.

"Hold it right there!"

I froze. The pain was spreading down my arm, and I felt the wetness. I stood up and faced an old man holding a gun trained on me, and supporting himself with a silver headed cane.

"So," he said, his accent heavily Southern. "This is the face of a spy."

"What the fuck are you talking about?" I spat back.

"You, sir!" he snarled. ""It was you who dared to invade the sanctity of our meeting!" It was then that I recognized the voice of the Leader of the Gold Circle. This old man was the cause of all the misery so many had endured.

"It was you," I said quietly. "You're the crazy bastard who had those people killed. It was you that spoke those vile, hateful words that night in the valley, wasn't it?"

"People?" he said, a look of amusement crossing his face. "People? You could never understand, could you? The colored races are not people! God would have smote them down centuries ago were it not for the benevolence of the white race! It is our bound duty to keep them in their place and protect them from themselves. They are property to be cared for!"

"You're deranged!" I yelled. "You didn't care who you had killed."

The Leader kept the gun trained on me as he held his cane up to the heavens. "Thou shall not begat with inferior races! It is the law of our God!"

"*Our God?* I don't think so, you lunatic."

He wasn't listening to me. "But *you* have taken the pure blood of Southern Patriots," he said. "And then you had the nerve to summon me here, like some lackey! You dared to summon me to a duel on holy ground!"

"You're crazy. I don't know what you're talking about!" I said. "I just want the girl back!"

"Do not deny!" he said, still not listening to me. His voice rose and his eyes bulged with hatred. "Do not deny, sir! Your Niggers and your *His-pan-ics*," he spat out the word. "They cannot save you!" he pointed the gun at my chest. "You have interfered with our plans one time to many. You should have learned how we deal with spies by how we dealt with that policeman in Nashville, and that lawyer in Atlanta. We cannot be stopped! We will have what is, by right, our destiny!"

I fought the rage that was erupting within me as I heard the dismissive talk of Carl Lee Wiggins and Willie Patton. But I knew I was powerless to do anything about it.

"You are charged as an enemy of the Confederate States of America, and are here so adjudged!" he sneered. "Your sentence is death by firing squad; the sentence to be carried out immediately!"

I stared at the gun pointed at my chest and waited for the kill shot. Instead, I heard a "grunt" and a sharp cry. Suddenly, the old man's hand dropped to his side, his eyes lost focus, and the cane fell from his hand. He fell to his knees, pitching forward in a heap. The unexpected movement caught me by surprise, and it took a few seconds for my brain to register that there was someone standing where the Leader of the Klan of the Gold Circe had been standing only a moment ago. He was a smallish black man, maybe seventy or more years old, dressed in a dark suit, but tieless. In his hand, which was now pointed in my direction, was a silenced handgun.

We stood looking at each other. The blood continued to trickle down my arm, and I was feeling a little lightheaded, but when he said: "Good evening, young Mr. Patrick," I knew that it was the voice that had called me to say that he had Abby. He was flanked by two large black men.

"Who the hell are you?" I said quietly.

"My name is Walter Sampson, and I am pleased to lead an organization that shall go nameless for the moment. I am your host for this evening's festivities, of course." He dropped the weapon to his side. "I don't think we will need this," he said. "But perhaps you will step away from your weapon while we talk?"

I knew that this man would not be here alone, and that I was being watched. I had no choice but to step further away from the Glock lying on the grass. "Your 'festivities' include murder, I see," I snapped back. "Where's Abby?!"

The man held up his hand and said, "All in good time, sir. First, I will explain why I sent for you to come here tonight."

"I know why, God damn it! You brought me here to use as bait to catch that sack of shit!" I yelled, pointing at the dead man lying before me. "You told him I'd be here!"

"Guilty as charged," he said, "at least in part. And by the way, that 'sack of shit,' I believe you called him was about to kill you, but yes, I knew he'd come here himself if he could kill you, and it was he that we wanted. In any case, I don't believe you have been formally introduced to this man." He nudged the corpse with the toe of his shoe and said: "I'm pleased to introduce you to the, ahh…recently deceased Senior Senator from the Great State of Tennessee, Arthur Ellis."

I was dumbfounded; shocked into silence.

"I believe," Sampson said, "you may also know him as the Leader of the Gold Circle Klavern of the Ku Klux Klan. You recently attended a little event he presided over near Pulaski, did you not?"

"I…I know about that," I stammered. "But you're telling me he's a U.S. senator?!"

"Was," said Walter Sampson, lightly. "You and I have been pursuing the same ends, Mr. Patrick. We have both been attempting to end the reign of terror Ellis and his cohorts have been inflicting on the South. That is why you are here. I wish to have you share in the finale of this sordid affair."

"What about the men he brought with him? There must be some of his men around."

"Let's just say they are not an issue at this time," Sampson said.

My head was spinning; the implication of his words, clear. And the continuing drip of blood from my wound was having an effect. I leaned back against the monument. "Why should I believe you?" I said, bitterly. "You kidnapped Abby and almost got me killed."

Sampson smiled. "Perhaps we should take care of that wound, and heal the distrust in your heart as well." He raised his hand, and there was a rustling in the bushes nearby. And then, suddenly she was there. Abby was there, then in my arms, and I held her tightly.

"I'm okay, Thomas," she said as I kissed her. "Really, I'm fine. Let me see your arm."

I let her pull the sleeve of my windbreaker gently down my arm, ignoring Sampson for the moment, and basked in the nearness of her.

"I though I'd lost you....," I said, and she touched my lips with her cool finger tips. "I'm here, Thomas." Then I heard someone step from the direction from which Abby had appeared.

"How do, Mista' Patrick," a voice said.

CHAPTER 42

▼

Memphis, Tennessee

I thought that I must be dreaming. But I knew that voice, and I squinted into the darkness and searched out the face.

"Cletus?" I said, quietly. "Cletus? Is that you? What are you doing here?"

Cletus Mackey, proprietor of Mo Kelly's Bar in Nashville stepped out of the shadows. "Been in it all the time, Mista' Patrick." Abby tore the hem of her skirt away, and tied it around my wound to staunch the flow of blood. Cletus came over to us, and gently took my other arm and helped Abby walk me over to a bench a few feet away. I sat down heavily.

"I don't understand any of this," I said to Walter Sampson. "What's Cletus doing here? Who are you people, really?"

He moved closer to us, and Arthur Ellis' body no longer lay between us.

"Cletus is my grandson, Mr. Patrick," he said. "And I am the great, great grandson of Horatio Mackey."

I shook my head. "Is that supposed to mean something to me?"

He sat down on the bench next to me. "Horatio Mackey was the manservant to the President of the Confederate States of America." He looked up. "The very man under whose statue we sit at this moment. In truth, he was a life-long companion to Jefferson Davis. They grew up together, and as was the custom of the time, Horatio learned to take care of his young master, and eventually his whole family. Three days before Mr. Davis suffered the first of the strokes that would deprive him of his physical and mental abilities, he gave Horatio a map; a very detailed map; which showed the location of the hidden Treasury of the Confederacy."

Sampson stopped, and let me absorb this information. He had my undivided attention, at least as much as my light-headed state would allow. Abby put her arm around my shoulders and we waited for Sampson to continue.

"His instructions were to deliver the map to Davis' most trusted general, Nathan Bedford Forrest, who had resumed his residency here in Tennessee after the war. But Horatio never delivered the map. To do so, he would have had to travel from Louisiana, where Davis died, to Tennessee. That was a very dangerous undertaking for a Negro even in the 1880's. In any case, Davis died. Horatio was unable to read, and not knowing what the significance of the map was, decided that it was unimportant, and kept it as a keepsake of his years with the Davis family. It has been passed down in our family all these years."

"The map Carl Lee Wiggins found?" I asked.

"He didn't find it, Mr. Patrick. We provided him with a copy of a much less specific map meant only to keep his interest in pursuing the crimes he was investigating."

I shook my head. "So Cletus fed him false information, and he got himself killed because of it." It wasn't a question.

"Regrettably, yes." Sampson said simply.

"But how did Ellis get a copy of it?" I asked.

"We arranged for him to find another copy of the doctored map. We had known about his obsession with a new Confederacy and the Confederate treasure, which has been a magnate for treasure hunters and conspiracy theorists since the war ended. In fact, the Gold Circle was actually formed to *protect* the gold from being found by persons disloyal to the ideals of the Confederacy." He smiled. "It wasn't hard to pique the senator's interest. He *wanted* to believe the map held the secret."

"But it does exist, doesn't it" Abby asked.

"Oh, yes, dear lady. The gold does indeed exist."

"You said Ellis would be here to retrieve the gold," I said. "Why this wasted trip to Irwinville? The guys that showed up there weren't looking for treasure."

"In a way they were," Sampson said. "Ellis told his chief partner in crime that the gold was there because he no longer trusted him. Ellis felt he had been poorly treated and his leadership threatened by his partner, and began to understand that others were in this venture for the money, not the Glorious Cause. Irwinville was a test. His partner, the man who showed up at the meeting grounds late the night of your escape sent men down there to capture the gold after Ellis' men dug it up. The partner failed the test, of course, so the Senator now knew he was expendable, and took action to protect his dream."

"And now Ellis is dead, and I never got to find out where *my* partner is being held." I said, ruefully. "Now that you've blown this thing up, Bobby Hemphill is expendable to them."

"Mr. Hemphill is not with them," he said, and smiled again. Walter Sampson motioned to Cletus Mackey, and the tall man disappeared into the bushes again. In a moment he was back, along with another man I hadn't seen before. They were holding up an obviously semi-conscious Bobby Hemphill between them. I started to jump up from the bench, but Sampson put an arm on my sleeve.

"Do not be alarmed by Mr. Hemphill's appearance," he reassured us. "He has been kept under sedation to insure his....cooperation. I assure you, he is fine."

But Abby ran to Bobby, and helped the others lower him to the ground. "But how....?" I stammered.

Sampson held up a hand. "The night of your escape from the Klan meeting, you luckily ran into the protective arms of your friends who had been observing the meeting from the woods," he explained. "Mr. Hemphill was lucky enough to fall into our hands."

"You were there too?"

"We have been watching these people for a very long time, Mr. Patrick. I assure you, we have become quite good at it."

My anger grew as I remembered the anxious hours we had all endured worrying about Bobby. "If we're on the same side, why didn't you send him back to us, or at least let us know he was okay?!"

"Simply put," Sampson said calmly. "We still had doubts that we *were* on the same side. We must be overly cautious. In any case, it was not time to inform you of our existence. As it is, we nearly had to give ourselves away to come to your rescue when you rather foolishly followed Charles Murphy into that house. Luckily, your two friends showed up in the nick of time to help you."

"Not one of my better days," I mused. "But now that I do know about you, aren't you afraid I'll make your existence public?"

He gave me a steady look. "No, I don't believe you will so that, because you know our cause is a righteous one."

I knew he was right. "But, even if that is a fair assumption, you had Bobby, why kidnap Abby?"

Sampson waved a hand. "Perhaps that was a miscalculation on our part, for which I apologize. But we needed to insure your cooperation."

"I'm curious," I said. "How did you know we were on the same side?"

"You may thank my grandson for that, Mr. Patrick. Had he not believed you to be what you professed to be, you would most likely be dead by now." He gave Abby a slight bow. "Forgive my bluntness, dear lady."

Cletus stood forward. "Carl Lee, he believe you, and that good enough for me."

"I'm glad," I said. "But I promised Grace Wiggins I would find the man who killed Carl Lee."

"Ahh," Sampson said. "That would be one Eddie Cooney, a rather distasteful man. He was Charles Murphy's...companion....shall we say? He was with him in Atlanta the night you were attacked as well."

"I want him," I said my anger building again.

"And I would like to give him to you. But I'm afraid Mr. Cooney is no longer with us. Senator Ellis considered him a liability, like Mr. Murphy. The Klan doesn't like loose ends."

So that was that. But at least I could give Gracie some closure, and Sabine Metaine was avenged as well. That would help Bobby.

Abby stood and came back to us. "He's okay, I think. His breathing seems normal, and his pulse is strong."

"How are you going to get away with having killed a U.S. senator in the middle of a park in Memphis," I said. "This is bound to piss off somebody."

"Oh, the Senator did not die here," Sampson said with a smile. "He will die in a terrible explosion and fire when his car hits an abutment on a lonely highway near Nashville in the early morning hours. The ensuing fire will make the cause of death impossible to determine. Outside the car, the authorities will find a fireproof metal briefcase which will have been thrown from the car on impact. Inside will be all the information necessary for them to dismantle the Gold Circle, once and for all."

"But if you have all this information, why not just go public with it?" I asked.

"The nation has suffered enough from this terrible ordeal, Mr. Patrick. This way, the authorities can deal with it quietly, and we stay in the shadows.

I sighed. "So why me? What did you need me here for tonight?"

Walter Sampson took a sealed envelope from his coat pocket. "This is a copy of the information in the briefcase," he said. "Names, dates, crimes; it's all there. If there is any attempt by the government to suppress the information in the briefcase, we wish you to then make this public." He handed me the envelope.

"I will," I said. "*Deo Vindice,*" I added, quietly. I shook my head again. "You've thought of everything, haven't you?"

Sampson shrugged his shoulders. "Not everything, young man. If we had, many more people might still be alive. But we will continue to try." He stood up. "Now, Mr. Patrick, you will excuse me, but as you can see," he glanced at the body of Senator Arthur Ellis. "We have much work to do, and you should return home to your loved ones."

"Just a minute," I said, as he started to move away. "About the gold? I'm not going to ask you if it's here, because I have a feeling it never stays in one place for very long. But if you know where it is, why not take it? Why not use it for whatever good it can do?"

He looked up at the silent statue of Jefferson Davis, then he reached inside his jacket, and pulled out a folded Klan hood. He looked at it for a moment, and then he laid it on the bench next to me. "Because, sir," he said. "The country is not ready for it. Not yet. When the worst kind of racists can be protected by law enforcement officials while they perpetrate the most heinous of crimes, the country shows itself to be unwilling to accept change."

"So, when?" Abby asked. "When is the right time?"

Sampson smiled. "When it is time, we will know. It is very possible that the people who will benefit from the gold of the Confederacy are yet to be born. The gold is in no hurry, nor are we."

I sighed. "What now? What comes next?"

Sampson thought for awhile, as if unsure he could, or should, tell me. Finally, he said, quietly: "Retribution, Mr. Patrick. Retribution comes next."

"More killings," I said. It was not a question.

"I prefer to say that the innocent must be avenged. It is a sad fact of life," he said. "But there are always some people out there who do not deserve to live." With that, he turned and walked away.

Fifteen minutes later, the blades of the Bell Jet Ranger piloted by Jimmy Winston, with Arnie Peevy riding shotgun, cut the air above Confederate Park. Ten minutes later, Jimmy, Abby, Bobby, and I were on board, and Peevy was on his way to pick up his car. We met back across the river, where Peevy's wife bandaged me up and fed us. All the way home, Abby slept, her head on my shoulder, her hand cupped in mine.

At 5:20 a.m., the lights of a still-dark Atlanta came into view. We were home.

CHAPTER 43

▼

September 4, 2003
Atlanta

My arm was healing, and Bobby was going to be okay, but he had absorbed an awful lot of whatever he had been given over the time he had spent with his captors. He was asleep now, and Abby and I were taking our turn on watch in his hospital room at Grady Memorial, waiting for him to come around. I'd had little chance to speak with him since Memphis, and even then he hadn't been very coherent. But the doctors said to just let him sleep as much as necessary.

I was standing at the window watching the traffic eight floors below on I-75/85 flying by, not really paying much attention to the CNN broadcast playing softly on the overhead TV. The news hadn't been something I wanted to be aware of the last few days. Instead, I had spent most of my waking hours, and a goodly number of the hours I should have been sleeping, replaying the terrible, heartbreaking events of the last few months. Bobby lay in a sickbed for the second time since we had undertaken the frightening task of finding and saving Abby from her Cuban abductors. Now she had been kidnapped for a second time, and although she seemed not to be suffering any ill effects from the ordeal, I relived the moment over and over again daily when the voice had reached me at the Jefferson Davis Memorial Park. I felt again the pinpricks of a million firing nerves. I felt again the fear that I would never be able to protect those closest to me.

"Thomas," I heard Abby say. I turned to see her staring at the TV. She put the volume up so that we could hear. Andrea Mitchell was reporting from in front of the Capitol Building in Washington, D.C.

"*…..And rarely has this country experienced such a loss of national leaders over such a short time span. It's really quite remarkable. First came word just two* *days ago of the fiery crash that took place in the early morning hours on a lonely Tennessee highway, taking the life of Senator Arthur Ellis, the state's Republican senior senator who was evidently on his way to his estate near Nashville, when it is thought he suffered a massive heart attack, and crashed into a bridge abutment. And then yesterday, the body of Representative Gerald Greenway, also a Republican, who was serving his fifth Congressional term representing the 10th District of Mississippi, was found dead from a gunshot wound to the head, in his study at his home in Arlington, Virginia, apparently a suicide victim. As you know, Chris, Greenway was said to be despondent over a recent diagnosis of a malignant brain tumor, but that report has not been substantiated by the Medical Examiner at this time...*"

"But it will be," I said quietly.

"*...And now comes news of this tragic plane crash, which took place just outside the boundary markers of a privately owned airstrip near Waycross, in southeastern Georgia. The plane, a Cessna six passenger, twin engine prop model was carrying the pilot, Senior FBI Southeast Regional Chief, John Saxbee, and three state FBI directors on a hunting vacation trip. As you may know, that part of Georgia has many quail ranches set up as private hunting preserves, and the four were to be the guests at the home of former FBI Director William Lindsay. Eye witnesses say the plane appeared to lose all power during the approach to the one-runway air field, and nose dived into the ground about two hundred feet short of the runway, and burst into flames.....*"

I looked at Abby. "Who says our government doesn't know how to clean up its own messes. They sure covered this thing up fast enough."

She lowered the volume and put down the controller. "Is it really over now?" she asked.

I folded my arms, and stared out the window. "I don't know," I said. "Now that the FBI knows how complicit Saxbee and the others were, I don't think they'll stop looking for the people that actually committed the murders, if only to protect their own asses. And," I added. "I don't think Sampson and his people are going to let the perpetrators go unpunished, either. Then there are the local cops that turned a blind eye on all this that need to be dealt with. I don't know if it will ever really be over." I thought about the envelope Walter Sampson had given me; the one detailing the names of the people who had initiated this monstrous plan. I hadn't opened the envelope, but I could guess that this Greenway, and Saxbee and the others would be on the list. I had decided to keep it for now, in case the government faltered in its internal investigation. I sat down next to Abby, took her hand and kissed her. "For us, though," I said. "For us, it's over."

"God, I hope so!" I heard the groggy voice of Bobby Hemphill say.

I gave him a grin, and he gave me that old "Bobby" look. "I hope the rest of the nurses are better looking than you," he said, and was instantly asleep again.

"How does he do that?" Abby asked.

* * * *

But the more I thought about it, I knew I wasn't done yet. There was something that continued to eat at my heart; something that made it impossible to sleep without the nightmares coming back. And so, the next day, with the welcome relief of a cool September morning that gave a promise of the coming autumn, I found myself standing in front of a tall condo building on Peachtree Street in the heart of Buckhead, just a mile and a half from our little apartment above Ireland's Own.

I took another deep breath, walked into the lobby and took the elevator to the tenth floor. I found Suite 10E and knocked on the door.

I waited a few moments, then knocked again more forcefully. Finally the door opened wide enough for me to see the haggard face of Marti Patton's mother looking back at me. I could see there was no chain on the door, so I pushed it gently, and met little resistance, I pushed harder, and walked in past the startled woman.

"What are you doing?!" she said, in a shrill voice. "Who are you? What are you doing?!"

"Where's your husband, Mrs. Harrison?" I said as I strode through the living room.

"Wait! I said, who...."

But I wasn't stopping to discuss this with her.

"Edgar!"

And suddenly Edgar Harrison came into the room. He was carrying a folded newspaper in his hand, his shirt unbuttoned at the top, and looked like he hadn't slept much lately. Gone was the confident indifference of the man I had first seen at Marti's wake.

"What is the meaning of this?! Why are you in my home! Leave now, or I will call the authorities!"

"Why don't you do that?" I said, stopping to face him. We stood two feet apart, and he looked at me closely, as if trying to remember if he knew me. I heard Ethel Harrison behind me. I looked at her, but she stood stock-still, and posed no threat.

"I just wanted to look you in the face, Mr. Harrison. I wanted to look into the eyes of a man who could kill his own daughter."

I heard a sudden, heart wrenching sob come from the woman, but I kept my gaze on him. His eyes were vacant, and his face took on a sudden pallor, as if the blood had suddenly drained from it.

"What do....," he stammered. "Get out of here," he managed to say, but the volume of his indignation had subsided to a near whisper.

"Maybe you weren't there that night," I said. "Maybe you didn't pull the trigger yourself, or jamb that wooden stake...that precious symbol of the 'cross' of hate that you worship, into your son-in-law's heart, or cut the child from its mother's womb, but you killed them, Mr. Harrison. You are responsible."

Ethel Harrison was wailing now, and I heard her drop to her knees. She fell forward, burying her face in the carpet, repeating, over and over, "Oh, God, Oh, God, Edgar!"

He stood still, unmoving, and staring not at, but through me. "Stop!" he said. "Stop this!"

"It was you, wasn't it?" I kept after him. "It was you driving Benton Fielding's car, wasn't it? You picked up Charles Murphy when he was released from jail! You paid him off, didn't you?!"

He didn't answer, and I turned on the prostrate woman who was crying quietly now, her body shaking with every sob. "Did you know, Mrs. Harrison? Did you know what he did?!" I was shouting now, and I could feel the pent-up anger brimming just below the surface. "I think you did. You knew, and you let him kill your daughter. You let him kill your grandchild." I stopped. I was shaking, and felt the weakness of spent emotions coming on. I turned back to her husband. "For what?" I asked, quietly. "For what?"

"You don't understand," he said. "You could never understand what they took from us." His eyes were glassy, and he was staring at some distant object, or some distant time. In the background, his wife still cried. "The grandeur, the culture, the grace," he said in a faraway voice, and I knew he was no longer in this room with us.

"You killed your daughter for the ideals of a world that should have never existed in the first place." I said.

"They took away the beauty! They made everything we stood for seem common! And she married a nigger!" he raged, not hearing what I had said. His voice was rising again, and sweat began to run down his face. "She knew! She knew what this meant to me, and she married a lowly......"

I slapped Edgar Harrison across the face as hard as I could, and he staggered backward, but stayed on his feet. Mrs. Harrison wailed some more.

"Yes," he said, finally, the words coming in a whisper. He looked at me, and I knew that this time he was seeing me. "I did what I had to do," he said. "I did what I had to do."

I reached behind me and pulled the bloody Klan hood that Walter Sampson had given to me that night in Memphis from my waistband, and dropped it at the feet of Edgar Harrison.

"And so do we all," I said. *"Deo Vindice"* I turned, and walked out of the condo.

*   *   *   *

Outside, I walked up to Jake Berger and two uniformed cops who had been waiting near the entrance to the Harrison's building. I took a deep breath of the blessedly cool, dry air, opened my shirt, and unhooked the wire and listening apparatus Jake has given me earlier.

"You get all that?" I asked.

He nodded. "You want to hang around for this?" he asked, quietly.

I looked up at the front of the imposing building, and then shook my head, slowly.

"I'm going home to Abby," I said.

Jake nodded again and patted me on the shoulder, and the three of them went to arrest the Harrisons.

I walked to the curb of Peachtree Street and hailed a cab.